MW01197043

Some more sounds came from inside and then the noise of the heavy trunk being yanked across the floor. The door finally opened – but only a little way, and the occupant, an affable boy of no more than twenty, tried to talk his way out of his corner. "Morning, Mr. Armstrong. How can I help?"

Ah, now he remembered who had this room, the Admiral's boy – Geoffrey Something – that's who was in Number Eighteen. Spoke like a younger version of the Admiral, too – a buttery, well-bred voice.

Not like the porter, who spoke like an iron rasp on a rough piece of timber. "You've got a girl in there, I heard her, so you may as well admit it."

"You heard what, did you say? A woman? Are you sure about that?" The boy raked his fingers through a frond of hair that fell over his forehead.

Then, the girl herself spoke in a clear, light voice. The owner of the melodious laugh. "Don't fret, Armstrong. It's not what you think."

"Cathy," the young man protested with a smile, "I was handling it."

"No, you weren't. You were just about to flannel." Then the door swung open and there she was, a girl with soft brown eyes. And beyond her, glimpses of the night before. Armstrong did a quick stock-take of the evidence. The unmade bed, the flowery scent, her shoes discarded on the floor.

She smiled. "It's not what you think."

"It's not?" said the porter – fixing her with one of his truth stares.

"No. not at all," said the girl, sincere brown eyes shining. It was disarming, the way she wouldn't be ruffled. "Don't you see? Isn't it as plain as day? He's my twin brother."

The porter stared from one to the other. They were indeed rather similar. Two peas in a pod, as like as any brother and sister could be, same soft brown eyes, same auburn hair, though hers was longer – but not by much – and they were obviously extremely close in age.

"They all claim to be a sister or a cousin, Miss," he said, but he spoke more respectfully. The Admiral was well-liked. And this was his daughter?

"Yes. Of course. But it happens to be true. Cathy Bancroft-Smythe, at your service." She held out a small, slim hand for him to shake, and he took it, marveling at her confidence. "Would you like to see my driving license?" she said. "Just to reassure yourself?"

Armstrong shook his head, and smiled. "I remember your father. Name was Julius, wasn't it? He had room number twelve along there."

"He did. He's told us stories about that room." Those memories delighted her. "Gosh, how sweet of you to remember him."

He did not say that he remembered their father's nickname too – derived from the initials of his surname – Bancroft-Smythe.

The porter collected his thoughts, scattered as they were by this slender but determined young reed. Cathy. The brother hardly took his eyes off her the whole time. Twins, eh? Yes, he could believe it. She flattered him with her kind comments, though, hoping for leniency. "You can't stay in the rooms overnight. There'll be complaints. You don't want to be the reason your brother gets sent down."

"I understand. But my brother will be leaving soon. His papers have arrived." Her lovely young face saddened at this. She went all shadowy and soft. "He's going to sea. I came over to help him pack."

So, the students were starting to get their call-ups now, and the colleges would grow quiet, and before long the news would filter back about this one and that one, the medals, the daring deeds... The place wouldn't seem the same without them. "Very thoughtful. And you missed the train home?"

"No. I'm an undergraduate *too*, Mr. Armstrong," she lifted her chin. "Dangerous territory, making assumptions." Playfully, she reached for her striped jacket which was slung over the back of a chair, and put it on, to demonstrate that it fitted. "I should've gone back to my digs but we ended up talking all night."

"Ah – you're at the ladies' college, are you?" Armstrong conceded.

"Either that or I stole someone's jacket." She did a twirl.

"Where's mine?" said her brother, looking around in distraction, "I need mine, so we can be twinny."

"On the floor, sir." Armstrong aimed for a tone that conveyed parental disapproval. The boy's room was a shambles.

"Ah yes – with my commission papers." It was chaos in there. The only thing naval about it was the old sailor's trunk, bearing the words J. Bancroft-Smythe in chipped white paint.

"He's going straight in at the rank of Lieutenant," the girl said, gazing at her brother.

Armstrong wasn't surprised. What else for the son of an Admiral? But he hoped they didn't put him in charge of organizing the fleet.

"I haven't received my call-up yet," said the girl. Cathy.

"Perhaps you'll be needed at your mother's side, if she's sending both her husband and her son off to sea to fight for our freedom."

"I am not going home to knit socks, Armstrong."

"I didn't imagine you were."

"Cheeky."

He scowled at her – but with more good temper than when he first banged on the door. "May I remind you, Miss, that you are here without permission, absent without leave from your own college, careless of your reputation, and in breach of the fire regulations."

"Yes – I'm a renegade, aren't I?"

An auburn-haired little fire-cracker, yes. The bells were about to ring. Any minute a stream of undergraduates would be crossing the quad and he'd be missed at his post in the archway. He winked at Cathy. "Help your brother pack and I'll turn a blind eye."

"Thank you, Mr. Armstrong. You're a pal!"

"Tell the Admiral I said hello."

Cathy

Only moments before the Porter's visit, the twins had leaned against the single bed discussing this latest attack on their togetherness. The closeness that everyone thought so adorable when they were children was now something they had to conceal. They were nineteen. Too old for sharing clothes and dreams and being the only other person who mattered.

She'd been parted from him once before, when he was at Britannia Naval College and she was not allowed to go. He had written her a letter every night, and she had answered every morning. She had learned French and musical counterpoint; he had learned seamanship and gunnery. But the college, though styled as a ship, never plunged through a turbulent sea. It sat in a manicured patch of green, just like this one. Safe, sound, and full of comforting naval tradition. A place where things would *never* change – until warplanes flew overhead. And bombs fell. And everything was different.

"What if you never come back?"

"I will," he said, "Don't dwell on it, Cath. Live for today and be happy."

He'd told her every joke he could remember to see if he could make her smile, while she began packing his books and clothes. His pictures and letters, his model boats. She emptied his wicker wastepaper bin – and he'd danced around with the bin on his head. That's when they'd got caught by the porter.

Cathy thought he was the craziest, funniest, best brother in the whole world.

It took half the morning to get him ready.

"At last," Cathy said, closing the lid of his seaman's trunk. "Shipshape and Bristol fashion." She padlocked it and gave him the key. "Don't lose it."

He put it away carefully in an inside pocket on his tweed jacket. Feeling reassured. But then he patted his other pockets. "Panic stations, Cath. Did I give my train ticket to you?"

"No. It's in your wallet on the window sill."

"Phew." He walked over there and picked them up and put them in his pocket. His ticket to Greenwich, in London.

"Oh my gosh, we nearly forgot this, too." He picked up a framed photograph. A trio of happy people. In the middle, a tall distinguished man in naval uniform, with his two children, standing solemn on either side. Cathy and Geoff, in miniature, wearing nearly identical sailor suits. Geoff smiled and touched the embossed silver leaves that decorated the edge of the frame.

Cathy reached out her hand. "Give it to me. I'll put it in the middle of the trunk with the soft stuff, so it doesn't get broken." She began to unlock and unpack the box.

"You're an angel, Cathy, an absolute angel."

Since there were two of them, they didn't trouble the porter to help them with Geoff's trunk. They each took one of the old rope handles and carried it down the stairs and through the archway. Out to the road beyond, where a car was waiting for them. Their lift – a long, low, sleek car – driven by an equally smooth young man, dark and smiling, waited with the engine running. He called to them from the car window.

"Hurry up. That pernickety porter says I'm not allowed to park here."

Cathy waved for him to come. "Give us a hand then, lazybones. Open the boot."

Geoff's friend Guido Palamara – or 'Guy' as he styled himself now – opened his door and leapt out in one fluid movement. He wore what all the students wore – a wool sports jacket over a white shirt and grey flannel pants, only he always managed to look Italian in his. The cut of his pants was different somehow; his sports jacket a rich sensual blue instead of tweedy and brown. His white shirt fitted close to his body. Cathy had known him since they were nine. He'd appeared one day on the steps of their London home, solemn and bearing two wrapped gifts, with his dark hair wetted and combed, for one of their birthday parties. Heaven knows why he'd been invited. That was half a lifetime ago. Since then, he'd become like Geoff's other twin.

They heaved the trunk into the back of the car, and Geoff patted his friend on the back. "Thanks for everything, Palamara. Good luck with getting a commission."

But all three of them were aware that Guy's hopes of being an officer might not be possible. His prospects made him gloomy. "With my name, I'd almost expect to get interned, not commissioned." It was not an irrational fear. Since the war broke out, everyone seemed much more aware that he was, in some way, Italian. *That oily foreigner*, their father would call him, but Geoff kept him under his wing. "He was born in England, father. Same as Cathy and me."

Guy went back to the open driver's door, got in, and started her up, and the twins sat in the back seat – together. "I'll miss Cambridge," Geoff said, as they drove to the station. "Hey look, Cath – isn't that where I fell in the river?"

A vista of the River Cam had appeared as the car rounded a corner. Then the alluring glimpse was gone and the river was shrouded by willows and buildings. All three of them had loved punting on the Cam. Cathy saw images of Geoff, leaning back with his hand trailing in the water. Guy had been a pal and stood at the stern, being the one doing the actual punting. He could be relied upon not to jam the punt into the riverbank, or scrape it along the inside of a bridge. Geoff couldn't. He was fun and frolicsome, and if he took charge, he'd be overboard with the pole in ten minutes, claiming – with wet hair streaming over his eyes – that he *wanted* to cool off and get a quick swim. That's why Guy would step in and be their gondolier. She smiled. He did look rather Venetian.

The station loomed too soon. Too soon for Cathy. They hauled the trunk out of the car and said goodbye. "See you after the war, Palamara."

"I'm hoping we'll catch up long before that," Guy said. "You people get shore leave, don't you? And Cathy – you won't abandon me? We can go out to tea, perhaps, or study together?"

Cathy looked at the fender of the car. At the vista down the street. The shape of a church spire in the distance. *Not without Geoff*, she thought. And as for studying together – well, really – as if her English Lit would have anything to do with what he was doing in the Physics department?

"Good God, man, you're about as subtle as a brick," Geoff said, but he shook his friend's hand warmly.

Cathy gave him a desultory glance. "Don't wait, Guy. I'll walk back to my college."

He looked surprised. He clearly hadn't expected to be dismissed as easily as that. "It's so cold today, Cathy. Let me drive you."

"No. I'm staying here til the train goes, and after that, I need some time alone."

The brother indicated with a firm shake of his head that it was no use arguing with her. "Hop back in your car, man, don't stand around in this kind of weather." He indicated with a glance and a raised eyebrow that he apologized for his sister. "Yes. The trees are *hinting* at spring, but the air is still *rather frosty.*"

Guy smiled, put on his hat, and turned away. He got back into his car, started her up, and drove away.

"Do you have to be quite so mean? Any one would think you were afraid of him," Geoff said, as they did their thing with the seaman's trunk again, so they didn't have to keep waiting for a porter.

"I'm not afraid of him. Or anyone," she said. "And I like Guy, but not in that way." So what if his olive skin was warm and his legs were long? She wasn't blind, she was just impervious. "Will they put him in an internment camp, do you think?"

"Does he look like a threat to British security?"

"He looks the way Guy always looks," she said. "Like he's been on a skiing holiday."

And had every success on the slopes and in the bar afterwards, she could have added. But Geoff was protective of his friend. "He looks like a man in love with a statue of cold marble."

"Who are you calling a cold marble? I am not a marble."

"No. You are a lost cause. And *Guy* has lost his marbles." Geoff had always said Guy was insane for even *considering* a campaign to win her unresponsive heart. She was unrepentant. It wasn't her fault if a man gazed at her, wanting something she wasn't about to give.

Again – at the station – people mistook the twins for a courting couple. "Has your young man got any more luggage?" the railway porter asked her. She smiled and said, "No, just the trunk."

He loaded it into the guard's van, leaving them to look for a first-class compartment. Geoff found the carriage that would take him away from her, and they stood on the cold grey platform together.

"I want to go with you," she said, and she hugged him. Tears misting her eyes as they stood in that last embrace beside the train.

"You will be with me. I have pictures. And letters. In my trunk."

The train was waiting, and the time came for Geoff to jump on board. "Next time I see you, you'll be in uniform," she said. Resolving inside, that if he was, she would be too.

He nodded, and read her mind. "It's the Wrens for you, surely?"

Yes. The Women's Royal Naval Service. A good choice for a girl like Cathy. There were recruitment posters everywhere, some of them right here in the station. They featured women with porcelain faces and trim figures, lighting cigarettes for smart young sailors. "Maybe I'll surprise you and join the Land Army."

"Moooo," he said, and smiled. Being silly. She wanted to say moo back, but her eyes felt too misty for mooing. She held onto his hand tightly, waiting for the final whistle. Framed by the opening in the door of the railway carriage, he was a beautiful version of her. But he was so much more. He was everything she wished she could be.

She held onto his hand, as if she could hold that moment of parting forever.

"Free a man for the fleet," he said quietly. But he let her keep hold of his hand, until the train pulled away and she had to let go. Then standing tall and wanting to be brave, she waved and waved – ruggedly cheerful – until he was gone.

Anne

Portsmouth, Hampshire

Anne looked up at the house with some apprehension, and got a cool look from a man with greying hair standing at an upstairs window. *It's alright*, she told herself. She was an officer – the equivalent of a lieutenant in the real Navy. She had a right to be there. She set her course for the front porch, and walked purposefully through the gates. Spring flowers brightened the driveway; they were beautiful, but to Anne they were also a sharp nudge in the ribs, telling her it would soon be April. Three Aprils had come since the war broke out and all her best laid plans went up in smoke. But an exciting new job might open up all kinds of new possibilities.

A crunchy gravel drive led to some steps, and up into a big square porch supported by white colonnades.

This was nothing like any other naval training facility she'd seen before. The Wrennery – everyone called it, since the girls moved in. But it was far more than a mere barracks. Her commanding officer, Penelope Phillips, who greeted her at the door, knew it's true title. She called it 'a stone frigate'. The sign beside the front door said HMS *Resilient*.

"You'll like it here. The workload isn't heavy – the house is glorious – the only drawback is that you're all packed in like sardines upstairs. You won't get a cabin on your own."

The house *was* glorious. A lovely home set in a patch of green, giving it a countrified feel, but in one of those privileged leafy streets that exist not far from the city. The exterior was white stucco and very light – contrasting with the interior of dark wood panels and dark green walls. Once inside, the curved stairway beckoned them upstairs. The hand-rail that followed the curved stairs was a rich glowing mahogany. There were oil paintings, gleaming brass fixtures, and a white marble bust in an alcove.

The woman spoke as if Anne had already got the job – but she knew she still had to get final approval from the powers that be in the 'proper' Navy.

It was reasonable to assume the man in the window was that body's earthly representative today. A suspicion soon confirmed by Penelope. "We'll go and meet Commander Redcliffe in a minute. He used to run the show you'll see today, when it was men who were stationed here. You're not intimidated by naval personnel – are you?"

Anne crossed her fingers behind her back and said that she wasn't.

"Good. Don't let a bit of gold braid scare you. Let me show you the house."

It was part hostel, part training facility. Four Nissen huts housed blackboards, desks, basic radio equipment and morse transmitters. For training purposes only. The house itself had been turned into a comfortable place for the women to stay, with ample living areas and spacious kitchens. What used to be a large yard with stables beyond was now a parade ground, where the women practiced marching in formation and held their daily Divisions.

This is great. She walked from room to room, enjoying every minute of the tour. Her commanding officer seemed to think Anne was exactly what the place needed. And at this moment, Anne was in complete agreement. *If Jim could see me now.* Being considered for sole charge of a place like this. Not bad for a girl who used to run a shoe shop.

They headed up to the first-floor accommodation. The huge, gracious rooms each housed as many single beds as they could fit into them. The largest room held two rows – five beds on either side – and each girl had a small chest of drawers – placed at the foot of the bed – in true naval tradition.

Anne's senior officer looked approvingly at the neatness. Only one framed photograph was permitted to stand on each girl's chest of drawers. Even personal things had to be regimented, like everything else in the Navy. When she spotted a *second* picture on one, she whisked it out of sight. She opened a drawer, and popped it in. "You didn't see that."

In the doorway, a young woman stood and saluted when she saw Penelope Phillips. Her commander gave her an indulgent smile. "Come in Binky, and meet Anne Foxton. Feel free to tell her a little about your life here."

Encouraged, Binky turned to Anne. "This is where I bunk, actually. It's rather jolly up here most nights, as long as there isn't a raid – in which case we all go down to the basement in our pyjamas. Mostly we listen to the wireless, practice our dance steps, and talk about boys." She took a furtive look at Penelope.

"It's alright dear, I was young once, you know."

So Binky said, "We've got some nice boys nearby at the flying school, and they're Navy people like us – training for the fleet air arm."

Penelope made a noise of partial approval, then said to Anne, "Yes, it's best to let the girls have a *bit* of fun," she said, "but always keep a watchful eye. Especially after the dances. Our youngest Wrens are only seventeen. Most of the trainee fliers are wonderful boys, but we don't want them getting up to mischief."

Anne tried to reassure her that she was competent and well-versed in navy discipline. "I take my responsibilities very seriously."

"That's why we were so glad to find you, Anne. We want someone who will 'mother' the Wrens, but won't let them get out of hand. You're perfect dear. Experienced... Mature."

Oh dear. *Mature.* Anne knew what that meant, and it brought her pleasure in the possible promotion to a crashing halt. At twenty-eight, and still dreaming of a different life after the war, she'd rather be *demoted* than mature.

By the time they had finished looking at the Nissen huts in the back garden and returned to the main house, it was time to visit the male naval officer in his spy-glass location on the upstairs landing. He was on the phone. Talking about Anne – much to her horror. "Yes. Is there anyone else you can suggest? I saw the woman coming up the drive and she looks like a bit of a mouse..."

Mrs Phillips barged in, determined to put a stop to his nonsense. "She's not a mouse, Ralph, and you're jolly lucky to get her. She's got two years more experience than anyone else I can find, and she does come *highly* recommended."

He blanched, and got off the phone. Anne smiled politely, and Penelope announced this was her brother. "That's why she thinks she can still boss me around," he said to Anne. "Sorry about the telephone call, you weren't meant to hear that."

"It's alright, Commander. Personnel choices are never easy." She could see she'd struck a nerve – his mouth tightened. This was a man not entirely happy with Wrens in the Navy, even if it was helping to win the war. But he held out his hand. "Ralph Redcliffe."

Anne shook it, accepting that to him she'd seem insignificant. She was not an imposing woman like Penelope. She was an English sort of a girl, and her hair was indeed that shade of light brown that some people call 'mousy'. But from the way Redcliffe shook her hand she knew she was not entirely repellent, and when he lingered, looking into her eyes, she smiled and felt a lot prettier.

They all three sat down, and Penelope took over the talking. She outlined Anne's experience in Quarters – two years supervising new recruits and six months overseeing a Wrennery for nineteen girls back in bomb-damaged London. She told him that Anne was well-organized, tough, an all-round survivor – despite her mild-mannered exterior. He outlined the demands of the job, and how urgent it was to get the women trained fast to read and send morse code and to operate the radio equipment. Signals was desperately short, he said, with so many men being placed on active duty. The teaching here would be done by a navy man, until he too, could be replaced by a woman.

"No personal ties?" he wanted to know. "No distractions to get in the way?"

Anne glanced out of the window. Breathed in, breathed out, and stayed impassive. "Not anymore."

Penelope Phillips pressed her lips together. She looked across at Commander Redcliffe. "Anne lost her fiancé at the start of the war."

"I see." The naval captain's voice mellowed.

"To her credit, she's never had a day off work. She's given her all to the Women's Royal Navy. She's a no-nonsense type of gal. hardworking with lots of maturity."

Ah, that word again. Maturity. But it was becoming clear that they didn't have much choice but to appoint her.

Ralph asked, "Is there anything you'd change, if you were running this show?"

Anne decided to be bold and tell him. "Yes. I would move this office downstairs. I can see why you like it up here – it's like the bridge of a ship, which would be wonderful if it really was a frigate. But I'd want to work in the open area downstairs, in the middle of it all. Keeping tabs on what's going on."

A look of surprise, on Ralph's face. Penelope raised an eyebrow. It was a good idea, and spirited of her to tell him to his face.

At the end of the interview, Ralph stood up and shook her hand. "Welcome aboard, Anne. The job's yours. Apologies for my misgivings. Had to be sure you've got what it takes to be in charge of a stone frigate."

"And you think I do?" Anne smiled, a sudden natural smile. "Thank you, Captain. Nicest thing I've heard all day."

She saluted, and accepted the position.

When she left to go home to her billet and pack, she walked down the drive with a lighter heart. She reached the road and saw an old car parked there, with a young man leaning against it. Navy boy, of course. Hands thrust casually into his trouser pockets, rucking up his nice blue jacket. He looked tired, like he hadn't slept. She guessed he was probably a flier. He was gazing up at the Wrennery windows, waiting for someone. Her footsteps made him look her way, and seeing her, he straightened up smartly. He smiled and gave her a practiced salute, and she saluted him in return. And because she was happy about the new job, she smiled the way she used to smile. At Jim.

She went home to her parents that night for a visit. They lived in a small red-brick house not far from the middle of the city. It was easier to visit when she had good news, and tonight, she could tell them she'd got the promotion.

"Oh, Anne, darling, that's wonderful." Her mother – small and thin – fetched a tea tray and took it into the parlour. The net curtains needed washing, the rugs were frayed, and Anne was filled with doubt – maybe she ought to be helping here, instead of running a stone frigate.

"Well-deserved," said her father, weak and pale by the fireside. Anne's father was a veteran of the previous war, and he had weak lungs from being gassed. He'd survived the last war – just – but Anne sometimes wondered if he'd live to see peace again. Frail as he was, he sparkled with happiness to see her.

She told them all about the Wrennery, and the girls, and her commander Penelope Phillips. She didn't mention Ralph of the lingering handshake and smiling eyes. Or the fliers that seemed to hang around the place like a plague of bluebottles. In her parents' parlour, with the fire burning in the grate, and the saggy brown couch with the white crochet arm-rest protectors, she was back in those happier days. When her father was less frail and her mother less worried, and there were no air-raids and ration books. No sirens or piles of rubble. And if she closed her eyes and listened, Jim was knocking on the door to take her to the pictures.

Linda

Linda zoomed along the road like a bird set free. She loved riding a motorbike for the Navy. She was on her last assignment – riding through the dawn, heading towards the Fleet Air Arm training facility at Lee. Dodging rubble in dark streets to get messages from the docks to the Admiralty was dangerous work. But she thrived on it. Her longest ride had been over two hundred miles, and had included an icy road through Dartmoor. Mostly she worked locally, relaying messages to the captains of the ships at anchor in Portsmouth or Plymouth. She was based at HMS *Resilient* - an elegant house - which she loved. The only thing she didn't love was being on the night shift.

She'd been in the Wrens for five months, mostly working nights. This morning the dawn was so staggeringly beautiful, if she hadn't been on her message run, she would have revved the bike and roared up to the highest point overlooking the town – from where you could see the sea in all its glittering glory. The calming sight of the sea and the sunlight through watercolour clouds was truly beautiful. There was a lot happening down at the Admiralty rooms – and in the harbour the ships were getting ready to leave. She was lucky, most Wrens never even saw the sea, let alone got to board the big ships, but she was up and down the gangways all the time – and there were days when she'd be escorted up to the bridge – inner sanctur of power – to wait for an urgent reply. She would stand there, revel it, enjoying panoramic views of the harbour. But she *must* put into the right hands, to fail in that duty was treason. Her jo man named on the front of the sealed envelopes she carried, no matter how important that person might be. Today it was the Air Commodore at the training facility near Lee-on-Solent.

She was having a terrific war. New clothes, nice pay packet, freedom from the constraints of her parents' home for the first time in her life, some transport in the form of her Triumph, purring under her, and she got to hear all the Navy gossip. It made her feel important. She heard things, taking despatches from one department to the other. Pieced things together in a way that others couldn't, because they didn't hear one part of a conversation here, another part there. They didn't think she was close enough to learn any secrets. But she heard all the words, knew all about the special places. Room Forty, Station X, Service Y. Sometimes, it wasn't hard to put two and two together. A new operation was mooted in the Mediterranean. A really big one. She even knew the codename, but that was sealed in her heart as it should be, a place where many official secrets lay.

She weaved through the streets catching admiring glances. She loved seeing people do a double take as she went by. Yes – a blonde girl on a motorbike. She'd give the bike some revs just to show them. Va-va-va-voom. Beethoven's 5th symphony – motorbike style. Her uniform was trousers and a smart cadet-style cap held on by a slim leather strap. Her blonde curls peaked out from under the cap, curling prettily just below her ears. She had lipstick on, and she carried a compact with face powder in it. Sometimes, bike purring between her legs, she'd sit there and touch up her makeup. She always got a few wolf whistles doing that.

Linda rode out to the training facility at Lee with the letters in her satchel for the head of operations. She was under strict instructions to give her letters only to him, which meant that the message was important. She rode up to the building, braked, put the bike into neutral, turned the engine off, and put down the kickstand.

She showed her pass at the front desk and went inside. On her way she passed some of the classrooms, catching glimpses of life on the base. In one room was a full-size model fuselage and pilot's cockpit, where the men stood in a queue to practice their start up procedure. In another room there was a blackboard, where a much older pilot stood in a jacket cuffed with gold, and lectured, po-faced, pointing with his stick, on everything from the principles of flight to the avoidance of certain embarrassing diseases. And overhead the drone of airplanes in the sky as the boys came in, learning how to obey the cues from the batsman, brave man, who stood armed only with a pair of flags, hoping the trainees wouldn't run him over.

A trainee pilot swirled by and tried to kiss her on the cheek. "Got my wings, Liz."

She shoved him away. "It's Linda. And any of that and I'll have you reported." She gave him a good thump as she tried to get past with her leather satchel. He was a bit of a rogue – Dicky Tavistock.

He touched his arm protectively. "Don't thump my nice new wings." He stretched his arm out for her to see. She admired the red and gold motif in the shape of a pair of wings that now adorned his dark jacket. "Very nice. But you've only been here a month. Can you actually fly yet?"

He nodded. "Tomorrow we're flying from Gosport to practice our deck landings. And we've been night flying all week. It's killing my social life." He shook his head. "It's in tatters, Linda. Tatters. Have you got good news? Is there going to be one of those marvelous parties?"

The official messages Linda carried were rarely good news. Especially not for the flyboys. Sometimes, before she left the building, she'd witness the effect a message had on the person she gave it to. A heavy sigh, a man's hand passing over his sweating forehead. Or he might jump to his feet, barking orders as she left the building. But, hey, don't shoot the messenger.

But what *he* meant was that he was hoping to get wind of one of the social events they held at the Wrennery, the hostel where she lived. The social calendar at the women's quarters was a source of great interest to the flying school trainees. A honey pot of total fascination.

She made him wait, crossing her arms for effect, while he looked at her with hopeful, restless eyes, his body full of nervous energy. "Come on, Linda, tell me?"

He didn't deserve to be invited. With him it was one girl after another. But she uncrossed her arms. "As it happens there will be one before too long. We're getting a new team leader."

His face lit up. "Thank God for the Wrens. Wonderful girls. But, oh dear, *what* shall I wear?"

Linda laughed. Crazy guy. He would, of course, wear his pilot's uniform. Wings prominent.

Shouts came from outside. A shadow passed over the aerodrome. An aircraft coming in, flying far too close. A hideous noise – rattling the windows beside them. He ran to look. Then out through the open door, sprinting onto the tarmac. Linda followed, magnetized by the sight. A pilot in trouble. Coming in too fast.

Despairing cries, yelled instructions. Frantic signals from the batsman. But no use. The hopeless angle, the edge of one wing scraping the concrete. A doomed landing. The plane careened into the runway. She scraped, spun, and crashed. Slumped like an animal. Hissing, leaking. Smoking.

"Dicky, don't!"

But he wouldn't listen. He ran into the smoke to the wreck, calling out "Cyril."

Chapter Two

The Message

The Commodore opened the message while the girl who'd brought it waited beside him. She was shaking like a leaf. Outside on the tarmac the heat wagon and the meat wagon – fire truck and ambulance van – were dealing with the prang. Pity about the pilot. He'd shown some promise, earlier in the week. Must have got flustered. The message, typed on wafer thin paper, was from the Admiralty to the Air Commodore at Lee.

Reduce training time for FAA pilots. Swordfish pilots and support crew urgently required to join ships in both Home Fleet and Indian Ocean. Must be trained in night flying. Select operational crews and advise by return.

He ran through the list of young men in his mind. Mentally forming a squadron. Fine fliers they'd make – given time. But time was a pre-war luxury. It was on the ration now.

Select operational crews. Advise by return...

Cathy

London, April, 1942

Cathy had gone straight to a recruiting office on her way back from seeing Geoff off at the station. She'd survived the scant but obligatory three weeks of basic training – during which time the girls all wore their normal everyday clothes, learned square-bashing on the parade ground, and ruined their hands scrubbing floors that were already shiny. They called this 'scrubbing the decks' in a nod to Navy vocabulary. She looked down at her work-reddened hands, wishing she'd applied a bit more beeswax like the more experienced girls had advised.

She didn't tell her parents where she was, although on the face of it, there should have been no reason for them to object. She was from a Naval family, and in a time of national emergency it was the natural progression to join its support service. Why would there be any objection? But for some reason she was afraid that there would be. She let them think she was still at Cambridge, and supported this little white lie with a well-timed postcard, to be dropped in the post by a girl she knew in Hall, exactly half-way through her basic training.

As far as the training went, she'd endured it rather than enjoyed it, she knew everything from her daily exchange of letters with Geoff while he was at Dartmouth being an amiable Naval Cadet. The lessons for the would-be Wrens had been an insult to her intelligence. Semaphore she knew. Morse too. And very little time was spent on those fun things, anyway. Most of it was basic stuff covered in frightfully dull lectures, by a man with a false hand and a terrible stutter. A whole morning on the ranking system in the Royal Navy... oh, *please*. The only thing that had kept her going was the thought of the uniform.

Today was the day. She was at the outfitters – which was temporarily set up in an old cinema with a bomb-damaged façade and boarded up windows. She reached the head of the queue and after being sized up and measured for a hat band, she was handed a pile of dark clothes. She hugged them to her body like a long-lost friend.

She could barely see over her pile of clothes, and there was nowhere to change in the hot stuffy hall full of female bodies. But she was excited, because perched on top of her mountain of clothes was a smart new sailor cap, pert and pretty, issued with instructions how to wear it. At a jaunty angle pointing down to starboard. She suppressed a smile. As if she'd wear it any other way.

She moved through the hall looking for a place to change. The dark corners of the room were all taken – full of girls wriggling out of their clothes. Noise, artificial light, makeup being reapplied, everyone as excited as she was.

"Mother and Daddy are in for a surprise." She looked forward to that wonderful moment when she would appear on their doorstep as a fully-fledged Wren, but she hoped they'd be alright about it. She knew they wanted her to finish her degree, before taking up any sort of war service. "Geoff will understand. I can't sit around with my books while he goes off to do what needs to be done." But that brought up worries. She hadn't been there to receive his letters, and her roommate had not sent any on, although she was sure he would have written, and not receiving word from him was a worry and a conspicuous lack. She needed that communication, that lifeline. The absence of it was unsettling.

There was nowhere except the middle of the room to change. She'd just have to stand there and put it all on. Cathy wasn't shy about shedding her civvies, and nobody was really looking. She stripped to her bra and cami-knickers and started by peeling down her ordinary stockings and exchanging them for the black ones – she fastened the tops of each leg to the press-studs on her suspender belt. She put on the white shirt and the long black tie, which she imagined might look a bit saucy when worn with only the stockings. She pulled on the skirt, a demure A-line model, and then added the double-breasted jacket. She stroked the folds of the navy cloth. Felt the hug of the dark wool jacket across her shoulders. Enjoyed the cool touch of the buttons. They were dark and did not need polishing. That was a blessing, in Cathy's opinion – she'd polished her father's brass buttons for him on many occasions. These buttons were blue-black and each one was embossed with an anchor. Lovely.

A roly-poly girl next to her was changing into an identical set of kit. "Wish I was an officer. Those new hats look way better than these sailor bonnets, don't they?"

Cathy couldn't understand what the fuss was about. Some examples of the coveted new navy tricorne had pride of place on the tables where the uniforms were laid out. And everyone oohed and aahed over them, and said they were 'très chic'. Cathy conceded that the incoming style did look nicer than the current model, which could only be described as an unflattering sou'wester.

But Cathy liked her sailor bonnet more. Loved it, in fact. To her, the officers' hat looked like something any woman might wear to shop in Oxford Street or Tottenham Court Road. But it was not something a sailor would wear. "Wear your sailor cap with pride," she advised. "You'll get your tricorne soon enough, when you get your commission."

"I'll never get one, Miss. I'm a cook." She didn't seem to think this fact could ever change.

"Well, I hope you know a good recipe for steak and kidney pie."

"Learned it last week, along with the Admiralty's Instructions."

Ah, the big book of secrets, kept in a lead cover so it would sink and not be surrendered to the Germans.

Cathy laughed. "I reckon it's *in* the Admiralty's Instructions, along with the secret formula for plum pudding."

"You sound like an officer already."

"Sorry, I'll try to tone it down. I'm Cathy," She stuck out her hand, in comradeship, hoping she'd made her first friend. "I've volunteered for transport."

The girl paused, but then she shook hands and smiled. "Mavis."

Cathy expected to be commissioned, she was a realist. Everyone had heard of her father, Julius Bancroft-Smythe. Once her secret was out, it would follow the logical progression. As soon as she was old enough, she would be asked to go to Greenwich to receive officer training, and she would leave the enlisted ranks. But for now, it was nice to blend in with the crowd. She was seized with the idea that she could stay like this – an unknown Jenny Wren among a thousand others – and *see what happened*. She'd be liked and loved for her very own self, and not for who her father was.

The minute the uniform was on, Cathy felt at home in it. She had a moment in front of a speckly old mirror, angled against the wall. She couldn't linger. A queue of noisy girls wanted a turn. But she got her moment – and when she finally stood in front of the glass she saw an auburn-haired girl in smart navy blue and felt unaccountably happy. She added the sailor beret, her fingertips touching the black tally-band. The place where, in peacetime, the name of the ship would be sewn. It read simply HMS at the moment, in gold letters. A ship. A *ship*. Geoff was so lucky to be appointed to a real ship. The only HMS she was likely to be appointed to would be an onshore country house, or some other dry land location, when she would love to be at sea.

The sea had been a central part of her upbringing. Holidays as a child always involved a sail boat or a putt-putt somewhere – Buckler's Hard, Cornwall, Scotland. As they got older, there had been elegant yachts in warmer locations – the coast of France, Greece, the island of Capri. And, of course, she'd been taken to visit her father's ships often. Up and down steel companionways, racing across smooth wooden decks with her brother, and always ending up on the bridge, where they would fight for first dibs to read the instruments housed in the binnacle. The sea called her like any other matelot. It piped to her like the pied piper of Hamelin. It sang to her like mythical Sirens – while the Admiralty kept her lashed to a mast.

But it was good news when she got back to the training facility. Their Chief Petty Officer had pinned up a list on the communal noticeboard. A whole crowd of wrens were gathered round, all trying to find their names and their postings. "Ooh, Cathy. Be careful what you wish for. You've been accepted for Boat Crew."

Linda

Shaken from witnessing the crash, Linda went back to the Admiralty with another message.

"One Swordfish unserviceable. Pilot dead. Trainee observer injured. Enclosed paperwork for requisitioning replacement aircraft. Please expedite."

They would have had two dead if Dicky hadn't climbed onto the wreck to make a last-ditch attempt to get Cyril. The maintenance crew sprayed foam at the plane, while he undid the boy's straps and pulled him dazed from the wreckage. The other man was a broken mess. Too late for anything except a difficult letter to his mother. On a clear day in spring. Not an enemy in sight. Linda shuddered. And that was called training.

"Sorry you had to witness that, my dear."

Those were the words she'd heard, as she stood too stunned to move, watching the incident unfold on the runway in front of her. She'd turned and given the flying instructor a wan look. Then someone had herded her inside – for the inevitable hot, sweet tea, and a fifteen-minute wait for the message.

Now she was back at the yard, trying to put it out of her mind by cleaning her bike. Squeezing the rag in the warm soapy water was soothing, almost hypnotic. The bike wheels were gleaming. But the images were still there and couldn't be washed away with soapy water.

It hadn't been anyone she knew. There was no reason to let it shake her.

'Hey, you!'

That was not the recommended way to address a colleague in the Royal Navy. Linda looked up across the Admiralty Motor Yard in the direction of the yell. She saw a man in a navy greatcoat staring at her as if she'd done something wrong. Perhaps he was thrown by the fact that she was a woman, which he registered only when he saw her blonde curls. She got up from where she'd been kneeling, she'd been washing the wheels of her bike with a soapy rag. She wiped her hands on her trousers, and made a careful salute. "Sir?"

"Sorry." He began walking briskly towards her. "Can you drive a car?"

"I've driven a delivery van. Stick shift, is it? Three gears?"

"You can drive a van, can you? Even better." He looked at her with interest now. "I'm looking for a driver with skill, stamina, and a certain amount of discretion. Day shift, can you take it?"

Day shift. Music to her ears. A change of scene. "Yes, please."

"I need you to take some experts to a site."

"Experts, sir?" She'd developed this art of repeating orders, instead of asking searching questions. It often worked a treat, and she learned a little bit more. But this man wasn't taking the bait. "Look – you'll know soon enough. It's not *exactly* classified, but best not to talk about the details. I hope you understand."

"Perfectly."

"Good girl."

He was a little condescending, given that he needed a driver with skill, stamina and discretion. But she had to let it pass. "Am I allowed to ask where the site is, Sir?"

He smiled. "No. We don't know ourselves until we get a telephone call. Locations all over the show."

"Sounds fascinating. When do I start?"

"I'll add you to the roster for next week." He handed her a memo he had in his hand. Driver to report to Gate Four and await further instructions. "Go there, and they will issue you with clearance papers."

"Sir. I've had a bit of a day. I was just about to clock off."

"Sorry. But if you can do it, I'll put a good word in with your commanding officer."

She nodded. She put her cap back on. "Agreed."

She left wondering if she could have said no, even if she wanted to. Sometimes this war seemed like that. Duty was inescapable. But it did sound intriguing.

Chapter Three

Anne

Anne unpacked her few possessions at the Wrennery. Laying her clothes carefully in the chest of drawers beside her bed. She didn't mind that she would be sharing. In some ways it might help her to sleep. There was a wardrobe at the far end of the room, that the girls all used to keep their jackets in. The rest of her uniform went in the chest of drawers. Lingerie in the top drawer. Picture of Jim.

She had one suitcase and a carpet bag – the bag was an 'unauthorized' item according to the Wren's rules. That was the sum total of what she carried with her, and yet she still told herself she ought to pare it down. She could always send a box to her mother's home if she wanted to lighten the load. At the bottom of the carpet bag was an uncut dress pattern. The wedding dress for the event that didn't happen. She had chosen the fabric and got as far as taking it round to the dressmaker, and choosing the style. It was heartbreaking to have to say she didn't need it any more. The dressmaker had been kind and resourceful, she had sold the white silk to another client. But she gave her back the pattern. Anne looked at the line drawing on the packet, depicting a willowy 1930s bride. It was out of style and out of date. There was no point in keeping it now. She could treat it like any other bit of paper – nothing sacred about it. She could put it, if she chose, in 'the Round File'.

She couldn't though. It went in the top drawer, with Jim and her French knickers.

Anne's work downstairs involved handling all the administration for the Wrennery, with one other admin Wren to assist her. They ordered supplies, balanced budgets, and made sure the Wrens were all at their desks or their posts at various times during the day. The Nissen huts buzzed with activity and the parade ground was alive with the sound of stomping. The instructors who came to teach the Wrens signaling and morse code seemed surprised how fast the women learnt. The place was like a hive. Anne secretly liked to take some credit for that. A good Wren is a happy Wren – a Wren that's well looked after. Every few weeks there were new Wrens arriving, and 'old' Wrens – fresh faced twenty-year olds – leaving for far flung parts of the country, with six weeks training under their belts. They were trained in many skillsets. Signalling, or morse code, plotting – and if they didn't have talent they could learn. With the war into its third year, Anne had seen the Navy accept more and more changes.

She went to her new admin area beside the foyer and the saw the postman arriving. There were always a great many letters for the Wrens – their friends and relatives seemed to spend every waking moment sending them wads of tittle tattle in scented envelopes with elegant sloping writing on them. The boyfriends more often sent postcards – brief and to the point – "Forty-eight-hour pass on the 14th. Can you get the weekend off?"

"You're a bit of an improvement on the last Mother Superior, I must say."

Anne looked up sharply. The postman, standing there with his sack of mail. Smiling. But his cheery smile fell when she said, "I *beg* your pardon?"

She didn't know why she was so stand-offish, when really, it was nice to be noticed. She was not one of your glamour-girl types, with her light brown hair in a bun, but she did have red lipstick on, and she was well aware the Wren outfit suited her.

"Sorry, Miss. Just me being cheeky. Here's the mail for yer." He plunked the sack down on the polished counter in front of her.

"Thank you," she said, in a tone of voice that repels all boarders. Oh, dear. The mailman would never smile at her again – poor fellow. And he'd only meant to be friendly. He turned and went, leaving Anne wondering why on earth she'd been like that. He'd given her a compliment, that's all, on a bright Monday morning.

Cathy

Cathy walked from the station wearing her brand new uniform, feeling both conspicuous and happy. Her family home was in a leafy suburb in Middlesex, and they had lived there since her father got his first real command. The Georgian sandstone façade was beautiful, symmetrical and perhaps a little rigid – like her family. She went up the drive towards the house and saw a man waiting at the top of the front steps – the photographer her mother had booked. He had a wooden stand and carried a large square bag with his portrait camera inside. He looked like he'd been ringing the bell for some time.

"You won't have much luck. The maid left last week – she's gone to work in a munitions factory." Cathy ran lightly up the steps. She had a key. "I'll let you in if you like."

Inside her mother was standing with her back to her, in the cool splendour of their entrance hall. She was on the telephone arguing with Geoff. "Can't you tell them who you are and get a shore-pass, darling? I've made all the other arrangements."

The hallway, with its polished mosaic floor, was quieter than the street. The chandelier hung at a wonky angle, but the room was gracious and clean. It smelt of home and lavender-scented furniture polish.

Cathy gestured to the photographer that he could sit down and wait in the hall until someone was free. The negotiations with Geoff didn't seem to be going well, and Cathy's mother was getting upset. "Your father is on his way. Cathy's coming home specially, and the photographer is all organized."

"Actually, mother, he's here."

The photographer thanked her, wordlessly, for trying to announce him.

Her mother's grip tightened on the phone. "Trust you, Geoffrey, to botch this when everything else has been organized -" But then, the lady lifted her eyes to the mirror in front of her – and in the reflection, saw, for the first time, her daughter in the uniform of the Women's Royal Naval Service.

In the looking glass, Cathy saw an expression of incomprehension, then a frown, and then an understanding, all in an instant on her mother's face. The gasp came a second later, as she whirled round to look at her daughter. "Oh, Cathy! What have you done?"

Geoff seemed to be asking a question on the other end of the phone. The photographer was weighing up whether he could put down his bag and his stand, which must have been rather heavy. And Cathy was standing there. Being a Wren. Feeling quite pleased with herself.

Her mother looked very stressed and ran a hand over her face. She stared at Cathy, but she spoke into the phone, "Darling, I'll ring off now. Your sister is home in full kit. And I'm assuming you *knew* about this."

Which gave Cathy a start. "No, no – don't ring off – I'd like to speak to him!"

"If Cath's there, I really need a word," she heard her brother say via the telephone receiver.

But her mother had finished that conversation. "Later," she said, and put the phone down.

Cathy crumpled with disappointment. But Mrs. Bancroft -Smythe was unrepentant. "It's alright, you'll see him soon enough, if he can get his 24-hour leave sorted out. He was supposed to be coming home so a photograph could be taken before he was posted. But I expect you planned this."

"Geoff wasn't in on it, Mother. I've hardly heard from him since he went away."

"A likely story." She turned her attention to the photographer. "I'm terribly sorry, but my son will not be joining us. I fear you've had a wasted journey."

The photographer clutched his bag, obediently, and picked up his stand. "Oh, right you are, ma'am. Did you not want me to photograph your daughter?"

Mrs. Bancroft-Smythe held her long elegant fingers to the bridge of her nose, as if she felt a nosebleed coming on.

And at that moment the Admiral came waltzing in through the open door – singing heartily – he spotted Cathy and whirled her round in a hug that turned into a jig in the hallway. "Jenny Wren, Jenny Wren – what a sight to see." He was in full naval regalia.

Cathy knew she could rely on him, at least, to be pleased. She kissed him. And he gave her sailor cap a tweak. "Lovely to see you, darling."

Cathy's mother turned on him sharply. "Julius. Were you in on this? If you were, you can eat with the servants for a week."

"We don't have any servants left, my sweet. The cook gave notice this morning." He kissed his wife affectionately on the cheek.

"Oh, dear God. This bloody war." She looked about ready to commit murder. "My home is full of liars, and my servants are deserting a sinking ship."

"Keep calm, Mother," Cathy said. "The recipes are all in the Admiralty's Instructions."

The Admiral laughed and gestured that he would like the photographer to go into the sitting room and set up. "No Geoff?" he enquired. His wife shook her head. He shrugged and went in anyway.

unless she was wise enough to start lending it out. Most of the girls only had their uniforms, even for dances and picnics with their sweethearts.

The pilot she was dancing with – now Anne remembered. She'd seen him leaning against an old car, the day she first arrived. But Delia hadn't even been here then, he must have been waiting for one of the other girls. Anne turned to the girl beside her and asked, "Who's Dee dancing with?"

Speccy Wilson, real name Sarah, looked at the man on the dancefloor. "That's Dicky. He's a shocker," Speccy told her. "He's Fleet Air now – he was promoted up from Temporary Midshipmen – it's gone to his head I think."

"Promotions often do," Anne said self-consciously.

"You're not like that," Speccy told her. If not for the difference in their ages and ranks, Anne would have loved to be friends. With Speccy and all the other girls. They were so much fun. But her new role required ... distance.

Anne gazed at Dicky. He looked alright. Pleasant, friendly, tall. "Why is he a shocker?"

"Usual reason. Got his wings. Thinks he's God. Tries his luck with everyone."

Anne asked her to spill the worst. If she was in charge of the moral welfare of the girls, then she needed to know who the troublemakers were. Speccy told her what had been deduced so far from Dicky's erratic behaviour. "He turned up a few weeks ago. He was quite open about it – I'm going to find myself a nice little Wren – he said."

Anne smiled. Well, that was fairly standard operating procedure for the FAA boys. "What else d'you know?"

"His family is Old Navy – on warships ever since Trafalgar or something. But Romeo over there got out of it – said he had some experience clocked up before the war. *Flying* experience that is. Can't speak for the other kind – I've decided to steer clear of him, myself. I'm not ending up as an officer's groundsheet."

Anne looked shocked – of course she'd heard the phrase before – but Speccy was so young she hadn't expected her to say it. "Sarah, *please.*"

"Sorry, Officer Foxton, but I'm doing the liberty boat run out to the warships now. I've had to toughen up," Speccy said. She tilted her head towards Dicky. "Anyway, he got himself moved to the Fleet Air Arm. Which made him rather dazzling, and he's been buzzing round the Wrens ever since.

He proposed to a girl called Lucinda last week, and now look at him dancing with Delia. We've all warned her. She says she doesn't pay attention to his lines, but she likes going out in his car. He's promised to take her out for a nice lunch at the George Hotel."

"Which one is Lucinda?"

"Oh, she's gone now. Demanded a transfer."

Anne looked at him, trying to work him out. With his fresh face and shining eyes he didn't look like a monster of seduction. But a man driven by the idea that he's sailing towards death or glory could be very persuasive, as she knew. Delia hauled him off the dance floor and over to the table with the cold drinks, fanning herself, laughing, and he poured two cups and offered her one. As they chinked and raised a toast to each other, Anne looked on with a heart full of sadness. *You are so lucky, you two. Don't waste a single second.*

Speccy looked too, but her interpretation was different. "Womanizing cad. Delia's robust enough for anything. It's the next person he picks on I feel sorry for."

Chapter Four

Cathy

At their home in Middlesex, the Bancroft-Smythes sat down to a lovely last supper – provided by the cook who had given in her notice. Julius whispered to his daughter. "How will we survive when your mother takes over the cooking?"

Cathy savoured her last mouthful of creamy dauphine potato. "Doesn't bear thinking about, does it?"

They decided their best hope was to be tremendously appreciative, and they kept sending down their compliments to the kitchen, in the faint hope that the cook would change her mind.

Her father had invited a friend – Commander Ralph Redcliffe – in all his naval splendour. He was seated opposite, and had perfect table manners. Cathy knew he was there because of her, which was quite absurd, he was much too old for her. She was nineteen. She guessed him to be about forty, greying at the temples like an aging star of stage and screen.

He was very polite and very attentive. "Where are you posted, Cathy?"

"Pompey," she said, using the Navy nickname for Portsmouth.

Ralph knew the Wrennery where Cathy would be going – in fact, it used to be *his* stone frigate, when the place had been full of young men. He assured her it was a lovely place and he'd met the young woman who was running it, and she seemed sensible and kind. He was on his way back to Portsmouth tomorrow, and he could take her down there, if she liked?

Two hours alone with Ralph in the car? She shook her head, politely. "I'll get the train."

"You'll have luggage, dear, let Ralph take you." Her mother's voice was firm.

"No, no. I'm travelling light." It was true, she was taking only what she'd been issued, plus writing paper and stamps. No ballgowns, no complete works of Shakespeare.

Ralph smiled, pleasantly. "I practically pass the Wrennery, it seems *absurd* not to take you along for the ride."

Cathy opened her mouth to say no for the third time, but Julius stopped her. "Cathy, some battles are too *rude* to fight."

"Sorry, Daddy." The meal passed in quiet politeness after that. Just pleasantries and the musical tinkling of silver cutlery on china plates. But then – just in time for pudding – a wonderful surprise.

Geoff arrived.

He appeared in the doorway of the dining room – posing like a minstrel with his hands on either side of his cherubic face – so they could admire his new Navy look. A general hooray went up, and Cathy squealed, jumped up from the table, and gave him a hug. She didn't even have to say she loved the way he looked. Dark jacket, single band of gold braid round each cuff, peaked cap and gold badge of a commissioned officer. Gorgeous. He knew and his eyes shone in the reflected admiration. It had only been three weeks since they'd parted, but she held onto him like he'd returned from the Napoleonic Wars.

"For heaven's sake, Cathy, stop making an exhibition of yourself and sit down. Geoff, dear, you must have known we were about to serve the crème brulee?" His mother smiled at him, and gestured to a chair.

Julius leant forward and said in a teasing voice, "and you still expect to get some pudding – after not turning up for the family photograph?"

Geoff grinned and said that he did. He sat down next to Cathy. "Gosh, you look the part in that Wrens uniform." She squeezed his hand under the table.

Oh, bliss to see him again.

"Your sister has been posted to Pompey." Julius said. With a note of pride in his voice that made her happy.

Ralph leaned forward. "Would you like me to put in a good word about a posting closer to home, Cathy?"

"No, I'll go where I'm needed. Like any other Wren."

"What about a posting that might take you closer to Geoff?"

Sly old thing. Now she'd have to say no to that too. "It's alright. But thanks awfully, Ralph."

Her brother smiled. *You're welcome horribly.* That's what he would've said if the remark had been fired his way. He sent her a quick eyeball telegram to indicate that he understood her discomfort. Her parents seemed determined to push her off onto grizzled old Ralph. He was such a traditionalist too. And a landlubber. Lamenting the loss of his stone frigate when he'd been offered the chance to command a *real* one. *The petticoats are invading the Navy*, he'd said when he saw her – and thought he was being witty. *Alright, Ralph, I'll accept your kind offer. But any ideas about invading my petticoats, and I'll have you decommissioned. On the double.*

The Admiral was on to the deep red contents of the decanter on the sideboard – and Cathy's mother turned to her and said, "Darling. We should withdraw. Leave the men to have their port."

Cathy hated being told that Navy talk was only for the men, when there was no one she'd rather be with than Geoff, and Julius was a fairly close second. Even the company of Ralph Redcliffe seemed preferable to being sent away as if she was too silly to understand what was being said. "No, Mother. It's my last evening at home. I need to hear what the fleet are doing." She looked up at her father. "Daddy – you *must* tell me what's happening at Scapa."

Cathy knew that most of the Navy's treasured home fleet was stationed at the huge natural harbour up near the Orkneys.

Julius smiled indulgently and got his daughter a small glass of port. "Well, yes – dear old Scapa – but that's not where our concerns are, at the moment." When her father said 'concerns' he usually meant 'battleships', so Cathy felt she'd learned something already. "But listen, my darling," he said, leaning forward. "All eyes are on a certain little island in the Med."

"Malta?"

"Yes m'dear. Poor old Malta."

Malta. She had been there as a child – the whole family had lived there on a posting during the early phase of the Admiral's career. Cathy remembered being there – a golden place saturated in Mediterranean sun, full of beautiful buildings and courtyard gardens of vibrant colour. For her it had been a magical playground, and her mind went to a happy memory of running around the footings of an ancient monument high on the hill, in a rowdy game of hide and seek. Geoff's chubby face peering out from behind a pillar. "I won!" he would say when he found her, which took about ten seconds because he always knew where she was likely to hide.

Her father was deeply worried about the island. "After so many days of bombing, it's a miracle there's a monument or a building still standing. If something doesn't change – the only flag flying over Malta will be the white one of surrender."

"Our efforts to supply her have been dismal." Ralph Redcliffe stroked his chin, pompous old thing, and spoke of the losses. "Two convoys – both failures. No fuel got through. The enemy is sending all our best tonnage to the bottom of the sea."

And Geoff stroked *his* chin in imitation of Ralph. Trying to look sage and naval, but reminding Cathy of a gnome in the garden. "Do you think the Italians will invade?"

"They are very well placed to do so," Julius said.

Ralph tried to ask how long Malta could hold out, but Julius wouldn't say any more. Ralph changed the subject and said that now Cathy and her schoolgirl chums were in the Navy, the enemy wouldn't stand a chance. *Patronising old buzzard.* But Geoff squeezed her hand. Geoff's good opinion was all she needed to ever feel happy. He said, "You really *are* going to free a man for the fleet."

Cathy almost glowed. She hoped she could be truly useful, with all the nautical knowledge she'd picked up from Geoff over the years.

"Do you get a choice what duties you do?" Her brother wanted to know.

"You can put down a preference. I've applied for Boat Wren, and as a back up I've said I could do signals or gun-emplacement maintenance if they're short."

Julius smiled. "It could be Wardroom duties, you know, dear. Waiting tables and making beds."

And Ralph Redcliffe ventured another possibility: "Some Wrens take care of the naval officers' clothes. Brush them down at night, that kind of thing."

Cathy's mother, vigilant on the evening watch as usual, raised an eyebrow.

"I'd leave," said Cathy. "And if they make me empty the Admiralty chamber-pots, I'm going to be very upset."

"Cathy! Not at the dining table."

Julius reached for a wooden box containing his cigars. "You'll be sent somewhere safe and comfortable, if I have anything to do with it."

"Don't you dare," Cathy said, smarting. "Let me do my bit. This war needs talent, not nepotism."

Julius smiled and lit up a fragrant cigar. Several aromatic puffs of smoke emanated from his mouth as he leaned back making no comment on his daughter's ambition.

Cathy turned to her brother. "Any news of poor Guy?"

"*Poor* Guy?" Geoff laughed. "Asking after him now, are we? I can't wait to tell him you did that."

"Oh, please *don't*." It would only make things worse. Guy had already got quite the wrong idea.

"Why not? It might lift his spirits for another six months siege warfare on the impenetrable fortress of Catherine."

She nearly pushed him off his dining chair.

"Stop it! Unacceptable behaviour." Mother had her hand on the bell ready to ring for her ever-diminishing fleet of servants. "*I'd* like to know where Guy will be sent, too."

Mother sounded solicitous, but Cathy suspected it was more like a keen housekeeper wanting to know the exact whereabouts of a fly or a spider.

"He could be sent anywhere with a name like Palamara." Julius was always charming and polite to Guy and his family in person, but behind his back he spoke rather differently. "The most sensible plan *would* be to intern him. He's too much of a risk. Sentimental attachment and youthful radicalism are a dangerous cocktail."

Cathy thought this was a little unfair. Guy abhorred Mussolini. Called him a posturing tyrant. And it was hardly Guy's fault where his parents had been born.

"What does your friend study at Cambridge?" Ralph Redcliffe wanted to know.

"Physics," Geoff said. "He's obsessed with Cathode ray tubes, he says. Anything that sounds like Cathy, if you ask me."

Julius laughed. But Commander Redcliffe's face took on a very serious look. "Cathode rays. Really? Are you sure?"

Geoff nodded. "Absolutely. He's been obsessed with them for years."

Cathy saw Commander Redcliffe take out a small silver pen, and write the name Palamara on the back of one of his own calling cards. Which he slipped back into his pocket. She could've asked why, but she didn't want to spend the evening talking about Guy.

Besides, she didn't want to give Commander Redcliffe any encouragement. As it was his eyes darkened whenever he looked at her. And while it was flattering being admired, she resented his predatory stare – it made her feel awkward. She reached for her wine glass and swirled the contents, hoping it made her look worldly and strong. "Daddy? Tell me how we're going to keep hold of Malta."

Anne

Bright and early at breakfast time in the Wrennery Mess Hall. Anne presided over fifty wrens, led prayers, and made the announcements. "Good news," she said. "The new girls are arriving today."

The girls gave a mixture of cheers and groans. Some were expecting friends and looked forward to seeing them, but others were more worried about queues for the bathroom. The Wrennery had only one room with a bath in it, and two old-fashioned water closets. There was only one other lavatory the girls could use, and that had been placed – heaven knows why – in the stables.

Each bedroom had a pedestal handbasin, thank goodness, in which the Wrens could wash their hair. Anne thought there would have been a mutiny if not for those basins.

Only five new girls were joining them today. But even five extra to be fed and looked after added to the complications Anne was facing. She wished Linda, with her no-nonsense approach, was here to welcome them with her. But she was on a double shift doing some mysterious driving assignment. And Anne's duties were stacking up around her. The man who taught Morse was unwell today, and they were trying to find a replacement. The gardener had found a wasps' nest near one of the Nissen huts, which had the potential to cause a lot of excitement. A tap had gone wrong in the scullery. The whole place had gone crazy, and Anne was rushed off her feet.

The new consignment of Wrens would be employed as Boat Crew in the harbour, so she expected hearty, outdoorsy girls. The Boat Crew category was sought after – so many girls applied that they could afford to be choosy. Initially, the proper Navy had been very reluctant to put Wrens on the boats, and it had been a victory when Mrs Laughton Mathews persuaded the Navy top brass that women could indeed manage a boat without falling in the drink or becoming pregnant before the shift was up.

The new girls would be put to work the following week on a runabout – taking mail out to the Navy ships at anchor, and ferrying passengers to and from the shore. Until they could start, they would be undertaking training opportunities with some of the other girls.

Mid-morning, four of them arrived on the same train from their basic training facility at Mill Hill. They were the tough athletic girls she was expecting, but the last one. She was different. A slender girl, with pale skin and rather lovely dark red hair. She turned up in a polished Navy staff car. With soulful eyes, she gazed up at the Wrennery from the passenger seat, while the driver ran round to open the door for her. And the driver was none other than Commander Ralph Redcliffe. Today, oddly, he was wearing civilian clothes. He looked wonderful. Nobody ever accused a man like *that* of being too 'mature'.

Anne almost saluted him when she greeted them outside the house. Which would have been a mistake. "Hello, Commander."

The new girl with the lovely eyes looked up at the sky in irritation. "Oh well, it was worth a try."

Anne knew she'd trodden on a nerve or something. "Delighted to see you, Officer Foxton," Redcliffe said. "No need to salute when I'm in civvies. This is Cathy. I want you to take *great* care of her."

He gazed like a melted caramel biscuit at Cathy – lucky girl – and Anne's heart sank a little bit lower.

Cathy

In the end Cathy was quite glad Ralph Redcliffe drove her down, because they'd passed the station on the way and she'd seen how chaotic it was. The war seemed to require everyone to change places, like some gigantic board game. So Ralph drove her to Pompey, and all the way he was utterly charming. Cathy felt almost sorry she couldn't like him, but there it was.

He *even* wore civvies to turn up there, at Cathy's request. Which was actually rather sweet. She hadn't seriously expected he would do that for her, but then, to her surprise, he did. She'd been worried about how it would look, arriving there with him, and meeting the other Wrens. "If you turn up wearing brass buttons and gold braid, everyone's going to know about Daddy."

To Cathy, Ralph looked even older in his casual clothing. It was all English tweed and old leather brogues. But it was a kind gesture. His Navy finery travelled down with them in a suitcase in the back of the car.

When they were inside the building, the woman who'd met them outside picked up a clipboard from the front desk. The sign on it read "Anne L. Foxton, W.R.N.S". And she was just as Ralph said she would be: welcoming and nice. She pulled a clipboard from under her arm. "Your surname, please?"

"That one." Cathy pointed at the name, which appeared near the top of the list. "But can I be known as Cathy Smythe? Or even better, Cathy Smith."

Anne didn't comment, she seemed to be a professional person. Nothing like the dreadful old dragon at the basic training school. She obliged and pencilled a correction over the top of "Bancroft-Smythe".

Ralph folded his arms in disapproval. "Why hide who you are?"

"Because after a lifetime of living with what comes after, I'd love to know what it's like to be Cathy Smith."

He didn't understand. "But you're very proud of your father."

The woman on the desk was much more understanding. "Actually, it might be for the best if it isn't common knowledge, sir. And it is quite a long name, isn't it?"

Ralph opened his mouth to speak but Cathy decided to cut him off. "Thank you so much, Wren Officer Foxton, *hugely* appreciated."

And the woman had sent her an eyeball telegram to show that she understood, bless her. "We'll get you settled in your cabin, shall we?"

"Which room?" Ralph asked, lifting up the case, fully intending to take it up there for her. Anne stopped him. "Oh, we don't allow men in the ladies' cabins, Commander. Cathy can take it up herself."

Thank God. Images of Ralph in her new bedroom was something she could do without. "I'll take it, Ralph. If I'm here to train for a man's job, I'm sure I can manage a suitcase."

Reluctantly, he put it down. But didn't turn to go. "I was hoping to take you to tea somewhere. I don't have to get back to the Admiralty for an hour or so."

Why on earth is everyone so keen on having tea, all of a sudden? All they talk about is having tea.

"Tea is available, here, Captain. One of the Wrens in the galley will be happy to make some for you."

Cathy shook her head. "Just go, Ralph. Please. Just go."

He put the case down, reached for her slim arm, and pulled her awkwardly towards him, so he could give her a peck on the cheek. She allowed this, as she had many times before, but only with an eye-roll and a look of resignation. He smelt like all Navy men in her circle. Soap and cigars. She pushed him away. "Good-*bye*, Ralph."

She noticed that Anne Foxton stood by looking wistful. Silly old Ralph. He should have asked *her* out for tea.

Then he turned and went, and Cathy stared at his departing back. Watched him get into his car. "Foolish man. If he'd offered to buy me a stiff drink I might have said yes."

Anne stared at her like she was from another species.

A pair of girls walked in through the main door, having seen Ralph Redcliffe in the driveway.

"Who was *that*?" they wanted to know. "He was rather gorgeous."

"No idea," Cathy lied. "I met him at the station."

Cathy saw Anne raise an eyebrow, and knew she'd gone too far, but the woman didn't challenge her for sounding so brazen. "Take Cathy to the main cabin, please. There's a bed for her, made up and ready."

The bed in the dorm room or cabin was covered in a nice candlewick bedspread. It had an anchor motif on it, but apart from that the room was very suburban, very girly, very cosy. There were three other beds in the room, with just enough room for a small cabinet and lamp between. It was like a small hospital ward in a cottage hospital, perhaps, nicer than a boarding school, but not quite as soft and squishy as a good hotel.

She was happy to see a friendly face – Mavis the cook, from the day she got her uniform – who had the bed next door but one. Cathy smiled and patted her arm. "Shipmates."

Mavis took her through the rules. No clothes on the floor, no smoking in bed. But they were allowed to listen to the wireless. They could go out to the pictures as long as they were back in good time. Walks were permitted, with other girls or with the boys from the aerial training ground. Some things were out of bounds. "We're not allowed to go down to the Docks – they're out of bounds – unless you have Admiralty clearance."

Cathy had no problem getting through Admiralty barriers, but now was not the time to say so.

Anne came round to see if she was unpacked and settled. The other girls in the room, Delia, Binky and Mavis were all in a state of excitement, because they had a visit to Lee in the morning – the Fleet Air Arm base. A feasibility exercise – to test their aptitude to perform ground crew work. How exciting, thought Cathy, and ran downstairs to get permission to join in – which to her delight, was granted. She spent the whole evening studying the information sent through by the instructor, so she would be well prepared. So nice to have something to look forward to – and what a wonderful thing to put in a letter to her brother.

Chapter Five

Cathy

On a crisp morning at the FAA training station, Cathy and the girls gathered in a nervous group waiting for their instructor. They had been trucked to the base in a Navy transport truck, told to wait on 'dispersal', an area of the runway where a squadron and its crew disperses after a mission. The weather was brisk, the April sun above them. The girls were in brand new dungarees, issued that morning by their quartermaster. A Spitfire – recently landed – stood warm and waiting for them on the grass. Ready for re-armament. The maintenance men that normally did this task were sitting on a long low trolley over by the hangars, watching. There were five or six of them. They passed round a packet of cigarettes and prepared to enjoy the performance.

Delia – with her straight blonde hair scraped into a cadet cap, said, "They're much bigger when you get up close to them, aren't they?"

Binky, red lipstick perfect, stared at the aircraft. "Do we really have to climb up onto the wing? With all those men watching?"

Cathy said, "You've got breeks on, for goodness sake. They won't see your knickers."

Mavis looked worried.

Binky glanced across dispersal towards the hangar. "Shhh! Wet your lips, girls. Here he is."

Their instructor came towards them across the grass, with a look of doomed resignation. He was an officer, and wore a peaked hat, but for today's mission he was in a dark blue boilersuit and a pair of rubber boots. Cathy and the other girls stood to attention. Stuck their chests out as they'd been taught to do – and saluted.

And the boys on the bomb trolley whistled.

The instructor scowled at the spectators, but he didn't reprimand them, which Cathy thought was a great mistake. If there's one thing the men should never be allowed to forget, it's that the Navy requires absolute discipline.

"Reggie Hall. CPO. Maintenance Unit," the man said, by way of introduction. His voice sounded shaky. Another mistake, thought Cathy.

But at least he was trying. "Today, we're going to learn how to re-arm a fighter." He glanced doubtfully at the girls, and they, in turn, shifted uneasily in their new boilersuits with the fold marks still on them. "Well, ladies. This is a first for me too."

Oh – fatal. A ripple of laughter from the men. *We can see that*, somebody murmured. They nudged and swayed, barely hiding their amusement.

Poor Reggie was dying. "I mean the training. Not the re-arming." He glanced at Delia. "And obviously, I've trained lots of cadets before, just not..."

Just not anyone from a ladies' finishing school, thought Cathy. *With red lippie and a bullet bra under their boilersuit.* He speaks too quietly. She willed him to be a bit tougher. *Sock it to them, sir, so they sit up and listen. The women are nervous, can't you see? And the men are bordering on disrespectful.*

Maybe it worked. Her twin-like attempt at telepathy. He turned to the men. "Yes, yes. This Wren-training lark may be amusing, but I must remind you – you are still on your shift, getting paid for doing nothing. You are here to offer support, if required."

Some of the men seemed to like that idea. Others looked dismissive and scathing. The instructor – Reggie Hall – said, "remember, too. These girls are all volunteers."

One smiling man passed a hand over his eyes as if he couldn't believe he was witnessing such folly.

The instructor asked the girls to bring to mind the memo he'd sent across to the Wrennery. Training instructions for today's exercise. Cathy had studied hers in great detail. Her first and only chance to learn about air-sea battle.

He pointed to the Browning guns on the aircraft – to port and to starboard. "So what's the first thing we do before starting work, when the fighters return to the Fleet Air airfield?"

"Check to see if the gun firing controls are at 'safe', sir." Cathy answered.

"Good girl."

Delia next, "And then one of us works above the wing, the other underneath."

"Correct. Armourer on top, his mate underneath. Each unscrews a panel. But before that. Before we take the magazine out, who remembers?"

Silence. The men on the wall let go some smoky breaths from their cigarettes and waited – with an air of expectant amusement.

Everyone had read it, but no one would say it. Cathy murmured a curse word under her breath, worthy of any sailor. In a clear tone, she recited from the training memo. "The *cocking* lever must be held in the '*cocked*' position, sir."

Which released a ripple of laughter from the displaced ground crew, and irritation from their beleaguered instructor. He rounded on the men. "Yes, yes, boys. The vocabulary of aircraft engineering does rather lend itself to double entendre. I'm acutely aware of that. But this morning, I would like to educate these ladies properly – "

One young man leaned forward and ran a hand over his face to hide his amusement. "Wouldn't we all…"

"In the correct re-*armament* procedure," Reggie said, pale with annoyance.

"So why don't you buzz off and get yourselves a cup of tea in the Naafi?" suggested Cathy. Which was sensible. But nobody moved. They weren't allowed to. "Go on, then, laugh. But we'll be doing your job, if you get seconded to an aircraft carrier."

The poor maintenance boys looked glum. They wore blue coveralls today – but on board ship they would do this work in the garb of an ordinary seaman. All of them were, technically, sailors.

The instructor, however, looked a tiny bit happier. Perhaps dreaming of a day when the men on the bomb trolley had gone to sea, and *he* was left with the ladies. He turned to the men. "Right, you and you," he said choosing two of them. "Get up there and make that lever safe so we can get the magazine out properly."

The men ran lightly onto the wings of the plane in their rubber boots, and one made the necessary adjustment, while the other, in a practiced movement, started undoing the hatch cover. Under orders, Cathy noticed, they were at least reasonably compliant.

Reggie got into his stride and pressed on with the clearing process for a Browning gun. "Now we'll move to the gun on the starboard side and have a go at implementing the procedure. Turn around needs to be fast, ladies, we want this airplane re-armed and ready."

Delia climbed up onto the wing, wobbled a bit, but walked along and leaned into the small cramped cockpit. Looking for the cocking lever. The maintenance man – still up there on the port side – leaned across and pointed to it. Gave her a languid smile.

Risk-taker, thought Cathy, as the lovely Delia gave him a look that could have curdled aviation fuel. "Don't even think about touching my hand, sailor. Or anywhere else, for that matter."

Reggie talked them through from the very beginning. "Next step, please?"

Delia called out from up top. "Armourer reports 'guns clear!' sir."

"Yes. Nobody moves til we hear that. And what does it mean, girls?"

"Safe to work in front of the gun?" volunteered Binky.

Reggie nodded. "Less risk of accidental firing." Poor man. No wonder he was nervous. Dead Wren on the dispersal? No thanks, not this morning.

"It's actually perfectly straightforward," Mavis said, surprising Cathy. "It's a bit like maintaining a sewing machine."

Even dizzy little Binky was starting to enjoy it. "Quite a responsibility, isn't it?" she whispered to Cathy. "Making the guns ready for battle."

Reggie asked them to gather round. He picked up a roll of what looked like pajama material, and got a small oil-can out of his top pocket. "Next, we put oil on a piece of flannelette, mount it on the dipper, and lubricate the shaft. Come on, girls, who'd like to try it?"

The sailors on the wall convulsed with laughter. And Cathy turned on them and roared – "You chowder-brained bunch of fish heads. We are learning how to clean a Browning gun whether you like it or not. Do you want me to report you to Admiral Bancroft-Smythe – with whom I am well acquainted? *Silence* from all of you – or you'll be on lavatory block duty."

And Reggie added weakly. "Yes, boys. That's right. Do as the lady tells you."

Linda

Linda pulled up outside HMS *Nautilus* – a large country house – to pick up her experts. She expected a team of brass hats, but the first one out of the house was a man in a boilersuit, Wellington boots, and dark knitted hat. Two others followed him – a man of about forty in a greatcoat, and a sailor in standard blue tunic and bell bottoms.

"Where's Toby?" said Greatcoat.

"There, sir. Coming in on his bike."

A young man in civvies cycled towards them, dismounted, and spent several moments removing bicycle clips and chaining his bike to the railings.

The Greatcoat got in the front alongside Linda. "Hello Jenny, thanks for turning up at short notice."

"It's Linda." He was one of those men who liked to call all the Wrens by the generic term: 'Jenny'.

She'd love to ask what happened to their last driver, but tact demanded she say nothing. Greatcoat did the introductions while the other three men all slid across the bench seat of her car. Greatcoat's real name was Captain Ted Morrison and the others were Clegg and Frye.

"Linda Tomkins," she said, and touched her cadet's cap in salute. "Where to, sir?"

"Dockyard, please."

The experts were not chatty. But Captain Morrison, in an effort to be polite, made a couple of attempts at conversation – did she have 'people' in the royal navy, and was she comfortable in her current billet? Linda said the Wrennery was the nicest place she'd ever lived and no, she didn't have any people in the Navy. No brothers at sea. No uncles who'd won any medals. She was an only child and her father owned a greengrocer's shop.

She glanced in her rear-view mirror at the men in the back. Clegg was the one in the boilersuit, Frye was in the ratings uniform, and the one in civvies – Toby Wallis.

They tootled through the lanes as if out for a picnic, and then the streets as it became more built up near the docks, tall buildings punctuated by bomb damage – the docks seem to be a target for many sticks of bombs. They went past a checkpoint, Captain Morrison waved a pass at the two men on duty, and Linda drove them through.

It was daytime, but she was tired from the nightshift. She longed to park the car, pull a nice tartan blanket over her legs, and go to sleep.

One of the men in the back tapped her on the shoulder. "Put that in't glove box, will yer?"

She looked round to see what he meant. It was Toby. He held out a moleskin notebook, tied up with a brown cord.

"Certainly." She took the book, leaned across Morrison's knees and opened the glove compartment. She stowed the book inside.

"Thanks. Now if anything appens, like. Give that to my commanding officer."

"What?"

"That there book. It's important."

"Alright ...um, sir." She wasn't sure what rank Toby held, if any, or how to address him.

"Let's get at it, then" said Morrison, who was already opening his car door and swinging his legs out. "Sooner we start, the sooner it's done."

The men got out and thanked her, asked her to wait, and she was left on her own in the Navy issue car. It was black, shiny, with bulging fenders and running boards – a pre-war model – as they nearly all were, the factories were all making spitfires.

It seemed to be taking an awful long time. It had been okay at first. A welcome break, and she was happy to sit in the car and daydream, or touch up her makeup. And then as the afternoon ticked on, she decided she'd settle back for a snooze. So she settled back in her seat, loosened her chin strap and pulled her cap down low to shade her eyes.

Cathy

"Now, *that's* more like it." Cathy pulled on her white square neck top and bell bottom trousers, relieved that she wasn't expected to work the harbour boats in a skirt. She fastened on her 'HMS' sailor cap, taking care to make sure the chin strap was tight so she wouldn't lose it if the breeze rose. Last of all she added the double-breasted jacket.

Her days followed a classic pattern. After breakfast – which was usually tea, toast and sausages – she and the Boat Wrens would wait in the porch until the transport arrived. They would pile into the vehicle and drive a short way down to the dockyard. They would show their passes and be admitted past the chain link fence and through into an area that the Navy commandeered. Then the day would really begin...

This morning the tide was low. Their boat was tied up by the old stone steps that led directly into the water. If the tide was out – as it was today – the seaward edge of the bottom six steps would be visible, covered in thick green seaweed. They made their way down the slippery steps and hopped on board the boat. While one wren got the engine running, the other three made ready to cast off. While the engine was turning over, the mail van would be driven up close and the Wrens would first get the bags on to the quayside, then throw them onto the deck of the boat. Cathy got to be at the helm and everyone said she was a born leader and would soon be recognized as their Leading Wren. She steered her craft into the middle of the harbour. – proud to be at the helm. And be it only small and unimpressive – it was her first command. They would putter out into the harbour – and come alongside one of the Navy ships at anchor. As the grey side of the ship loomed up, they would wave at the waiting sailors – who would help them tie up the boat. Then she and the three other Wrens would offload the mailbags so the boys could have their letters.

Her father, the Admiral, always told her what a hush came over the men as they stood or crouched down on the deck, perhaps with a cigarette between their fingers, to read those all-important letters. "Jack loves his letters," he used to say. "And no matter what you hear elsewhere – take it from me – Jack loves his womenfolk too. And I don't just mean the girl-in-every-port story. I mean he idealizes them. His sister. His mother. His sweetheart. If they write to him, their letters can bring a tear to the most battle-hardened man." Well, that's what the Admiral told Cathy, anyway.

Cathy looked up at the men who had come to help the girls get the mail bags slung over. It was usually the same trio of boys. All in ratings uniforms, complete with sailor collars and dark round caps with HMS on the tally band. For the first few weeks the arrival of the Boat Wrens in the harbour had been a huge novelty for the boys on board. Wrens oiling heavy chains or taking control of the tiller. Girls dulling the engine to a low throb and handling heavy ropes like any sailor. But after a few days they got comfortable and by the time a ship had been in for a week or two, they were on first name terms.

"Hand it up, then, Cathy-girl." A young man with a good set of shoulders and close-cut blond hair under his cap leaned over the rail to speak to Cathy.

She hurled the heavy sack at him, teasingly, and he pretended to stagger back under the weight.

He said, "You'll be getting muscles like Pop-Eye, darling."

She made a strong-arm pose for him, and combined it with a provocative pout. "You've noticed."

He grinned. He'd noticed her, alright. Him and nine hundred other sailors. "Last one." He pointed to the last mail bag, slumped half empty on the deck of her boat.

She'd found that the lighter ones were actually harder to handle, the fabric flapped and made them hard to throw. This one was no exception – she nearly missed, but he was skilful and caught it before it went into the drink. "Oooh – nice save!"

"See you tomorrow, Patrick."

Chapter Six

Anne

That morning Anne Foxton was fielding a call from Vera Laughton Mathews – the indomitable leader of the Wrens – who had taken the group from nothing and made them into a force of more than sixty thousand women. There was talk of getting another ten thousand recruits signed up by the end of the year – so yet more men could be freed up to join the fighting fleet. Anne was quite enjoying reporting all her progress to Mrs Laughton Mathews. She was proud of what she had achieved. But today, 'Skipper' had news of her own.

"Anne – this is news alright – are your girls up to an inspection?"

"By the Admiralty, do you mean?"

"No. Even higher."

Anne laughed. "Nobody's higher than the Admiralty, are they?" In the circles she moved in, the glorious Navy played second to none. But a thought struck her. "You don't mean.... Do you?"

"Yes. I do. I mean *royalty*."

Anne gasped and wanted to hear all the details. But two people came through the double doors into the entrance hall of the Wrennery – arguing hammer and tongs – right in front of Anne's desk. She knew them from the supper dance the other night. Delia Finlay, the girl who looked like a petulant starlet, and her enthusiastic flyboy. Last seen whirling round the dancefloor while Anne had a chaste lemonade and soda – and now ruining her telephone call with Mrs Laughton Mathews.

They'd looked so happy then, only now the young man's ears were red and the girl looked cross and spiteful. By the sound of it, their lunch date had not been a roaring success. Delia was telling him- in no uncertain terms – that they were 'through', as the Americans would say. And bizarrely her boyfriend wouldn't take no for an answer. He trailed her across the gracious entrance hall of the Wrennery, begging her to explain.

"But Delia... Delia! You said you liked me. Loads of other chaps are getting married. Why not us? What's wrong with me?"

"What's wrong with you?" said the girl. "Well, quite a number of things, actually. I hardly know where to begin."

Anne expected that sort of reply, coming from Delia, who was always complaining. Nothing about the Wrennery was good enough for her. Food. Towels. Roommates. All unacceptable and sub-standard. Delia was difficult to please. It pained Anne to see the way she wheeled on her chap and spoke to him so unkindly. "You're rude and you're moody and you've got a dreadful temper."

"But there's no time left. You *can't* make me start at square one. I've only got a few days."

"It's preposterous to ask me to marry you at such short notice, when you've never even *met* my people and I know nothing of yours." She folded her arms, a pretty child in a stubborn mood. "I don't want to get into something I might regret. What's the big secret, Dicky, is your pa in the clink or something?"

He looked like he'd been stung. "There isn't time for all that meet-the-parents rubbish."

"There isn't time to get married, either."

He looked desperate, tried to grab her arm. "But Delia. I've already asked for leave."

"Get your hands off me." She raised her elbow, pointed and sharp, at the poor boy's face.

Anne rose, covered the telephone receiver with one hand, "Excuse me? Can you do this somewhere else? I'm taking an important call."

They didn't seem to register that she was there. They were too wrapped up in their personal drama.

He said she'd lied to him all week and Delia said she'd never lied and he could go to hell. Voices rose. Tempers too. Things got loud and ugly. But no matter how horrible she got, Dicky didn't seem able to accept the rejection. "But I don't understand. You have to tell me why?"

Delia turned on him. "Because I don't want to be a widow at twenty-two! And you fliers don't tend to stick around that long. I'd much rather wait until the end of the war and see who actually makes it."

Makes it. Some girls derive all their vocabulary from the cinema.

"How pragmatic of you," he said. "And will you marry a Nazi, if they win?"

The sound must have reached Mrs Laughton Mathews via the telephone line. "Hello? Hello?"

"I'm still here." Anne was torn between one duty and another.

"My dear, it sounds as if you have some kind of an incident going on."

"Yes, there is. I'm afraid I'll have to go and sort it out."

"Go. We can't allow people to air their dirty laundry in public. Phone me back as soon as you can. It really is rather important."

"Thank you, Skipper – I'm terribly sorry."

She replaced the telephone receiver in its cradle, and came out from behind the polished wooden reception desk.

"Tavistock, isn't it? Lieutenant Tavistock?" She judged his rank to be *second* lieutenant, from his peaked cap and the single gold stripe on his sleeve, but she used the generic term of address – and it worked. She said, "I must ask you to leave. We've all got more important things to do than have arguments in the hallway."

He looked visibly upset. She softened, experiencing an unexpected wave of sympathy for him. "You seem like a nice young man, truly you do. And I don't know why this silly girl won't marry you. I'd marry you like a shot if I was in her position, but she obviously doesn't want to, does she? And have you *never* heard that expression about bashing your head against a brick wall?"

"Well of course I have," he said, turning his pilot's cap round in his hands. "I'll be shipped out next week, so I won't trouble any of you again."

He seemed crestfallen, staring at Anne's nicely polished shoes, his young face blank with disappointment. She wondered if he'd turn on his heel and leave, now that she'd told him off and explained how foolish he was being. But then ...his gaze travelled, taking in the shape of her legs in their black silk stockings, the hem of her A-line skirt, the curve of her hips, the way her crisp white shirt fitted her upper body. The slim black tie pinned neatly to her shirt. She wasn't wearing her regulation jacket – it was over the back of her chair. She felt almost naked without it, while he made this all-too-obvious appraisal. His gaze finally arrived at her face.

He had found his new prospect.

The nature of his thoughts, as Anne imagined them, made her blush to the roots of her hair.

He smiled slowly, and his eyes lit up with a kind of amusement. "*What* did you say – about marrying me yourself? Are you available next Thursday, by any chance?"

Delia gave a roar of irritation. "Dicky, you incorrigible beast! You think you can just turn round and ask the next bit of skirt you see? Honestly, someone should report you to your senior officer."

Anne was flustered. She had only meant to soften the rejection. And as for Dee referring to her as 'the next bit of skirt' – well – she was surprised that Delia even knew the phrase.

Dicky turned to Delia again, giving as good as he got. "I don't see how I can be reported for proposing *marriage* to women. That's hardly indecent, is it? And since you've made it plain that you're not interested, how can it be any business of yours?"

"You don't know her from a bar of soap. You're laughable. You really are. I know I'm not the first woman you've chased and given your little 'marry me' speech to. Everyone knows you're a cad."

"I object to being called a cad simply for pursuing the opportunities that come my way. There is precious little time and you know it. Now, if you hadn't led me on..."

"I led *you* on? That's ironic, when all you've done is chase me all week," Delia stepped forward to laugh in his face, a bad idea, and Anne seriously wondered if she might need to call for reinforcements.

"Stop it!" She rose to her full height, which was not as tall as him, unfortunately, but she made the most of what she had, and she put her hand like a barrier between the mismatched lovers. "Stop this silliness, immediately. You may live to regret it, Delia, if you part on fighting terms. Lieutenant, did you say you are being sent to sea next week?'

"Yes. Aircraft carrier – destination undisclosed."

"Well, then, be sensible, and don't ruin your last week on shore. Shore leave isn't much fun if you have to spend it explaining things to the disciplinary committee." She paused for effect, while the silly boy took this in. She outranked him – and as the commanding officer of HMS *Resilient*, she could report him – and she would, if she had to. Then she turned to the girl. "Delia. Thank this man for taking you out to tea, and say goodbye like a lady."

The girl didn't want to, but she looked sulkily at the young man and then smoothed a strand of hair behind her ear. "Goodbye, Dicky."

And Anne took a formal tone with him and said, "We wish you well, Sir, and pray for your safe return."

He nodded, more polite now, and put on his peaked cap. "I'll be off then. Goodbye, Delia, and thank you, this has been fun."

Delia rolled her eyes and walked away with as much dignity as she could muster. She sashayed up the lovely curved stairs that led to the dormitories on the first floor, obviously hoping he was watching.

He was. But he waited until she was only half way up before he winked at Anne, and gave her that look again. "I rather liked your idea. Could we talk it over tonight, at the Waterman's Arms?"

He was impossible. She leant forward, almost as conspiratorial as him, and said "A lady's feelings are not to be trifled with, even if you do have to go to sea next week."

"Eight o'clock, then?"

"I am in no mood for jokes, Lieutenant."

He looked at her, and smiled. "Neither am I."

He turned, pushed through the double doors and ran lightly down the steps to his car. Anne stood there, in the middle of the entrance hall, wondering what had hit her, with the memory of his hopeful eyes vivid in her mind. Through the glass panels – each taped with an 'X' in case they got blown in by a bomb – she watched him drive away.

"Crazy man," she said to no one in particular, and sat down to phone Mrs Laughton Mathews.

•••

It was confirmed that afternoon. A member of the royal family was coming to see them. Not the king. They were told it was definitely not the king, to avoid disappointment. But a card-carrying royal – probably a woman – would be coming to inspect the girls. It was such exciting news that Anne came into the Nissen huts and interrupted their training session – an unprecedented move – but she had to let the girls know. They must be ready.

The visit would occur on Wednesday, and urgent preparations must be made. The Wrennery and the classrooms must be made shipshape. And the girls must all look their best. Only a few days – and so much to do. It was enough to send anyone into a tizzy.

Ralph

From a vantage point on the bridge deck of a Hunt-class destroyer, Ralph Redcliffe stood, and saw Cathy and her team heading towards the ship across the rippling water. The harbour vessel she loved so much was known to the men as The Boatload of Beauty. Or booty, as some of the men would say. Cathy was at the wheel, and she was a sight to see, steering jauntily towards the warship, with a crisp white wake curving away on the sea behind her. Her white square neck tunic fluttered in the morning breeze, and her sailor cap was lashed tight under her chin. Ralph would definitely have sighed if he hadn't been trained to keep his feelings battened like hatches in a rising swell.

Was he really 'too old' for Cathy? He was only thirty-eight – although he suspected that Cathy thought he was considerably older. Her parents would certainly give their blessing, but with a high-spirited girl like her, their blessing might even be a hindrance...

He watched her manoeuvre alongside, admiring the panache with which she did so. Her girls ran to the heavy coiled ropes. They tied up smartly – throwing lines up to the waiting sailors. She didn't look up; she didn't see that Ralph was watching. He had half a mind to call out to her, just like the other sailors did. Instead, he watched her throwing the heavy mail sacks across to the men. He saw them laughing and joking with her. One of them – a man with blond hair like a Norwegian – was particularly friendly. He ran along the deck, bell bottoms flaring, leaning over the rail to exchange some banter with Cathy. He frowned at this sight, and resolved that he must do something. A girl like Cathy, consorting with common sailors in that easy familiar way?

He rationalised his thoughts, even though he knew them to be selfish; he re-packaged them as 'his duty'. It wasn't difficult to convince himself and find a more logical rationale. Cathy had military strategy as second nature, there were many other ways that she could be used.

He watched her laugh as she threw the last of the mail bags across to the Norwegian – who probably came from Woolwich or Hull. He was full of laughter too. He blew her a kiss. "See you next time, Cathy-girl."

Not if I can help it.

Cathy was too valuable for harbour work and Jack Tar was not to be trusted.

Linda

Linda got worried about how long this 'inspection' was going to take. Her experts had been gone for hours and now the sun was so low, she wondered if they'd got another lift and gone home without her. She looked at her wristwatch. Everyone at the Wrennery would be having supper, and her tummy was grumbling, letting her know it was very sorry to have missed out. Nobody had even had the courtesy to come round to the car and tell her what was going on. But she couldn't drive off without telling the team, could she?

So she got out, locked the door of the car, and went for a wander. The area had been bombed last night – there was fresh bomb damage everywhere she looked. They were working in the Admiralty controlled area, which contained terraced office buildings made of small red bricks – a lot of which were scattered all over the road. Three buildings had been blown to bits last night when the Luftwaffe left its calling card. On the other side of the road there were warehouses– old Victorian ones – and some were so badly damaged that whole walls were blown out, window frames too – they were lying on the road among the scattered bricks.

She rounded the corner, and saw the four men deep in conversation, two of them leaning on their shovels, the other two – Toby and Greatcoat – real name, Captain Matthew Morrison –were in a tense discussion.

She gingerly stepped into a warehouse through the open side blown out by a bomb. Part of the roof was missing, and she could see the three men gathered around – the sailor and the man in the boiler suit both leaning on their shovels.

"Hello?" she called out. She struggled to climb over a pile of wreckage and some bits slithered down.

Their faces whitened with alarm when they saw her. Hands went up to warn her not take a single step more. A gasp, an agonized whisper. "Stay right where you are."

A flash of irritation from Captain Morrison. "You were supposed to wait in the car."

Linda said, "Sorry – but it's getting so late I was worried ... Oh." She saw it. The tail end of a bomb, wedged deep into the concrete, and they were all gathered around it, excavating as carefully as if uncovering a beautiful floor in a Roman Villa. "Oh my God. Is that thing...a *bomb*?"

They nodded. Almost in unison. Silent.

Until Toby answered in his broad North Country accent. Deadpan calm. "Yes, Wren Tomkins. It's an unexploded bomb."

Morrison wiped some sweat from his brow. "And we'd like to keep it that way."

Frye said. "We're trying to formulate a plan. A make-safe."

She nodded. Swallowing hard. She tried to form the words "I'm sorry, I didn't know."

"It's alright, love, just leave slowly," said Frye.

Heart thumping. She took two steps backwards, making the pile of rubble slither worse, if anything, than when she had picked her way over it to get in.

"For God's sake be careful," said Morrison.

"Sorry," she breathed. Her throat felt raw. A mixture of brick dust and emotion.

How could they do it? How could they stand there, calm as you please, around an unexploded bomb? The image of them, Frye scratching his head, Toby with his wire clippers, and Morrison with sweat on his brow, stayed in her mind. They were trying to make it safe. *Trying*? Even the word was loaded with uncertainty.

What if they failed?

Chapter Seven

Anne

Anne had been so busy with preparations for the not-so-secret Royal visit that when supper time came, it was like realizing Christmas had arrived un-announced. She laughed it off at supper in the Wrennery dining room, addressing the girls as they sat at long tables for their evening meal – "The enemy need no better invasion strategy than to spread a rumour that Royalty is on its way – our defences would be down in minutes."

As it was, supper was a riot of gossip and excitement. What parade would they do for the Important Visitor? What flags would they fly? Would Her Majesty want a demonstration of signalling, perhaps – like an official military tattoo? The girls clinked their teacups and opened the special pots of jam to celebrate.

Finally, the hour came when she was 'officially' off duty, making cocoa in the scullery. She had come to realize, since taking this promotion, that an Officer Wren in charge of a Wrennery is never completely off-duty. But she was about as relaxed as she could be, under the circumstances. She'd unpinned her hair, and it was curling softly over her shoulders. She never bothered with curlers. For daytime wear, she would twist up her hair, secure it with four or five pins, and put it in a semi-invisible hairnet. When she let her hair down at night, she often found it held a bit of curl from being twirled up like that.

She was in the kitchen, where low sunlight came in through the glass panels in the back door. It was lovely now the evenings were lighter, and there was no need to blackout the windows for another hour because the clocks had just gone forward. The peace and light in the room reminded her of the year she met Jim – 1937 – before all this madness began. She had her cup of cocoa ready on the kitchen table – too hot to sip yet, but giving out a warm aromatic scent. She'd changed out of her sensible navy-issue brogues and into her slippers. They were the only truly feminine shoes she possessed, as they were meant to be part of her trousseau – the treasured set of clothes she had put together to wear on her honeymoon with Jim. Most of it she still couldn't bear to touch, although the clothing shortages were getting so bad that eventually she'd have to. When her old slippers fell apart, she'd had no spare coupons, so the honeymoon ones had been pressed into service. They were very pretty – open toe, pink fluffy band over each foot, and kitten heels, as they were known in the trade.

She was still fielding anything that got thrown at her, dealing with the girls' problems, helping them, sending them into the scullery to fill up their hot water bottles if they still wanted them. Heavens it was April now, and some of the girls *still* wanted to take hot water bottles to bed with them. Like Mavis, who appeared in her curlers, to fill her hot water bottle on the dot of 8pm every night.

Binky ran in from the main entrance hall. "Miss Foxton, I mean, Ma'am, or whatever I'm supposed to call you?"

They were supposed to call her Wren Officer Foxton, but she'd talk about that when she read the notices at Directions tomorrow. "Yes?"

"There's a man at the front door, says he's got an appointment with you."

If she'd been holding her cocoa, she would have spilt it. *Dicky Tavistock?* Good grief. If she was a sailor she would have sworn. Epithets came to mind but did not pass her lips. She just stared in stunned horror at the bringer of the news, and felt sure she'd gone rather pale.

"He's very insistent. He wanted to waltz right in here but I told him he had to wait."

Anne shook her head. "I can't see him like this."

"You can, Miss, it's only your slippers. You'll have to speak to him. He's got a bunch of flowers."

That made Anne laugh. "Oh, a man can do anything he wants, can he? As long as he's got a bunch of flowers. How ridiculous."

Dicky Tavistock. Catching her off guard like this. "I'm not dressed. Tell him to go away."

"But you are dressed. It's only slippers and a mug of cocoa."

"My hair," Anne touched a lock of her shiny light brown hair, falling over her shoulders.

"It looks nice, Miss. It's much nicer like that than when you've got it in a bun."

"Or you could donate that to somebody who doesn't have a date," he pointed at her cup on the table, "and come with me to the Waterman's Arms."

Anne looked up at him, desperately torn, but too scared to take the gauntlet. "I didn't say yes. Earlier."

"But you didn't say no, did you?"

He held out the flowers. "So, what's it to be? Either we can sit here and discuss it, or you can hop in my car and we'll go to the Waterman's Arms."

She looked at her rapidly cooling cocoa. She didn't like to waste things. But she didn't like to waste opportunities either. It would be tempting to let him sit down and have a warm drink, it would be a laugh, in fact. A handsome – if crazy – young flyer, right here, right now in the kitchen. Chatting her up in a way that made her feel truly alive. That would be nice, but she couldn't bear the embarrassment of the other women watching him tease her – and they'd be interrupted every ten seconds by the girls, the evenings were always spent like that – another request and another hot drink, another argument erupting upstairs about whose turn it was to have a bath. She looked at the flowers, and then into his eyes. "We'll go to the Waterman's. But I'll have to get my shoes."

"That's my girl," he said. "Now, what about the flowers?"

Mavis reached for them. "I'll sort them out, if you want to go and get ready."

"Splendid idea."

Anne watched, as her flowers – the beautiful, extravagant bunch of flowers she had never even touched, let alone smelt or enjoyed – went from Dicky's hands to Mavis and away into the scullery to be plonked in a vase. It was like an omen. The sweet things in life would always pass her by, if she didn't wake up and start living.

"Will you wait while I run upstairs for my shoes?" Anne said, seized with the feeling that she really wanted to go out with him, all of a sudden.

He smiled his openly seductive smile, and raised his eyebrows. "Yes, and I'll behave myself. Don't worry."

She started to thank her lucky stars that Mavis was a plain stodgy girl in a bathrobe and curlers. But knowing Dicky, that wouldn't stop him.

Knowing Dicky? Am I really thinking like that? Knowing Dicky? When, actually, I don't know him at all.

She ran up to her 'cabin' on the first floor, grabbed her shoes, kicked off the slippers, did nothing to her hair, didn't even stop to look in the glass because she really thought that if she took too long, he'd be proposing to somebody else before she got back down again.

She ran down the stairs, as she was always telling the girls not to, shoes in hand. This was actually fun, being chased by this insane man. Insane *boy*, really – he must be a good five years younger than her. No, definitely a man – but with a boy's eagerness, and ears that went red when he was excited.

"Great," he said, when she reappeared, and started putting the shoes on her feet. "This way – my car's at the front steps. Don't worry about the laces *now*, Anne, do them up in the car."

There was a sense of urgency with Dicky that you simply couldn't argue with. He steered her through the house and down the front steps. Laces flapping. "Don't rush me – I don't want to fall to my death." But she was laughing for the first time in years.

Cathy

On an evening clear enough to see the Isle of Wight, the wind freshened in Portsmouth Harbour. There was a frigate out at anchor in the deeper water, and that evening Cathy was on Liberty Boat Duty taking groups of men from the ship to shore and back again. As they approached the quayside they were greeted by the sight of a crowd of men, about seventy of them, waiting for a lift back to their ship. Even from out on the water, it was obvious some of them were roaring drunk.

Speccy Wilson went pale. "I don't like the look of that lot."

Cathy grinned. "Quite simple. Imagine you're an infant school teacher."

Two girls tied up for her. From the wheel, Cathy turned to the swaying men on the quayside, and gave a roar of command. "All aboard, ratings. Look lively." Voice like a foghorn.

Speccy winced, but the men responded. Some even straightened and attempted a salute.

A familiar voice carried on the sea breeze. "Don't put your effing elbow in my eye, you bastard, I need that for doing my watch." Cathy searched for his face in the crowd. Patrick Clarke, from the mail bag run.

He came forward and stood at the edge of the quay. "Fancy meeting you here."

"Hello, old friend. How was your liberty?"

He grinned and raised an eyebrow. He helped her get the metal gang plank down, and stood by it to get the men aboard. He took this rather seriously. "They fall in if you don't watch them, Cathy. You have to watch them all the time. I saw a man drown once who fell off the plank."

Speccy blanched again and looked at Cathy – who patted her on the back to encourage her. "It's alright. If one goes in the drink, we'll fish him out with the boat hook."

They got most of the men sitting down. Less likely to lose one over the side if they got them sitting quietly. They counted them and Patrick called out, "Seventy-five souls." Speccy found the battered boat log and recorded the number in the appropriate place.

Cathy went to her place at the helm and they untied again and puttered out into the water.

Patrick joined her before too long and they stood together by the wheel. She found his presence mildly disconcerting. She'd never been on the same deck with him before and was glad to see he was reasonably sober – just a slight pink flush on his cheeks. He glanced back with a laugh at Speccy, who was finding a bucket for a sailor who said he needed to get rid of some rum. "She's a trooper. Never thought I'd see the day they had little posh girls running these boats." He looked at her, blue eyes finding hers. "You're doing well, Cathy."

"Thank you." She had to concentrate – the harbour was busy and although there was moonlight, it was vital to steer carefully between the other craft. She had her harbour lights on – red to port, green to starboard. They glowed as they made their way through.

He put his hand on the wheel and made an adjustment for her. She returned what she hoped was a cool, amused gaze. "I know when to helm up, thanks."

But it was nice, working with a friend. Something she'd never experienced. She risked a quick glance at his sleeve to see if she could see his badges and work out what he did. "I'm an armourer," he told her – reading her thoughts and her gestures – which reminded her of Geoff.

"We did some armoury training at Lee," she told him, thinking of how she'd learned to clean the Browning guns. And she enjoyed seeing the look of surprise on his face. "Did yer?"

She nodded. She didn't tell him it was only one afternoon.

Another larger liberty boat went past too close in the other direction and the boat rose sharply in response to the wake. Speccy fell and landed in a man's lap – and a cheer went up – which made Patrick smile again.

"On your feet, Sailor," Cathy yelled. "No time for that on this run."

The men laughed and started to sing. Poor Speccy righted herself and went into the cabin to recover. Patrick faced into the wind, beside her. And all the way to the ship, he would glance at her and then look away, almost shyly. "What is it?" she asked.

He blew out a breath. "Never had a shipmate like you, Cathy-girl."

Anne

Anne and Dicky arrived at the pub and he pushed the door open for her. She entered a room full of noise, thronging with men from the army, the navy and the air force. She wanted to turn and run away from all that banter and laughter. She wanted to run away from all the men. The whole place smelt of cigarettes, beer and men's cologne. They were everywhere, standing at the bar knocking back pints, sitting in booths or around barrels in the main bar, leaning in doorways, or lurking in shadows. A sea of men. There were only a few Waafs and Wrens, and a scattering of people in civilian clothes. The rest were all servicemen – including *lots* of sailors dressed exactly like Jim.

The tavern was old, and the room had a low ceiling, exposed beams, and an inglenook fireplace. A piano lurked in the corner, but no music came from it, the stool being used as an extra seat for a sailor with a beer. A place for male bravado, clinking tankards, and happy laughter. All the chairs were taken, especially near the fireside, but Dicky headed for a corner near the piano, and offered to buy some men a pint if they agreed to move.

Before long she was sitting opposite him, with their drinks between them on a small upturned barrel. *Oh, heaven help me.* She was out with a man, for the first time since Jim had died. She felt like she was doing something illegal. And she had nothing to say, she was certain they had nothing in common. For a second, he seemed lost for words too, now he'd got what he wanted and they were out together. But finally, he found some. "I must say I really like your hair."

"Thank you."

Awkward. She felt so bloody awkward.

"And your eyes are lovely, too."

Did she need to respond and find something nice to say about him, she wondered? Perhaps it was better not to. He did not have Jim's muscular attractiveness. He was a nice-looking boy, but he was not like Jim. Oh, how she missed Jim's dark eyes and expressive eyebrows, and his lazy, shore-leave smile. *She closed her eyes for a moment, in pain. No, I can't do this. I can't face the heartache again.* She swallowed and stared at the gin and tonic Dicky had bought her.

"Are you alright, Anne? Is there something wrong with your drink? Can I get you something else, if you don't like gin and tonic?"

She looked up, thinking that was kind of him. She smiled and said her drink was fine, and tried to make the best of it. Many girls would be envious, if they could see her out with a flier. She should be grateful she'd been asked. There were lots of things to like. The smart cut of his hair, the clean shave, the scent of his skin as he leaned close to talk to her over the noise, and his sparkling, hopeful eyes. Well of course he has *hopeful* eyes, she warned herself. But they seemed brim full of sincerity now, despite his reputation. And she wondered if he truly deserved it. "Why are you doing this, Richard?"

"Call me Dicky, everyone does."

She couldn't. She felt silly, saying it. "Tell me about the flying school. Did you enjoy the training?"

He shrugged. "I could fly already." He leant forward. "I was in a flying club before the war. When it started, my friends there joined the RAF, but I'm from a Navy crowd so that's where I went, and I was happy as a midshipman, quite happy, but somehow my commanding officer found out I had flying experience, and then they sent me back here to update my training. Not that it needed updating, given the old kites they want me to fly. But at least I got six weeks on shore."

She nodded and wondered how much of her gin and tonic she dared to drink.

"They want me to fly a Swordfish," he said, without much enthusiasm.

"A Swordfish?"

"Out of date *before* the war, Anne, but no expense spared for the Fleet Air Arm," he grumbled. "Bloody Swordfish. I'll be a sitting duck in one of those."

"Really?"

He nodded. "They call it a stringbag, you know? An old shopping bag. And the construction. Fabric – not metal. Good engine, but in many ways, painfully slow. I don't like slow."

She'd gathered that he didn't.

He went on, "the training's alright. But it's criminally brief. They expect us to fly into battle when we've only had a few hours in the air. We're here for weeks but most of that's in a classroom doing calculations. And flying's a physical skill, not just theoretical. Too much schoolroom and not enough time in the cockpit." He flashed her a smile. "A few flips up there, and before you know it, you're in the middle of the sea firing at the Germans."

"Are you allowed to tell me which ship you've been assigned to?"

"Maybe I can tell you at the end of the week."

Wartime secrecy. She tried a safer topic. "Tell me about flying before the war. Did you enjoy it?"

"Oh, I loved it. Soaring over the countryside gives you the most tremendous sense of freedom. You feel like a God. Looking down on villages as if they were part of a model railway set, you know, buildings made out of match boxes and bits of green fluff. Everything looks so perfect from above. You feel like you own the whole of England. I never thought I'd have to shoot anybody or lay torpedoes. I thought it would always be like those last two summers, before this began. Flying for pleasure. Wonderful. Have you ever flown?"

"No, not at all."

"If I ever get the chance, I'll take you up for a flip. It may scare you, if you let it, but I promise it will enchant you. It always does that to me."

After getting the second round of drinks, he broached a hard question. As if he'd talked himself into it while he was standing at the bar. "Whose ring is it that you wear, Anne?"

"What?" Her fingers were naked. She didn't wear any rings. But he knew. She put a hand up to her neck, where normally her white blouse was fastened high with a Wren's tie, but tonight, her top button was open.

"Sorry," he said, acknowledging her embarrassment, "I saw it fall forward in the car. When you were fastening your shoes." *Jim's ring, on a gold chain around her neck.* Tucked away where no-one was ever meant to see it. Only this pushy fellow *had* seen, and now he wanted to get the full story out of her. "Look, I have to ask. Are you spoken for? Are you engaged?"

How could she possibly tell him? Jim's ring. A tiny little sapphire. It had meant so much to her. *Blue like the sparkling sea he'd said,* when he placed it on her finger before he went off on that last voyage on the cruiser *Exeter.* She'd worn it for a year after he was killed. Her fingers slid inside her shirt and she touched the chain that had betrayed her secret. "No. But I was. He was on HMS Exeter."

Dicky looked at her. "A fine ship. I saw it once at anchor in Plymouth. Your chap – was he killed in action?"

To Anne, a 'fine' ship would have been one that didn't cause the death of her fiancé. But then, it wasn't really the ship's fault, was it? She nodded. "At the Battle of River Plate. He was a gunner."

Both gun turrets were blown to smithereens, they told her.

"River Plate? In '39. I know a bit about that."

"Most people don't. They only know it was a success, and the victors had a special lunch at the Guildhall to celebrate. Only my chap didn't get to go."

"I'm sorry." Dicky shook his head, sadly. "There is a high cost paid, for every victory."

One small line on a list somewhere. Her Jim. A casualty of war on the 13th December.

She was glad he didn't tease her for still wearing the ring, two and a half years after the man was gone. But he got other things out of her. That she'd joined the Wrens early, hoping to help get the war over with, and that she and Jim had been planning to marry, when April came around, in 1940 – which they'd naively imagined might be 'after the war'. She told him how she loved being in the Wrens and it had saved her, after his poor parents got the telegram and told her the news. How she had lost herself in her work, and got several promotions for her dedication. How she'd come to make the hard decision that she would have to stop wearing the ring – on her finger, at least. And he nodded, understanding. "You realised it wasn't doing you any favours."

"Yes."

"But you still treasure his memory," he said. "That's very sweet."

The gin must have loosened her tongue. "I have so many regrets. He didn't want to wait. But it was just before Christmas and there was so much to arrange, it only seemed sensible to wait for the Spring."

"And then he was killed."

She nodded. He sensed the gravitas that came with her confession. And he honoured it, even though all around them people were bellowing with laughter and their red faces shone above their pints, as if there was nothing finer you could do with your life than give it to a fierce, unpredictable war.

He took her hand across the table, or rather, the barrel. She let him. She didn't pull away. She had been so starved of physical contact – and his touch was gentle and warm. He was mercurial – vivacious and sparkling one minute, and shaking his head in sorrow the next. But his moods, though changeable, seemed genuine. "Most of my RAF friends are gone too," he admitted.

"What is it you really want?" she asked him, acutely aware that he was holding her hand, stroking it, trying to forge some kind of physical link. "Is it a weekend in a hotel, pretending to be Mr. and Mrs.? Before you go to sea?"

"I shall have to pretend I'm offended," he said. But he smiled – he couldn't help it. He stroked his thumb across her fingers. "Naturally, I'd love a weekend away. I was thinking the Lake District. Or somewhere closer. At the end of next week."

"Oh, so you admit it?" In mock reproach she tried to pull her hand away, but he was too quick and he held tight, capturing her in a good-natured tug of war across the top of the barrel.

"Absolutely."

"Well, don't you go saying I suggested it." If she wasn't careful, he'd turn up at the Wrennery saying she'd promised him a whole weekend – not just a casual drink.

He gazed at her, with unashamed directness. "D'you think you can get some leave?"

He was teasing her. She shook her head, and answered in the same teasing spirit. "No, I don't. The Admiralty would think me very uncommitted if I asked for leave so soon after taking up my position."

His eyebrows lifted, flirtatiously. "How unreasonable of them. The papers are always telling us the needs of the men must come first."

"Dicky! Clean up your conversation, please." She laughed, finding that she *could* say his name. In fact, she liked saying it. "I should walk out on you and take myself home to the Wrennery."

"The nunnery." He smiled, and stroked her hand again. "No. Stay and have another drink."

Oh, she was weakening. The way he touched her. The way he looked at her. "Dicky... about you and me...I mean... we could never..."

"Whyever not?" he dared her. "You seem to be just the girl I'm looking for."

Flatterer. Besides. She could never be his girl. She was Jim's girl. Even if that meant sitting on the shelf for the rest of her life. Waiting for someone who'd never return. "I couldn't possibly..."

Or could she?

He leaned forward, and his eyes shone as he spoke. "You can't go home in the dark, darling – I've got the car keys. And you're having too much fun, aren't you?"

She was. She couldn't deny it.

Chapter Eight

Linda

Linda was in the car, no longer sleepy. It was hard to feel anything but edgy while waiting for her experts to finish defusing their bomb. She'd never seen one up that close before, and it was huge. A dark, menacing thing, with a metal tail like a shark or something. She wondered how far away she should have parked, in order to keep herself and the Admiralty's van out of danger. She sat, for another ten minutes, fidgeting with things, in a state of tension.

Then she heard a cheer from inside the building.

A few moments later, the men appeared. All smiles. First Greatcoat – who she must remember to call Captain Morrison, then Boilersuit Clegg, then Frye in his sailor suit, and bringing up the rear was Toby, with his shirt off – looking rather good, she had to admit – carrying a small wooden box with the detonator in it.

They loaded the dirty shovels into the boot, and Morrison hopped in beside her. "Right, my girl. A good day's work. Off to the pub, I think."

There was no way she was going to deny these boys a drink after what they'd been doing. She started the engine, and drove. The Waterman's Arms was not far away. She couldn't help wondering, as she was driving, what the drill was on the days that didn't go quite so well as this one.

Outside the pub, she parked the car. The three navy men leapt out, wanting to slake their thirst. So, for a moment Linda was left in the car with the enigmatic one, Toby Wallis. She wasn't sure if he was shy, or aloof, or what. Some of the time she thought he was from another planet, but other times he was down to earth and direct. She asked him, "Are you coming in to have a drink?"

He shook his head. "No."

The way he said it, with his Lancashire accent, it sounded like 'gnaw', not 'no'.

She waited for him to volunteer a polite excuse but he was silent. "Why not?"

"I don't drink."

"On duty?"

"Ever."

Linda didn't think that sounded like fun. "Why not?"

"Signed t'pledge."

"You've signed a *pledge* never to have a drink?" What a pity. She'd always thought that having a drink with the boys at the end of the night was one of the best parts of working with the Navy.

"Aye." This time – stone the crows – he actually added something. "Me dad and me granddad. They've all signed t'pledge too."

Obviously from a long line of people who really knew how to have a good time. Linda's mind wandered to other possibilities. "Is there anything else you've signed a pledge not to do?"

He gave her a dark stare. "Naw."

"Sorry. Kidding."

With the humour of an undertaker, he nodded. Another dark stare.

Riveting as this conversation was, she decided she'd rather have a drink in a nice lively pub than carry on. She could murder a port and lemonade. She made a move to exit the car, and Toby reached for his moleskin notebook, although there was not enough light to read or to write by. But he held it like a teddy bear, or a talisman, or something. He sat, leaning his angular face against the rounded frame of the car window, with the notebook in his arms. Linda felt bad about leaving him, but she decided that injecting a bit of fun into Toby's hollow existence could wait until another day. "Will you be alright to wait here while I have a quick drink?"

"Aye."

Inside the pub – she was amazed to see Wren Officer Foxton out with Dicky Tavistock, seated near the piano in the far corner. They were leaning forward, talking intently, and they were *holding hands*.

"Would you look at that," she breathed. She had to stare to convince herself it was actually them. Talk about a moth and a candle.

They were so wrapped up in their conversation, she decided she'd better leave them to it. Instead, she headed to the public bar, where Captain Morrison and Able Seaman Frye were waiting for her, and Clegg was buying a round of drinks.

"Linda, love. There you are."

"Oh, sorry. Were you waiting for me? I was trying to persuade Toby to come and have a drink with us."

Clegg shook his head and smiled. "No chance, love. He's a bit of a rare breed is our Toby."

Linda looked at Clegg and then Frye and Morrison. Searching their faces. "What's the story, then. Do tell."

Anne

In their corner of the pub, Anne and Dicky were onto their third round of drinks. Anne was feeling light and happy, listening to all his after-dinner stories. His was a world of pilot's luck and flying stunts, of tests sat drunk, and boots lost in the Solent, and subsequent outrageous bluffs to get through kit inspection. He liked making her laugh, he said. And she was rather liking it, too. Until his face changed and he was solemn again. "Without wanting to cast a moment's gloom on our evening, can I tell you something?"

"Yes?"

His lips parted to speak but words failed him, and instead, he lit a cigarette, the flame from his silver lighter illuminating his face for an instant. Then he changed his mind. "Oh, it doesn't matter."

"It sounded like you wanted to tell me, only a second ago."

He looked at her, studying her, deciding what to say. "I lost someone too. We weren't close, my brother and I, he was older than me, and we didn't even have the same mother."

She nodded, trying to follow his disjointed narrative. "What happened to your brother?"

"He was in the Navy, like me. We all were. My father, my grandfather. Family tradition." He looked at her. "Is tradition important to you, Anne?"

"Well, some of it."

"This war has a way of ending all that – sweeping things away – the end of an era."

She nodded and waited. *He needs time. He's trying to get to it.*

He put the cigarette to his lips and drew in a breath. Anne had never found smoking attractive and really wished he would extinguish it. He turned his head away to release the aromatic smoke, perhaps sensing her discomfort. "Survey vessel. Arctic circle. Sunk by a German U-Boat."

"I'm so sorry," she said, thinking about how he could only manage to say it like that – telegram style – with no investment of emotion. She wanted to touch his hand, give him some comfort, but he still had the lighted cigarette glowing between his fingers.

"When my brother died. It changed everything." His gaze fell back on her. "Turned my whole life upside down." He shook his head. "This war. It's such a lottery, who comes back. Who lives, who dies. In the end, I thought, well, Tavistock, you have to compress your life into the space of a few short weeks. And I got to thinking, what *should* be in my life, if it's going to be very short?"

If what she'd heard about him was true, he'd decided it should be a relentless pursuit of pleasure. That had been everyone's assumption, but judging from the sober look on his face, she was starting to wonder if there was something more.

The pub was full now. And loud. The airmen at the bar thumped for another round of beer, and burst into a song. A dirty one. Sung to the tune of *The Drunken Sailor*. Dicky frowned, as if the bawdy song was interrupting a more serious train of thought. "Sorry. Does all this sound familiar?"

She struggled to find an answer. It sounded as if his experience was almost the exact opposite of hers – he'd dived into his love affairs to forget about his troubles, and she'd dived into work to forget that she didn't *have* a life or a love, outside of what she was doing for the Wrens. But she believed she understood. "I'm so sorry about your brother."

Dicky nodded, accepting her condolences, tapping his cigarette ash away. But then he looked impish all of a sudden. "Did you go to bed with your sailor, before he went away?"

She spilt an inch of her drink on her skirt. "Dicky! What a question!" Her face betrayed her and her cheeks felt hot.

"Ooh, you did! I knew it. Well, I *thought* you had, and now, I'm absolutely certain." He laughed, while she blushed hard, and thought she would lose every last bit of her composure. *Evil man, to read me like that.* And just when she was starting to feel something for him. To like him, even. She wondered if she should abandon the rest of her gin and tonic, and walk out in a huff. Didn't he know when he was going too far?

"Sorry," he said, grinning. But he wasn't sorry at all. He was pleased with himself, for guessing. "It's alright. Since you know how nice it is, maybe you'll take pity on me."

"Stop it, Dicky, for goodness sake." Her face flamed. And all he did was gaze at her, with laughing eyes, before drawing another breath through his horrible cigarette. She was stunned at how mercurial he could be. One minute, the conversation was about his brother, and his melancholy thoughts on death in combat, the next, he was digging up the most personal events in her entire life – discussing them as lightly as one might talk about a new flick at the cinema. She fumed for a minute at the intrusion, but in the end, what was the point? He wouldn't care. He couldn't be reformed. She raised her glass to her lips and took a long drink to keep herself steady. Another ten minutes and she'd ask to go home.

But she looked at him, sitting there with his eyes glittering. She put her drink down on the barrel, and bolstered by her gin and tonic she decided to ask him why he was like this. "I want to ask *you* something, but I don't know how to put it."

He flashed her another smile. "Put it any way you like, I'm a grown man and I'm in the navy, I can cope."

"Look. Most of my Wrens are away from home for the first time in their lives. They're very young and very proper. I'm sure you must know how to find yourself a fast girl, if you are in that much need of a...a...release." She struggled with the words, which amused him and made him suppress a smile, but overall, she was glad she was being matter-of-fact. "So why do you keep proposing to my girls?"

But then he became deathly serious. "My children, if I leave any, must be legitimate." As he spoke, he stared right past her. His face took on a look of considerable anxiety. "That's become rather important to me, in these last few weeks. If I die, leaving someone with a child out of wedlock, it would be the most dreadful mess."

No wonder people found him too intense. The thousand-mile stare, the formal turn of phrase, the talk of 'leaving' his children. Not a conversation for a casual first drink.

He sensed it. "Sorry. I'm being maudlin. When you are so intriguing, and deserve to have so much fun." He extinguished his cigarette and took her hand again – across the barrel. "Tell me how you keep that gaggle of impossible girls in order. When I can't even handle one."

She didn't know what to make of him, with his rollercoaster moods and his overly familiar manner. She'd never met anyone like him, never would again, she was sure. She told him all about the running of the Wrennery, and he acted like he was riveted by it all. Service was important to him, as it was to her. And his time at sea gave him a maturity the other trainees lacked, the boys who had never flown before and never been to sea. She was intrigued when he told her he had a love-hate relationship with the Navy. It was a fine life, full of camaraderie, although the night watches could be rather tedious. But the sea was sometimes cruel, and the war, even crueller. And he didn't relish the idea of dying so young. "When I came on shore to do this training, I thought, *six weeks*, six weeks isn't enough, to do all the living I'd like to have done. And now even that's gone."

She felt a wave of empathy for him. "You're too young to be thinking like that. You'll be alright."

There *was* something they had in common – the feeling that time was running out.

"Anne, listen to me." He gave her hand a squeeze. "You don't have to forget him. The man you loved before. But you're an attractive woman, surrounded by men. You could be with someone new."

"I don't know what you mean."

He brought her left hand up to his lips and kissed it, he kissed the place where the ring used to be. "Oh, *come on*. I think you do." He kissed the same place again, and for longer. She was sure she felt his tongue against her skin. He lingered and looked up into her eyes. "For luck," he said, when he had finished.

Was the luck meant for her, she wondered, or for him?

The men in the pub were singing, banging on the counter, red-faced and loud. The Navy songs were rowdy, each verse getting more and more colourful as the night went on. One of the boys had a fine tenor voice and when he joined in, some ripe swear words sang out with perfect clarity across the room. The publican came out from behind his flap. "Save that one for the naval base, lads, we've got *ladies* here tonight."

Dicky yelled, "Can somebody play the piano? Some of us would like to have a dance!"

An ARP man swayed towards the piano, saying, "I can play the old Joanna." He placed his pint, with care, on the top, where there were many white rings on the wood from previous beers, and sat down to tease out a tune.

Dicky held out his hand. "Care to dance?"

She was about to say no, but he pulled her to her feet before she had time to answer. The tune was familiar. The girls played it all the time – *Ain't Misbehavin'* – although she felt like she was. A smoochy little foxtrot.

And now, she was dancing – in public – with Delia Finlay's young man. There was no room for whirling, not here. In the crowded pub it was different – smoky, intimate and more like a shuffle than a dance – but ultimately *comforting*. It was so nice being held like that. Dicky's idea of dancing involved more than the recommended amount of body contact, but even that seemed alright – in fact, it seemed completely natural. She felt relaxed and secure. He wasn't a monster. He was lovely. He held her close, with his clean-shaven face next to her cheek, and she rested her hand on his uniformed shoulder. "Wonderful," he murmured, and let his lips touch the side of her face.

She knew he was taking liberties and she should make him stop. But he would soon be gone – posted to some far-off sea. What harm in giving him a dance?

Linda

Linda came out of the pub into the cool night air, with Frye in his sailor suit on one side, and Captain Morrison in his peaked cap on the other. Clegg brought up the rear. They were laughing, now they had a drink inside them, but it was late and they needed to stay sober in case they were needed tomorrow. Theirs was a job you couldn't do with a hangover, although Morrison said one or two had tried.

"Wasn't that your C.O. in there, love?" he asked, and smiled at her. "Didn't you want to say hello?"

"Did you see the way they were dancing?" Linda was still very surprised to have seen Anne there at all. And with *Tavistock*, of all people. Cheek to cheek.

Morrison grinned. "I should have cut in and taken her, just to see the look on that soppy boy's face."

Linda turned in surprise. That seemed like a mean thing to say, when Anne and Dicky were obviously enjoying each other's company.

"Take no notice of him," said Frye. "He hates the fliers coz they get all the girls."

Morrison made a face. They were beside the vehicle now. With a flourish, he opened the car door for Linda, and put a hand on her back to 'help' her get in. Toby, with notebook, was under Linda's blanket. Fast asleep.

"Wake up, sleeping beauty. Time to go home," he said.

Linda had to drive with extreme care on the way back to HMS Nautilus because she wasn't allowed to put the headlamps on. Her 'boys' as she called them thought she was brilliant at this, but in truth night-driving in the blackout was enough to scare anybody. She had mastered the art of driving along in a very low gear so the squealing of the car gave the impression of speed but she still had time to take care as she wended her way along the dark roads – mainly navigating by the glint of the rain on the pavement. As she drove she stole another glance at Toby – thinking about what the men had told her about him. A man of high principles who hated the destruction of war but still wanted to see it over and done with... that's what they'd said about him. A genius in some ways, with his knowledge of explosives – but not savvy in others.

"Has he got a girlfriend? She'd asked. More curious than anything else...

Chapter Nine

Anne

Anne slipped into the house and went upstairs, hoping the girls would be asleep, but they weren't. They were making the most of her absence. Delia, Binky, Cathy and Mavis. *A gaggle of impossible girls.* They had the radio on, a card game spread out on someone's bed, knitting set aside, mending basket abandoned. The conversation ranged over two main themes, FAA boys and American movie stars. Anne spoke from the doorway of the main cabin. "What's all this? Some of us have important work to do in the morning."

"You're back, Officer Foxton. We were waiting for you!" The girls all looked up – bright young faces, full of girlish excitement and fun. The question on everyone's lips. "Well – did he? Did he propose?"

Anne laughed. "No, of course he didn't."

There was a hoot of disappointment from several girls. One said, "He didn't? That's *most* unlike him."

"Yes," said Mavis, "Delia Finlay got proposed to over lunch."

Anne vowed to remain good-humored. She needed to keep things light. "Well, I'm not as pretty as Dee."

Delia flicked her hair back from her shoulder. "It was a ploy to get me tipsy, so I'd agree to get in the back of his car."

That made Anne feel awful, but she tried to hide it. "It was a friendly drink. Nothing more. I don't expect him to propose. Not now, not ever." She hadn't even let him kiss her, although God knows he'd tried.

Binky was persistent. "You're seeing him again, though? Tell us you're seeing him again?"

"Oh, I don't know. We left it rather open." Anne said. "Delia, is this conversation upsetting you?"

"No. You're welcome to your turn. He wouldn't want to leave anyone out."

Cathy gave her a thump on the arm. "Don't be mean Delia. You didn't want him. You've been saying the most awful things about him all evening."

Which Anne thought was hardly surprising.

Mavis asked, "Cathy, do *you* have a boyfriend?"

"No. I'm free as a bird."

Anne was still thinking about Dicky. "Has anyone ever tried saying yes?"

"Yes, Captain. Yes, yes, *yes!*" Binky feigned passion rather knowledgably for a girl of nineteen – which worried Anne. Some of the girls had no understanding of the facts of life – imagined you could get pregnant just from kissing – and others were much more worldly wise.

"He's not a captain. He's a subby. He's only just got his wings," said Delia, lying on her tummy on one of the beds.

Mavis frowned. "What's a subby?"

"Subaltern," said Cathy, in a bored tone. "Or second Lieutenant, on the same level as a flying officer in the RAF. You need to swot up your ranks, Mavis."

"Yes. How are you ever going to net a good catch if you don't know your ratings from your subbies?" Giggles from the girls and blushes from Mavis, who had probably never been kissed.

Cathy looked at Anne. "He might have more luck if he stopped aiming at debutantes that don't really want him."

Anne shook her head, and felt a stab of sadness. "He's not for me. He's only twenty-one."

Delia said, "I expect somebody'll have him, now he's got those stupid wings."

"Or he'll have them," said Binky.

"Maybe he actually wants to get married?" Mavis said innocently.

Most of them doubled with laughter, one girl even fell off the end of the bed. "What a hoot! Where's he taking you next time? Has he offered to buy *you* a big boozy lunch at the hotel?"

Laughter rippled. "Maybe he'll book a room with a nice double bed."

Anne knew it was time to call the evening to an end. She stood up, in managerial mode, because pleasant as this was, they all had jobs to do in the morning. "Bed is where we all should be. Dreaming of our boys in blue and khaki."

She started shoo-ing them all back into their rooms. Cabins. She had rounds to do, cabin doors and 'portholes' to check. It was getting very late. She was so happy the girls liked her, but she hoped she'd not been too open with them. Kind but firm was what she must aim for, not giggly friendship.

She must not allow the girls to turn her into one of them. But as she said goodnight to everybody and got herself ready for bed, she almost felt like she was seventeen, and in her heart burned a strange mad hope.

She *had* agreed to see him again. He said he'd pick her up at first light tomorrow morning. And this time she didn't doubt him. Be ready before seven, he said.

"So early?" she'd protested.

"It's the only way I can make this work. There's so little time. Bring a coat and squeeze me in."

Cathy

Cathy changed into silk pyjamas, hoping there wouldn't be a raid tonight. She wanted to spend the whole night between nicely laundered sheets and wake up to a piping hot Navy breakfast. She liked the Wrennery – it was familiar, it was efficient, a home away from home, and it took the edge off missing Geoff. She was planning to keep all his letters in her pyjama case in her top drawer. She'd had one from Guy – a brief letter smelling of minty Italian cologne, saying he was leaving Cambridge – the war office had come up with something. He was starting work soon, and thankful to be part of the war effort.

Good for him – no internment camp.

She'd also had a card from Ralph Redcliffe, or rather from his secretary at the Admiralty – a small, gilt-edged card inviting her to a naval dinner in Greenwich. He'd written a line on the back that there was just a chance she might see Geoff there. She decided to see if she could get off boat-cleaning duty to go, just to be closer to Geoff.

She slipped into bed and nestled on the pillow. She heard Anne call "Lights out," and someone flicked the switch. The room went dark.

Should she tell Anne, that she knew Dicky Tavistock? The poor woman had no idea what she was getting into. But Dicky was a friend, and she hardly knew Anne. Although she would like to. If it wasn't for the difference in their ranks and ages, she would have hoped Anne could be a good friend. She thought of Anne's kindness to her on the first day, over changing her name, and what that had meant – that anonymity – and she thought, let Dicky have his secret.

Anne

Early morning. They sped along the road to the airfield in his car, which had an open top. Anne's hair whipped against her face one minute, streamed out behind her the next. She should have tied it up. There had been rain in the night and the road was wet, which terrified her, but the sky above was crisp and clear. She'd like to ask him where he got the petrol, but she guessed he must have bought it on the black market like the flowers, unless the car ran on nervous energy like its owner.

"Glad you kept your hair down," he said, above the noise of the engine. "Did you do that for me?"

She refused to admit it.

He sped along the country lane, making the engine roar. "It's like an old pram, this thing, isn't it?" he said, foot to the floor. "Not enough torque."

She'd never driven a car and wasn't likely to get the opportunity, so she wasn't sure what to say. She had a good grasp of navy administration and management, but she didn't know about things like torque. He took his hand off the stick and touched her knee. "I wish we had more time. I'd court you slowly. Like your other chap did."

No, you wouldn't. That was a sailor's promise. She had a feeling he'd never done anything slowly in his life. And he was 'her chap' now, was he? But in a way, he was. For today, for this short drive, he was hers. He gave her another smiling glance and her whole body responded. *You want him. You do. You want him.*

"It's alright," she said. Feeling nervous inside. "I'm enjoying the drive."

He floored the pedal and bombed along the empty road. He was grinning. "So am I."

He parked the car at the far end of the runway. *Best place to see them land,* he said. They waited in silence for several minutes. Only the birds singing and a soft breeze ruffling the trees. The air was fresh, mixed with the damp scent of the woodland beyond, and they were quiet in each other's company. Until they heard the sound of a Swordfish approaching.

"There's one," she said as it came into view. She shaded her eyes to watch the dark speck of a plane come towards them, getting slowly bigger, the droning engine ever louder as it came near. "Are they fun to fly?"

"Yes – except for putting her down on the deck of a carrier instead of a nice long runway like this."

Quite a circus trick, she thought. Part of the world he lives in and wants me to understand. They could see the plane heading straight for them, prop buzzing, wings outstretched like an ungainly bird. A biplane – surprisingly old-school – open cockpit, fabric fuselage, fixed landing-gear splayed and ready.

He watched the aeroplane. "You see how long it takes, to get to the landing strip?"

"Yes," she said, smiling, "it seems almost leisurely. You said the Stringbags were slow."

She felt relaxed now, sitting beside him in the open-top car with the sun on her back, she was almost starting to enjoy it, but he was slipping into one of his serious moods. Staring ahead, eyes fixed on the Swordfish.

"To place a torpedo in the hull of an enemy craft," he said, making a slicing gesture with his hand, like a surgeon talking about an incision, "I have to fly straight and level towards the target – like the aeroplane coming towards us – until I get near enough to do the release. Then I reduce my altitude to mast head height, not much higher than the trees, and prepare to fire..."

The plane ahead of them was dropping altitude too. Coming in, lazy and slow.

"Now imagine this car is the target – and you see me – you see the torpedo, clear as day, hanging there under the aircraft."

She could indeed imagine. The Swordfish came closer, ever closer. The note of the engine changed. If it was carrying a lethal cargo, it would be enough to chill anyone's heart.

"Well, what do you do? You've got an Ack-Ack gun and you've got me in your sights as I make the approach. You can't stand by and do nothing, or the ship you stand on will sink."

She nodded. The plane was so low now she could see the man in the front seat, the glint of the sun on his goggles, the scarf of the man behind. Even the struts between the wings were well defined in the morning light. "I take aim."

"Yes. And with all that time to take aim and your own life to save. And the lives of others. Do you think you'd miss?" He glanced at her, and then back at the incoming aircraft.

"No," she said. "Any gunner with a good eye could take down a target like that." A huge wave of empathy swept over her. She understood why he said he was a sitting duck.

His face clouded with a kind of despair. "Four weeks," he said. "That's how long the average pilot lasts." He touched the starter button on the dashboard, and she believed she saw his fingers shake. His voice was confident enough though, when he turned to her and spoke. "Marry me, Anne. Before I go."

It wasn't even a question. It was put in the form of a command.

Her heartbeat – rapid and uneven – told her this was a chance that would never come again. The biplane swept in and bumped once or twice as it touched the landing strip in front of them. Air crew came running in to help. A classic landing, in perfect weather. This one would fly again.

Without taking her eyes off the runway, she nodded. "Yes. Alright. I'll do it."

As if he'd asked her for some small favour. Something she could easily give. Her heart skittered inside her. She was afraid to turn and face him even after what she'd said she would do. Face burning with a kind of shame – that such recklessness could exist inside her too. He leaned in close, and scooped the hair back from her cheek – warm breath on her skin. "Now kiss me and make me believe it."

A whole second passed. A moment of shyness, but she turned and let him pull her into a long, hard kiss. She was caught in the passion of his madcap proposal, surprised by the strength of his kiss. The fierce warmth of a warrior – not a boy, not a fool – a fighter, a defender of the realm. The wind ruffled her hair and his hands tangled there, guiding her, holding her – making her stay with him and experience this fully.

He deepened the kiss – tightened his hold over her – and her heart thumped so loud she was sure he would hear. She made a sound – a soft acknowledgement of pleasure. Only then did he become gentler, taking time to savour her, to take a softer pleasure than when the first surge of need joined them a few moments ago. His hand strayed to the front of her dress. As his lips parted from hers, he murmured – "Success." He was smiling, exhilarated, triumphant.

"Oh, what have I *done?*" She didn't realise she had spoken until he answered. "You've made me the happiest man on the airfield." He grinned. He leant back in his seat – smiling at the sky.

Kiss me today, miss me tomorrow. Love me til they shoot me down in flames.

"I need to get back to the Wrennery." She was so distracted she almost said *nunnery.* "I'm sorry. I'm dreadfully busy. We've got a special visitor this week."

"I understand. I'll drive you," he said. And true to his word, he did nothing more. They barely spoke on the drive back. But when they stopped outside the Wrennery and she made a move to get out in a hurry, he caught her arm. "Wait, please!"

She panicked. "Don't kiss me here. The girls will be watching."

"I know." He reached inside his jacket, finding what he wanted in the inside pocket. Pulled out a document, neatly folded, and handed it to her. "Sign it. I'll see you at lunchtime."

Chapter Ten

Linda

Alone in the car, with the experts doing their stuff and not due back for some time, Linda was tempted to have a look in Toby's notebook.

She shouldn't. But she was curious.

She picked it up. The moleskin notebook was tied up with brown ribbon tape – frayed and much-handled. First, she studied how he had tied it. After all, if she was going to pull one of the tapes and untie the fastening, she was going to need to know how to replicate the way he'd tied it.

When she was satisfied that she could make it look as if it had never been broached, she slowly, carefully, untied the ribbon. She looked out of the window of the car, to see if anyone was coming.

Then opened the book, on her lap.

Every page she turned was densely, carefully illustrated. Black ink drawings, both simple and complex. Intricate details, faithfully recorded. Sometimes a word or two – noted and underlined – and always in a cartoon speech bubble with a small human figure holding a spade – standing beside it.

But it was more than a cartoon story. It was a handwritten treatise on how to deactivate every single bomb that Toby had ever encountered. On one page labelled "Rogues Gallery" was a row of different types of bombs, each one given a smile and a personality, and beside them, a tally of the destruction they'd done in various cities. A devastating, deathly tally. On the next was a series of steps and checks, some underlined, showing how to de-activate each 'rogue'.

And then he was there, standing by the car window. Toby.

She gasped, closed the book, and said she was sorry. He stared at her for a long moment. Then, he took the book from her hands with a disappointed frown, and a look of incomprehension. "Why do people always look when you tell them not to?"

Human nature, she thought, and bit her lip. "Sorry, Tobe."

Anne

Anne put the huge bunch of flowers in a vase on the front desk, and everyone who passed by commented on them. She told them that Dicky had proposed to her on their second date – both occurring in less than twenty-four hours – which had to be a record even for him. They all cracked up laughing and said he was after *anybody* and wasn't it the most terrific wheeze? The 'serial proposer' had struck again.

She smiled, but inside she was crumbling.

When she was with him, it all seemed real. When she wasn't, it seemed like a farcical prank. A joke left over from April Fool's Day. She didn't know what to believe, so she let the girls think she was taking it all in her stride. It was just a bit of fun – a diversion that made office work less boring. But inside. Turmoil. Humiliation. Longing.

She couldn't accept the proposal of somebody she didn't even know. She was a woman who did things properly. But she was dithering. Leading him on. Not wanting it to be over. She groaned, inwardly. Feeling physically sick.

She was behaving *exactly* like the girls she was here to protect.

She unfolded the application form he'd given her. Spread it out on the blotter. An application for a special licence to marry, on Thursday, the day after tomorrow. She looked at all the details he'd filled in. Richard James Tavistock. She hadn't known until that moment that his middle name was James. A popular middle name – but in her heart, a name that belonged only to Jim. Sadness welled inside her. She sat alone, with treasured memories, until tears ran down her face and onto the blotter.

A polite cough. Cathy was standing there. "Do you need a hanky?"

Flustered, she shook her head, and dabbed her eyes with her own lace-edged one. She pulled a blank sheet of paper out of the tray in front of her, and put it over the embarrassing document. Composed herself. "What is it, Cathy?"

"About Dicky Tavistock..."

Anne gave her a dismayed glance. "Oh, not you as well?"

"No, *not* me. I can honestly say I have never been romantically involved with Dicky Tavistock," then she stopped, remembering something. "Although, I did dance with him once. At a house party in Suffolk."

"Oh," said Anne, looking rather thoughtfully at her flowers. "So you know him?"

Cathy was in danger of making things worse. "He was at Naval College with my brother."

"Have you come to tell me I'm making a fool of myself?"

"No." Cathy was stiff and awkward. She was in dangerous waters. "Look. He'd kill me if he knew I was doing this, but I wanted to say... if you've decided to give him a chance, then that's to be applauded – not laughed at."

Silence, from Anne. Still gazing sadly at her flowers. Not sure what to believe. "Thank you, Cathy. I'm trying to keep an open mind."

"This is difficult – what with you being my commanding officer." Cathy said. "And I never thought I'd be giving Dicky Tavistock a character reference."

"Is that what you're doing?"

"It looks like it." Cathy exhaled and glanced away.

There was a pause. Neither woman knew quite what to say. "Wren Foxton – Anne. What do *you* think of him?"

"I think he's a troubled young man who puts on a lot of bravado, but inside he might be quite deep."

"Ah. So you like him?"

"Oh, yes, very much." That was quite an admission for someone like Anne. She blushed and looked down at the blotter.

So Cathy said. "Then enjoy it. He's a smug bastard sometimes but he's actually quite a good bloke."

Anne laughed and looked up. "So that's your official assessment?"

"Yes. And tell him the Stringbags are not as bad as he fears. They're brilliant on the carriers – look what they did at Taranto. The Navy loves those planes, and they keep serving us well. It's so important he has faith in his plane."

Anne clutched at this piece of hope. "I'll tell him that."

"Please do," Cathy said. "It might help to keep him alive."

When Cathy had gone, Anne sat at her desk, alone with the form. This was not a decision to take lightly.

She thought about her work at the Wrennery – what would happen to that? The life she had worked for two and a half years to build up. The people who depended on her. But...

I've already said yes. And Cathy said enjoy it. She was kind and sweet and told her to ignore the others. But Cathy was a silly goose who couldn't see that Commander Redcliffe was in love with her...

Who should she listen to, instead? The girls who thought it was a complete hoot when Dicky had made a play for her? The finishing school girls – like Delia, who'd rejected him – they thought everything was a game of strategy. War. Courtship. Love. Marriage. Points to be scored and victories to be made – like tennis or cricket – but all mixed up with other games like charades and blind man's bluff.

She looked at the papers he'd given her. At the dotted line where she would have to sign, if she was going to let Dicky talk her into this. It would be a hurried affair in the registry office, no doubt, in their everyday uniforms, while the next couple waited outside in the corridor. A cross between a formality and a duty, like filing taxes or going to the dentist. And all for a couple of nights away?

She appealed to Jim to advise her – although it seemed hardly appropriate to ask *his* permission to marry another man, but she needed an answer, and she couldn't quite trust herself. Was this alright, or should she crumple the paper now and file it in the Round File? She asked for Jim, but she got Richard. Dicky. His voice, warm and resonant, spoke to her as if he was present in the room. "Go on. Do it. Be *my* April bride."

She reached for her fountain pen, ready on its polished metal stand. And signed.

Cathy

The ink was barely dry when he came to pick it up. Cathy, passing through the entrance hall on her way upstairs, saw him whirl into Anne's office for a brief kiss, where he gave the form the onceover and emerged with a satisfied smile.

She stopped him – pulled on his sleeve. "What are you *doing*, Tavistock?"

"I'm finalizing the details of my wedding. Want to come?"

"Finalizing the *details*? Like the bride's name?"

"That position has been filled. Anne Louise Foxton. Rather pretty don't you think?"

She stared in aggravation at the ceiling, and then at Dicky. She shook her head. "You'll never get the license in time."

"I will," he countered. "I will get the license, even if I have to ask the Archbishop of Canterbury to help me."

Probably would too. Insane man. She wanted to say, *don't hurt Anne.* She only known Anne a very short length of time but she was such a kind woman, and she'd already been through a lot. She had her own views about Dicky's haste, but those were sentiments too difficult to telescope into a conversation in the entrance hall – especially as Anne was at her desk and quite probably within earshot. "Can't stop. Got to get changed. Boat-cleaning duty this afternoon. See you in the Registrar's office."

"Chaplain's doing it. All arranged. It's on Thursday. Don't worry about bringing a gift."

Chapter Eleven

Ralph

Ralph, in full naval commander mode, knew all about the frantic preparations for the Royal Visit, but that didn't put him off. His plans were more important, or so he believed, than the public relations exercises that occupied Royalty. He decided to pay a visit to the Wrennery that afternoon. He swept up to Anne's new desk just inside the entrance foyer.

"Lovely to see you again, Officer Foxton."

He expected her to blush prettily at him. But this morning, she seemed rather distracted. He put this down to the impending Special Visit.

She was brusque. Professional. Gestured for him to sit, in her new office. "How can I help you, Commander?"

"Catherine Bancroft-Smythe. I need to reassign her." He needed to reassign lots of people, but Cathy's name always swam closer to the surface than most of the others.

He saw the concern on Anne's face. "Oh, what a shame. She loves her work down at the harbour."

"In time of war, we can't all work where we want to." Ralph took the seat that Anne offered. Held his peaked cap on his lap. "She has special qualities. She needs special training."

Anne smiled.

He could see that the woman thought that his physical interest in Cathy was doing much of the talking. And of course, she was right, it was there. He did yearn for Cathy. But there was so much more. Oh, *official secrets*, how he had come to hate them. How he had come to rue the day he had signed never to reveal them.

If not for that signature, he could tell Anne everything. And wouldn't that be a relief? She would instantly understand his aims. His goals. She would help him today, and others would help him tomorrow. He could requisition all the places and the people he needed. He could enlist Guy with no questions asked about his wretched background. He could persuade Cathy to move without a murmur. He could even harness the efforts of her useless, but amiable brother. But all he could say was, "send for Cathy, if you don't mind, and please, Officer Foxton, *for the sake of the war*, help me to reassign her."

Anne rang the bell on her desk, and a young girl from the galley answered. "Find Cathy Smith for me, please. The commander has a new posting for her."

That was clever, Ralph thought. Cathy would feel the impact of the news while being fetched – even before she got downstairs to speak with him about it. She would process some of the shock while she was pulling on her jacket, and dragging a brush through her lovely auburn hair. She could even let out a few sailor oaths – if she had to. He smiled. Anne was good with people.

"Cathy's aptitude tests – taken during basic training – revealed a highly strategic mind. She has qualities of leadership, and a certain... idealism." He guessed Anne knew all of those things – the only things he was allowed to tell her.

She smiled and nodded. "Lovely girl. We will miss her. Such a pity, she was just getting settled."

He wished he could explain. He wished he could tell her. *I have to think ahead, Anne, to a part of the war I may never even see. The part where we start winning, not just defending.* If only he could take Anne for the short drive round to Fort Southwick, into the tower, and down, down the 168 steps to the earth-works underneath – where the tunnelling company of the Royal Engineers had been working for nearly three months now – constructing a secret lair, or nerve centre. Anne's best Wrens, trained in their safe little world in the Nissen huts in the Wrennery garden, would first be assigned to gain experience around the country, and then brought back to staff his rabbit warren. His task, this year, was to scout the finest, the best, to fill those desks – in that eerie, subterranean hell.

Instead, they waited in awkward silence, trapped in a 'pistols at dawn' moment of British politeness.

"What's all this, Ralph?" Cathy appeared in the doorway. Not very happy. He rose, and she automatically saluted. She was a Navy girl, born and bred, that was clear. She was ideal in every way for the two purposes he had in mind for her.

He used the firm voice he would have used to address one of his finest men. "You're leaving Pompey, I'm afraid. I've a special ops job for you. On the East Coast. That's about all I can tell you." He nodded curtly and waited for her reaction.

Please, please. Don't let her cry. Hot wet tears on her pretty face. I'd want to kiss them away.

Anne spoke before Cathy had time to reply. "I've been asking Ralph if there is any way at all we can keep you here. We don't want to lose you."

He looked at Anne, who had done no such thing. But it showed great presence of mind to say so. She'd even thought to use his first name – the name Cathy knew – instead of the more impersonal *Commander*.

"Oh, have you?" Cathy said, looking gratefully at Anne, her saviour.

Anne nodded, but then her face became solemn. "But apparently, this has come from very high up, and no – it's not your father – I've established that. It's those tests you sat at basic training. You are a bright young mind, with *special* abilities. You will need to put your country first, and utilise those skills for the war effort."

Ralph paused, glancing at Anne. "I couldn't have put it better myself." Actually, he probably couldn't have put it at all, since his thoughts tended to dwell on Cathy's lips – or her hips – whenever she walked into a room.

"So I don't get any say in the matter?" the girl said, chest rising with emotion. "I felt so useful on the boats, Ralph. I don't understand."

Ralph wanted to yell at her. *If you agree to go – you silly girl – you can learn how to send our ships to war – not just take a putt-putt full of drunks across Portsmouth harbour.*

Anne tried to help again. "I think Ralph has done his best. And we all have to make sacrifices. I must remind you that you are an enlisted member of the W.R.N.S and so you don't actually *get* a say about where you are posted."

The girl was dangerously near to tears, he could see them forming. She makes me into an old fool, he thought. And after this, she'll never agree to come to that naval dinner party.

The girl looked like she hated him. Talk about sacrifices.

Anne helped him again. "Cathy dear, England expects *every* man to do his duty." Again, Ralph was impressed. Those were exactly the words that Cathy would need to hear, having learned them with her brother in childhood. Penelope was quite right about Anne Foxton. Exactly the right person for the job.

He nodded. Hoping he was radiating sage wisdom. Hoping his countenance was stern and his upper lip stiff. *Oh, Cathy.* He promised himself, that one day, they would work together, down in those tunnels. And she would forgive him. Of course, she would. But he was not sure she would ever love him.

Cathy

"At least I fought back," Cathy wrote, in her diary, that night. "I told him I would go on his wretched assignment, yes, but only on two conditions. I must be allowed to stay for the Special Visit, *and* for Anne and Dicky's wedding on Thursday. Told him I'd phone Daddy if he didn't."

•••

On the liberty boat run she was both glad and sorry to see Patrick. He waved from the quayside – excited to see her – and helped her with the gangplank like last time. His face fell when he heard she was being sent away. But he accepted it philosophically and he said he'd be shipping out too before long. "Convoy work. You didn't hear it from me, though."

She nodded. No one was ever supposed to tell anyone anything. It made life difficult.

They stood at the wheel, like last time. But in a different mood. There was never enough time. To say what needed to be said. He came straight to the point. "Will you write me?"

Write to him? She glanced out over the murky waters of the harbour. She couldn't. Could she?

He waited. The hesitation was too long for it to be good news for him. He glanced away and looked like he wished he hadn't asked. "You said you used to write to your brother, that's all."

Yes. She still did. And Geoff hadn't written her a single letter since he took up his commission. Lazy imp.

Maybe Patrick only meant to be kind. She certainly ought to be, anyway. "Of course I'll write to you. I'd be happy to."

He smiled in quiet jubilation. Ever practical, Cathy turned and shouted for Speccy Wilson to bring her the logbook, stubby pencil attached by a thin bit of cord. "Write your serial number down for me, then. And the name of your ship."

Speccy brought it out, and Patrick licked the pencil and wrote on the endpaper at the back of the book. Name, rank and serial number. Everything she would need to write him a letter. "There," he said, putting it on the shelf near Cathy. "I won't ask for yours. You can tell me when you write me."

•••

Cathy decided to go to the Admiralty do in her Wrens outfit. Which she thought was great – no worrying about what to wear. No fussing about what was suitable or in style. She'd often asked her mother, before going to one of these things, must she *really* wear a long frock and a fur? So much easier to stick on the uniform and get on with it, just like the men.

"How will you ever meet a husband with that attitude, darling?" Her mother had often said.

"Hard to see how I could avoid meeting one, mother. I'm always surrounded by Navy men, and that's the sort of hubby you want me to find, isn't it?"

Which was blunt but true.

Ralph looked a little disappointed that she wasn't wearing a dress, when he came to pick her up, but he was pleased enough that she'd agreed to go.

"I can't believe your C.O is marrying that fellow Tavistock," he said, when Anne was out of earshot. "He's a bit younger than her, isn't he?"

Cathy turned and gave him a stern glance. "And who are you to talk about a disparity in age, Ralph? When your penchant for younger women is well-known. You do realize, don't you, that you are exactly *twice* my current age?"

Ralph gave a kind of chuckle and led her down the front steps of the Wrennery. "Point taken."

They arrived in a Navy staff car, mercifully *not* displaying an Admiral's pennant, which was what happened when she went to these things with Daddy. The door was opened for them at the front steps though, and she and Ralph got out and went inside.

She left Ralph in the main hall, fluttering his eyelashes at the girl with a silver tray of hors d'ouvres, and went off to look for Geoff. Someone had pointed through a pair of paneled doors. "I think he's through there – he went to get a pre-dinner drink."

But he wasn't – so she went through another set of doors and into the next chamber – and then again through some more doors and into the garden – and there – on a bench seat in an alcove, she found him. Kissing a girl she'd never seen before. A girl in a pink chiffon dress.

It was a shock. Seeing him like that. She couldn't even *believe* for a minute it was him. But it was. She'd know her twin in a dark alley. She'd know her twin blindfold. It was him. His body was pressed against the girl, who had her fingers in his hair. His dark red hair, the exact same shade as her own. Pale fingers threaded through it. And he was so *involved* in the kiss that he didn't even notice. Until she spoke. "Geoff?"

He moved all right then. He and the girl separated in surprise and he looked up with a start. He actually looked a bit irritated. "Cathy! What on earth are you doing here?"

"I was invited, by Ralph Redcliffe. He said I might see you."

"Ah. Good, good," he recovered his dignity. He stood up, looking a bit foolish, and the girl stood up too. Smoothing her dress, which seemed to have got rather crumpled. This was hugely awkward, for all concerned – though really, there was no reason for it to be. He gestured to the girl, whose face was pink from excitement and mild humiliation. "This is Alison Hargreaves. We met... um...quite recently."

Cathy nodded, feeling strange. Geoff, with a woman, in a passionate kiss? And even though she was sure it wasn't his *first* kiss; it was certainly the first one she had ever witnessed. "And getting along famously, by the look of it," she said, ruggedly cheerful, though inside she was falling apart.

Her world slid into the sea, like the collapse of some ancient monument. But she summoned her manners and extended her hand, politely. "Great to meet you, Alison. I'm his twin."

Cathy didn't know how she got through the rest of the event. The dinner. The speeches. The bravado about how well the war was going. The stewards endlessly re-filling the men's glasses while the tried and trusted after-dinner stories were rolled out, just like the trusty old dessert trolley and the box of cigars. Ralph asked if she was alright a couple of times, and she nodded and smiled. She was *fine*. Perfectly alright. Nothing was wrong. Everything was as it should be. Except that it wasn't. It was complicated. The rest of the evening was all a bit of a blur, really.

She kept thinking about Geoff. All pashed up with a girl. It had to happen sooner or later.

But she felt… adrift.

On the way home she actually found herself wondering if she should let Ralph kiss her goodnight. But she decided not to rush into anything. She was thrown by the new developments she'd witnessed. She needed time. She didn't want to do something she might later regret. She was indeed adrift, and she wondered where the wind would take her.

•••

The following day it was full steam ahead with the preparations for the Important Visit. Cathy was glad to be part of the flurry of activity. All morning they worked on getting the Wrennery, the courtyard they used as a parade ground, and the Nissen huts where they did the training into a state they'd be happy to show to Royalty. This meant linoleum had to shine, even if girls laddered their black stockings and got work-reddened hands doing it. The copper pots in the galley were polished pink as the day they were made. Family photos tidied away – they were going for a neat, almost surgically neat, sense of order in the bedroom. The floors were brushed and the rugs were banged. Everyone got filthy dirty and spent a lot of time arguing about baths and putting their hair into rags and rollers. Somebody had an iron that you heat up and singed a bit of Binky's hair, but they worked out how to hide it by putting it into a Victory Roll.

By lunchtime, Cathy was on the stairs, with a tin of brass polish – polishing the metal rods that held the stair carpet in place – when a man slipped past her. Polished shoes. Well-pressed trouser legs. A large bundle of whitish yellowish clothing hanging over one arm. He was heading for the *bedrooms*.

"Hey? What are you *doing*?" Cathy said. He turned halfway up the stairs, and she saw who it was. "Oh, hello Dicky."

"Ah. Cathy. I'm leaving this for your C.O. Anne Foxton," he said. "I need to find her room."

"She's not here – she had to go and see her parents." *To tell them she's marrying an insane Fleet Air-head,* she could have added.

"It's alright, I only want to leave this for her."

Cathy hesitated for a split second. Then ran lightly up the stairs. "You'll get me into trouble, showing a man the way to a Wren's cabin. Come on. It's this way."

She took him to the doorway of a room with three beds.

"She shares?" Dicky asked, looking in.

Cathy nodded. "How are you getting all this time off? Explain yourself, Dicky."

"We're training at night. The Admiralty insists we log some night-flying. So, I've got time during the day to pursue... other things."

"And when do you sleep?"

He grinned. "Yes, Nanny. And I'm eating my vegetables, too. I promise."

Cathy laughed, but she was concerned. "You must be exhausted."

He looked into the room at soft beds with the candlewick bedspreads. Yes. He was tired. His face was almost grey with tiredness. "Which one is her bed?"

"That one, just inside the door."

Dicky went into the room. Reverently, he laid the dress on Anne's bed, and placed the veil, and a letter, on her pillow. "I'll telephone tonight to see if she likes it."

"You owe me," Cathy said. He did too. More than he knew. "Get some sleep this afternoon, you twit. She's said yes to you, now, hasn't she?"

When he was gone, some of the girls went to up to have a closer look. They laughed and said it was loathsome – egged on by Delia Finlay. "Look at it. Horrid thing. It's awful – so dreadfully out of style."

The girls gathered round the wedding dress and veil. An early 1920s style, lace-edged, with delicate, handkerchief points. The veil all torn and yellow, the satin dress so out of fashion it caused a lot of hilarity, everyone laughing about it. *It's hideous*, they said one to another.

"Was Dicky's mother pregnant when she wore it, d'you think? There seems to be a lot of room in the front!" They picked up the dress and shook it. Some dust fell out and made Mavis sneeze.

Peals of laughter – Cathy wanted them to stop. "You're being mean." She smoothed the dress, and laid it out on the bed as Dicky had intended. "It's a dropped waist, that's all, and a wide sash that goes on the hips."

"Horrible thing – and look at the veil – it's almost gone yellow."

"It's torn too – did you see?"

"Like her husband tore it off her!"

"It'll be a surprise for Anne Foxton alright – I think it'll be the shock of her life."

Poor Miss Foxton.

Chapter Twelve

Anne

Anne's day had not been easy. The preparations. The stress. And the parents. She'd borrowed a bicycle and cycled over to see them. Her father, pale and ill, had been concerned to hear of the possible…marriage. That word didn't seem to cover the arrangement she was contemplating with Dicky. In the end, she hadn't had the guts to tell them the whole story. She said she'd known him for 'several months' – which they thought was much too hasty. She *had* admitted that she wasn't sure if he really intended to go through with it.

But keep Thursday, free. Just in case. Her mother had put a hand over her mouth. Her father had shaken his head, and said – "I hope you know what you're doing."

It was a relief to get back to the Wrennery. Although someone had taken the paint off the steps with over-zealous cleaning.

She went upstairs to hang her coat up.

When Anne entered the room and saw the dress, she gave a soft cry. Couldn't take another step. Stood and stared. "What's this?"

Binky said, "Surprise for you. From Wings himself."

A wedding gown. A real one. She gave a soft cry when she saw it laid out on her bed. An actual audible sound. It was partly the shock at seeing it laid out on the bed when the room had been spotless for the inspection this morning.

"Hideous, isn't it?" Delia said. Cathy gave her a sharp kick on the ankle.

But Anne was ecstatic. Tears came. A release of tension, disbelief and excitement. "A wedding dress," she said in amazement – as if they had just been invented.

Binky looked at Anne, sympathetically. "But not one that any bride would actually *wear*."

"Shut up," said Cathy.

The next thing Anne did was pick up the letter. Scanned the words with her hand clamped over her mouth.

Cathy ran to hug her. "It's his mother's dress, isn't it? Isn't that what it says in the letter?"

Anne nodded and showed it to Cathy. "He means it! I *am* getting married."

Heads together, they read the handwritten note.

Dear Anne,

This gown was worn by my mother on the occasion of her marriage in 1920. In that year it made her look like an absolute fashion plate, but I realize it's now out of style and may be completely unsuitable. If you have something you'd rather wear I will totally understand, but I'd be honoured if you would consider it. She would have been thrilled to see you wear that dress on the day I make you my wife. On that theme, I have one more request: I want you to wear your fiancé's engagement ring, and I will add the band of gold that he did not live to deliver. We will honour our dead as we honour each other.

Please do this for me, Anne, he was dear to you, and his sacrifice need not be hidden.

Most sincerely,

Richard Tavistock

Her heart leapt with excitement and tears of joy sprang easily. She was overcome by emotion. *He means it – and he understands, about Jim's ring.* "Oh, Cathy. Thank you."

Cathy hugged her. "What for? I didn't do anything."

You did. You helped me make a decision, and I'm beginning to believe it was a good one.

Then Mavis came running up the stairs – "He's on the telephone, Miss."

"Now?"

"Yes – he wants to know if you've got the dress."

She ran downstairs, light as a girl, and picked up the telephone receiver. Cradling it in both hands, she said. "Dicky? Is that you?"

"Yes, darling. Look, if the dress isn't right – I will understand, truly..."

"Oh Dicky, now I know it's true! I *am* to be married! I really, really, am."

"Thank God. I must say I'd become rather worried. I learned this morning that Wrens can borrow from a selection of rather stylish wedding gowns owned by the Navy for just these – *emergencies*."

"No – of course not! I'd be honoured to wear your mother's gown."

The letter. It had set something free inside her. The unfulfilled longing had gone on so long she'd accepted its heavy presence, its shackles had held her and brought her down. But seeing that dress on her bed had unlocked her, unleashed a new hope that made all things seem possible. If they could just have enough time.

The phone line seemed to crackle with emotion. "You know what, Anne?"

"What?" she was breathless with excitement. She could have hugged herself and everyone else around her. Impossible dreams. Doors that had seemed jammed shut, swung open and beckoned her inside.

"I've finally got the right girl."

Her heart soared. "Oh Dicky, I hope so. I don't even know how it happened, but I'm so happy, I think I actually screamed."

She could sense he was smiling, even on the phone. "Darling, it was *your* idea."

Linda

That afternoon, Linda was getting an outing to the seaside. She drove along the road to the coast, feeling ever so glad she'd volunteered for motor transport. It opened up all sorts of opportunities. But this was no ordinary day at the beach. She was with the bomb disposal team – and for the usual reason.

The men were in a buoyant mood. On the way down they'd sung "I do like to be beside the seaside." She'd even glanced in the mirror and seen Toby's lips move ever so slightly in time to the words. Though no real sound came out.

Captain Morrison wondered out loud – "Is there anywhere we could get scampi in a basket, d'you think?"

"Be lovely to have a good plate of fish and chips," said Frye. "And a beer."

But first – more pressing matters.

The beach was a mixture of pebbles and sand. The seafront was deserted because the locals were not allowed to walk there – it was sectioned off with barbed wire and controlled by army checkpoints, only sparsely manned. Linda had been given permission to drive through, so she took the car down the slipway and onto the beach. She parked well back from the waters' edge where the sand was still firm. She didn't want to risk the precious vehicle getting stuck. It was lovely to be out – even in British weather. She savoured the smell of the sea and the uplifting sight of the frothy white breakers bursting onto the sand. The beach looked perfect.

Yes. Perfect – if not for an ugly great mine in the middle of it. The mine – a menacing black ball with short spikes sticking out of it – stood as high as a man's thigh. All five of them looked warily at it, as they opened the doors and got out of the car. Linda got out too and went round to the back of their vehicle – a 1938 Hillman Minx, with 'BDS 12' on the plate (short for Bomb Disposal Squad), and stamped "Navy" in various places. She opened the trunk and started helping them unload the things they would need. "Right boys. Here are the shovels. Do you want the rope and the tool box?"

"Let the dog see the rabbit," Clegg said. Meaning that Morrison would need to 'inspect' the mine first, before they decided how to tackle it.

Captain Morrison asked his men to shed any metal items they had with them. He put his screw driver and pen knife on the front seat of the car, for fear that the metal in them might set off an explosion if the mine was a magnetic one. Then he walked over towards the mine – remarkably blasé, Linda thought. For half a second, she thought Morrison was going to kick it like a beachball, but once he was right beside the mine, he *did* treat it with the respect that such a dangerous object deserved. Without touching it, he looked at it from every angle, and called out that the detonator was underneath – which was not good news. "She'll have to be dug out, I'm afraid."

Frye grunted, not liking the sound of that. Toby and Clegg just stood there leaning on their shovels, enjoying the sea breeze.

"Toby – come and have a look at it with me," Morrison said. "Leave your shovel up there."

Toby nodded. Mute as usual. He gave his shovel back to Frye, saying nothing. His angular face revealed very little at the best of times. He didn't have a hat or a muffler today. He crunched across the beach looking sheepish in his fisherman's jersey and what might have once been a pair of bell-bottoms, tucked into his wellies. Captain Morrison was in his greatcoat – he seemed to live in that. Nobody wore any gloves – too risky – they needed the fine control. Hands in pockets were permitted in this corner of the royal navy – the men had to keep their hands warm somehow. The two men conferred quietly. The mine looked harmless. Its black paint caught the sun as it sat there like an out-of-place tourist on the beach. But Linda knew it was powerful enough to disable a small vessel – and definitely powerful enough to kill the two men standing beside it.

She shuddered as she watched them touch the mine. One man steadied it – the other one dug with his hands. They took turns doing this, working with painstaking care, until they could roll it slowly – inch by careful inch – to look at the detonator cap.

"Any thoughts on this one, Toby?" Morrison knew he had to ask, or Toby would stay silent. Without a direct question to answer, he wouldn't say boo to a goose, Linda noticed. Strong silent type.

"The detonator cap's the same as the last one we did." Toby said, kneeling down and looking closely.

"Yes – I spotted that. Perfectly standard. Anything else?"

"I don't like the way the caps been put on – looks like they've buggered it up – jammed the thread."

"Oh, yes. It's on a slight angle. Oh, bother."

Captain Morrison was always cheerful. Nothing fazed him. "I expect it can be eased off anyway, I'll try a little tweak under the edge with my dental probe." Morrison's father had been dentist and he'd inherited a bagful of old dental tools – invaluable for de-fusing bombs, apparently. He went and got it and then asked, "Will one of you hold her steady?"

Toby offered to do the holding. And Morrison told the others to move to a safe distance – preferably a position behind the van. Linda did the same. Everyone looked at one another, but they were used to obeying orders, so they went. They waited in a companionable but tense silence – crouched in a row behind the vehicle. Clegg looked at Linda. "Keep your head down, love. They don't call em murder mines for nothing."

Ten minutes passed. Linda thought this ten minutes seemed to last even longer than the last one. She didn't think she'd *ever* be relaxed again doing this kind of thing. And yet she *loved* being this team's driver.

"She's off!" Morrison called out – sounding rather pleased with himself. And the release of tension was palpable. Everyone relaxed and smiled at each other.

The whole team – except Linda – could now work more comfortably near the mine, and they followed their usual procedure. Toby took out the whole detonating mechanism – and finally the charge – bit by bit in the form of cylinders. He stuck his arm deep inside the mine and pulled out each container of explosive.

Then – the bit Frye said he liked best – they made a pile of the cylinders some distance away on the beach. And let them off. No major bang – just a pleasant fizz. Like burning phosphorus on Guy Fawkes night. Evening Fireworks.

Morrison sighed in contentment. "Time to find the pub then..."

Chapter Thirteen

Linda

On the day of the Very Important Visit, Linda was on call for the bomb disposal guys again. Anne touched her shoulder at breakfast time and told her that she'd received a telephone call asking for Linda to be ready in twenty minutes. "Do you want me to try and get you out of it?" Anne said in a conspiratorial whisper. "So you can stay and meet ...our guest from the Palace?"

"No. Don't do that," Linda said, looking up from her breakfast plate – wondering if she had time to finish her sausage on toast. "I'll drive for the boys. It's much more important, really."

Anne patted her on the shoulder – impressed with her dedication to duty. "Good girl."

Truth be told, Linda wasn't all that sorry that she would miss seeing the Royal Person. She'd never really been obsessed with the royal family – not like some of the girls were. Nor was she especially keen on meeting what her dad would have called 'big wigs'. She was even quite glad to be missing the last of the frantic preparations at the Wrennery, where the whole thing was sending everyone into a tizzy and bringing out the worst in people. All her thoughts these days were for her team and their work. Before this, she hadn't even realised that the Navy had its own disposal teams. Now she knew them and loved them like friends or family. Even when she was delivering messages on her motorbike she thought about them, and she was secretly glad that she'd been placed permanently 'on call' for those times when her boys needed a driver.

So, half an hour later, Linda was behind the wheel whistling a happy tune, on her way to a bomb site. Morrison was sitting in the seat beside her, looking calm but focused on the duties that lay ahead. The other three men were sitting in a row in the back of the car. Toby was in the middle. He caught her eye when she looked at him in the rear-view mirror and she thought she saw a smile – but it was so subtle she told herself she was imagining things. He rarely expressed even a flicker of emotion. But anyway. It was a fine morning. They had work to do, and they were together again. Her red lipstick smile was wide today.

She turned to Morrison. "What news, sir?" She was hoping he'd tell her a bit about what to expect today.

He gave her a quick glance and then continued looking out at the road ahead. "It's a bomb that was aimed at the dockyard. It missed and went into a row of offices inside the Admiralty's area. That's about all I can say."

She nodded. "Good luck, sir."

"Thank you."

They drove in silence the rest of the way. They passed through a checkpoint. The street had been closed to the public. A man from the Admiralty – wearing a uniform with quite a lot of gold braid on it – was already there. He was pacing nervously in the road – glancing up at the building beside him as if it might explode at any moment. He leaned into the open window of the car – even before the men had a chance to get out. "I hope your men can work quickly, Morrison. Speed is essential. We need this sorted out pronto."

Linda heard that, and felt worried. The team worked in a way that minimised *danger* – not in a way that maximised speed. They couldn't just 'speed up' and work more quickly.

Morrison looked at the man from the Admiralty quite crossly, too. He stood up to him, despite the fact that the other man outranked him. "We can't do a bomb like that – we can't 'hurry up' or we might pull the pin on the thing and be blown to kingdom come."

"I'm afraid you simply have to. We have an Important Visitor coming this afternoon and we need to make the area safe for her."

Ah. So that was it. There was no escaping the royal visit, or the tizzy it was causing, thought Linda, and smiled to herself. Of course, the VIP might want to see the Admiralty headquarters while she was here. And the *last* thing they needed was a UXB in the area that might threaten the Royal Person's safety. But they still couldn't just 'speed up'.

Morrison scowled. "It doesn't matter how important your visitor is, sir. She'll jolly well have to stay behind the barrier like everyone else if she doesn't want her hat blown off. Or her head. The work we do simply can't be hurried, I'm afraid."

Well said, thought Linda. Feeling a small surge of admiration for Morrison that she didn't usually feel.

The Admiralty man looked like he was sucking on a cough lozenge with a horrible taste to it. "Well, I'm disappointed in you, Morrison. I would have thought-"

"Yes, yes, yes. Awfully sorry. We'll do our best. Just show us the UXB, will you?" Morrison looked very determined and started getting out of the car, which meant the Admiralty man had to step back to let him out. Linda knew Captain Morrison well enough to know that he didn't suffer fools gladly, and that dicing with death every day had made him bold about standing up to people who were too 'officious' as he called it.

It wasn't a good start though. Linda would have preferred to have kept the mood light, as it had been en route to the site. She had a firm conviction in her heart that her boys – yes, she definitely thought of them as 'her' boys now – worked best when they were calm and relaxed. As far as that was possible.

She saw them off and watched them heading into the building carrying their shovels over their shoulders like four of the seven dwarves off to work. Not that any of them were small – Toby was the tallest, but they were all strong and muscular. The digging helped with that. She settled down for her long wait in the car.

She had – wrapped in greaseproof paper inside her pocket – a piece of bread folded round a sausage that Mavis had given her when she had to leave the breakfast table in a hurry. She didn't need it right now, but she was looking forward to a mid-morning snack a bit later. She gave a little sigh of contentment. A late breakfast, washed down with some hot tea from her new thermos flask – a military issue one in black with a wire handle. They were great those things. It was so nice to have a warm drink on an assignment like this that might last for hours.

She was just having a little day dream about things like picnics and thermos flasks when...

The three men came racing round the corner like men possessed. Linda had never seen Toby move that fast. His gangly body sprinted round the corner – he seemed to leap the last ten feet and then – through the window – she saw his head duck down beside the car as he sheltered behind it.

The other men came running out at a pace an Olympic runner wouldn't be ashamed of. "What's going on-"

"Get down!"

A loud bang. Brick dust flew around her. She screamed. Bits of brick were coming down like hail. Showering noisily all over the car. The windscreen broke – but even that did not shatter. Bricks landing on top of the car made Linda scream again as the roof bulged in above her. Heart pounding, she crouched down, cowering as low as she could get. Hoping the roof of the car would hold and protect her.

Chest heaving, she thought. *What the flip just happened? Did it blow? Are the team alright? Where is everyone?*

She got out gingerly. The car's fenders were covered in brickdust. She stood stunned for a moment, until she noticed that Morrison was right there – with his greatcoat covered in a fine brick-coloured powder.

"Everyone alright?" he said cheerfully.

The three other men popped up from behind the car and peered out over the top, like three chipmunks coming up out of their burrow. It all seemed rather comical... and Linda found that she desperately wanted to laugh – perhaps just to relieve the tension. *Oh, the relief.* Everyone was accounted for. The car was a bit dented, that's all. No harm done. Linda's heartbeat began to slow down.

"Blimey," said Frye, looking at the dust and debris all around them.

"That's what happens when you rush," said Toby. Stoical as ever.

The other men were elated – they'd been let off Scot free with their lives. Clegg was grinning like an idiot.

Morrison stared at the lumps of brick on top of the car. Some of them were quite big. "Bloody lucky we're all going home. Let's hope those stuffed shirts at the Admiralty don't charge us for the damage to the car."

"No real harm done," said Clegg, happily. "Look on the bright side. We can tell the Admiralty the bomb poses no danger to She who will be secretly visiting the dockyard later today. No danger at all. And all accomplished *fast* – as per our instructions."

Morrison smiled. "That's true. We've never de-fused one *that* quickly."

"Lucky it was a ticker," said Frye. Leaning close to Linda.

"A what?"

"It started ticking – Toby heard it first – he gave us the shout, and we had those few seconds to run."

Yes, she thought. That *was* lucky.

"This calls for a pub lunch," announced Morrison. "To celebrate our survival."

Linda smiled. Morrison thought everything called for a visit to the pub.

"Too right it does," said Frye. "That was a close one."

Today's encounter had been so close that even Toby agreed to go and have a drink – although his was a fruit juice and soda. They found a place with that had a little 'beer garden' out back and all sat down at a scarred wooden table. Toby passed the time waiting for his drink to arrive by writing some notes in his beloved notebook. When the barmaid came out to them with a tray of drinks, Toby set aside his little book – placing it reverently on the seat beside him as if it were a small child he was looking after.

Linda plucked up the courage to ask him about the book and why he kept it. Even though he wasn't tiddly, he was in a good mood, happy and relaxed after the near miss, so he showed her. She was able to get a much better look inside the book than the time she'd tried to leaf through it without his permission. She turned the pages, slowly. She gazed at the detail – marveled at the intricacy of his notes and illustrations. It really was a remarkable thing. "You're so talented, Toby. These are *great*."

The book was a chronicle of everything he'd ever defused or seen. All done in his inimitable artistic style. Cartoon bombs with smiley faces on them – each given a personality. Each torpedo, each bomb, with its own goofy little face. She smiled when she saw a cartoon torpedo that he had named Trevor. He'd given it an expression at every stage of its journey. There was a heading on one double page spread in the centre of Toby's book:- The journey of Trevor the Clever Torpedo. Linda followed along carefully as Toby, in his biggest speech ever, explained what happens to a torpedo from the moment it is 'born' in a factory, to the moment it 'does its job'.

His finger – with a bit of dirt trapped under the nail – traced the progress of Trevor the Clever Torpedo as he spoke. "The girls in the Shadow factory make em, see, and they put em on trucks or trains. Off they go on their little jaunt." He made train noises, like a child, and that almost made Linda giggle. But he frowned so she kept a straight face and followed the rest of his explanation.

"They send em to the dockyard at the Admiralty, like, and sometimes there's Wrens waiting – yep – it's often you girls that put em on the ships, and then the lads on board take over and they strap em into cradles and look after them."

"Look after them?" Linda smiled. In cradles? Bomb-care for beginners?

Toby looked serious. "If you don't take care of bombs, Linda, bad things appen." He paused, dark eyebrows drawing together as he thought about some of those 'bad things' and how hard he worked to prevent them. Then, he continued. "Time comes for an op, and the lads load em onto trolleys and take them up to the aircraft deck – onto the planes they go. Locked in place underneath – but ready for release at touch of a button. Armourer checks them and makes them ready. Pilot takes em up into the sky and out to the enemy ships. Press that button and torpedo shoots out and into the sea. Mechanism inside makes it level up and travel at the right depth. Arms it too. And if the aircrew's done its sums right, Trevor the Clever finds his mark and goes slicing into the hull of the ship. Explodes on contact. Job done ...See that torpedo there – the big one?"

Linda nodded.

Toby looked solemn "One of those in the exact right place – and bingo – nine hundred souls lost. And t'other side's busy doing the same thing... dropping their bombs on our ships and our folks here."

It was a sobering thought. The waste of human life. It obviously troubled Toby deeply. He started telling her about how they worked on bombs that fell onto civilian targets. And how he dealt with those. "If I can just clip the right wire, then the whole thing stops. It's disarmed and it can't hurt anybody. It's just a harmless metal shell. But there's bombs dropping all the time, Linda. Tons and tons of them. They hurt folks who never did anything to anybody. And I can't work fast enough – that's the trouble. They're dropping them too quickly for me."

"You're doing your bit," she said. Encouragingly. She patted his arm and he gave her one of his 'almost' smiles. It troubled her that he couldn't see the war in quite the way she did, though. To him, there was no 'just war' – no good reason to fight. Ever. She studied him, carefully. "But Hitler *has* to be stopped, don't you agree?"

"Oh, yes. Someone should have clipped *his* wires a long time ago."

Cathy

On the parade ground at HMS *Resilient* the atmosphere was tense. Fifty Wrens stood to attention, every girl holding a firm salute for several minutes as the car swept in through the gates of the Wrennery and rounded the corner into the courtyard. Even the car looked Royal. An impossibly shiny black car, exaggerated in length, with silver headlamps that caught the light and gleamed – even on a day of intermittent sunlight. Small patches of pale blue appeared between clouds in a dappled mixture of white and grey. Although forbidden to speak or relax their salute, Cathy could hear the words rippling in the air, as the lady – a small women – stepped out of the vehicle. Her gloved hand took the helping hand that was offered as she stepped out of the car...

"Oh, look – it's *her!*"

The consort of the King – the mother of the two princesses – had come to see them. Elizabeth Bowes-Lyon before she was married, and now, since the abdication and the unexpected installation of her stuttering husband, she was, quite simply, the Queen. She had come to the city to inspect some bomb damage down by the docks, and she had kindly offered to extend her itinerary to include the girls at HMS *Resilient*.

She stepped forward, perfectly matched to the weather, wearing a dove-grey hat, angled sharply up, with a huge brooch on the band underneath. A grey coat dress, open at the front, to show a pale blue frock beneath. She carried – and placed under her arm when she wanted to inspect something closely – a clutch bag, leather, like her gloves, same dove grey as the hat.

The girls launched into an enthusiastic display of their marching skills, The tightest, neatest version of their daily parade that any sergeant major would be proud of. Their parade master – who'd been frazzled all week, had a ruddy face that glowed with pride. Ma'am smiled beautifully as if it was the first parade she'd ever seen and told them they marched exceptionally well. Then into the Nissen huts where the girls learned morse and teleprinting, and she even touched – no *pressed* – the polished knob on one of the morse code machines. "A very useful skill. Does it take you long to learn?"

Off into the house and through the kitchens – finding a kind word here or there for the galley Wrens. The lady was gracious in the extreme, and wanted to see *everything*, even the cabins.

"The feverish cleaning wasn't all for nothing," Mavis whispered, as they stood to attention on the landing, wondering which room ma'am would like to visit. She peeked into all of them – which was very diplomatic. Penelope thanked her profusely for coming and encouraging them all.

"Offering encouragement is something I *can* do, and in time of war we must all do what we can."

The Queen seemed magnetically drawn into the doorway of the room that Anne shared with two other girls, and they all sent up a prayer that the room didn't smell of damp tea leaves from their efforts to get the crumbs off the floor. Then Anne saw what had drawn their Esteemed Visitor in. And caught her breath. The wedding dress, to her embarrassment, had *not* been put away, someone idiot had hung it up on the outside of the wardrobe, instead of putting it out of sight. The Queen looked in and saw the dress. "Is someone preparing to get married?"

Anne could have died. She should've made sure it was put away, but she'd been busy downstairs and twice she'd asked the girls to run up and check. She'd expected them to have folded the dress and shoved it away somewhere, but here it was, because they were trying to hang out the creases.

"Our Commanding Officer, ma'am. I believe the gown belonged to the groom's mother."

And to their surprise 'ma'am' went over to look at the dress – and she touched it. "Delightful. It's actually rather similar to the one I chose for my own wedding day." she touched the aging silk, fondly. "I never thought to see a modern bride getting married in such a dress. What a treat."

Delia Finlay was the first to speak. "Breathtakingly beautiful, isn't it, Ma'am?"

"Lovely, lovely style," Binky said.

"Simply heavenly," Mavis agreed.

Cathy had one word on her lips and she murmured it, only to herself. "Hypocrites."

Anne touched her wedding posy and gave him a sidelong glance. "Ah yes. Lovely girl. You didn't tell her you were a *captain*, by any chance?"

Now, that made *him* start blushing.

The marriage by special licence wasn't bleak at all. The chapel at the Fleet Air training wing was in a plain low building, but it was as much like a church as she could have hoped, and a good choice under the circumstances. Her father, too ill to stand, was just inside the door to grasp her hand and wish her good luck.

The trainee fliers were marvellous at impromptu celebrations, they looked so smart in their navy-blue jackets, and their military swords looked dashing. They had bunting and confetti at the ready, and they made two lines to marshal her in. The old-fashioned dress fluttered prettily as Anne got out of the car, and the boys wolf-whistled at her slim ankles. Her feet felt light and nimble as she walked up the steps in her borrowed satin shoes with pearl button fastenings. The day was bright, but cool, classic April. She wasn't sure if she shivered from cold or excitement. She went down the aisle with her uncle, who was white with nerves, as if she was getting wed at St. Paul's Cathedral.

Her five-minute fiancé was at the altar waiting for her as she walked to meet him. Her handsome, hasty young flier. He turned and smiled to encourage her. More of a grin than a smile. But it was an actual wedding, and even if he left her at the church door, no one could say he didn't mean it anymore. He was there, he was ready, he was waiting. She took her place beside him.

Jim's ring shone – catching the light from the minister's candles. So thoughtful of the chaplain to light the candles – extravagant too – but they did add a glowing, spiritual touch to a room that was war department plain. The naval chaplain got out his book, and blessed the ring and the union. Never commenting on the haste, in his chatty preamble. Never mentioning the fragility of marriage in general – and their mad dash to the altar in particular.

"All rise, and let us sing," he intoned.

> *Will your anchor hold in the storms of life,*
> *when the clouds unfold their wings of strife?*
> *When the strong tides lift, and the cables strain,*

will your anchor drift, or firm remain?

Rousing, stirring stuff – especially when sung by a squadron of lusty young fliers and a flock of Wrens all looking forward to a stiff drink in the Wardroom after. A *chime* – it's a chime of wrens, Dicky had told her, later.

The old-fashioned dress, the washed and mended veil. The shining pearls, sewn by a friend. Jim's ring, and Dicky's eyes, hopeful and bright, as he held her hands in his. Hands that were warm, comforting. His presence solid and reassuring. It was everything. Everything and more.

The memory she would take from this would be vivid. The scent of her flowers. Her satin shoes and his polished black ones, the slight tug of the baby-blue ribbon garter she wore on her right leg – for luck – though she already counted herself lucky. Her groom, looking so splendid in his naval uniform. Beyond words. The rich sound of his voice – resonant, warm, and kind, as he made his responses. The words she had always longed to hear. "To be my wedded wife, to have and to hold, from this day forward..."

The naval chaplain read out her lines for her. *I take thee Richard James Tavistock...* and she repeated them, clear and calm. *I take thee, Richard James Tavistock ... to be my wedded husband...*

Mrs Richard Tavistock, an awkward, unfamiliar sound, instead of Mrs James Bellwood, a name she had long believed would be hers. It almost seemed like a shock when she heard her own voice say, "I will."

There was an unexpected flypast about half way through, noisy and rude in the middle of the vows, but it made the audience laugh and lightened the moment. Congregation – not audience – she reminded herself. This is not a game or a theatrical production. This is a marriage. However long or short.

This is the start of my married life, and even if I lose him tomorrow, I will always have today. I will be happy. I will.

Cathy

Cathy was reluctant to leave the reception early – it was such a happy occasion. But her instructions from the Admiralty gave her no choice. She took one last look into the room – where the happy couple were now cutting the cake. Dicky Tavistock had pulled off the apparently impossible – a bride in less than six weeks – after two false starts, a slap in the face, and a cautionary talk with his wing-commander.

holding the edges of her jacket together. She relaxed her hand, fearing the woman behind the desk might think she was pregnant.

She was nervous, she could admit that, if only to herself.

Turning the new wedding ring on her finger, she tried to recapture that wonderful feeling that it was all coming together instead of falling apart. Jim's ring, she could wear it again, she could wear it forever. And the shining gold wedding band fitted so neatly beside it, as if the two were meant to be together, instead of being bought for her by two entirely different men. *Be hopeful.* Dicky had demonstrated more than once that he could be kind. She already had some inkling that he was deeper and more sincere than he at first appeared. He took both the cases, since doormen were a thing of the past.

The hotel manager led them upstairs to what surely must be the attic. She was apologetic. "It's a long trek – but we thought you might like to be a bit further away from the other guests, for privacy, like. What with you being a honeymoon couple."

"Very kind," Dicky managed to reply.

Their room was lovely, fresh flowers, more books, arranged on a desk in the corner. Comforting doorstops like *Our Mutual Friend* and lighter, happier ones, the *Just William* chronicles, the adventures of *Jeeves and Wooster.* Books from her childhood, and probably, from his. She ran her fingers lightly over them, and Dicky leaned close and whispered, "You won't need a book."

The hotel manageress decided it was time to leave them.

In the last moments of daylight, shafting in from the windows, she could see that the attic had a view of the lake. They'd go and walk beside the edge of the water tomorrow. The window itself was framed by wisteria. Curled woody stems, years old, grew up around the frame. It was a gabled window, and Dicky had to duck his head to look out. Lovely view. Last of the sunlight, fading fast. It was so perfect she couldn't speak.

He had chosen the perfect place, but even so, when they were finally alone, she felt a flood of awkwardness. He had planned this before he'd even met her. He'd imagined being here with someone else. There had been others. She was simply the one he'd ended up with. But she glanced at him shyly, and saw his tenderness, his longing, and how through all his craziness and haste, there was integrity, patience, and kindness.

He went and put his cap down on the dressing table. Asked her if she needed something brought up. A drink, perhaps? Some cocoa?

She shook her head. "Is that what you want?"

He gave her a soulful look. "People don't usually want cocoa on their wedding night."

A fire was laid in the grate and a taper and matches placed thoughtfully beside on the hearth. He reached for the matches; she didn't object. Even though it was spring, the weather was decidedly British, and they would be more comfortable with a small, flickering fire. He struck a match, and the smooth fireside tiles reflected the single fluttering flame. He held it close to the newspaper that formed the first fragile layer under the kindling. He waited for a moment, to see if it would take, until the first tendrils of smoke began to curl up over the wood and the coal. Some promising leaps of flame licked at the freshly chipped bits of wood under the coal. "Success."

The light from the fire brought out the organiser in her. "I must close the blackout curtains. We don't want to put everyone in the hotel at risk." She went and pulled them together, plunging the room into semi-darkness, which gave them a moment of blundering confusion, until he found and switched on the bedside lamp. They stood blinking at each other in the artificial light.

The awkwardness was intense, but he refused to allow it to take hold. He came back to her, and held out both hands. "I can't tell you how grateful I am to have found you."

Well, that was nice. But gratitude wasn't exactly the emotion she was hoping for. Suddenly, she was a nervous schoolgirl. "I don't know why you married me. I would have come here anyway."

What an admission.

He paused for a long moment. His hands were warm and smooth. "Anne." Such tenderness, in one quiet word. "It's better this way, believe me. It was brave of you to take me on."

She was blushing hard. The confidence she usually showed when she was running the Wrennery – it was not there. It was missing. It worked so well there, with impertinent tradesmen and difficult girls, but it didn't seem to have come with her on her honeymoon. "I don't feel brave at all..."

"You don't need to be. But you do need to trust me."

They had got to the place they both wanted to be. Standing opposite each other, beside a marriage bed. She looked up and met his gaze, calm and steady.

Chapter Fifteen

Cathy

Somewhere in England, as the Pathe News would say, Cathy was still on the train. 'Somewhere' always sounded so mysterious and alluring, so rich with possibility. But, for Cathy, she'd known the destination from the morning of the wedding. She was not optimistic that this was "Somewhere" she wanted to go. She'd rather go "Anywhere" but there – to be honest. She'd been issued with a rail pass – and it was stamped *Southwold.*

Where the heck is that? Suffolk coast? No navy there. Apart from the fishing towns, the closest port would be Ipswich. Miles away. *What on earth am I being asked to do?* And now – the conductor came and called out the name of the station – since all the station signs had been taken away. She got off the train in darkness, the daylight was gone. And went through the gate. She surrendered her one-way train pass to a man who clipped it invalid and then threw it away. "There's a car waiting for you, Miss."

"For me?" Cathy said.

"It's Navy – it must be for you."

Cathy went outside to the forecourt, and a vehicle, driven by a Wren, was waiting outside. The Wren wound down the window as Cathy approached.

"Station Y?"

"That's what they told me."

Cathy opened the door, stuck her case inside and hopped in. They drove to a place surrounded by barbed wire like a prison camp. The land around was dead flat – she couldn't see the sea, but she could hear it – and smell its salty presence only a short way away. The adjacent field was graced with two tall radio towers, slim fragile looking spires made of struts of metal. The hut was guarded by sailors, but walking through the camp she saw RAF uniforms.

"Combined Ops, is it?" she asked the driver.

"Yes. But the station's run by the Navy."

Standing in the middle of a hayfield was a two-ton truck, with a huge curved transmitter mounted on top, scanning slowly to one side and then the other. A man with a clipboard stood beside it, patiently recording details of some kind.

Chapter Sixteen

Linda

Evening. Eight o'clock. Knocking off time, thought Linda. Let's pull the pin and go to the pub, boys. But she knew that this was work that could not be hurried. The bomb disposal crew were in an office building, near the city centre. The room, the building and the street were all deserted. Inside it was dark, and they were working with lamps strung up in the ruined building. It was hot, dusty work. Linda peered in through the doorway and asked them if they needed water.

The trio of men were gathered around a square pit that they had dug – around the offending explosive. The sides of the pit were reinforced with bits of wood to prevent spoil from falling in and causing an unplanned detonation. The men's faces showed unimaginable strain, and sweat dripped through the dirt and the brick dust. Morrison nodded yes to the water, but said to leave it outside and not come any closer.

Linda left the water bottle on a wall away from the immediate site. A brown pottery bottle, with a cork stopper. A good thing to keep water cool. She put some tin cups beside it.

It was late and she was tired. She attended to the car to pass the time, folded back the bonnet of the car, checked the level of the oil with a long metal dipstick. She went round to the trunk and got another ceramic bottle, opened the tight brass cap on the radiator, and gave the car a drink. Stoppered the bottle and put it back ready for tomorrow. She got into the car, pulled her trusty blanket over her legs. Ready for much needed sleep.

Then came a shout and the men ran, but too late. The explosion.

The wall shattered – tin cups, bottle, and all. Bricks spilling across the pavement. She saw a searing flash of bright light in the road, and heard the blast as a crack of thunder. A spreading red stain splattered across the windscreen of her car. Red blood on the windscreen. Deep red blood.

She screamed. "*NO! Please, NO!*"

Someone's blood had been spilt. Light filtered through the unnatural red on the windscreen. The last of the evening sun. Through a filter of bright red blood.

Her heart beat like a startled bird in a cage, or a person trapped in a mineshaft. She turned her head to avoid looking at the blood on the windscreen in front of her. The side window was less occluded, only a few tiny splatters. Papers blew in an unsettling swirl from the office block where they'd been working. Sheaves of paper in turbulent gusts, no longer of any importance. A million papers blowing in the breeze. Secrets blown everywhere. Bricks. Lying across the street. Bricks. Newly broken.

Voices, feet running. A thin wail from somewhere.

Where's Toby? And George? And the Captain? But most of all, she had to know – where's Toby?

She put a hand on the door handle, but she was too scared to get out of the car. She sat there, frozen with terror. She sat there. Shaking.

Blood on the windscreen – some light filtering into the car through the dark red blood.

She couldn't hear her own scream – she was deafened, but she knew she had screamed because her throat felt sore. She was stunned – trying to decide. Do I get out of the car and find out who died? What will I see, if I do?

Heart pounding – do I need to stay here. Do I need to run?

Toby. What happened to Toby? And then someone came and rattled the car door. Calling to her. "Linda? Are you alright?"

It was George – the sailor named George Frye. Linda stared at him. Shaking. Needing to know. "Where are the others?"

"We lost Morrison," he said, shaking visibly. He was out of breath and covered in dust. And blood.

"Morrison?" She shook uncontrollably. Does that mean, oh, please let it mean....

It seemed so bad to think that way. *Okay, you can have Morrison, but please, God, don't take Toby.*

Toby. Oh no, she did not want to love Toby. Silent, awkward, unsmiling Toby. Humourless, plain clothes Toby, who held a moleskin notebook with more tenderness than he'd ever shown her.

But it was too late for that. The need to know that it was not his blood splattered on her windscreen told her that her heart had already chosen.

Cathy

Henry Rawton was one of those men who sticks out his hand when he was still on the other side of the room. "Ah, Cathy. Delighted to have you on board." He came towards her through the administration area, clipboard under one arm, other one extended in welcome.

"Hello, Captain." They shook hands, and he immediately made her do a hundred and eighty degree turn and led her back down the corridor she had just walked down. Placing a hand on her back, he guided her to the other end of the building. Opened a door.

"Our radio operators are in here," he said. She was given mere seconds to glimpse inside the room – where a row of Wrens with headsets on were listening intently for enemy messages, under the supervision of a naval officer. "And our direction finding takes place in Hut Two."

"Direction finding?" she said, as Rawton closed the door on the radio girls.

"Yes. Look. We'd better get your sig on the old OSA, before we talk about that, hadn't we?"

"Of course." Cathy assumed he meant the Official Secrets Act.

Rawton – always in a hurry – was already heading back to the administration area. "Mildred! Did you give me that blank OSA form I asked for?"

A tired-looking Wren with a mug of tea in her hand said, "On your clipboard, Sir."

Rawton pulled the clipboard out from under his arm – and seem to start with surprise to see the form there. "Ah yes. Good, good, good." He stole a pen from somebody's desk, and said, "Sign there, Cathy."

After she'd signed solemnly to say she would never reveal any details of her work at HMS Long Sands, Rawton gave her one of his two-second glimpses into the other hut – where there were a lot more personnel and a higher level of security. In there, instead of a row of radio sets – there were blocky looking units with circular screens. A bar of light in constant movement on each screen – a blip – a ping – an excited voice shouting "Contact!" and two or three people would run to check... disappointment – only a church steeple...

Then the door slammed shut. There was no explanation, no road map that might have helped Cathy understand what she was meant to be doing. Cathy had a zillion questions. *What is RDF?* But Rawton had turned to her and said, "Well my dear, you'll be wanting to get some rest – let me take you home to your new billet."

And he drove her, *personally*, in his staff car – to a modest house in town. They blundered up the garden path in the dark – Cathy carrying her own brown leather suitcase. Rawton handed her over to a Wren officer – nicknamed "The bosun" – who seemed to dislike her on sight. Intensely. She was shown into a cheerless room with two single beds – both empty – and told to go to sleep and wait for tomorrow.

Cathy felt like all the air had been sucked out of her.

Anne

It was the light that woke Anne as he twitched back one of the blackout curtains. She heard the sound of distant airplanes too. She touched the space in the bed where he should be. Missing that warmth already. He was standing in the gabled window watching a trio of warplanes burn a path across the morning sky, heading in from the coast.

"Hello," he said, looking sheepish.

Her heart did a double flip. Her mind was full of hazy fears she dared not give utterance to. Was last night a dream that dies with the morning light? She wished he'd been beside her, the first day she woke up married. "Have you been awake long?"

He nodded. The light suggested it was still early. The sky through the gap in the curtains was clear and pale – a classic English morn. He was half lit by it and half in shadow, until he opened the curtains some more. He was naked. "Breath-taking view."

She thought so, though she could not see the lake.

"I wanted to wake you," he said, glancing towards her in a rather sensual way. "But you were sleeping so peacefully. I thought I ought to wait."

She knew there would be plenty of time for peaceful sleeping when he was gone. Now was the time for having and holding. She reached out to him. "Come back to bed."

There was a knowing sensuality between them, because of what they had already shared. "Yes, please."

He crossed the room and got back into bed with her. Triggering a last moment of shyness, even though she had invited him to come. But from the second he rolled towards her and took her in his arms, she knew there was no need for doubts and do-you-really-like-me. All covered. All questions answered.

It *was* different this time. Urgent, needy kisses led swiftly into the act. Sweet sudden sex, expressing so much wanting and longing. His frantic search and her acceptance. His pent-up desire and her hidden desperation. *Yes, now, please.* Intense, striving sex, ending in a tense, aggressive race to the finish that flung them both – mercilessly, mercilessly – into a long moment of release.

Part Two - Storms of perfection

Chapter Seventeen

Cathy

One her first morning at the base, Cathy stood in Commander Henry Rawton's office, staring at him in incomprehension. He had drawn out an office chair for her. Pulled it out from the desk where he was expecting her to sit down and be a shorthand typist. He stood there with his meaty hands on the back of the chair, ignoring her protest that there must be some mistake. She was not a typist. She couldn't understand how anyone could have got this so wrong. And Ralph said she was *needed* here.

"I was Boat Crew," she said. As if that would explain everything.

Rawton smiled. "Yes, yes, yes. Quite an adventure for a gal. But this is the role for you now – and I'm sure it's one you'll rise to."

He seemed as baffled as she was. It was like the Admiralty's wires had got crossed.

"I'm not terribly good at typing – I might make mistakes."

"You'll be fine, my dear. You'll be good at anything you put your hand to – just like Julius."

Her father had never been a good typist and wasn't likely to become one. She remembered finding him in the study, once, smoking his pipe, having accidentally smashed together the 'f' and the 'j' keys. He'd got ink all over his fingers trying to prize them apart. And when he introduced the slim end of his pipe hoping that might help, he spilt the burning tobacco in the typewriter and the paper caught fire. A total disaster. Cathy had to grab the soda siphon he kept beside his whisky decanter. A quick squirt extinguished the flame, but the typewriter wasn't great afterwards.

So no, Cathy was not confident she was going to take to this 'just like Julius'.

She yearned to tell Commander Rawton where to put his typing job, and to insist that he move her somewhere where she could be useful. *Send me back to Pompey. Or if you won't do that, at least put me with the girls and the radio headsets. Or the room with the green blips on the dark screens silently tracking the progress of the enemy.* She needed and thrived on strategy.

But England expects and all that.

"Sit down, my dear. Please sit."

"This is a mistake," said Cathy, sitting down with a heavy heart.

"We'll just have to muddle along," said the Commander. "Do you think you could give my jackets a bit of a brush? I'll introduce you to the rest of my personnel later."

With that he went into his room – but he left his door open so he had a good view of Cathy, seated at her desk, just outside.

Cathy was left fuming. I'm not your bloody steward.

Linda

Linda went to the head of Motor transport and said the only duty she would be doing from now on was despatch rider – which was the role she applied for when she joined the Wrens – and the one she was trained to do. She would not drive another team of bomb disposal men to their deaths ever again.

"An enlisted man wouldn't be able to refuse duty like that," the man reminded her. "He'd be marked as LMF – lack of moral fibre."

"Yes, well, maybe this is one of the rare perks of being a woman," she said. She shifted in her seat, hands sweating. Face pale.

The man looked at her with a certain amount of sympathy. It had been a traumatic event. The report on his desk, that Linda had filled in for him, said she'd had to clean the blood of her colleague off the windscreen of the vehicle, before driving the other three men back to their quarters, on the day that Morrison had died. The ambulance had taken away whatever else was left of him.

"This has shaken you, hasn't it?"

She nodded. "I'm not a coward. Put me back on despatches. There's danger involved in that work too, but I only have to worry about myself, not... not..."

"Did you have some kind of relationship with Morrison?"

"Only a professional one." In her mind, though, she saw him smiling, buying her a drink, asking her to dance. Images that made her unhappy, even if her friendship with Morrison had been, essentially, platonic. She was glad that if he questioned her about the others, she could honestly say she'd never done *anything* with Toby.

Anne

The hotel people were wonderful – they kept a table for Anne and Dicky by a window overlooking the garden – so they could take meals at whatever hour they chose, as long as they were not too particular about what the kitchen could offer. A single tulip had been placed in a glass, to decorate their table for two. They sat and ate together, companionably. Often holding hands across the table.

He told her his mother had died when he was five. And when she asked how, he said he thought it was to do with having another baby. "I think losing her almost killed my father."

"And she was your father's second wife?" Anne wondered if it was alright to ask all these questions but she needed a bit more information about the family she had married into.

"That's right. His first wife died of the Spanish Flu, just after the Great War. Then the old man remarried in the summer of 1920 – unseemly haste, apparently – but I was born six months later so it soon became obvious why. And she was extremely pretty."

Anne thought about the effect of all this on the two boys, left motherless, and on Dicky's father. "The poor man. Has he found happiness again, since all that happened?"

Dicky shook his head. "He's the most bitter old buzzard you can possibly imagine."

"What else do you think he could've done?" She felt a wave of empathy for the man.

"Tried again. Like I did."

She smiled. It was something they had in common – they had both found the strength to try again.

After lunch, they walked by the lake for nearly an hour, but the clouds closed in on them, and heavy drops of rain fell and threatened to become quite a downpour. Dicky looked gratefully up at the sky. "Oh, thank *God*, now I can take you back to our room."

She worried about how that would look. "In the middle of the day? Won't the people at the hotel think that's odd?"

"I'd say they're used to honeymooners." The raindrops stippled the surface of the lake, like machine gun fire, as they ran for the path. He pulled her hand and made her run faster. "Come on. You're going to get wet."

"D'you think it's going to keep raining?"

"I certainly hope so. I *love* this rain. I hope it rains the entire weekend."

She laughed. *I love more than just the rain.* But it was best that the words were left unspoken. There was a song came back to her. *Love Unspoken.* She could hear it in her mind. A dallying count and a beautiful lady, on stage in Covent Garden Opera House. Before the war. When everything was different.

They ran towards the French doors at the back of the hotel. Dicky said, "I'll get them to send our meals up to our room, so we can spend the rest of the day in bed."

"You'll wear me out," she said, with no real trace of complaint. "Don't you *ever* run out of petrol?"

Chapter Eighteen

Anne

They had spent just three nights as man and wife at the hotel and they were on the drive back home to Hampshire – if you could call that home. The hotel room where they snuggled together listening to the rain had been the only place they'd ever shared, and it was quite a wrench to have to pack up their things and go downstairs and pay the bill. They had some sketchy plans for renting somewhere near to the Wrennery, so that they could be together on Dicky's next elusive leave. She willed herself not to dwell on the possibility that there might not even *be* a next leave.

They stowed their luggage in the car and set off.

Dicky said he couldn't really drive this way without visiting his father – who was alternately the Captain or the Old Man in Dicky's conversation.

Anne agreed. "It would be rude not to. Family is important."

He nodded but his mouth was pressed into a straight line. He got more and more edgy the closer they got to the town where he grew up. His driving slowed down. His mood was sombre. Anne wondered if she had done something wrong.

They parked at a lookout point where there was a lovely view of the rolling hillside, and a picture postcard view of the castle up on the hill. They got out of the car to admire the view and stretch their legs. And there, after giving her a kiss, he admitted his fear. "I'm worried the introductions won't go well."

She touched the side of his face. She had known that this conversation would come. "It did seem very odd that your father didn't come to the wedding."

Her mother and sister had been there, fussing over her hemline and her bouquet, and willing her to be happy at last. Her father, although quite unwell, had made a special effort to come along for her special day. Her next-door neighbour and two of her daughters, and an aunt who lived on the same side of London, they were all there too. Smiling and throwing rice. But Dicky only had his best man, that slim young man with red hair and an upper crust accent, who was also in the Fleet Air Arm. She wasn't surprised when the naval chaplain took Dicky aside before the ceremony and asked some very searching questions. She'd noticed how particular the registrar had been about checking the details on the special license. Comparing it carefully with Dicky's identity papers.

"I have a right to be happy," he said. "Why ruin what little time we have left?"

"What do you want to do?"

"I'm tempted to forget the whole idea of introducing you to my father. I'd rather drive you straight back to Portsmouth."

She said she would leave that up to him to decide, but whatever happened she was glad to have come this far. Even if they did just drive on, it was good to see the town where he grew up. "It's a beautiful part of the country – and from here you get such a lovely view of the castle."

"Probably its best vantage point," he said, giving it a baleful glance.

"Quite a landmark, isn't it?" She felt carefree and happy. Everything she saw was wonderful. As if it was all dusted with gold and laden with the potential to make magical memories. She shaded her eyes with one hand to look up at the castle ramparts rising high above the tops of the trees. "Spectacular. Have you been inside?"

He kicked a stone, restlessly. "Oh, God. Anne."

"What?" she asked. "Did I say something wrong?"

He shook his head.

"What is it, then?" But he couldn't manage to answer. He turned away from the castle and stared rather miserably out over the town below.

"Are you having second thoughts?" she said, bravely. Maybe that was it – after all, they were on their way back to the base and the Wrennery. Back to normality.

"Of course not. Best decision ever." But he gripped the lookout railing with both hands and bowed his head. "Happiest time of my life."

She came and stood beside him, putting her hand beside his on the lookout railing, almost touching his, but not quite. She had never seen him this nervous before, not even the day he proposed. He could be impetuous and he could be gentle, but he'd always come across as self-assured.

He was gazing down at the all the many houses in the valley. Lots and lots of houses, large and small. Some in green fields, standing alone, some closer together in leafy tree-lined lanes. Semi-detached ones near the sports field, old stone ones beside the parish church, and snaking terraces leading into the middle of the town. She looked at them too. She had thought that one of them was the house where he grew up. Until now.

Suddenly she understood. "Your father's place. It's not down there, is it?"

"No," he said, kicking a stone. "Sorry. I should've prepared you."

She glanced up at the castle. She took a slow breath in. And out. She would not show fear. "I assume that's what you're doing. Preparing me. Before we drive up there."

He turned his face toward her, with something like relief, now that she knew. "Preparing myself, more like. The old man can be difficult, but you're a marvellous girl, Anne. You'll cope."

She felt weak and shaky, now that he had confirmed where 'the old man' lived. In an ancient monument, perched above the town. She looked up at the castle as if an archer might appear at one of the narrow windows and shoot her through the heart if she didn't watch out. She fought the urge to ask him if he was joking, because she could see from his face that he wasn't. "Oh, Dicky. You waited until we were married to tell me?"

"It never seemed like something that would help."

She thought about this for a moment. His surname, Tavistock – her name now – had given her no clue. Of course, it was obvious that he was well-off, he had a car, and the money for black market flowers and petrol. For hotels, when most of them were closed. He even got leave, when others leave had been cancelled. But he knew that she worked in a shoe shop; she'd made no secret of that. He never seemed concerned about that.

The war brought people together, didn't it? All kinds of people. Smart new uniforms hid social differences that should never have mattered in the first place. It was a revelation, though...

"I think you were testing me, Dicky. After all, wouldn't Delia have married you if she'd known about that?" She looked at him, searchingly. "Wouldn't anybody?"

"Not if they were in their right mind, no. A place like that is an awful liability. The death duties alone will probably kill me – if the enemy doesn't do it first," he looked as if he wanted to say more, but for now he shook his head. "And for the record, I didn't want *anybody*. I wanted someone who took a liking to *me*, not a pile of old stones."

She nodded, weakly, then remembered her manners. "You shouldn't have to apologise. It's your family home. And it is... beautiful."

"It's very cold in the winter. The roof leaks. And it smells of old dogs." He turned his face to it though, as if a part of him still felt some affection. "My father is old and ill. This will come as a shock to him too."

She gazed up at the place – the place where Dicky grew up. The facts slotted into place. The sunlight still caught the old stones of the castle ramparts, but they were not as golden. Not as kind. She dispelled those thoughts. She looked down again, and her rings caught the afternoon light. She touched the golden band that Dicky had given her, as if the happiness of that moment could be her shield now. "Will your father be very angry?"

His face clouded with several emotions, he touched her hand at last, cupping his hand over the top of hers, protectively, for a moment. Then he straightened up and fished his car keys out of his trouser pocket. He threw them up in the air and caught them again. "Shall we go and find out?"

On the short drive up there, he tried to fill her in. "You've heard the expression 'the heir and the spare', I assume? Well, Sandy was the heir, you see, raised for the castle, and I was the spare."

"Stop a minute, Dicky. Who is Sandy?"

"Oh. Sorry. Sandy was my brother. Alexander."

It highlighted the brevity of their courtship that she didn't even know his brother's name. But he shrugged and continued. "Well, I was the spare and I liked it that way. I didn't have to worry about anything. My brother was the one trained for the responsibility. I wasn't. I could do whatever I wanted."

"But then the war came along, and you both had to fight."

"Yes. We were raised for the Navy. That was a given. I just never expected him to be killed, and then he was ...leaving me completely unprepared to replace him."

"When did this happen?" she asked.

"I was one week into my flight training. One bloody week. And none of it seemed real. He was buried at sea, so there wasn't even a funeral. But the responsibility. That rests on me. And on you, I'm afraid, now that we're married..."

Anne stared at him, feeling he should have said *something* earlier. "Cathy said I was going in blind."

"I wanted to tell you everything. But I didn't want to scare you away."

It was true. If she'd known, she never would've signed. Not because she didn't want to, but because she could not have believed she could rise to the challenge.

But he did. He'd shown a faith in her she simply couldn't match.

He warned her that the house was not the same as it had been when he lived there. The whole place was currently overrun by the Red Cross and being used as an army hospital. The army had requisitioned it during the second year of the war. Both outside and inside the keep, it was crawling with wounded men and vehicles painted dull army green. Nurses in their cloaks. A row of ambulances.

They drove under the gate house where Dicky had to show some identification to the men on guard.

They sat in silence in the car for a moment. As if wanting to prolong the calm before the storm.

"My father refuses to rent a house elsewhere so he's been consigned to some rooms above the gatehouse."

He led her up there now. Stone steps, with a dip worn in the middle of each one, God knows how old. Dark apartments, with some of his lordship's most treasured things squashed in for safe keeping. Through a carved wooden passageway, and into the gloom. They went into a square chamber where an old man was sleeping. He was slouched in a winged armchair, with a huge dog on either side of him.

The dogs got up as they came in. One of them emitted a low, hostile growl. She thought he was probably a wolfhound and the other a Great Dane. It was the hound that growled.

Anne looked at the old man, and then at Dicky as if to say, do we wake him? And he shrugged to tell her that he didn't know.

But then she looked up and saw a large oil painting – and gave a gasp. The painting – oh, what a painting. It was almost larger than life. A woman holding a single white rose. She was stunningly beautiful, all dreamy eyes and dewy white skin. She stood there, gazing out, soulfully. Wearing her wedding dress. The same one that Anne had worn only a few days ago – the wedding dress from 1920. Its proper owner had posed for hours and been *painted* in it – by someone who could paint in the style of Thomas Gainsborough. Anne stared at the woman with the beautiful eyes. "Your mother?"

"Yes."

"*Oh, Dicky.*"

The dogs growled louder when Anne spoke, so Dicky thought it was time for the introductions. "Hello Father," he said, in a loud voice, as if he'd only just come into the room. The dogs growled louder. The captain woke up at the growling, saw Dicky and grunted in acknowledgment, but being old and ill he remained in his chair. He reached deep in his pocket for dog treats to settle his canine companions. He fed one to the slobbering hound beside him.

Anne and Dicky sat down on a broken couch covered in an old blanket opposite.

The old man's rheumy eyes locked on Dicky. "Spit it out, boy."

"I'm being sent to sea soon. I've been assigned to a carrier."

"Good'o. Job needs to be done."

A horrible, tense pause. Dicky turned his peaked cap round in his hands. Then he set it aside, on the arm of the sofa, and took Anne's hand in his. "There's something else. Much more important."

Anne hoped his father was paying attention.

"This is Anne, who has done me the honour of becoming my wife."

The old man was in the action of fishing out a dog treat from the depths of his pocket and feeding it to the dog on his left. The dog, like the old man, was jowly and taciturn. The man slowly turned from the slobbering dog and looked at Anne – a suspicious and slow appraisal, before uttering just two words, loaded with derision. "Your *wife?*"

Then he began to ask the questions she was dreading. What family, what estate? what social position? And then, the assassination.

The next twenty minutes was so awful that she could only recall it in snippets, seen through a haze of tears.

Dicky said he was sorry about the news being sudden – it was only because he was being sent to sea – that the marriage was contracted in a hurry. But nothing helped. As soon as Dicky's father had extracted what he called 'the facts', he said that Anne was wrong, in every possible way. She was

London. Or what's left of it. The archetype of all big cities. Beautiful, but ugly as hell. Full of bomb sites, fag ends, and historic facades. Yes. London. A place of facades and dirty secrets.

Linda rode through shattered streets and showed her pass to get to the inner sanctum to deliver her message. She only knew the gist of it, but inside the envelope – sealed inside – the wording went like this...

2nd May 1942 Commander in Chief of the Eastern Fleet to the London War Office.

Prime Minister, you ask me why we have attempted so few offensive operations. This policy is forced on me by the very unattractive aircraft with which my carriers are equipped. The Japanese Fleet has modern aircraft fit for sailors to fly in, but our brave men have only a diminishing supply of Albacore biplanes, Fairey Swordfish, a handful of Martlets.

Please be aware I cannot stow fixed-wing Hurricanes in the hangar decks of my warships. Lacking modern aircraft designed for use at sea, my aviators face shore-based foe, flying higher and faster.

Yet you want me to strike?

Next came the phrase Linda had seen him write. With her own eyes. Despite the commander's concerns, it was polite and obedient. Like a public schoolboy, protesting an order from above, but then giving in and taking it.

"Fleet under sailing orders for the Indian Ocean. Now what about Malta?"

At her destination in London. Linda was asked to wait outside, but she caught a glimpse of the prime minister through a half-open door, while he was reading it. The great British bulldog gruff at his desk. The man himself. Churchill. So what? She was under oath – it wasn't as if she could go home and brag about it.

When the reply came. It was brief.

"Do it. Any cost."

The secretary, outside the door where the great man sat, stuffed it into an envelope, and sealed it. Linda stood, staring ahead. Pretending she'd never seen it.

She dreaded taking it back, to be honest.

She hoped the naval commander wouldn't shoot himself when he read it. She felt again the heavy weight of being the messenger. She knew where Dicky was going – to the Indian Ocean to face the Japanese. In a plane even his commander was in despair over. But she wouldn't breathe a word to Anne when she came back from her honeymoon. Instead, this obedient secrecy would carry on. Knowing nothing, saying nothing, the Navy – supported by its Wrens – would prepare for the next mission. A *costly* mission to Malta.

Anne

As Anne and Dicky emerged from their visit to the gatehouse, and drove their car back down the hill, they saw that one of the old oak trees was being cut down. The angry buzz of saws reached a stop and it came crashing down the grassy bank with the aid of some army engineers.

"Dear God, did they have to?" Dicky stared starkly at it. "Beautiful tree. Gone in an instant."

Anne turned slowly back towards the castle. Trying to understand why the army had cut the tree in the first place. "It must be to clear a sightline for the observation team up there." Anne pointed to the ramparts. "Maybe without the tree they can see all the way to the coast. I think there's more going on here than just the hospital."

"You may be right," he said, but sadly. He hated seeing the brutal way the army was 'looking after' the place. But Anne saw it differently.

"It's come alive, this castle. Because of the war."

He had to agree. "Yes. It's reverted back to its original, defensive role." He opened the car door for her. "Come on. We've paid our respects. Better leave the army to it."

Anne and Dicky rented furnished rooms near the airfield, for a handful of days and nights. The Navy chaplain sorted it out for them – while they were still on their honeymoon. "He's a good chap, our Holy Joe," Dicky said. The chaplain smiled kindly at Anne, when they found him in his study at the training centre. He had helped many young couples. He gave them a key, and a pencil sketch map on the back of an envelope, telling them how to get there.

It was very basic, a bedroom, a kitchenette and a sitting room – bathroom along the hallway. The carrier's departure – oh wonderful news – was held up while they took on more men. Anne got another four days with her husband. And four nights.

He was easy to look after. Navy food and boarding school beds – that's what he was used to. She made breakfast for him early – very early. "Up with the lark and to bed with a Wren," he would say, coming up behind her when she was tending food at the stove, wrapping his arms around her. Distracted, she would try to dish up two fried eggs on toast – their entire egg ration for a month.

"Mmm," he said, kissing her neck. "Adam and Eve on a raft."

He was still technically on leave, but he went off to the air station to do his last practice flights – mainly connected with the precision flying needed for laying torpedoes. She went to the Wrennery and worked there all day. Kind Mavis from the kitchen gave her meals to take home to him. "You don't want to be slaving over a hot stove, Miss? When you've only got a couple more nights together."

It's 'Mrs' now. But she didn't correct her friend. She was too grateful for the kindness, and Dicky liked Wrennery food – especially figgy duff and gammies – raisins the landlubbers call them.

People stopped teasing her. She was a married woman – a pilot's wife – and he was no longer the serial proposer. He'd gone through with it, against all odds and expectations.

She had to fight to keep her job. She knew that battle was coming. Ralph said he was surprised – disappointed. He asked her outright – should he 'anticipate' her resignation? But his sister Penelope, her commanding officer, said to wait and see what happened. *Wait and see if Dicky gets shot down,* is what that meant, which to Anne seemed horribly pragmatic.

But today, he was with her. Any excuse and he would wrap his arms around her. He was attentive, gentle. Not what she'd expected at all. He talked in Navy slang – which Anne understood some of, but not so much the slang specific to the Fleet Air Arm. But she was a fast learner. His world was full of Subbies and Wingcos and Fish Heads – and other terms much more unmentionable. He was still a Navy lad after all, from a hard drinking boys' club with a brutal reputation. "Bet you never thought you'd marry an FAA boy, did you?"

"Until I joined the Wrens, I had no idea they even existed."

His carrier was purpose built for the FAA, which was rare, he told her. The others were all modified – keels purchased half-finished, and a flight deck stuck on top. She was horrified when he outlined the landing procedure; the squadron circling the ship in tight formation, with only seconds between each airplane coming in to land on the deck. The accuracy required to get the thing down – the sudden engine cut – the sharp stop when the arrester hook caught the wire. "Better than the alternative," he told her, "Over the side, or nose first into the crash barrier."

It was a different war, this one – nothing like the great naval engagements of the past. It was a race to win Air-Sea battles, a deep dive into submarine warfare. Lord Nelson's ready boys had seen a few changes, but the culture was essentially the same. Eat, drink and be merry.

For tomorrow we die.

"If you need money, go to my wine merchant and purchase a bottle of Cognac," Dicky said. He was too young to qualify for the married man's pay allowance.

"How on earth will that help?" Anne asked. She didn't even like cognac. Dicky had to explain that the foul-tempered sea captain at the castle, had a long-standing arrangement whereby he would pay Dicky's tailor's bills and his wine merchant, but nothing else. It had been like that for ages. "So if you need anything at all, order a suit and then sell it, or buy some wine or spirits and swap it for what you really need. That's the way I used to get all my petrol. He won't help us, Anne, but he's never refused to pay my tailor."

What a bizarre system. What a father-son relationship. So, she would be well-supplied with Cognac, and she could obtain clothes from a men's tailor – if she had the coupons – plus whatever provision he was making for her from out of his Navy salary. "I don't think I'll need any of that, Dicky – I always managed before."

"You lived at the Wrennery before, this is different."

He'd be gone soon. And there were still so many questions she needed to ask him.

"What do you want me to do with the car?"

"I want you to learn to drive it," he said. "That way the battery won't be flat when I come home on my next leave."

But would that ever happen? Anne knew of one family that didn't see their pilot son for twenty-two months. And yet, she was supposed to rent a flat suitable for a married couple. In time of war, with so many shortages of accommodation, wasn't it wasteful to do that, on the off chance that he'd get a chance to come and see her?

The news came that night, when he came home after the last practice flight. Tomorrow was 'roll and go' day. She helped him pack his things. He shined his shoes. She mended his epaulettes for him. Reminded him to take his log book. He would go straight from the base the next morning.

It was customary to fly the aircraft on, but in this case that had already happened. The boys would travel by train to Liverpool to join the ship. Cyril would be with him – his new navigator, who'd been their best man. Twenty brand new Swordfish – not the battered training-school bombs – were on board the carrier. They were only waiting for the aircrew.

"We never flew together," he said, with deep regret.

"After the war we will." She crossed her fingers behind her back when she said it.

They stayed awake all night – stretching out their last bit of time – talking in bed together. Kissing. And the rest. One last time just before the dawn. Tangled sheets and total desperation. She wouldn't cry, she didn't want to give him that to remember. She held him close and stroked his hair. Told him she'd be waiting.

He heard the alarm click just before it went off, and silenced the bell, preventing it from ringing. If only, if only he could stop the clock. Stop the war. Stop the bombing. But the only thing he could do was wrap his arms around her, unshaven face warm against her cheek. *Stay with me. Stay here in my arms, forever.*

Chapter Nineteen

Cathy

Everyone around me is doing something important, Cathy thought. Except for me. I'm brushing Henry Rawton's suits. Or passing him his tea. Or sharpening his pencils. I've been seconded to the bridge and I'm not allowed to even *glance* at the binnacle.

Even worse, when he'd introduced her at his morning briefing, he'd placed a proprietary hand on her shoulder, and said to all the assembled people – both Navy and RAF, "I'd like you to meet my new right-hand woman, Catherine Bancroft-Smythe."

She could have killed him. In one fell swoop, he'd conveyed that she was both his property, and the Admiral's daughter, and therefore unapproachable. Her chances of even a friendly drink with a colleague were doomed. Possibly forever. No officer in his right mind would want to blow his chances of promotion by challenging his Commander or irritating Admiral Bancroft-Smythe. She was beached, on a landlubber's naval station in the middle of nowhere, with the potential social life of a cloistered nun.

She'd never felt so cheated. Ralph Redcliffe had given her the strong impression that her role in this place would be vital. But here she was, in a peaceful seaside town where she couldn't even SEE a ship. While Rawton made some of the most questionable personnel decisions she'd ever seen. She missed the ships. She missed Speccy and the liberty boat. She missed the sailors leaning out and smiling as she and the other Boat Wrens threw the sacks across the gap. She missed Patrick.

Here – the sea was distressingly empty. The seafront was a windswept strip. The town was undefended, except for two AA guns hastily put up in the front garden of a house on the seafront. The guns were manned on rotation by a small gun crew that spent most of the time leaning on the barrels, smoking, even on duty – which somebody ought to have stopped. She saw planes all the time. And she heard a lot of morse code all around her, tap, tap tappity tap all day long. Bleep bleepity bleep. Machine noise from the teleprinters. Static from radio transmissions – strange noises from the squawk box in Henry Rawton's office.

She picked up the telephone feeling disenchanted – wanting to say – "Hello, HMS Quicksand. Captain Insufferable's office." But knowing that she couldn't. It would be entered as a demerit on her record card. "Long Sands... Rawton's office..."

"Cathy. Is that you?"

A shock – hearing his familiar voice. But not an unwelcome one.

"Daddy?"

"Don't you *Daddy* me when you're representing the Royal Navy."

"But I've been having the most dreadful time."

She desperately wanted to *talk* to somebody. About the typing, and the mending, and the endless lists of electrical supplies with almost identical serial numbers. But her father was utterly unsympathetic. He retorted that everyone was having a rough time. War was not for the fainthearted. She had wanted to be a Wren and been placed at HMS Long Sands for a reason. To do good work and not to complain about it.

"I don't even know what we're accomplishing," Cathy said. "It's alright for you – you're important and they tell you things and you see top people all the time. You've even met Mr. Churchill. Most of us here have no idea what is happening next week and no clue how the war is progressing."

"Even at my level, yes – at *my* level – there is still a lot of uncertainty. I put forward ideas, but I still have to do as I'm told. If Churchill decided to send me and my fleet to the bottom of the sea, I would have to say aye, aye sir, and obey him."

She was saddened. The Navy was a hierarchical structure and it ran a certain way. But she was lonely, she felt roadblocked by Rawton, and she'd hoped her own family would understand.

Her father didn't. "You should thank your lucky stars you were selected for special ops."

"Special ops, my arse," she said, in a burst of naval crudeness.

"Catherine. A lady never swears. Do as you're told. Learn what you can. Act as if you were sent there for a reason."

"Yes, Daddy." The reason seemed clear – she was sent there to be wrapped in cotton wool.

"Yes, Admiral Bancroft-Smythe," he corrected. "Now put me through to Rawton. Immediately."

In a rebellious rejection of every naval protocol in the book, she leaned forward, yelled to Rawton – who was reading the newspaper – "Hey, Henry? I've got old Bullshit on the phone."

She popped the call back to the switchboard before the eruption began.

Dicky

The liberty boat took Dicky out to the Carrier. With four other officers and about twenty-five sailors. It was crewed by Wrens, which made him smile. *Thank God, Thank God for the Wrens.*

The men on board had hangovers, but they still sang "Leave her, Johnny, Leave her." The port slipped away. Shore-leave memories went hazy in the early morning spray as they bumped through the water towards the vessel.

As they approached the ship at anchor, they all fell silent. The ship was impressive.

Her name was HMS *Fortunate*. She was one of the only purpose-built aircraft carriers in existence. Her keel had been laid down in 1918, but her completion was delayed while designers haggled about what a carrier should look like – since there weren't many others to provide a blueprint. In the end she was surprisingly modern. She had a full flight deck with two lifts, and a superstructure positioned off to the starboard side to allow the runway to sweep the full length of the ship.

At that moment the ship was a long expanse of solid grey assurance. But out of sight of land, in the middle of a surging sea, she would seem like a postage stamp in an ocean of uncertainty. Dicky stared up at her as they approached. His practice landings had gone well, but he did not relish landing up there as the squadron came in at ten second intervals, and the rain came down in sheets and you could hardly see the batsman.

"Are you going aboard?" said another FAA boy. "Or just dreaming about it?"

He swallowed, stepped across the gap, climbed up the ship's side on a perilous metal ladder. The boat crew would hand up his luggage.

He was on board the carrier. His floating home for the foreseeable future.

People hailed him, friendly voices all around, other men from his training squadron. A friendly wave, a handshake, or a hand on another man's shoulder. "Tavistock! How was the honeymoon?" which he answered with a grin. *Mmm, the honeymoon.*

One man said, "sorry to hear about your brother."

That loss seemed a lifetime ago. Gaining Anne had eclipsed it.

His new Wing Commander shook his hand. "You'll want to see your aircraft."

Dicky nodded. One deck down, in the gloom, the ship had a belly full of airplanes, wings folded back like ladybirds. Off to the side, in ranks and rows, a deadly cargo of torpedoes waiting to be delivered.

His was the one at the back of the hangar, since he was the newest pilot. He walked over and introduced himself. Touched the fuselage. "Hello, darling," he said. "I'm Dicky."

She was new and smelt of the factory. Her struts were smooth and shiny. The roundel on her side was crisp. Perfect paint, perfect stitches. The leather padding around the edge of the cockpit looked fresh and firm. Her wing panels were shapely, even when folded. She was indeed a perfect Swordfish.

He ran his hand along her side, one more time, enjoying the feel of her. "Don't you dare let me down. Do you hear me?" *Because I've got someone waiting for me.*

Cathy

Cathy wasn't sure when she started to hate Henry Rawton. But hate him she did. The men and women at HMS Long Sands worked 'watches' as if they were on board ship. But some watches were as long as fifteen hours, which was rather gruelling. The RAF types objected to this – said their personnel were becoming exhausted. But there was nothing they could do. They were all under Rawton's command. Cathy tried to speak with Henry on their behalf. Was a person really much use in their fourteenth hour of service? She asked him, couldn't that be changed? Given that the work needs so much concentration?

"Of course not, Cathy. We can't go changing long-standing Navy protocol."

"Why not? It's winning the war that's important. Not preserving protocol."

He smiled. "Unlike you, little Wren, all my other personnel accept things without complaint."

Not true, thought Cathy. *You just don't listen.* In the mess, the WAAFs went on and on about how awful Rawton was.

But he knew better. "Don't believe all you hear either. The girls in the huts don't really mind those long watches. And they like getting their forty-eight hours off afterwards. That's what I've been told."

Maybe they have drinking buddies, thought Cathy. Although most likely they needed a weekend in bed just to recover. She watched Rawton closely. Trying to understand how he operated. He moved between the huts – scuttling like a crab from one to another, holding a clipboard or a sheaf of paper. One hut seemed to hold him some mornings, but then he would race across to the other. Sometimes, a man on a bicycle would ride into the camp and show him some flimsy bit of paper that excited him. He sat like a spider, presiding over piles of data and messages that had to be collated and sent away to a secret location.

Most mornings Cathy typed, and re-typed, requisition slips for small electrical components. She was allowed only two errors per page, which she could strike through with a row of letter Xs. If she made three errors, she had to rip out the page and start again. This happened often. She became good friends with the man who emptied her wastepaper basket and put the 'sensitive documentation' into the incinerator.

Cathy didn't think anything *she'd* handled could be classified as sensitive. But the wastepaper man took his work very seriously. His name was Arthur. Veteran of the Great War. Three kids. Two boys and one girl.

Gradually it became obvious what was going on in the radio receiving hut. The girls in the headsets were intercepting messages from enemy shipping. If the message was 'plain' – that is uncoded – it was translated on the spot and sent straight to the Admiralty. If they had the right linguist. If it was in code, it went to Arkley Park or Station X, which Cathy suspected meant Bletchley. It usually went by motorcycle courier, for security reasons, but if speed was essential – which it often was – they risked sending it via teleprinter.

The activities of the other hut remained for a time shrouded in mystery, but gradually the mist began to clear. The operators watched the darkened discs for blips of light that gave them the position of both aircraft and enemy shipping. They were helped by a handful of scientists who walked around with clipboards and studied all the readings. Skilled technicians adjusted the radar sets and made sure they were getting a signal. The metal towers picked up the incoming radio waves – from which a 'detection' could be made – or better still a location and direction. Everyone was *obsessed* with getting accurate readings. These were treated like the Holy Grail and compared with readings from other radar stations along the coast. If they could pinpoint the position and direction of a 'hostile', they could send Allied forces to seek them out and destroy them.

Some Y stations offered 'Interception' and others 'Direction Finding' – but Long Sands had both. For a sleepy seaside town, it was an installation of surprising complexity. And to Cathy's surprise, there was a bevy of other stuff happening off site too. Dotted all over the coast line – camped out in upstairs bedrooms and farmhouse attics – were the Vee Eyes, the Voluntary Interceptors. Keen radio enthusiasts, young and old. Some had their own radio equipment – hand built – others were given Royal Navy sets, hastily constructed. They spent hour upon hour crouched at home, headphones on, listening to endless static in the hopes of hearing someone on an enemy ship careless enough to reveal their position.

If that happened – it was all hands to the bicycle pump – and someone would cycle in with the precious message tucked in their pocket.

With a warm cup of tea in her hand, Cathy took her fifteen-minute break standing by the window. She gazed at the huge open sky beyond the metal receiving towers. Interesting idea – *direction finding* – and in a way, exactly what she needed. Cathy was adrift since seeing her brother in the arms of 'another woman'. Ridiculous. She was not upset. She wanted him to be happy. She did. But she needed a new direction too.

She tried to adjust. But at night she missed the Wrennery very much. The new place wasn't a nice big stone frigate – it was a much smaller Wren's Nest – in what had been a terraced boarding house two streets back from the seafront. Not nearly the same camaraderie. Cathy shared her 'twin' room – how ironic – with a girl called Faye, who was on night watch while she was on days. So at night she got very lonely. The 'comforts of home' were almost non-existent. She had an angled cupboard with hooks instead of a rail to hang up her clothes, access to an outdoor privy, and a view of the tiny bus depot.

She did the only thing she could think of to keep herself sane. She wrote a letter to Patrick.

Dear Patrick,

This letter will probably arrive like a paper doily – full of holes – cut by the Navy censor. I am no good at being subtle as you know. My work here is mainly administrative. Frightfully dull. I won't bore you with the details. There is a pub called the Lord Nelson where some of the personnel go drinking. The local girls are very taken with the Naval officers. They wear their hair in huge Victory Rolls and go home with smudged red lipstick and beer stains on their dresses. The girls that is – not the officers. I haven't been there much. I usually have to follow my C.O. around as if I were his lap dog, and most days I lunch with him in a corrugated iron hut optimistically labelled 'Senior Officers' Wardroom'. Today we had mock oyster soup made of fish heads (real ones).

As you can tell, I'm missing my old crew dreadfully.

I hope the tucker on board your ship is keeping you strong and fit. I hope the winds are favourable. I want to ask a million questions about your gun drills but I know you won't be allowed to answer. Tell me anything you can. What stars do you see on the night watch? When you write back – just put Cathy B. S. on the envelope and my serial number. It will find me.

G'night sailor,

Cathy

She left it unsealed for the censors and stood it on the bedside table. She would post the letter tomorrow. And check to see if she'd got any incoming mail. She *still* hadn't heard from a certain person – a certain lazy, good-for-nothing brother – but she told herself that here in this remote spot it might take a while for his letters to reach her.

She fell back on the bed, without even bothering to take her uniform off.

Cathy's room-mate burst in with exciting news. Exciting for *her*, that is. "Hey? Are you coming down to meet the new officers?"

Faye's face fairly shone with the possibilities a fresh batch of officers might offer.

Cathy didn't move from her bed – she carried on staring face up at the ceiling. "I'm not interested in officers – especially not shore-bound ones."

"Come on – free drinks," said Faye. "I've even heard a rumour about trays of welcoming snacks."

Now that was more tempting. The food wasn't all that plentiful at the Wren's Nest, supper had been small and she was still hungry. "Trays, did you say?" She raised an eyebrow, showed a leg, and got up off her bed.

Faye nodded and handed her a comb. Cathy pulled it through her hair, barely looking in the mirror.

"You want lipstick? Maybe a dab of perfume?"

Cathy shook her head. "Let's just go."

"Wait – let me at least spray you with cologne." Faye reached for one of Cathy's lovely silver-gilt bottles, with a tube and a spray, and released a cloud of eau de toilette in the room. Which caused them both to giggle.

Cathy had to wave her hands frantically to prevent it landing in her eyes. "Are you trying to blind me?"

They headed for the Lord Nelson – how appropriate. Where Every Man was doing his Duty, and the women would soon be Expecting. They walked along the seafront, where a brisk breeze was blowing in from the North Sea, and seagulls had decorated the pavement. They headed up the shallow stone steps and into the drinking establishment. The officers were clustered near the bar, most of them already holding a drink.

Not a snack in sight. Turn around and go back to the billet, Cathy wondered?

Not a chance. They were spotted.

"Gentlemen. The Wrens are here!" The officers' faces brightened and the circle opened to admit them. As the girls went forward to join them, all the newcomers looked their way – and Cathy saw that one of them was Guy Palamara.

She gasped. "*Guido,*" she murmured – using his pre-war name. Even from where he stood, a few paces away, he heard the word and looked in her direction. His face lit up with delight. "Cathy?"

She went straight to him.

With a casual disregard for the stiff etiquette of the young British officers around him, Guy did the traditional Italian double kiss on either side of her face, and she warmed with pleasure.

One of the other officers pulled him back by his shoulder. "Steady on old pal – you're a bit fast, aren't you?"

Guy smiled with amusement – his dark eyebrows mobile and quizzical. "Just a greeting."

"He's a friend," Cathy said, defending him. "I've known Guy since I was nine."

She'd never seen him like this though – in a naval officer's uniform. "Suits you," she said, pulling at one of his dark-blue lapels. "You never told me you'd been through basic training."

"I didn't," he admitted with a grin. "Ralph recruited me – by telephone. He said there was no time for training. Just stick him in a monkey suit and get him working."

"That sounds like Ralph," she said, sounding mellow. Although that morning, she had thought that she hated him. Along with Henry Rawton. "You're bloody lucky, Guy. To be excused basic training. They must think you're very special."

Oh, gosh, she thought, that almost sounded like *flirting.*

"And you, Cathy? You're stationed *here?*" he was grinning like an idiot. Couldn't believe his luck. And she was playing up to it. "Yes. For my sins. I had a good thing going in Pompey. Doing the mail boat run every morning. Happy as a lark. But Ralph told me I was needed here."

"That's wonderful," he said, with undisguised delight. "Good old Redcliffe."

Cathy shook her head. "Oh, Guy. Southwold's pretty but there's *nothing* here. And I'm not needed. Not needed at all."

"Oh, I'm sure you are." Visions of sharing his leisure time with her were obviously forming in his mind. Vivid ones. "And you don't like Southwold? I think it's rather nice, and the research here is ... cutting edge."

Tonight, though, looking into Guy's dark eyes, she had to admit she was awfully pleased to see him. Even Southwold's limited possibilities seemed to be improving – and this bar – the Lord Nelson – she was liking it a lot. "But Guy. What on *earth* are you doing for the Navy?"

He smiled. Dark eyes rich with promise. "A mixture of duties."

"Ah," she said. He spoke and read Italian, French, some German and even some Norwegian. Of course there would be work here for Guy. And he *was* a scientist. "Good for you," she said. "And good for the war."

"I hope so." He was gazing at her, radiating a warmth that she knew she had missed. She was lost in a moment too. Remembering how – when she was nine – she had asked him how to pronounce his name, when she'd first seen "From Guido" on the tags of the birthday presents – "Is it Guy-do, or Gwee-do?" she'd said, in a childish voice, smiling. "Come on. How *do* you say your name?"

He'd told her it was 'Gweedo', but then he'd paused and said he quite liked the name Guy and one day he might try using that name instead. Happy days. A golden childhood.

"Are you going to buy that little Wren a drink, Guy, or can I take that duty off your hands?" said another Navy man. Cathy smiled. She was popular tonight.

Flustered, and without taking his eyes off Cathy, Guy felt in his pocket for change. "No, no. Yes – Drink. Cathy, what will you have?"

"Oooh. What will I have?" She was seized by a never-before desire – unlikely to be satisfied in a Suffolk country pub – to ask for a large glass of Italian red.

Chapter Twenty

Linda

Linda's message that day took her to HMS Nautilus. As she went in through the portico to find the C.O. she took the opportunity to try and find out what was happening to 'her' bomb squad. She was asked to wait which gave her a chance to loiter by the noticeboard. Trying not to look as if she was reading it, she scanned the lists of names.

Yes – there he was. Toby Wallis. He was rostered on for duty today. Which meant he was still alive. Still sticking his hand into a bomb on a regular basis. She closed her eyes and sent up a grateful prayer – or something of that nature. *Please look after my Toby.*

Cathy

Cathy stood at the edge of Guy's desk looking at an Italian glass paperweight with a snow scene inside. He must have brought it with him. Cool glass, in her warm hands. She was helping him unpack. Rawton – not realising her connection with Guy – had even suggested she help him get settled. So she was spending a lovely morning organizing Guy's desk in one of the plywood offices in the main building.

He had brought some very 'Guy-like' items from home. In addition to the Murano glass paperweight, there was a small model of an Italian ship powered by many oars – a replica of one from the battle of Lepanto. And a morse code transmitter sat on his desk too. Not working. It was an antique brass one from when they were children. He touched it. "Remember all the fun we used to have – playing with that?"

"It wasn't wasted – all that time playing battleships," she teased him. "Now you're in the game for real."

He smiled. He seemed indescribably happy. "I'll play any game that brings me nearer to you."

She still had a hard time seeing Guy as a Navy Man. He was too smooth, too laid-back, too academic. He'd drifted in and out of the labs talking about scientific concepts with an amused kind of laziness. Never taking anything seriously. He wasn't gung-ho and full of military bravado.

Official secrets or no, he told her why he had come to HMS Long Sands. The allies needed Radio Direction and Range-finding like never before. In an unprecedented marriage between science and the military, the like of which had never been seen, many scientists like Guy had been recruited. "They have presumably told you the brand-new acronym?" he asked.

"Radar? Yes. Rawton told me. He also said I could be shot if I uttered that word outside the perimeter fence."

"Quite so."

She had thought he was there because he was a linguist. But it was obvious now, and she felt like such a fool. He was here to build radar for the allies. It felt a bit clandestine, the discussion, but each supposed it was alright. To share something of what they were working on, to enlighten each other. It created a secret-sharing mood, an intimacy.

"But you understand, don't you, Cathy? We have to build new, build better. It's a constant race to keep up. The more tools we have to detect the enemy, the more devious they get. All the main players have radar – England, Germany, Japan and America. All competing. Driving. Pushing."

"But we're still ahead?"

"Oh, yes," he said. "Very much so. Our receivers are so good we can get a contact from the minute the enemy planes take off from their bases."

"Can you track the U-boats with it?"

"No. We can't use radar to track the u-boats, the water absorbs the microwaves so we use sound waves instead – good old ASDIC. But anything on the surface or in the air – we can track it – the motor torpedo boats can be tracked quite easily. It's exciting, Cathy. The battle's played here as much as on the high seas. And the science behind it all – it's amazing."

She looked at him when he said that – his hand was on his heart, and his eyes lifted, dreamily. It *really* did thrill him. For her, science wasn't quite so orgasmic. But looking at him like that, she was almost tempted to reach out and touch his smooth brow. To soothe his fevered thoughts of physics. She would have done too, if she'd thought it could be done without giving him the wrong idea.

"The Navy's desperate to keep advancing its detection systems. The RAF too. The new machines go into both ships and planes. There are lots of combined operations – like we have here. A lot of scientists, like me, sitting in labs in the depths of the British countryside, designing detection equipment..."

"I owe Ralph everything. He found me, he telephoned me, he offered me this chance. If not for him I'd be mouldering away somewhere behind barbed wire. Churchill wanted to 'collar the lot' of us – I think that was the expression. I've seen good friends deported." Guy frowned. "But as long as I wear the monkey suit, as Ralph put it, I can put my understanding of radio waves to good use. I can assemble radar sets for our ships, our planes, I can test them, refine the designs, send back lists of improvements... And after the war there will be a million opportunities in this field... I feel energized by it, Cathy. I've never been happier."

She smiled at his boyish enthusiasm for a field she was only just beginning to understand.

He gazed at her. "But to find that you are here too..." he glanced away, as if the delight in seeing her was suddenly too much, too sweet. "Oh, Cathy." He smiled, glancing down at his feet. "I give myself away, don't I? Your brother said I was subtle as a brick."

She linked arms with him and kissed him on the cheek. "You're a fine friend, and I'm thrilled that you're here. I can show you round the place if you like?"

"Oh, yes," he said smiling. "Show me everything."

Guy

After she left his new office, Guy stood in the middle of the room and smiled. In the past, her insistence that their relationship was purely platonic would have upset him, disheartened him. But not today. She was changing like the temperature of water, slow to take on heat, but once warm, reluctant to cool. The way she latched onto him in the bar. The easy physical contact, the warmth in her eyes. Her greater degree of comfort when he was near. They were 'il fuoco et l'acqua' – the fire and the water. He was the heat and she was the cold grey sea. She would burn for him, he was sure she would, if he only had the patience to wait.

Guy had *endless* patience. He touched the place on his upper arm where she had linked arms with him. Imagining she was still there. Linking hands with her, in his mind's eye. Warm brown fingers, over her pale ones. She would give him a signal. She would tell him. It would take time, that's all, and the steady application of heat.

Chapter Twenty-one
Dicky

Operating out of Trincomalee off the coast of Ceylon, Dicky's ship, HMS Fortunate, had a squadron of twenty Swordfish lodged inside her. Nearly eight hundred souls lived there too – sharply divided along the usual lines. Officers sprawled around wardroom tables – sloping off at night to individual cabins. Enlisted men in bunkrooms and corridors – sneaking a fag behind the ready use lockers.

Dicky and Cyril were the last to join the ship, by which time all the single cabins had been taken, so they shared a cabin. They didn't mind, they were used to working together, eating together. And when they were flying, they relied on each other.

Each day after brekkie they got their instructions. In the ready room Dicky and his observer were tasked with running daily anti-submarine patrols – not that they'd seen any yet – although his aeroplane was armed to the teeth with depth charges, bombs or torpedoes.

The routine on board was predictable and reassuring. Three square meals and afternoon tea. Better than boarding school, but not quite as nice as the Wrennery. A slice of Britain in the middle of the deep blue sea. Or in this case – the Indian Ocean.

At night they drank gin and tonic in the officers' sitting room – where, lounging long-legged in sagging armchairs, they drank like fish and swore like sailors – dressed like British gentlemen. When the gong sounded there was a prep school stampede to get to the wardroom. The menu was chalked on a board in the corridor, unless adapted by some wit with a bright idea and a damp forefinger. Once seated for dinner, decorum reigned again. They dined – on traditional English fare – waited on by stewards.

They developed a routine. Range up for takeoff – look for subs – attack if found. Bomb the poor bastards. They did coastal patrols some days – flew through some flak. Daytime reconnaissance – flying low to get the best pictures. A radar man came up for a flip – to check the ASV – and get a feel for how the equipment was working. But mostly they were told to look for subs... look for subs... scourge of the sea... and bomb them to kingdom come if they saw any.

But the patrols were blissfully quiet.

Then fly home little dove. Find the ship. Follow the squadron-commander.

As they circled for the landing, Dicky would gaze down at the flight deck below and thank his lucky stars – they were home – a welcome sight for any sailor. *Arrestor hook down. Here we go.* Feel the sharp tug of the wire as she came to a rolling standstill. The deck swarmed with men to help her taxi forward – they'd unbolt her and fold her wings all in one seamless movement. Then down she'd go in the lift to the hangar deck below. Strike down complete. Goodnight sweetheart.

This is easy. I could do this the whole bloody war. All I have to do is keep myself out of mischief.

He closed his eyes. Maybe I'll be spared. Maybe I'll get to go home to her. He kept a picture of Anne taped beside his bunk. Sometimes he'd remember to kiss two fingers and touch them to her hair. Sometimes he was too bloody tired to do anything. Sleep would overcome him. Rolling shipboard sleep. Half-dressed in his flying kit – face in the pillow – with one hand trailing on the floor of the cabin.

Cyril shook him – woke him with the unwelcome news that it was already time for breakfast.

Cathy

Cathy had a new routine. It used to be work, eat, sleep, repeat, but now it included meeting Guy every time she had the night off. Cathy got ready at her billet, while her roommate Faye stood at an upstairs window, shielded by heavy net curtains, being her lookout.

Cathy was mortified to realize she was checking to see her tie was straight. *For Guy?* Who wouldn't care, anyway.

"Gangplank," Faye called out and caught a breath when she saw Guy walking up the path. "Gosh, Cathy, he's dreamy."

"What?"

"You heard," the girl said. Gazing at Guy. "Aww. He's besotted about you – bless him – look how he's smoothing his hair and checking his buttons are done up correctly."

Cathy had never seen Guy fuss over his appearance before. He didn't need to – it was always casually perfect. But today, as they spied on him from behind the net curtains, she could see that he was nervous. It made her feel uncomfortable, when the best thing about Guy being here was that he was a familiar presence from her past. A mainstay of her happy childhood.

Faye sighed. "Is he a good kisser?"

"How would I know? He's a boring scientist." He was just a pleasant person to talk with. With long, long legs and an easy stride. She'd noticed... But she was determined to paint him a different way. "The only thing he does in the dark is stare at the display on his oscilloscope."

"You've been dating him for a fortnight, Cath. Don't say he hasn't tried."

"He's a *friend*," she insisted. And no. He hadn't tried to kiss her. He wouldn't dare. It was almost disappointing.

The other girl looked at her as if she was certifiably insane. "I'll be friendly with him, if you don't want him. Oh, Cathy, you're so lucky."

Cathy watched him open the small front gate and look up at the house. She felt a blush spreading over her face, even though she was hidden behind the net curtains. She turned and picked up her sailor cap from in front of the mirror and fastened it on. Observed the difference the rosy blush made to her cheeks. She even added some lipstick.

By which time a girl downstairs was yelling up the stairwell, in a most unseemly manner. "Cathy! Get a move on. Your boyfriend's here."

◆◆◆

They walked along the concrete promenade beside the seafront. Access to the beach was restricted – but once you got beyond the beach huts, there wasn't much to impede the view, just a thin line of barbed wire – easily ignored. He smiled and patted her arm. "We could almost imagine we're strolling beside Lake Garda."

She had spent every leisure hour with him, since he'd arrived. She had given him several of the most thorough tours of Southwold that any young serviceman could wish for. And it was only a very small town. In the past weeks they had covered every inch of it. Walks around the duck pond. The location of the lending library. There was even one last drive in his car. He had no way of getting any petrol, so he parked it in a side street near to his billet, and hoped nobody would mind him leaving it there.

There were no more reasons to walk around the town together, unless they acknowledged what was blindingly obvious. They were 'walking out'. He offered to escort her back to the Wrens' nest, but she said she wasn't in any hurry. This was such an admission for Cathy that it made her whole body go warm.

What else could she do, he'd played along so well, with her insistence it was purely platonic? She willed him to try again. Seize his chance. Take the tiller.

They headed back to the Lord Nelson, with no intention of going in, but under the pretense that they might be in time for one final drink before last orders. Their pace slowed to prolong the opportunity. It slowed, like the rotational pull of the earth. But still, he didn't pull her round to face him. Still he didn't kiss her.

She looked up at the night sky in desperation, a gesture from childhood that always expressed her frustration.

And something changed. The sky. The street. The war.

Guy took hold of her hand, and she found the courage to allow it – to enjoy it – despite what it cost her. She had been so stubborn. How many times had he tried, and faced her scornful rejection? How many?

He squeezed her hand and smiled. He knew. He understood.

"Why did you never seem like this before?" she asked, voicing what had been a very private thought. He smiled. "I haven't changed."

He had though; she was sure of it. It was something she couldn't define. It worried her that perhaps she was falling for the uniform. Her life had been a sea of navy-blue uniforms – perhaps now he was wearing one it made him seem like he actually belonged. But it wasn't just his clothes. It was there in his eyes. Maybe it was the work – the way it made him happy and elated. Or the sea air. Or something.

He stopped walking, turned and looked at her intently. He touched her cheek. "You couldn't see me. I was invisible when Geoff was there."

Yes. That was all too true. Geoff shone like the sun while Guy waited in the shadows. "Oh. Guy. I'm so sorry. I must have seemed so heartless." Words she never thought she'd say.

"It's alright, Cathy. You and Geoff were such a happy pair – I don't blame you for wanting that golden time to last forever. But once we got to Cambridge, and you were all grown up," his eyes darkened. "I started hoping you'd come to me."

"I thought you were dreadfully dull at Cambridge. Always immersed in your experiments."

He smiled. "I am the same here, too."

Yes, it was true. When he wasn't at his desk studying diagrams, he was in the lab, with his calculations and his bits of wire. Or standing patiently over the screens and dials, getting them to work more efficiently. It was a familiar rhythm he fell into. It was not glamourous; it won no medals. It would never raise a ten-gun salute. But to her, it was gilt-edged heroism. The work of pure genius.

She looked at him. "You should have been at station X, Guy, you're so clever, you could have done anything."

"You know about station X?"

"One of the privileges of being an Admiral's daughter."

He was silent, and it was a silence heavy with significance. Then he said, "My own parentage carries different problems..." He paused for a long minute. This was a conversation where secrets flowed. Ebbed and flowed as naturally as seawater. "Cathy. My work here... it's no longer theoretical. It counts. Every advance, every mistake. It's nerve-wracking but it makes me happy. It was what I was born to do."

"Really? Your father was a banker. It always seemed strange – your endless obsession with physics."

"Cathy – I'm not ... I'm not the son of a banker."

"What?"

He took a breath and told her. "I learned last year that I am *related*, shall we say, to the family of Guglielmo Marconi, the physicist – the radio man."

"Oh, my *God*, Guy. Wasn't he a fascist?"

"Well, I think he had to be." Guy raised an eyebrow, ruefully. "His work on radio would have given the enemy the edge, if he hadn't died before the war."

"Does Ralph know?"

"Perhaps. Ralph knows a lot more than he lets on. But I am British born. I have pledged allegiance to the King. And I am sworn to the Royal Navy." He looked at her. "And you know my loyalties lie with you. They have always lain with you. And now ... it seemed like the right time to tell you."

"Did it?" she was stunned. "Why?"

"Because we are drawing closer." He squeezed her hand. Their fragile physical link. "And you have a right to know. Before anything happens."

This was far, far greater than finding the courage to let him take her hand. He was baring an unsettling secret, sharing his soul. She felt truly chastened by what she had heard. Impressed by his courage.

He asked her, "Does it change everything?" The tension behind the question was delicate, but intense.

She hesitated. Everything fitted. How he was – how he had always been. Scholarly, but seductive. Languid, soulful. Sometimes sad. The distance he felt from his father, the banker. The mother who was beautiful, but never very involved. Guy's eyes. The flashes of leisurely genius. Italian sophistication. A dash of Irish charm. It all made sense.

Did it change anything?

She stroked his lapel. Enjoying the feel of the soft, dark cloth under her fingertips. Her Navy man, but unlike any other. Guy, who had shared her childhood, her love for her brother – and now, his darkest and most vulnerable secret: that he was not his father's son.

He smiled. "Well, does it?"

She answered, "Hell, no."

And he burst into a laugh. Exasperation. Relief. But he sobered up fast. "You can't tell anyone. It's to be an Official Secret. Between you and I."

Cathy stroked his lapel, provocatively. "And how will you keep me quiet?" She was close now, teasingly close.

His hand closed tightly over hers and gazed at her intently. "I do believe you want me to kiss you. After all this time."

She glanced up at him. Challenging him. "You'll have to silence me *somehow.*"

That was the trigger. He pulled her towards him, a firm hand at her waist. "Right. Come here."

A squeal of delight. A laugh cut short. And a long, long kiss. She heard herself make a soft appreciative sound – and wondered why on earth she'd waited. She melted deeper into the kiss while he held her, confidently, quietly, as if they had been lovers for a lifetime. Warm lips, strong shoulders...

"What – no room key?" one of a trio of servicemen called out, laughed at his own wit, and walked on by.

When they were alone again, he pulled her close, taking the weight of her body against his. The street was almost dark – no streetlamps here – an incoming blanket of darkness. The sea air cool; the sound of the waves coming in. "Do you want to go somewhere?"

"I don't know what you mean," he said. In a voice that gave away that he did.

"I mean what I say. I usually do. Shall we go somewhere?"

"Cathy. Don't say things like that." But he sounded absurdly happy. "One kiss and you'd... you'd..."

She blushed. Actually blushed. Realizing he was leaping to conclusions. "Good God, Guy. No. Of course, I intend to fight you off all night. My defenses will remain at their current status – unbroached and unbreachable. But we don't have to kiss in the middle of the street, do we?"

He made a soft sound. "You will kill me, Cathy. With wanting you."

"Come on – I know where – your car with no petrol – have you got the key?" He nodded, and she hauled him along the road – holding his hand – laughing and joking. "Come on, Navy boy."

Boy plus friend. Equals boyfriend. Perhaps it would be alright.

•••

That next day, back at work, she was busy. She typed – and re-typed – some lists and letters until she got a call from the men on sentry duty. An important requisition had arrived.

Cathy left what she was doing, and ran out to see what it was.

On the back of a flat-bed truck – there it was – a smashed up fuselage from a plane. The driver leaned out of the cab window and spoke to Cathy. "Special delivery. For Guy Paloomera."

"Palamara." It wasn't that hard. Pal-a-MAR-a.

"That's the one," the man grinned. He pointed with a thumb at the aircraft on the back of his truck. "Where d'you want it?"

Cathy made an executive decision. "Over there by Hut Three. There's a workshop inside. I should imagine he'll want it there."

"Right you are love."

The man drove on, and Cathy stared at the plane. It was a smashed-up Swordfish. Crumpled metal. Torn fabric. Wires hanging out. And was that ...*blood*...near the cockpit? She shuddered. *How awful.*

She went to get Guy.

He was standing at a scarred wooden bench, testing something. Twisting a dial on one of the units – concentrating so intently that he didn't notice until she was standing close by his side. She touched his arm gently – not meaning to startle – but he still seemed mystified to find her there beside him. "Your Swordfish has arrived."

He woke from his thought coma with a jump. "My Swordfish? Oh, yes, my *Swordfish*. How exciting."

They walked together across to Hut Three to see it was being unloaded.

Cathy turned to him. "Well. Guy. What does Henry want you to do with this thing? Get it flying again by tea-time?" She was teasing. But he didn't seem to notice.

"No. I'm allowed to practice on this one, that's all. Someone at the top had an idea – about slicing up the dome and mounting it on the fuselage. Just about there." He pointed at the underbelly of the aircraft.

"The dome?"

He nodded, and lowered his voice. "For the radar."

They both knew that even inside the compound, it was not a good idea to speak openly. The truck driver threw the last crumbling bits of the plane out of the back of his truck and closed the tailgate.

"Thank you!" Cathy shouted, as he got back into his cab and slammed the door. He gave her the thumbs up. She and Guy waved him off, feeling a sense of relief once he'd gone.

Leaving the wreck of the Swordfish in a sorry pile in front of them.

She turned to Guy. "Does Dicky Tavistock have good comms? On his plane?" She thought about Guy's work and what it must mean to the Fleet and to the fliers. It was a constant race against time. A race to stay ahead of the enemy and give our fighters the best chance. Out there – in the middle of the ocean – lonely and bleak. A plane could be piloted. Guided.

Guy was drifting back into deep thought mode. He ran a hand through his shining dark hair. "Yes. He'll have something. But it could be *so* much better..."

Anne

At the Wrennery, Anne felt new confidence and the frigate was flourishing under her command. She had a knack for keeping the girls happy – though she modestly put this down to keeping the tuck shop well-stocked – but whatever it was, the place was ticking along nicely. Her new name sign arrived and she got it out of the box and put it on her desk – setting it down on the golden wood carefully. She rather liked how it looked – Anne L. Tavistock WRNS. Her *married* name. She touched the lettering, lovingly. Thinking of him. Of course, half the girls still called her Miss Foxton, and the other half dubbed her 'skipper' like Vera. But her true rank was the equivalent of a Lieutenant Commander. She smiled. *Not bad for a girl from a shoe shop...*

A new parachute officer training course had begun, and she was asked to select nine bright girls to be trained in aircraft recognition and Intelligence. Wrens were taking up work no one had ever dreamed they were capable of before the war.

After brekkie and divisions on the parade ground, she inspected the work going on in the Nissen Huts. She watched in awe as the signal master got all the girls in his class to tap out a message in perfect formation. It was almost deafening hearing all the machines at once... Dot Dot Dot, Dash Dash Dash. Dot Dot Dot.

"The universal distress signal," she said, smiling at the instructor. "I hope we won't be needing that one anytime soon. Well done, girls. Or should I say – Carry on regardless!"

"Thank you, Skipper," they all chanted – in unison – like the morse code.

Anne sailed out like a galleon, hoping she'd struck the right note. Friendly but firmly in charge.

Vigilant as a hawk, she soon noticed that all was not well with Linda. She passed by the door of Linda's cabin one day and saw her sitting on the edge of her bed, staring into space. The poor girl had never been quite right since the accident that day. Dreadful – to lose a colleague that way. But she'd made discreet inquiries via Mavis – since Speccy was a poor judge of people and Binky couldn't be classified as discreet – and she'd found out that Linda was 'worried' about someone. Not just troubled about the man that died. *Worried.*

Anne guessed that Linda must have become fond of another member of her team. She knocked softly at the already open door. "May I come in?"

Linda nodded. She'd been putting on her shoes when her thoughts took her miles away. "Sorry Skipper, I'm not good company at the moment."

Linda's pale face and wan smile had told Anne that already. Anne sat down beside her, and for a few moments they said nothing. She waited til Linda was ready to talk.

Finally, Linda asked – "How do you deal with it? Not knowing what's happening to your husband?"

"I try to hold on to hope, that's all... I do know he might not come back to me... but you have to keep on hoping," Anne said. Then she thought she'd better ask her. "Linda. What's his *name*?"

There was a long pause. Linda looked up at Anne with worried blue eyes. "He's not my boyfriend or anything."

"Isn't he?"

Linda looked very dejected. She stared at the carpet. "No. And I don't suppose he ever will be."

"Oh, you never know..." Anne said. "Life's full of surprises...Come on, Linda. He must have a name?"

Linda smoothed a blonde curl behind her ear. And gave in. "His name's Toby."

Anne looked at her, poor pale worried Linda. She patted her hand. "Toby. Now, that's a nice name..."

And that did it. Linda was shaking, and speaking, all at the same time. "Yes. It's ever so nice, isn't it? But he's in so much danger. Every single day. And he's so intelligent. And brave. And ... and..."

"Nice-looking?" Anne said. "Some of those bomb squad men can *really* pull off a boilersuit, can't they?"

Linda laughed – "Blue dungarees – no shirt – straps off." She pretended she had to fan herself to cool down...but then her face fell and she shook her head. Anguish in her eyes. "Oh – I don't suppose I'll ever see him again. And it's all my own fault because I wouldn't go on driving for them... not after what happened." The poor girl shuddered – thinking of her colleague's death. "And it's not like I'm going to bump into him in the pub or anything. He's one of those clean-living types. A teetotaler."

"Is he?" Anne said sympathetically. "Is he a religious boy, or something?"

Linda lowered her voice as if she was about to say a dirty word. "Well, I'm pretty sure he's a *pacifist*," she said. Pacifism was not a popular philosophy in her world. "I think he's one of those Quaker Oats people. He doesn't drink. He doesn't dance. He barely even speaks... he just sort of stands there... *smouldering* – if you know what I mean."

"Hmm." Anne had encountered Quakers before, and 'smouldering' wasn't the word that usually sprang to mind. But Linda was obviously smitten...

"My parents wouldn't want me seeing a boy like that, Mrs Tavistock. They'd be mortified. They want me going out with a nice boy who's fighting for his country."

"Of course. That's understandable. But they might come round."

She shook her head. "No, I don't think so."

"But you'd like to see him again, I think?"

"Oh, yes. Course I would. But I'd have to keep him a secret. And short of marching round to his barracks and demanding to see him, I can't see how to get the chance anyway ... Oh, it's all too complicated. I can't get too involved with someone like him...." Linda looked down at the carpet.

"Sounds like you're quite fond of him already."

"I am. But that just makes it worse... he might be blown up in a couple of weeks."

Anne gave her a thoughtful look. "No time to waste then, is there?"

She decoded his location – no problem. "See hell, why don't you" was a common way to send a cryptic message in a letter like this. See translated to C, hell to the letter L, why to Y, take the first letter of the word 'don't' and get D. Finally, change 'you' to 'ewe' and you get E the same way...

Sleep tight, sailor. I know where you are.

The letter smelt faintly of cigarettes and Patrick. She folded it up and put it back in its torn envelope. Stared out to sea and felt confused.

She walked back to the base. Stared at the map they'd pinned up on the noticeboard. A big nautical map of the world and its seas and oceans. She studied it. She needed some answers – and some could be had – by studying the names, by thinking hard, and by connecting the dots with all the information she had in her head ... from a lifetime of being an Admiral's daughter.

Where's the home fleet? Because wherever the home fleet was, surely Geoff must be with it... Why was Patrick's ship sent north? Convoy work he said. Her fingers traced the routes... often the home fleet used the shelter of the Orkneys for the big Naval ships ...but cargo doesn't travel on Navy ships... and they'd need cranes and the dockhands to load them... they'd want a local escort, a group of cruisers, a destroyer or two ...to make them feel safe as they left for open water... and *where* is the flagship of that old friend of Dad's – Admiral Burroughs – he's running this show, isn't he? She'd met him at parties – nice chap – *Harold* – a vicar's son. Good question – where's that flagship?

Oh, for a glass of port and chat with some boozy old Naval commanders... She'd know everything by the end of the evening.

Anne

It was July, and it was hot in the Wrennery dining room. Anne bustled around preparing for the dance. They'd opened the double doors to the garden and that was letting in a lovely breeze. It helped dispel the whiff of the cabbage soup they'd had at lunchtime. Two wrens carried in the radio and tuned it in and the clipped voice of the speed-reader who read the news came crackling over the airwaves. The news was cheery – win or lose – with an 'inches-from-Victory' spin put on everything. But everyone in Pompey was more concerned about why the South Downs were full of Canadians and what those warships in the harbour were doing. On a nice day, all the locals could see across to the Isle of Wight where several warships lay, and it was obvious 'something big' was going on. But that was definitely NOT going to be mentioned anytime soon by Mr. Speedy.

The hour came for the supper do to begin...and Anne waited with bated breath to see if the bomb squad would arrive. The servicemen trickled in in twos and threes. Canadians. FAA boys. Canadians...

Aha. She saw them parking. Percy Mackenzie was doing the driving himself tonight. She watched them getting out and walking towards the house. Dismayed to see they hadn't dressed up. Two of them were still in their *wellies*. She guessed which one Toby was. Dark. Silent. Handsome.

But as they came up the steps Toby broke his silence and spoke to the others – in his broad North country drawl. "They haven't even put barriers up. We can't have all these people around, sir..."

The four men came up the steps, to where Anne was waiting in the entrance hall to welcome them with a drink...

"Bomb safety team – at your service madam," said Percy. Slightly tongue in cheek. "Where's the object of concern?"

"Through there. She's over by the gramophone."

The dining-room wasn't full yet – just a few people, a sign saying 'Welcome', and a record starting to play ... the sound of a trombone's sultry mating call.

"Oh no." Toby said, seeing he'd been tricked. He tried to do a quick one-hundred-and-eighty-degree turn. But Frye and Clegg were expecting that and they grabbed hold either side and manhandled him in through the door.

Frye, through gritted teeth, said – "Don't be a coward, Toby Wallis. And d'you think you could try and force a smile?"

Toby turned on Frye. "Who are you calling a bloody coward?"

"Well go in and say hello to her then, y' big lump."

From the doorway, Anne saw the look on Linda's face – she was *thrilled* to see him. "Toby!"

She looked. He looked. She stared as if she couldn't quite believe it, then she gave him a huge radiant smile. The men on either side of him let go. Toby went forward slowly, and said, "Hullo Linda."

"Didn't expect to see *you* at one of our parties, Tobe."

He folded his arms. "They lied. They told me there was a bomb."

Linda wasn't fazed. "Pleased to see me then, are you?"

"Aye. That I am."

"*Are* you?" she said, touching his arm gently. He didn't show it. He looked like one of the standing stones at Stonehenge.

"Aye."

Then Linda saw Anne standing in the doorway – and caught her eye – Anne gave her a friendly wave, and went back to the entrance hall. There were Canadian soldiers arriving en masse... what looked like a whole *platoon* of them were coming up the steps.

Ralph arrived too. Seemed surprised to see Anne on the front desk – handing out paper cups of orangeade. Possibly not something he would have done when he was running HMS *Resilient*. He would have stood upstairs, looking dignified, like Horatio Nelson.

"Hello, sir. Can I offer you some refreshment? It's such a warm night."

"Could have done with this weather a month ago..." he said darkly.

She'd heard a rumour about a cancelled operation, but she let the remark slide by. The last thing he'd want is to be grilled about military secrets in the front entrance hall. Mavis ran through the hall and clattered up the stairs almost before Anne could say -"Wren rating. Walk, don't run!". The girl poked her head over the banisters and looked down, smiling. "I've just had a *dance*. He's from *Canada* and he's ever so nice. He's asked me to write down my address for him – so he can write to me when he goes to France."

Ralph bristled. "Tell your girls they must be more discreet. Nobody is supposed to know that we may ...*one day*... go to France."

"I'll speak to her," said Anne, to mollify him. "But given that France is only the other side of the Isle of Wight, and the ships have practically got their engines running, we can't blame people for working it out."

Ralph adjusted his stiff naval collar. He was – as ever – impeccably dressed. "Now where's this book of drawings you want me to see?"

"Come this way, Sir."

They rendezvoused with Percy Mackenzie in the carpark and had a surreptitious look at Toby's drawings. Which, as per his usual habit, he had left in the car.

"Impressive, aren't they?" Anne said, as Ralph rifled through the pages.

Linda was right. They were very detailed plans of the inner workings of bombs and torpedoes. The boy said nothing, but he saw everything. He was very talented.

"I wouldn't want these falling into the wrong hands," said Ralph, with a glance up at the house, in case anyone was looking. "There's information about our counter-measures in here."

"That's not why I asked you to take a look – and you know it." Anne hoped she hadn't made things worse, when she desperately wanted to make things better. For Toby, and for Linda.

He handed her the book. "Look, Anne. I'll talk to someone – but no promises. I'm awfully busy with this mission I'm working on with Dicky."

"Dicky?" she said, looking at him sharply.

"Not Dicky *Tavistock*," he said scathingly. "Dicky *Mountbatten*. There's more than one Dick in the Royal Navy."

Anne nodded sagely. "I've noticed."

Anne crunched back up the drive and into the house, to check on how Linda was doing. After that unpromising start, she'd been worried he'd run away – Linda's bomb safety man. But he stood there like a rare and magnificent animal, exuding silent sex appeal. It seemed impossible that a man who had no gift of the gab, no smart uniform, no stunning dance moves, no witty repartee... could be of any interest at all to the ladies. But he was. Even Delia was fluttering round him with little cups of non-alcoholic punch.

But as Toby stood there, gazing darkly across at Linda – who left his side for a minute to change the gramophone record – it was obvious there was a mutual attraction. Anne wondered what on earth she could do to help things along. She wanted to rush up to him and say – "Toby, Toby? Would it kill you to ask her to dance? Or to take her for a moonlit walk in the garden of the Wrennery? Music and *moonlight* – Toby – opportunity knocks."

His mates thought the same. She heard Clegg say. "Go on, let your hair down... have a bit of a boogie, why don't you..."

He didn't. He stood there with his arms folded across his chest. Welded to the spot. Such a shame. But Linda – a happier version of Linda – was back. And that was a real blessing. She flashed smiles – red lipstick smiles. She tossed her head prettily, and her blonde curls bounced. "Good to have you here, boys."

Of course, it was not a joy without sadness. Linda spoke to the other men and they exchanged quiet words and sympathetic nods – about losing Morrison. They stood in a circle and drew strength from each other. Anne came and stood with them and put her arm around Linda's back. No words could truly express the raw feelings – of witnessing a random, brutal loss – but these men and this woman had shared that experience and formed a bond through that suffering and that was a comfort in itself. Linda said how much she missed working with the team. But all the good memories were mixed up with the bad. She told Clegg she felt bad about letting them down, and he told her he understood. It had been a fearful shock for everyone involved – there was no need for guilt. None at all.

Clegg introduced her to their new man – Percy Mackenzie – who said he couldn't stay long, he had a wife and two little girls at home. He didn't need to go to Wrennery parties. But he'd been happy to be part of the plan to get Toby along... and it was great to see the boy enjoying himself. At which point they all looked at Toby – who'd been given a cucumber sandwich by a girl passing by with a silver tray. He put the whole sandwich into his mouth, and stood there, eye's glazed, like a cow chewing on the cud.

Anne took Linda aside on the pretext of needing her help with the drinks in the foyer. For a rash moment she was tempted to tell Linda to take Toby downstairs to look at the reinforcing steel in the basement – but then she thought – no, don't interfere, don't make things happen – you've got them together. Now let nature take its course. It's their romance. They can work it out. But she couldn't resist whispering to Linda. "What's the plan of attack?"

"There isn't one," Linda said, 'Do you even think I'm in with a chance? He's barely said a word. And I'm not exactly having to fight for my virtue, am I?"

Anne laughed. "He's not like the Motor Boat Torpedomen – that's for sure. But he's lovely. He's a man with a conscience, too, which is rare. Maybe that's why he hasn't wanted to get too involved. But still waters run deep, you know..."

"You really think he likes me?"

"Linda, dear – he's an unexploded *bomb*."

Linda blanched for a second and then she burst into a happy grin. "I don't know what's got into you, Mrs Tavistock. You're quite different since you came back from the Lake district."

I'm happy, that's all, thought Anne. *Dicky made me happy, even if it was only for a few days.*

Cathy

A day or two later, Cathy was at her desk outside Rawton's inner sanctum when Faye put something in the in-tray beside her typewriter. "Letter for you – marked *personal*."

Her heart sank. Oh, no. Another love letter from Patrick? Who was supposed to be a *friend*. She had messed that one up, good and proper.

Faye said, "Well, don't bother to say 'ta' then, when someone goes and collects the mail for you..."

Cathy looked up. "Sorry Faye, I was miles away. Thanks awfully."

But then she caught her breath as she looked down at the envelope in front of her. *At last.* It was from Geoff – she tore it open.

"Dearest Cathy," he began. Nice touch. But she suspected she was no longer his *dearest*.

She read on.

I'm sorry. I'm useless, aren't I? But I love you. The letter-writing thing – it's difficult at the moment – and I can't tell you much about what I'm doing. Preparing to go somewhere sounds a bit vague – but that's about the size of it. There are some nice chaps on board that I mess with. Two friends from our Dartmouth days – and one I wish I could throw overboard. Utter bastard. Reminds me of Captain Hook from Peter Pan and Wendy.

Well, old girl. What are you up to these days? I heard Pompey had been bombed. Got ever so worried. Then mother's letter arrived and she said you've been moved to the country.

Must go. They want to darken the wardroom now. They're screening Rita Hayworth's latest offering. Hope this finds you well and happy, your ever-loving brother,

Geoffrey

P.S. What do you want for your birthday? I have to say I don't know but mum always likes to ask.

She sat at her desk in stunned silence. It wasn't working any more. Twin telepathy. The letter told her almost nothing. Nothing about what he was doing. Nothing about the new love in his life. Nothing about his ship, even. When they'd always shared everything.

Never before had she felt so alone. As if she was sailing through uncharted waters. Irritated with Geoff, she screwed up the letter – which seemed to convey so little – and threw it into the corner of the room.

She stared at the list of electrical components she was typing and felt the prick of tears. She looked up and gazed out of the window. She could see Guy out there – with the breeze ruffling his dark hair – in the middle of a big expanse of grass – looking up at one of the two radio towers, then looking down and writing something on his clipboard.

Cathy saw little of him during the day. His work was absorbing and intense. She couldn't interrupt him when he was thinking or when he was in one of his deep discussions with the other scientists. He was obsessed with things like interference, soundwaves, and the optimal position for signals. He had become a great problem-solver since he joined HMS Long Sands. He was the one who suggested moving hut number four so the transmissions there didn't mess up the signals for hut number three. Troublesome, but necessary – and Guy had endless patience.

He had supervised the move personally, seeing that the hut was re-assembled in the proper place and all the equipment was up and running before nightfall. He stood with the lab techs at long wooden benches, examining electrical components and bits of wire, that made no sense at all to Cathy. He leaned over an operator's shoulder in the darkened confines of Hut Two – staring intently at those bright green lines that told them if enemy planes were approaching.

He never seemed to notice the operator's red lipstick and sunny smile – or the waft of perfume she emitted. If he hadn't been so obsessed with what was on the screen, he might have seen that all the Wrens liked him.

Then he looked her way – as if he finally sensed that someone – his someone – was watching. They looked at each other for a long moment, and he smiled at her. He wrote something on his clipboard and held it up – a single word – made large by cross-hatching the letters. LUNCH, it said.

She smiled – and nodded. She finished typing her list, said hello to Arthur who collected the rubbish. Then she got up and went to the wooden coat-stand in the corner of the room, got her jacket and sailor hat – She even paused to check her lipstick in the mirror of her powder compact.

Arthur bent down and picked up the scrumpled letter. He added it to the rest of the wastepaper he was collecting. "Off out with your boyfriend, Miss?"

"Oh – lunch at the officers' mess that's all. Nice of him to invite me."

And who could resist that mock oyster soup? Poor Guy – he thought British food was bad enough – but powdered egg? Margarine? It was a far cry from Italian cooking. She checked out of the window – yes – Guy was walking back towards the hut now, so she gave him the 'thumbs up' signal.

They were seated in the Officers' Mess by the time she realized her mistake. It dawned as the steward placed a bowl of steaming soup in front of her – pea soup – bright green. Irresistible.

Guy smiled at her. "Hey Cathy – you've got a birthday coming up..."

She nodded. Thinking this would be the first birthday in her whole life that she and Geoff would not be spending together. That's when it hit her.

Geoff's letter. They never called their mother 'mum'. She was always called 'mother'. She had missed something – and it was really important. "Oh no!"

She leapt to her feet. Threw down her white linen napkin.

"What's wrong?"

"It'll be in the *incinerator.*"

Guy looked up. His pea soup untouched. "What will?"

But she was off. She ran through the Officer's mess, out of the door of the hut and raced across the grass looking for Arthur. Sprinting as fast as her A-line skirt would allow her.

She ran into the main office. "Has Arthur emptied the bins yet?" People looked up with a frown and nodded. She ran back outside again. Fast across the tarmac out front and over the flat grass to the hut where the incinerator lived. She could see smoke coming from the small metal pipe on the roof. Oh no.

What do you want for your birthday?

He would know. Geoff would know what she wanted...to know he was safe. To know where he was, and what he was doing.

Guy had followed her – and with his long legs he caught her up easily. "Cathy? You can't go in there... What's happened? Have you burnt something of Rawton's by accident?"

She hammered on the door of the maintenance hut but it was locked for security reasons. "Arthur! Are you in there? Arthur?"

No reply. Cathy turned around and looked at Guy in despair. She had been blind and she felt so stupid. Of course her brother wouldn't write to her and tell her *nothing*.

But then they saw Arthur – in the distance – making his way across the base, carrying his bin beside him.

"There he is." Without a second's delay she began to sprint towards him.

"Cathy?" Guy called out to her. "Wait!"

But she was already half-way across the open space. Running towards Arthur.

Finally, she reached him, stood panting and – between breaths – told him she'd let him take away an important letter. "Don't worry, Miss. We'll find it."

On the grass, they emptied out the contents of the metal bin and went through every bit of rubbish until they found Geoff's letter. Guy joined them and saw her relief when she had the crumpled ball of paper in her hand again. They exchanged glances.

Kneeling on the grass, surrounded by bits of wastepaper and other rubbish, she uncrumpled the letter. She smoothed it out and traced her finger over the last line. It was obvious now. What he'd meant. She re-read the last line: "I have to say I don't know but mum always likes to ask."

He meant he was *required* to say he didn't know where he was going – to keep 'mum' like everyone was supposed to. But...

Mum Always Likes To Ask...

She looked up at Guy and he knew too. She could see it in his eyes. She knew where her brother was headed – on the next deadly convoy through the Med – and he had even told her when.

Guy said, "Poor Geoff. What a way to spend your birthday."

Chapter Twenty-three

Dicky

The lift on board the aircraft carrier purred into life, and Dicky – in the cockpit of his Swordfish – rose up onto the flight deck – like a rabbit out of a hat, operated by an unseen magician. His flight observer was already on board, and today they were flying without a TAG, a Telegraphist Aircraft Gunner, because although they had bombs on board, they were not laying a torpedo. His airplane was surrounded by a swarm of duty boys, preparing for immediate takeoff. As they ascended up out of the belly of the ship and onto the flight deck, the carefully choreographed work began. Within seconds the wings were extended and secured. The prop was checked and a man cranked the engine into life. A cloud of fumey smoke blasted forth, and they taxied into place and prepared for takeoff.

The ship was already steaming into the wind, so they soon got the green flag from the monkey island – the superstructure on the starboard side – and began to accelerate for takeoff. Dicky throttled hard and cursed under his breath as they lumbered towards the bow of the ship and took gentle flight at the end of the runway. Even at full power, the takeoff was never rapid. He always had the feeling she might let him down, sending them off the bow and sputtering down into the sea. Then they'd have to do a spot of swimming. But so far, it had to be said, she'd never disappointed him.

Cyril, who loved their Swordfish like a favourite maiden aunt, shouted into the tube – "Vindicated again, eh, Dicky? She did that like a perfect lady."

Now they were airborne, they eased back and let her gain altitude gradually. The patrol went smooth as silk since they were only required to do one hour out and one hour back. The sea sparkled and the sky above was clear. A benign sunny trip, almost as easy and peaceful as his prewar flying experiences. What a doddle

They saw nothing. No axis shipping, no slim superstructure of an offending submarine. No other aircraft in the sky.

Then they found an enemy cruiser – which sent up a lot of ack-ack fire. They took some flak and had to break their flight formation with the rest of the group.

Dicky circled round and tried again. Cyril lay on the floor inside the fuselage and prepared to drop their payload. On cue he released the bombs and watched as they fell and hit the sea. They both saw plumes of water go up when the bombs exploded, but didn't think they'd done anything to the ship. Another staccato blast of enemy fire came up so Dicky flew out over open sea where they couldn't be hit.

Cyril spoke to him through the tube. Bright cheery voice, Cyril had, but it carried bad news. "Bullet through the R/T unit, Dicky."

Dicky frowned. They wouldn't be able to radio home. Cyril's navigation was excellent. He always got them back to the ship. But there was no need to make things too challenging. "Call it a day, then? What d'you think?"

Polite as ever, Cyril said, "your call."

"Play it safe, I say. Let's go home." The Swordfish was easy to maneuver. He'd give her that. They headed back to HMS *Fortunate*, in bright sunshine under a careless blue sky.

They both got edgy as they approached the spot, where they expected to see *Fortunate*. Cyril didn't make mistakes, but this time he must be way off. There was no sign of the ship.

Even over the drone of the engine, Dicky knew that all was not well. Flustered, Cyril went over his papers and calculations again, scuffling and making strange noises through the headset. "What is it, man?"

"I don't know, Dicky. The ship should be here."

They circled the area again. Finding nothing. Nothing but the glittering sea. No flight deck, no airfield, no coastline. No sign of *Fortunate* and no sign of any other vessel.

"Where *is* she?"

Then the horrifying realization.

They traced back along the vector she'd been travelling. Searching for a sign, or a clue.

No words were exchanged, the men flew on in eerie silence. Perhaps, if they kept flying, kept looking, they might find her again – their floating home – and today would end in the wardroom with a warm meal and a gin and tonic, just like any other. They nurtured this hope. Even as it faded.

"Look. There. See that?"

They flew towards flecks of something on the surface of the sea. They knew from a long way off what they were. They were traces of her. The ship. Bits of debris from the flight deck and the superstructure. Bodies in the water. They circled in silent despair.

They were too late. *Fortunate* was gone, fathoms deep. The voices and the cries of his shipmates were silenced.

Eventually, they saw some bits of ship. Some bodies, floating in the water. They were alone and their ship was sunk. They circled. Looking for signs of life. Hoping to see survivors.

All lifeless. Their luck was at the bottom of the sea.

Cyril was silent. They both knew what this meant. They were a long way from the coast. They already knew they were alone.

Before long the engine would give that faltering splutter... it was inevitable... they couldn't fly on like this indefinitely. The dream would soon be over. On this day, under a careless sky and in bright sunshine. Dicky Tavistock would run out of fuel.

Cathy

Cathy and Guy took a long walk along the coastline, only pausing to kiss, to talk and to look out to sea. "Does Malta have good radar?

Guy shook his head, almost imperceptibly. "You can't say that word off base."

"I was just wondering about their early warning systems – and about the ships, too-"

He stopped her with a kiss. Then as he broke away, he said, "I know you're worried about Geoff. But we can never afford to forget that careless talk costs lives."

"I know," she said. "But I want to understand better. About Malta."

Of course she did.

He relented. "Malta needs all the intelligence she can get – being so close to Sicily. Enemy planes take off from there and bomb the Maltese almost daily. Far worse than we have to endure. One of the only reasons they've lasted this long – is because they've been using radar."

"I see."

"And yes, there's work going on – people trying to make the systems better. But nothing I can *share*, unfortunately."

"I understand. But what about the ships – trying to get through hostile seas? What about *Geoff's* ship? Does she have good radar?"

He nodded and lowered his voice. "They put new equipment in last October, when she came in for a refit. Cutting edge stuff. But it's driving warfare under the sea. They're diving deep to hide from us." He looked nervously along the windswept strip of land that ran along beside the sea. "Always think hard, Cathy, before you say anything to anyone."

"But they go all the time. Convoys. To Malta. The enemy knows that already."

He glanced down at her and nodded. "I know, but be careful. Don't trust anyone. Not even me."

She gazed out to sea. "I've never dreaded a birthday before. Is Geoff in danger?"

They both knew that three convoys had already failed to get fuel and food through to Malta. *Was it even worth a fourth attempt?*

He put an arm around her. "All I know is that keeping that little island out of enemy hands is very important. And Geoff would want to be part of that. Come on. Let's get back to the base."

She knew they must trust nobody. But sometimes, it helped to see how it was all connected. How her life and her brother's were still, inextricably linked. Through working with Guy she was gaining a new understanding of what she was part of – and it helped. Even if she was stuck in Rawton's office, fetching him tea when he wanted it, typing his boring lists. She began to see more purpose in the dull forms she filled in – requisitioning bits of equipment from other parts of the country. Sourcing obscure and sometimes almost unobtainable things. For the team. For Guy. For the war.

He stopped to kiss her. Pulling her into his arms and lowering his head to give her a tender, solemn kiss. Oh, she was so fond of him now. So serious. So handsome. Being here had changed her opinion of him forever. All her life she had been drawn to men like her father – confident, authoritative types. Loud voices. Obvious leaders. But now she could appreciate a different type of authority; a quiet command based on facts and drawn from the cutting edge of science. Another way of leading a field. Another type of pilot.

Guy didn't have to fly anywhere to perform his reconnaissance missions. He knew – the instant the warplanes took off from Germany – he knew how many, and where they were headed.

Things were becoming more intense between them. They spent a lot of time together – closer than ever. Talking and kissing – nearly always ending up in the dark, in his car. Warm Mediterranean hands all over her. And although she continued to fight him off, her desire to abandon that strategy was becoming hard to ignore.

She felt a frisson of fear as they approached the base – people were running from one hut to another. They saw and felt the tension even as they showed their passes and hastened across the grass.

"What's this – is the enemy approaching?" Guy tried to ask a passing Wren.

Cathy thought that was unlikely. She didn't think the enemy even knew where Southwold *was*.

Faye came running out of the main administration block. "Cathy – get in there. Half the girls are in tears and Rawton's in a blue funk – a message just came through the teleprinter... Apparently we had a taskforce in the Indian Ocean – and three of our best ships have been sunk."

The mood in the office was frenetic. A crowd of people stood exchanging news and views about what might have happened. Whether they knew anything about it or not. They stabbed anxious fingers at a map spread hastily over the clutter on somebody's desk. Three ships in the Indian Ocean. All discovered. Blown to smithereens. A carrier and two cruisers. *What about the Swordfish on board the carrier?* Cathy wanted to know. Flown off – some got to Trincomalee. Some didn't. The navy men were angry, some of them. "The ships had no air cover, you see, with the squadron flown off. *Fortunate* was a beauty. But they left her unprotected."

"...and the Japanese had duck for dinner," one of the RAF men said, nervously fingering his light brown moustache. Henry Rawton thought it was broad daylight when they went in for the kill. *How?* Everyone wanted to know. Torpedoes? Was it? No. Dive bombers. Same lot that attacked over Pearl. Our boys held them off at first, dodging anti-personnel bombs – those evil explosives that wouldn't sink a ship but would kill and maim her crew. But the deathblows came ... and the ships sunk fast...though some men were dragged out of the sea. There was a girl crying at her desk for her chap – ship's engineer, second class. *Dry your eyes*, everyone insisted. *Don't blub*. There was a hospital ship making fast for Ceylon. He'll be on it, everyone said. He'll be *fine...*

Cathy was shaking. Guy put an arm around her shoulder, right there in front of Rawton. Which was unwise. "It wasn't your brother," Guy said gently.

Mildred said it must be a relief to know her brother was safe.

"Yes, it is." Cathy said weakly. "But I did have a friend on HMS *Fortunate*. He was Lord Glenlark's only living son."

Anne

The sitting room was warm and sunny. But it was not a place of cheer. Anne now had a telegram on her mantelpiece. A 'Missing' telegram.

It brought pain that was all too familiar. The man who had coaxed her off the shelf and back into life. The man she had come to love and trust. The only man tenacious enough to persuade her that she was *good* enough, *strong* enough, *young* enough – and that there was *still time* to live a little. To have all the lovely things that falling in love can bring. Tender feelings. Secret smiles and holding hands. Moments of delight in bed together. That cheeky grin of his as he smoothed back his hair and pulled on his flying jacket.

Taken away from her. Just like Jim.

She had a system. For dealing with this. She stood the telegram on the mantelpiece where everyone could see it. Then when people came to visit, she didn't have to explain. She didn't have to answer questions. Her guests would read it, and understand. They would shake their heads and say – "Oh, my dear. I'm so sorry."

Binky came to see her just after the news came, and they stood in the doorway and hugged each other, saying nothing. For a long, long time. Then they talked and made tea, and wiped away tears. They bolstered each other's fragile hopes. She told Binky that Cyril would be fine. And Binky did the same for her. Dicky was indestructible, she said. "He'll be back before you know it." Anne had smiled and poured out second cups of tea. "I hope so."

It was good to be with a friend who understood her predicament. But mostly, when she wasn't at the Wrennery, she was alone.

The hardest thing was receiving a letter from him. She ripped it open with trembling fingers, hoping for the best: -

My darling,

Had to write. Despatched a hostile ship today on our twilight patrol. We think it was a submarine depot ship, but from above it looked like a toy left out on a lake after a day's play. She spotted us and sent up flak but we were too high for her. Ha-ha! Circled first with the squad. Then back into arrowhead formation. Our WingCo radioed to say throttle back for a sec, then push the stick hard over – all the way to the stop – and go for the dive. What a rush! Wind blazing past us. Slipstream battering the old goggles. Cyril was yelling like a kid at a fairground until I saw sense and levelled her up.

What a sight to see tracer fire in the twilight – tiny beams of orange light spearing past us so the enemy can see where his bullets are going – but you mustn't worry. They always miss, my love, they always miss. Came in for the approach like we practiced over the Solent – but have to say the flak made it much more exciting. Grouse shooting has nothing on this.

The sea ahead of us was speckled white, gunfire roughing up the surface, but we held our course. Kept Swordie steady, flew in for the drop at a lovely angle. Textbook stuff. Dropped the tinfish and Cyril leaned out to watch it zim through the sea and find its mark. Success! Oh, there'll be some gin on the tab in the wardroom tonight. The noise from the men singing is deafening me even as I write. Reply by return and tell me you miss me.

I'm doing this for you, and for us.

Your darling,

Dicky.

The realization – the thud in her heart – that he wrote it a full two weeks before the telegram came.

The flat seemed awful now. A place of emptiness and dread. She tried to tidy things, make things, mend things. Listen to silly songs on the radio. But when she could bear the happy sound no longer, she'd switch it off and sit by the window, holding the morning paper folded to a convenient size, but mainly gazing at passers-by in the street. Sadly, the paper didn't help. Didn't hold her attention. The headlines screamed of near victory, loud as ever, but the word from the telegram on the mantelpiece always seemed to drown out the upbeat babble of the press.

Her husband was 'Missing'.

Missing, she thought. She was missing him already. Missing his chatty letters. Missing a period too. She looked at the date printed small but clear on her folded newspaper page. She was long overdue. She put the paper aside – and got up and went across the room – touched the 'Missing' telegram.

Standing in front of a picture of him, she ran her hand down the front of her dress until it rested over her womb. She spoke, into the empty room. "You did it."

And there was no one there to say – "Success."

She felt so lonely knowing there could be no reply, when she had such important news. Oh, yes. She was missing him. Intensely.

In the end she decided to pack up her things and move back to the Wrennery. She needed a place of warmth and safety. She'd stay there as long as she possibly could – and hide the fact that she was having a baby.

Chapter Twenty-four

Guy

In a clandestine meeting arranged at short notice. Guy met a man in an Ipswich tea shop. They both spoke perfect English. They ordered scones. They drank tea from china teacups. But the way they sat, the way they moved their hands, the way they inclined their dark heads toward one another. Recognisably Italian.

The man was a friend of one of Guy's cousins. *With friends like that...* Guy wished he hadn't agreed to meet him.

The fellow was certainly persistent. He leaned forward and spoke with fire in his eyes. "We're almost family," he said. His outward appearance – neat hair, polished shoes, shiny briefcase – gave no clue to his radical views – which were hidden from all except the most trusted. Guy knew he was sent to recruit him.

"The Navy is my family now," Guy insisted quietly.

"Come on. You want to be on the right side when this show's over, don't you?"

Guy wondered how he could shorten the meeting and get back to the base and to safety. He hated being put under so much pressure to be disloyal to his country – which *he* counted as the one where he was born – although of course he felt the tug of his family connections and strong links with the places his forefathers came from. He could see why some people would succumb. The war was not going well. It was a productive time for those who wanted to stir up doubt and disloyalty. They sounded so sincere – these men. They always did. They offered all sorts of perks and promises. A chance to be part of something glamourous and secret.

But Guy shook his head, and said he was not the man they needed. Guy had Italian blood, and loved the language, the wine and the culture, but he was very much made in England. He wouldn't shop them, the people who wanted him to betray his country, but he wanted them to leave him alone. "My mind is made up. My promises are made."

Leave me in peace, amico, so I can love Cathy.

"That's a surprise. You never struck me as a man of *principles*, Guy."

"I don't have many, it's true," said Guy, with a Groucho Marx shrug. He couldn't be bothered with being offended. "But I'm a Navy man now – and win or lose – I'm sworn to serve my ship."

"And you'll go down with it, will you? If the other side wins?"

"Yes. If required."

The man smiled. "We know why. We know of your attachment to the Admiral's daughter."

But Guy shrugged again, casually throwing the attention away from the one and only thing that could hurt him. "No. Science is my first and last love."

"Is it?"

"Yes." Guy smiled. "And maybe it will be *you*, not me, who changes your allegiance. Maybe the war will start to go *our* way, and Italy will sue for peace."

"Can't see that happening, friend."

"You might be surprised," said Guy, with a flick of his dark eyebrows.

They shook hands and parted. Two men who looked like brothers. On different sides.

"If you ever change your mind, we'll be happy to hear from you."

Cathy

They were outside Cathy's billet. He held her close and kissed her long and slow. Cathy knew he didn't want to let her go, but soon he'd to have to say goodnight and walk home alone. She shared his intense longing for their relationship to become even more than this. No need for words – it was a given. The long, loving looks, the insistent kisses. The push of his body against hers. But the doorway of the billet was not the place, and the Petty Officer in charge would probably appear soon and start breathing fire.

His lips brushed against her forehead. Warm breath in her hair. He said, "The supply hut up by the receiving tower. I can get the key."

She went quiet. A place to be alone together. Not a car parked in a public street – with drunken men walking by and slapping the glass when they saw there was a courting couple inside. A secluded place with a door you could lock. Oh, a real temptation, to be alone with him like that.

Worse though, he'd left important papers out, on his desk. A buff-coloured folder lay tempting her on the top. Cathy was drawn by the word "Julius" on the front. She read it – and saw things in it that scared her – about last month's efforts to supply Malta – executed under the codename "Operation Julius". She saw the name of her brother's ship mentioned and wondered to what extent he'd been involved. And what about her father? She knew he was concerned about Malta. Was he part of this? But surely, the codename *must* be a coincidence. It occurred to her that, since she'd joined the Wrens, she knew almost nothing about what her father was doing anymore.

They say a *little* knowledge is a dangerous thing. She wanted to sit down and read the whole file, but Rawton would soon be back, so she left the report and went back to her desk.

She risked a forbidden telephone call to Anne. Rawton couldn't put her on Captain's defaulters for making a compassionate call – surely. Minutes were precious, so they had to be fast. Secrets had to be spilt quickly, if they were to be spilt at all.

"Any news of Dicky?"

"He was reported missing after Fortunate went down."

"Oh, *no*. I'm so sorry." The words were so inadequate somehow. And Anne was having a *baby* – that news made Cathy gasp. If Dicky didn't come back, Anne would have to give up her job and raise the child alone. "That's *exactly* what Delia was afraid of. Being left like that, with a photograph and a widow's pension..."

"I welcomed it, Cathy. And I'm glad I did it. You told me to enjoy it, remember?"

Poor Anne. Cathy shook her head. "Dicky Tavistock was extremely selfish."

"No, Cathy. He's wonderful. And please don't say *was* when you talk about him. He's only missing, after all."

Cathy felt terrible – hearing that note of desperate hope in Anne's voice. "You love him."

"Yes, I do."

A pause. Cathy's news and questions didn't seem important anymore. But Anne was kind and she got it out of her. "Are you meeting new people? Enjoying the work? And dare I ask – do you have a beau?"

She told Anne, yes, she was falling for someone. All getting a bit intense. But she didn't want to have a baby just yet. Anne said straight out that she must use some protection. She was motherly and sensible, but she didn't treat Cathy like a child. *Such a relief.*

"He can get them, can't he?" Cathy asked. "The Navy gives them out, to the men?"

"Yes. I did ask for the same privileges to be granted to my Wrens, but apparently that would be seen as condoning a lapse in morals, instead of taking sensible precautions," Anne said. "Very aggravating really. When we've got much more to lose by 'loving unwisely' as Mrs Laughton Mathews calls it. But there it is."

Cathy hesitated. Thinking. "But if I ask him about something like that – he'll think I mean yes..."

"Indeed he will." Anne was pragmatic as ever.

"And he keeps saying it's my birthday soon..."

Anne laughed. "Well, it's not *his* birthday, and you don't have to be the gift."

To Anne it was simple. Very black and white. But Cathy was still completely torn, and drew worried faces on the paper blotter in front of her. Torn between wanting and waiting.

Anne counselled waiting if there was any doubt at all...

But then came the good news: *Linda was on her way to Long Sands.* Cathy would see a friendly face from Pompey at last. Anne said, "I only know this because she came back to the Wrennery to get some things she needed for the journey... I've told her to ask for a billet for the night. It's too far to ride there and back in one day."

◆◆◆

"Hello, Cathy. Working hard?" Rawton patted her shoulder as he passed by. And Cathy shuddered.

At least as hard as you are, she thought. Picking up the next piece of paper from her in-tray. She typed about three words before she made a mistake.

She went back and typed over it in heavy black letters – XXXX. Other four-letter words sprang to mind first.

During her tea break, she composed a difficult letter: -

Dear Patrick, forgive me, I'm a poor correspondent. You are in my thoughts and I hope this letter will reach you before you sail – or if not – that it will be waiting for you when you arrive in port. In the office we heard the news of three ships lost, you will probably know which three. Many of the men are still missing. It made me understand how brave you are, and how much I value your friendship...

She hoped that conveyed the gist of it. She didn't attempt to 'encode' anything. She wanted it to be a plain text message. If only she *could* speak plainly. He would understand then, wouldn't he? Oh – this was so difficult! Can a woman ever be 'just friends' with a man? Or was she hoping for too much? She finished the letter and put it in the bag to be sent out with all the others. She could always fish it out later if she thought better of it...

•••

Her lunch break was spent on a picnic blanket – with Guy. He asked nothing more of her than 'be with me, keep me company'. She thanked her lucky stars for his endless patience and agreed to spend a few stolen minutes lazing in the sun with him. He'd been working on the design of some large radar units that could be retrofitted into existing ships. He'd looked tired standing in the lab, but here, under the warm sun, his skin was golden brown and his eyes shone.

He was still her brother's best friend. Only now it was just the two of them and he lay beside her holding her hand. She could let go anytime she liked – secure in the knowledge that he'd hold hands with her anytime she wanted to. Rolling onto her side, she watched a tiny bug creeping up the stem of a buttercup, and wondered if she would remember this moment with him forever. The scent of grass. The feel of the blanket under her fingertips. The warmth of the sun.

"Is it okay to talk about solar flares at a time like this?" he asked. Only he could make physics seem irresistibly romantic. She nodded and let him tell her all about the energy of the sun – about storms of bright perfection and intense white light. Of a natural fusion that kissed the earth with its life-giving heat. He made it sound positively sensual. Even if it was only happening millions of miles away on the superheated surface of the sun. He made it come alive and seem real.

"Millions of miles away," she repeated softly. "Like our life before the war. So far away now."

"Our life after will be even better," he promised, and he kissed her hand. He told her all the wonderful things that would be possible after the war. He told her how the wave frequencies he was studying – microwaves – would one day be used in all kinds of ways, at present unimaginable. How they would speed things up and help humankind – or they would if he had anything to do with it. "Scientists dream of the future too, Cathy."

Yes, she thought. They dream of life-saving advances, of efficiency and progress, of gadgets so small you could lose them in your pocket, yet so powerful they'll let you rule the world. She smiled at him. His enthusiasm. His certainty that amazing things would come to pass. "Oh, Guy. Who knows where all those crazy ideas will take us?"

"Into a world of peace and plenty, I hope."

Cathy smiled and waved a buttercup under his chin. He was such an optimist. He reached out a hand to stroke her face, and an overwhelming feeling came over her. She let the buttercup slip from her fingers. Seeing the look in his eyes. Acknowledging its meaning.

Her uniform. Its near-black severity. Its nun-like monochrome. It didn't seem appropriate for this kind of thing. A summer day like this called for something soft and pale and dreamy. For the first time in her life, she felt she needed a pretty dress. She would be like Delia and ask her mother to send her one. She knew the one she wanted. White cotton lawn sprigged with green leaves. A delicate feminine thing for him to toy with. Something for him to undo, button by button. Yes. A pretty dress with a row of buttons down the front. He kissed her again and she revised that thought – maybe she needed something with a clasp that undid all at once. She almost laughed – catching herself thinking like that about Guy – after all the years of just being friends.

As it was, he was running his hand over the robust navy-blue skirt that sheathed her hips as if it was silk. But she'd rather have been wearing something softer, smoother, more yielding. Oh dear. *Yielding.* That's what she was doing. Bit by bit by bit. She was *yielding* to him. Letting him get close. Almost giving in.

He pulled her closer and spoke soft words to her, to reassure her. His body felt deliciously firm under the white shirt he wore. His shoulders were strong, and his forearms were scattered with little golden hairs that bronzed in the low afternoon sunlight. He kissed her neck and tried his luck. "Let me, Cathy. You won't regret it."

It would be so easy. His fingers were on the fastening of her skirt and it was such a warm afternoon, it would be so nice to take the ruddy thing off. But then sanity flashed a warning. *Stop him.* There's a war on. You can't afford to get carried away. "No. Guy. I *can't*. Not yet."

Chapter Twenty-five

Linda

Voom, voom – Linda roared along the country highway on her motorbike, feeling a sense of exhilaration and freedom. She couldn't do her *top* speed – not with Toby riding pillion – but close enough. Toby was grinning over her shoulder, saying he loved it, and holding on tight. He was wearing leather today – to protect him if they fell. It looked a lot better than his fisherman's jersey – but not quite as captivating as the blue dungarees. They leaned in perfect union as she roared around a curve in the road. Toby laughed out loud like a child. She smiled and squeezed the accelerator. They rode on and leaned in for the s-bend up ahead.

"Hey Linda," he yelled above the roar of the bike. "Were you one of them stunt riders, before the war?"

"Delivery girl." she yelled. "Some customers are impatient, though. Where's the gate?"

"Up ahead. See. Over there."

As the roar of the motorbike engine died away and was still, the sounds of the countryside took its place. Happy birdsong. Crickets. Hardly a car on the road because of the petrol problem – it was bliss.

Linda was on her way to HMS Long Sands. Or she was supposed to be. But right now – the messages for Henry Rawton – marked 'important' but not 'urgent' – were tucked away in her trusty messenger bag. She took the bag with her, over her shoulder. She would never risk leaving that hanging on the handle of the bike. Besides – today it had a picnic blanket inside...and a few other vital supplies.

She climbed over the gate, but Toby vaulted it like an athlete. He was in high spirits – although the untrained eye might find his elation hard to spot. But she was used to him now. She took his hand and they walked for just a few moments, to get out of sight of the road. A field of golden oats swayed in the breeze.

She skimmed the tops of them with her free hand as she walked. *They reach ripe perfection at the height of summer. Just before they're picked. And they're tall enough to hide two people who want to lose themselves in each other...*

There, she lay down on her blanket with Toby Wallis, and with her head resting on her messenger bag, she tested her theory that as long as the task didn't require conversation – he performed well and didn't disappoint.

They didn't have long. It was a stolen moment. She felt so decadent, doing this. She was normally such a diligent messenger. But she was entitled to a lunch break, same as anyone else. They'd planned their little diversion carefully. Ride out from the Wrennery. Pick up Toby on the street corner as she passed HMS *Nautilus*. Ride out into the countryside. Find a nice place to stop for some...lunch... and then afterwards, he'd make his own way home while she rode on to Long Sands.

After she and Toby had lain spent on the blanket for a while – they sat up and ate cheese sandwiches and drained two bottles of lemonade that Anne had given her for the journey.

Toby looked at her and gave her a smile. "Do you think about Morrison, at times like this?"

"No," she said. But she wasn't offended. That was just offbeat, oddball Toby. Saying Toby things. "Do you?"

He nodded. "Sometimes."

But he didn't elaborate. He never did.

After the sandwiches were gone and the drinks drained down to the last drop. Toby pulled her down on the blanket again. She giggled as he ran his hand up her thigh and pulled at the fastening of her trousers. "No, Tobe. I can't do round two. I have to go to Southwold with the messages."

But he was over her now, gazing down. Dark fronds of his hair fell over his forehead – which was warm and smooth. He gave her a long, arousing kiss. Made her sigh. Then came tickling, nibbling kisses into the curve of her neck – they made her laugh. A luxurious sense of well-being came over her. The blue sky above was peaceful and serene. The war effort seemed... far away... someone else's struggle. Serenity was here, in an oat field.

Toby loosened her shirt. Slipped his hands inside and cupped her breasts. "Maybe they can wait."

After that they really did have to make haste. She'd need to ride hard to make up the time. He folded the blanket and she grabbed her message bag. They packed up their empties and stowed them away in a pouch on the bike. She dropped Toby at a train station so he could get back to Pompey. The station was alive with Canadian troops. Like her Toby, they were heading south. Their uniforms were slightly different from the standard British Tommy – the hats, the boots they wore, the guns they carried – and they had lilting Canadian accents. But they were the same fresh-faced young men full of bravado.

Toby – jostled like a traitor because he was in civvies – got himself a ticket and waved goodbye.

She heard fragments of gossip from the soldiers as she puttered her bike slowly through the gates of the train station. They were excited. Soon they'd get to test their combat skills – for real – the ships were waiting to take them to France.

Poor lads – if they'd seen the messages she'd seen, they'd be running for the hills.

They whistled at Linda as she rode by. "Hey – baby! Wanna give a lonely soldier a ride!"

•••

Linda zoomed on towards the radar station, hoping for a nice clear run. She'd better make up a bit of time on the open road, or she'd arrive at Long Sands later than originally planned. She was thrilled this morning when she realized she'd get to see Cathy. She held the knowledge tight in her heart and looked forward to a wonderful time – spilling secrets of the unofficial kind – one of the perks of friendship in the Wrens.

It was only when she was heading for the checkpoint outside Long Sands, that she got to wondering about the message *she* was carrying, and the effect it might have. She frowned and brushed those thoughts away. She eased her speed and came to a stop.

Cathy was there to meet her at the sentry point on the way in to the base. "Linda! How was your ride?"

Linda looked at her and almost laughed out loud. "Excellent thanks... exhilarating."

"Well – let's get your clearance sorted out," Cathy turned to the sailor manning the checkpoint. "All approved. She's here to see Rawton."

"Yep. That's right. Show me the way..." Linda hopped off the bike and wheeled it in, so she and Cathy could talk as they walked. Cathy had work to do – typing Rawton's responses. But after that, they could go to the Lord

Nelson, if Linda felt up to it. There'd be officers there who'd be pleased to make her acquaintance...

Linda smiled lazily, and said she'd love a chat and a drink, but no officers, thanks. She was kind of 'taken' now.

"Oooh. Tell me more."

Cathy

Cathy told Linda to go into the inner sanctum, where Rawton opened the despatches standing at his desk. A "hmmph" sound came from him as he stood there and read them. He was so engrossed in the messages he seemed surprised that Linda was still there. "Oh, you can ride back to Portsmouth, if you like..."

Linda reminded him, very respectfully, that she'd been promised a billet for the night. Her commanding officer didn't want her to make the journey home across country in the dark. Not unless Henry had a response that was extremely urgent. In which case, she would. But, for tonight, she believed Anne Tavistock had said they would probably put her at the Wren's Nest – with Cathy – was that right?

He waved his hand absentmindedly and said Cathy would have to sort it out...

Linda emerged giving Cathy the thumbs up. They would get their girly conversation and their visit to the pub. Cathy was longing to hear all Linda's news. And all about Pompey – well, anything Linda was allowed to tell her ...which might not be much. Cathy told her to go back to the Wren's Nest where The Bosun would find her a camp bed and might even let her have a bath or a shower if she was lucky. She'd love to come back there with her – and hear all about Toby Wallis, but ... Cathy still had her typing to do first.

So Linda went off on her own, and Cathy resolved to *fly* through her typing.

She loaded paper into the barrel – eying the machine like she was eying up a Hun. She was getting better at typing, but it was still a loathsome task. She managed the first two pages with no mistakes. She was quite proud of herself. After a while, Rawton emerged with a scribbled pencil list for her. It was attached to the despatch that Linda had brought with her...

Cathy read it. The message that Linda had carried – it said to select twelve men and send their names through straightaway so that letters of appointment could be issued and the men could be signed on to specific ships. Trained Wrens could now be found to replace them – in both service and technical fields. Cathy knew that the pool of enlisted Wrens now numbered over sixty thousand. Rawton had selected the men – written a list out by hand that she was to type up and send via teleprinter. He'd arrange a transport to come and pick up the men.

She put in a fresh bit of paper ready to type, she wound it through the carriage.

Started typing the names. Atkins, Ellenby, Harris, Palamara...

She stopped. "Palamara, Sub Lt. G."

Oh, God. They're sending him to sea.

She sat back in her seat, and stared for inspiration at the ceiling.

No. They can't. He's never even been to basic training.

After a moment, she pulled out the sheet of paper from the barrel of the typewriter, and went to confront Henry.

She knocked, but didn't wait. He looked up with irritation, but mellowed when he saw it was Cathy standing in the room.

"The Admiralty's request for men," she began. Nervously. "The men selected for active duty."

"Yes?" Henry's eyes narrowed.

"Erm – are all these men really suitable to go to sea?"

A shocked pause. "I beg your pardon?"

She was speaking out of rank. And fired by emotions she couldn't even have named five minutes ago. But she shook with the need to make this go away. "Well, some of them – they're linguists.... they're specialists...they're *scientists*... they're not really the sea-going type, are they? ... and aren't they more useful *here*?"

He looked stunned. He acted as if she'd said something highly irregular. "Are you questioning the Admiralty's choice?"

She paused. If she mentioned Guy by name now, it would only make things worse. And it was *Henry* who had made the selection, on the Admiralty's behalf, wasn't it? A long hesitation. Struggling to accept what she had to accept. "No, Sir."

Rawton smiled. *Evil man.* "Sorry, Cathy. I think *some* of us know what we're doing. There's a desperate shortage of men. Several ops are about to sail, my dear. We have to supply them."

Now he was even *bragging* that he was sending Guy to Bomb Alley. The convoys would take everything from her. It was too much – *Geoff, Patrick, Julius, Guy... everyone I care about.*

And in that moment, she knew it was all inevitable. The parting. The loss. What she had in her hand was Guy's death warrant.

"Get that typed up. There's a dear," said Rawton spitefully. He stood and waited for her reaction.

She nodded. Distressed that Henry had the power to do this. But powerless to do anything about it.

"Get on with the transmission, Cathy – I've got a transport coming in the morning to pick up twelve men."

She wanted to scream at him. *Does it have to be these twelve?* But if she asked that, he would ask why. And she wasn't ready to admit it. Not even to herself. That this was *unbearable.* All she could do was stand there, white-faced, with the list in her hand – on paper so flimsy it was almost transparent. Slowly, she straightened up, and keeping what was left of her composure, she turned and left the room.

In the hallway, she leant her head against the cool glass and thought about her options. There was a way it was meant to go. She would, with tears pricking her eyes, sit down and type the list and Guy would be appointed to a warship. She would run across the camp and tell him, and see the grim lines of concern settle on his face. He would abandon his ground-breaking work, and pack his things ready to leave on the transport the following morning. She would tell him he was brave and wonderful, and they would end up spending the night together. Somehow. She would kiss his soft piano-playing fingers and his smooth scientist's brow, and let him have his lover's way with her. And like Anne, she wouldn't care if he made her pregnant, because she would want something of his – something to keep and to treasure. And in the morning, the Navy would take him away from her. Forever.

He would never survive it – the fiery hell of battle – he was too gentle, too sensitive, too unique.

No. That is *not* how it will go, thought Cathy.

When she got back to her desk, she already knew what to do. She took out the sheet of paper that was loaded in the machine, and put in a fresh sheet. She sent the names to the Admiralty. Knowing that in the morning, fate was sealed for those names she had typed.

The teleprinter buzzed with the replies – here were the signing on papers for twelve men.

Rawton came out of his office. "All done?"

"Yes, sir." She held the pile of letters tightly in her hand.

"Why don't you go and meet your friend at the pub," he said, aping the kind tone of an actual human. "You can take the letters with you and distribute them. After all, that's where all the men are, I expect."

Typical. Make me do your dirty work and ruin everyone's evening for them. Thanks very much.

•••

In a daze, Cathy went to find Linda and they headed for the Lord Nelson to get a drink. Cathy felt like she needed one.

"Piano sounds nice, doesn't it?" said Linda, as they approached the pub.

That's Guy, Cathy thought. That's Guy playing the piano. Cathy had no idea where the men got a piano from – it hadn't been there last time. But she could hear it as they walked in through the open door on that warm July night, the sounds of the chords came out to meet them, inviting them in. The men were gathered around the piano, and when they saw her, they called out "Here's Cathy!"

They nudged Guy, who was playing for them, and told him to serenade her, which he obviously thought was a splendid idea. He began with one of those rippling, attention-seeking arpeggios up the keyboard which made everyone in the room shut up and listen. Beer mugs stayed put. People turned to look, with their cigarettes angled from their fingers and smoke curls rising in the air. While Guy played effortlessly well.

"You'd like a song?" he said, with a pianistic flourish.

Cathy nodded, weakly, and tried to smile. "Yes, what are you going to play for me, Guy?"

"You'll see."

He began with smooth, mellow chords and it took only a few of them before she knew the name of the song. Then it went through her like a knife.

Slicing into the depths of what she'd thought was her *un*-romantic soul. He played "Our Love is Here to Stay," and he knew all the words.

"That's a Gershwin song, isn't it?" Linda said.

Cathy nodded. "Yes. The last one he wrote before he died."

"It's beautiful."

Oh, it was. Both the song and the singer. The words and the music. The look in his eyes.

Cathy was dying. Confusion. Embarrassment. Love. Wait. No. *Not love.* Surely not *love*? She had always said she would *never* love Guy. But he was gazing at her, all wolf eyes and mellow sensitive music, while his hands ranged provocatively, expertly, over the keyboard.

The men laughed "Aww. Cathy! Come on! Smile."

Linda said to the crowd. "Alright, alright. He plays a nice tune, and my friend appreciates it, yes, I know she does. Thank you, gentleman. Thanks. But what we really need is a drink."

She steered her friend over to the bar and bought her a stiff one. "There. Get that inside you."

Cathy choked, taking a sip. Coughing. Turning away from the sound, the sight, of Guy playing that hopelessly romantic song. Linda banged her on the back. "Sorry. I thought it would help."

Poor Cathy. Drowning, in a mouthful of gin and lemonade. And Guy was *still* playing that bloody song.

Cathy recovered. "Yes. It is helping. Thanks." The drink *was* helping. But inside her mind, turmoil. Attraction was bad enough, arousal had been worse, but love would take her straight into the fires of hell. She leaned close to Linda over her drink. "I can't. I can't love Guy."

"You can. It's alright. It's allowed."

"I can't." Cathy's eyes stung. The drink, the choking, the song. *Dante's hell. With him. I can't do it...*

"I thought that, too. Until I fell for someone." Linda said quietly. "You think I want to be in love with someone who shoves his hand inside bombs for a living? Thank your lucky stars that you've got Guy here, safe, in the middle of nowhere."

Cathy shook her head. "The messages, Linda. The *messages*." The song's last chords sounded, and there was a raucous round of applause.

Linda's eyes widened. "Oh, No. I hate those bloody messages sometimes."

Then someone else, not Guy, started playing a much noisier tune. Cathy could tell the pianist had changed, even though her back was facing the piano. Different touch.

Linda warned her. "Look out. He's coming over..."

Cathy straightened up and turned around to face him as he came and joined them at the bar. "Linda has ridden all the way from *Portsmouth*, Guy, isn't that amazing?"

He nodded politely. Acknowledged Linda. Extended a navy-clad arm. "Portsmouth. That's quite a ride. Glad you could join us." He shook Linda's hand. "Cathy, are you alright?"

She nodded and returned to her drink. Trying to pretend nothing had happened. Guilty as heck.

He looked so, so crestfallen. Linda tried to rescue the situation. "Sorry, Lieutenant. I think Cathy's a bit *overcome*."

He nodded. He was used to it. He glanced away – hailed the barman and ordered a drink for himself. Cathy said she had orders to give out letters of appointment and would he see they got to all the people named on the list? Would he do that for her? She couldn't face seeing the men's faces, she said. She pushed the pile of letters across the polished surface of the bar, and Guy looked at them in dismay – knowing what they meant, for him, for his colleagues. She murmured that she was sorry, and then ran out of the bar.

Guy stood there, confused. Appealed to Linda, who looked at him with motherly pity. He said, "Well, what do I do? Go after her?"

Linda nodded. "Yes. Go after her. On the double."

He ran outside and caught her up. He caught hold of her elbow. "Cathy. What's wrong?"

"Nothing, Guy. I love you. I *love* you." She said it with a kind of amazement. As if she hardly believed herself capable of love.

"Oh." He broke into a smile. "I've loved you since I was nine years old."

"I know."

Outside the Lord Nelson, they stood and kissed, and kissed. She didn't care who saw them or what anyone thought. But then when they broke apart, she said she had to go back to Rawton's office. "Tell Linda I'm so, so sorry. I can't celebrate tonight. I'll see her back at the Wrens' Nest later. Or tomorrow morning..."

There was some paperwork she needed to finish. Urgent. And utterly secret.

•••

She had printed the letters of appointment. Yes. But she'd kept one back. *When the transport comes in the morning it will pick up eleven men. Not twelve.*

She made sure she was up before Linda. She set an alarm and slipped out at 5.30 in the morning. The transport was due to pick up a dozen men at six a.m. sharp.

When it came, it picked up eleven men. The driver asked about the last one, but Cathy shook her head and said, "Reassigned." She watched the men stow their bags and get on board. Some were red-eyed from lack of sleep, like her.

She waved and said. "Good luck, boys. See you when you get back!" On the outside she was rugged and cheerful as ever. On the inside, she was scared and desperate. The driver slammed his door and the engine started. She waved at the men until she could no longer see the transport. Then she ran all the way back to her billet.

She didn't have much time.

Linda

Eight a.m. Outside Rawton's office. Linda sat on an army issue chair in a corridor that smelt of linoleum polish. Through the open door she could see Cathy's desk, which was, as she feared, empty.

The rest of the room was neat and demure. But something was definitely wrong.

Captain Rawton's phone went unanswered. It screamed like a child wailing to be fed, but Cathy didn't come to her desk. There was a sound from the teleprinter, which Linda guessed was what happened when the messages backed up. Rawton appeared in the doorway of his office, rubbing his unshaved chin. "Cathy! Cathy! Where the devil is that troublesome Wren?"

Linda got up, holding her cap in her hand, like any respectful messenger. She asked if there were any last messages she could accept, before she rode back to Portsmouth. He blundered around trying to see if Cathy had left anything on her desk, but it was empty, swept clean, like a well-scrubbed deck.

"I can't see anything," he said, frowning. And Linda, remembering how cluttered the desk had been yesterday, knew this was another sign that all was not well. This was not the way Cathy usually maintained things. It was too tidy and the in-tray was bare. The phone taunted her with its incessant ringing. The whole thing was off.

Rawton told Linda she was free to go.

She hurried outside and kick-started her motor bike, but instead of taking the road back to Portsmouth, she roared off in the direction of the officers' billets – looking for Guy.

Leaning the bike up on its stand, she hurried up the path to the front of the building. There was no one on the door. It was standing open. She headed straight inside to the officers' mess.

There were only three officers there, seated at a long table. Their colleagues had already gone. The breakfast table had a lot of spaces. Guy was studying a sheaf of technical papers, with an abandoned coffee cup close to his hand. Linda – who guessed she'd only got into the building because they were so short on staff, blurted out, "What have you done with Cathy? She didn't come back last night."

"What?" He looked up but his face was blank. Linda stared at him. Meaningfully. She'd been pinning her hopes on the idea that he and Cathy had spent the night together.

"What d'you mean, she didn't come back?" Guy frowned. "And how did you get in here?"

"Never mind. I'm worried about Cathy. I can't find her anywhere. And it looks like her desk's been cleared."

"No," Guy rose, abandoning his coffee and his work. "I have to find her." Then realizing he couldn't leave papers out for all to see, even technical stuff that nobody but him would ever want to read, he gathered the papers roughly together and stuffed them into a black leather attaché case that had been propped by the leg of his chair.

Linda said, "She can't be at the Lord Nelson because it doesn't open this early and I doubt she's got clearance to go into the radar rooms without you or Rawton with her."

He picked up his jacket from the back of his chair and indicated they should go. "I've got clearance. Let's go and find out."

They roared back to the base on Linda's bike.

It took all of twenty minutes to search Long Sands and find that she had gone, and so had Guy's car. It was no longer parked in a side street not far from the Lord Nelson Hotel on the seafront. They stood there, staring at the space where the car had seemed such a permanent fixture.

"Do you think someone towed it away?" Guy wanted to believe that anyone but Cathy had taken it.

"No. Guy. Look, I didn't go to Cambridge or anything, but I'd say she *drove* it away."

He nodded. "Yes. Of course. She could drive. She could probably get the petrol too. I just didn't want to think she'd taken it."

The Nissen huts were full of tension, Rawton was a mess. The men in the depot were agitated, too, with all their systems and orderly rosters thrown into confusion. By whatever 'big' was going on, it had some impact on many, whatever small part they had to play.

She ran back to where Guy was waiting by her motor bike. She really had to go. Guy begged Linda to tell him whatever she could about the sealed orders and messages she had brought to the base. And Linda said she didn't know. Truly. She didn't.

He said, "I've been thinking about where she got hold of some petrol."

"Local garage – black market supply?" said Linda, thinking that was the way things tended to operate in greater London, which is where she was from.

Guy shook his head "No – she's a Navy girl. She would have got it here at the base."

Guy rode pillion on the back of Linda's bike – he clung on and they roared across to the one of the huts where there was a man who dealt out fuel for the Navy's own vehicles – the car that had picked up Cathy from the station when she first was posted to the Y station. And other vehicles too – maintenance vans that went out to the transmitters and up to any receiver they had on the sand banks.

"Will I get into trouble?" said the young man there. After they'd asked some probing questions.

"Not with us. We're her friends," Linda said. "But it might be best to get your cover story sorted out – ready for Henry Rawton."

The man glanced away, but he admitted it. "I *did* give her some petrol."

"And what did she give you?" said Guy – hurt.

Linda touched his arm, begging him not to press for an answer he wouldn't like to hear.

"Nothing," the man said. And then... "Some money."

"Is that all?" Guy said.

The poor boy blushed. "I helped her carry the cans to the car. She was ever so grateful."

Guy clenched his fists and raised *his* eyes to heaven.

"Did she say where she was going?" Linda asked. Hoping to move the conversation away from Cathy's expressions of gratitude.

The mechanic shook his head. "No. But she said she didn't want to miss her brother's birthday party."

Linda looked at Guy for an explanation, and Guy went pale.

Chapter Twenty-six
Cathy

Cathy drove into the big, industrial city. There was traffic on the road into town – mostly cars – nearly all of them prewar models from the twenties and thirties. The trolley buses clanged and men and women swarmed along the street. A mixture of all kinds of people. Some rich, some poor. Men in overcoats and women in elegant hats – black velour with a rising point like the wing of a bird. Men in overalls. Women with prams full of children. A paper boy called out to people in a broad Scots accent. Unfamiliar names on the front of buses swirled around the street corner – Elderslie and Paisley and Rouken Glen via Giffnock. She drove past the University, secluded behind wrought iron fences and partly hidden by trees. It reminded her of her own college days, short as they were. Oh, how easy things used to be. With Geoff and Guy. Happy times. She thought of opportunities missed. Of golden chances.

She reached the docks. The people on the street looked harder. Hungrier. Poorer. A huge array of fine merchant ships lay at anchor in port, but there were a handful of Navy vessels. A steam tug belching black smoke from a low funnel crossed the water. The Navy ships – steely grey with darker paintwork visible round the bottom of the hull – had their own special area. The ferry was coming in, crammed full of people. Servicemen smoking, women and children, prams, heavy shopping bags. This city was alive and kicking.

The waterways teemed with ships. Huge packing cases on spindly ropes swayed across the sky towards the ships. Sacks and sacks of merchandise still being packed on board the ships.

The merchant ships – good fast ones – had been placed under Navy commission just last week, and loaded so heavy they were low in the water. Loaded with supplies. They were almost ready to sail... ready to sail for Malta.

One ship rose out of the river like a cliff, and swarming on its side were the small figures of men on ropes and flimsy platforms – painting the never-ending surface that was the side of the ship, while below them near the water line, torrents surged out of the bilges and back into the river.

There it was. The ship she was looking for. She was not too late.

•••

She pushed through the crowd at the Dockside Tavern. The music jangled and smoke pervaded the room. The air was thick with it. The pub pulsed with sailors of every rank. Boy seamen nursing pints they didn't look old enough to drink, men in bell bottoms in groups of four or five, and women in civvies. Officers didn't tend to go to places like this, but she saw one or two. Some NCOs – non-commissioned officers – were seated together near the bar. There was a Celtic band, with a fiddler and a squeeze box, playing a mixture of racy songs and traditional sea shanties.

She headed towards the bar. The cotton dress she wore was a bit big since she kept getting thinner, and made her feel like a child. But she quelled the voice that told her this might lead her to failure. *This is going to work. It has to.* She leaned against the bar, feeling like she needed higher heels. Even to get noticed and get a drink, she needed to be taller. She felt inside her bag for the money she'd stowed there. She strived to get the eye of the barmaid who was rushed off her feet. She needed a drink...

"On your own, tonight?" said the older woman as she poured the drink.

Cathy shook her head. "No. I'm meeting someone."

The barmaid smiled, knowingly. "You will be in a minute, love."

She handed over her drink, and Cathy gave her the money. She needed to sip the drink, not glug it down in one go, but she forgot. She knocked it back and replaced it on the counter.

"Downed like a true sailor," said a man to her left. And grinned. She looked at him, heavy set. Old and gnarled. Six o'clock shadow. She could get rid of him quick if she told him she was the daughter of Admiral Bancroft-Smythe, but again, she reminded herself, *think of the mission.* Sit tight and wait.

Come on. Where was he?

Another sailor approached her. A redhead, like her. Tankard in hand. He put a finger to his hat, in what didn't look like an entirely polite gesture. She forced a slight smile.

He had a friend with him – and he gave him a nudge – "Say hullo to the lady."

Cathy tried not to engage with either of them, and crouched over her drink for cover.

He leaned nearer – breathing fumes in her face. "You with anyone, love?"

"No. But I'm meeting someone." She wished he'd take the hint and go. The second one, mercifully, drifted away to the bar to try and get himself a drink.

"Where's your fella then. What ship's he on?" He held his tankard close to his mouth, but resisted taking a sip.

Cathy shook her head. "What makes you think I've got a fellow?"

"Girls like you don't come in the Dockside Tavern."

"You should be in intelligence," she said, which pleased him. He raised his eyebrows, appreciatively, and grinned.

"Is that what you're in?"

That stung, it was too close to home. But she weathered it. "I'm hoping to join the Wrens." She told him. Oh, how she missed her uniform. She felt almost naked without it, in the flimsy cotton dress. But she had to abandon her lovely uniform, for reasons she had carefully thought out. It was marked with her regimental number.

"Oh, you'll get in the Wrens, darling. Like a shot. They like girls like you in the Wrens."

She nodded and tried to look past him. *Come on, it's getting late.*

Then. She saw him. The one she was waiting for – coming towards her through the crush. She thanked her lucky, lucky stars. The bar seemed like a much nicer place all of a sudden, a place of warmth and fun. Instead of a place of intimidation. She saw the shape of her name form on his lips as he came through the crowd. "Cathy!"

"Oh, Patrick. Thank *God.*"

A broad smile brightened his whole face as he pushed through to meet her. "Look at you. I almost didn't recognize you in civvies."

She threw her arms around him. Her new best friend. Her blond sailor. He looked pleased and laughed. "Steady on."

"Patrick. You found me."

He grinned at her, and put his hands around her waist. Glanced around at his shipmates, who were over by the bar, trying to get served. He gestured at them with a tilt of his head. "You want to come and have a drink with my crowd?"

"No," she said, pulling on his hand. "Not yet. Let's go somewhere. I've got a car outside. And I saw a place where we could get a room."

"You *what*?" Patrick looked thrilled, but taken aback. "Cathy-girl. Have you already had a few?"

She reached up and kissed his cheek, turning it rosier than it already was. She did that thing with her lashes that she'd seen other girls do – often when they were talking to Guy. "Come on. Let me surprise you."

He raised an eyebrow. "You already have."

Minutes later she hauled him around the corner and showed him where she'd parked the car. It was lurking, long and low, in a darkened side street. On the windowless side of an old Victorian warehouse. She surprised him, even more, when they got inside and she pulled out a hipflask of whisky. She handed it to Patrick.

He smiled, but didn't raise it to his lips. "You ain't put anything in it, have you, darling?"

She was shocked at the very suggestion. She took the flask from him, and took a mouthful of the contents. "Liquid courage, that's all..." She'd filled it up from the bottle she'd found in the deep drawer of Henry Rawton's desk.

"Why d'you need liquid courage? Are you in some kind of trouble? When I got your telegram... I was worried." He looked at her kindly. "Cathy. What's this all about?"

"Have a drink with me, Patrick and I'll tell you in a minute."

He took his turn with the flask and took a drink. Then offered it, doubtfully, back to her. She nodded and took the flask. Drank from it again. This was it. She was putting her plan into practice. She glanced at him nervously and handed him the flask. He took it, but this time he didn't raise it to his lips. He leaned towards her instead, and hesitating just before he kissed her, he gave her a questioning glance. *Can I? Can I kiss you?*

She felt so guilty for leading him on, but if that's what it took, she'd do it. She nodded.

He needed no more encouragement than that tiny inclination of her head. He kissed her. Confusion and a frisson of surprise ran through her whole body. It ran through him, too, she sensed it. He was hungry for her after all that time thinking about her. But gentle. Surprisingly gentle.

Cathy broke the kiss first. It was good, but unfamiliar. He was gazing, gazing into his eyes, as they parted. She felt a crashing sense of guilt and dismay. To ruin a friendship only takes one little kiss, she realized. And that was not the only thing it could ruin. With a shiver, she thought of Guy, and imagined how he'd feel if he saw her doing *this*. She shook her head. "Oh, *Patrick*. I'm sorry."

"I'm not," he said, with a smile. He moved to kiss her again, but she shook her head and glanced away in an agony of turbulent feelings.

"Hey," her sailor-boy said. Noticing her pain. He touched her face. "You alright, Cathy-girl?"

She had to tell him. *Now*. "I need you to help me with something. Something big."

Everything was 'big' in this war – except beds, rations, and her chances of getting back to Portsmouth.

"Is that why you're trying to get me drunk?" He held up the hip flask, and raised an eyebrow.

She must have blanched. She didn't want to admit...that yes, that had been her idea.

"I didn't join the Navy yesterday, you know." He tossed the almost empty flask down on the seat and a bit of Rawton's whisky dribbled out of it.

She shut her eyes for a moment, deeply ashamed. "Patrick, you don't understand what I was trying to achieve."

He looked hurt and disappointed. "Well, it wasn't what *I* was trying to achieve."

"I'm sorry."

"I liked you, Cathy-girl. I really liked you." He shook his head. "When I got your telegram, I was so happy. Worried about you – but happy – thinking you wanted to see me...thinking you wanted to say goodbye."

"I *did* want to see you, Patrick. Ever so much."

"Yeah. Maybe. You don't seem to know what you want." He glanced away. But he was stoic and after a moment he turned to face her. "Now. What's this all about?"

She took a breath. This was it. The moment had come to nail her colours to the mast. "I want to go with you. On HMS *Tilbury*."

He almost laughed. "No, you bloody don't. You don't even know where she's going."

"I do," she said. "I know *exactly* where she's going." She guessed that none of the crew had been told yet. But she knew there would've been a lot of speculation – and a false destination bandied about. *All shore leave cancelled from tomorrow.*

"You don't." But then he looked concerned. "Do yer?"

She nodded. "My twin brother is on this convoy."

He looked at her. "I knew you must have *someone* on a ship. Twin brother, ay?"

She nodded, sadly. Missing Geoff. He was out of touch. Out of reach. Already under sailing orders. He wasn't even *in* the Clyde – most of the navy vessels were coming down from Scapa, ready to lead the merchant ships out to sea. Only a handful of the close escort vessels were with the merchantmen at the Clyde. But all that was classified, so she told Patrick the barest of details. "Yes. Lieutenant Geoffrey... er, Smith, on HMS *Eagle.*"

"*Eagle?*" Patrick's interest was aroused. "That's a big aircraft carrier. So that's coming with us, is it? Blimey, Cath. Me and the boys have been watching the ships load up for days. They've chalked up a code that makes it look like we're going to South Africa. But the rumour is we're going to Malta – am I right?"

She looked into his blue eyes and couldn't deny it. "They'll tell you tomorrow, anyway."

He whistled. "They'll be waiting for us – other side of the Straits."

She nodded. "It's going to be one hell of a party."

He saw all too clearly what she was thinking. He shook his head. "No, no, no. Not you. You ain't going nowhere. Except home."

"I'm going with you. On the convoy. To Malta."

He stared at her. "Why would you even *think* of doing that, Cathy?"

"Because Geoff's going. And I can't let him go alone. He's my twin," she said. But that was not the whole reason. Not by any means. Patrick kept looking at her searchingly. "Wouldn't your brother want you to be at home safe? While he does the fighting? I'd want that – for my two sisters."

She nodded. He was so sincere. Such a good-hearted man. But he took the time to hear her out. "It's not right that he was called to fight, and I was excluded. I have people I want to protect too."

"Have yer?"

She nodded. The closest she could come to telling him about Guy. "If you won't help me, I can go back in that tavern and find someone else who will."

"Get yourself left for dead on the wharf, more like." He shifted uneasily beside her. "Nice try, girl. But the answer is no."

"It's been done before you know. Does the name Anne Chamberlyne mean anything to you?"

"Can't say it does, no." He shook his head.

For a moment Cathy was lost in thought, remembering the day that she and her brother had run inside an empty church and seen the old brass plate with the story etched upon it. A story that enchanted Cathy and gave her hope. "She was twenty-three. She knew her brother had to face a terrible battle that he would most likely lose. So she went to sea to help him. She dressed in the same clothes as the other sailors and fought alongside him. At the Battle of Beachy Head."

"I never heard of her. When was this?"

"In 1690," she said. "Against the French."

"*1690?*" He said. "Some girl as crazy as you got on a ship and got away with it? In 1690?"

Cathy nodded. "You can get away with a lot if you've got someone who'll help you." She looked meaningfully at him. "Please. For me. For the war. For the convoy itself. For people you don't even know about, working day and night to get this right – to win this bloody war. For people who've already died. For people who are not even born. You have to help me. And if you do, I will do *anything* you want in return."

That troubled him. "Don't talk like that. It's not right. I wouldn't ask that of you..."

"No. You wouldn't. I've always felt I could trust you completely." As she said that, as she acknowledged the admiration she had always felt for him, the tears came. Outside the night had dropped dark. Her voice became a solemn whisper. "Please help me. *I am going in someone else's place.*"

It must have been the tears that did it. He became gentle, perhaps because he had always liked her, or because he was one of those men that didn't like to see a woman cry. Cathy didn't know. He held her in his arms, pulled her close. And she was grateful that at least he wanted to comfort her. He was strong and warm, a true shoulder to cry on. "Hey," he said, and kissed her hair. "Don't get upset."

But the gentler he was, the faster the tears fell. "I've done something very bad, Patrick, and when the Navy finds out ...I'm going to be in a lot of trouble."

"What, love? What've you done?"

She told him, through the tears, that everyone she'd ever loved was in danger. She told him that in a moment of inspired desperation – she had swapped places with someone. Someone whose work on the base was far more important than her own slack efforts with Rawton's typing. How she'd changed names and modified navy documents. She fully expected Patrick to tell her how foolish she'd been. But if he thought that he said nothing. Instead, he kept listening, soothing, stroking her hair, as the words tumbled out.

"Oh, Patrick. Lots of people know what it's like to have a brother, but it's so much *more* than that – having a twin. I thought I'd die if I couldn't go to sea with him. I don't think I can ever love anyone as much as I love Geoff. But I tried, I *wanted* to. I almost did. But we always did everything together. Me and Geoff. He was the first born – you see – and I was his second. So, wherever he goes, whatever he does, I feel I've *got* to follow..."

"Not where he's going, love. Don't follow him there." He held her – as if she was a child that needed comforting. "You can't play sailors with your brother all your life. You've got to let him go..."

As if she ever could...

She sat up, and wiped some of the tears away. Tried to sound business-like. "I have never been more serious than I am now. This means everything to me. You have to help me get on the ship, Patrick. I can crew. You know I can..."

"I'd do anything for you. But it's not even possible." He stared at her. "You *can't*. Besides. You have to have *letters* to join a ship. You have to be signed on."

"I know. I have my letter. I'll show you." And drying her tears, she reached in her kitbag which was in the footwell of Guy's car and showed him the letter of appointment – complete with the name of the ship – HMS *Tilbury* – a destroyer – complement just under two hundred.

He took the paper and scrutinized it – using his cigarette lighter to get enough light to read it – in surreptitious defiance of the blackout. "Well.

Look at that," he said, in amazement, seeing the words in the flickering light. "Just like the real thing."

The flame and the letter were so close.

"It *is* the real thing." She took the letter back before he was tempted to burn it. She saw the thought flash bandit-like through his mind and she wasn't having that. She folded it up and put it inside her bra for safe-keeping.

He stared at her. "Tell me how you got that?"

If he *was* going to help her, she'd have to put him in the picture – or at least, part of it. She told him how she'd managed to get the letter when the Admiralty put out the call, sending the names through her teleprinter and printing the letters of appointment alone in Rawton's office. And how she'd 'borrowed' someone's service number to put on the paperwork. She told him how she'd got one of the mechanics to give her the petrol to drive to the port, and used her Admiralty connections to get all the way into the zone.

He shook his head, hearing her confession. "You've got some nerve, haven't yer?"

•••

They got a room in a boarding house with a handwritten sign in the window saying "Sailors welcome." Patrick said he'd stayed there once before. The facilities would meet their needs, and best of all the landlady 'wouldn't say nothing'.

In the cheap dive of a room, over a porcelain wash basin, they did what they had to do.

She stripped off her cotton dress, and stood in her cami and silk knickers in front of the sink, staring into the mirror. Patrick – intensely uncomfortable – glanced away and folded his arms. "Did you bring clippers?"

"In the bag." It was tucked in the top of a sailor's kit bag leaning up against an iron bedstead. "Brown leather flannel bag. It's on the top."

He went and got it. He saw the name, embossed in gold lettering on the side – *Henry Rawton, RN.*

"The boyfriend?" he asked, pointing to the bag.

She shook her head. "Commander of a Naval research facility. Experimental radar."

"Oh my God, Cathy, you'll get me court-martialed."

"Just use the clippers, will you?"

"Alright, alright – how short d'you want it?"

"Same as yours."

Grim faced, he did it. He took the hand clippers and lifting the hair with a comb, he made quick work of the haircut. He shaved it short at the back and the sides, faded it in as best he could. Then he took the comb and some nail scissors and shortened the fringe for her. Bits of her dark red hair fell in the porcelain sink. He picked up a curl of hair, and put it in his pocket. They threw out the rest. She washed every trace of makeup off her face with a bit of soap from Commander Rawton's bag. Leaning low over the basin, she sluiced water on her face until she was sure every trace of lipstick and face powder was gone. And when she looked up, she was different. A boy of about fourteen, maybe – with the face of a frightened elf.

They hoped the uniform would make her look older. She kitted up – in her own bell bottoms because they fitted, and his spare tunic top, which was a bit too big. "Good thing you ain't got much on the foredeck," he said – adjusting the tunic for her. The tunic was too loose, really.

"It's the food – or the lack of it – I keep losing weight..."

He smiled. Almost sadly. He helped her with the square rig collar, tying the tapes the right way. But the tunic still looked too big. "I think I'll have to take it in a bit."

"Can you do that?"

"Yeah – I make repairs to my kit all the time. I expect the landlady will find me a needle. Are you alright, Cathy-girl?"

"You'll have to call me 'Smith' now."

"And how does Miss Smith like her new outfit?" He pretended he was an assistant in a shop.

She rolled her eyes. "Very much, thanks. Give me the cap." They only had one cap between them, but he said she could wear it, and he'd get another from the stores on board. "They'll dock my pay for losing it," he said, but she promised she would make that right for him.

The cap with its 'HMS' tally-band did it, and his spare tunic looked the part. It had gun grease on it and didn't look too new. She positioned the cap correctly, stationing the bow directly over her left ear. He didn't even need to remind her. He called out – "Rating Smith. A'ttenshun!" – to catch her out, but she saluted instantly, eyes level, shoulders back. He whistled. She was good at this.

She always knew she would be.

"Do you think they'll guess?" She glanced in the speckled mirror over the sink, and she was very pleased with the result.

"They will in the end, love. You can't hide much on a ship. You're still my Cathy-girl, underneath."

"It's *Smith*. You *have* to remember." She took the cap off, undoing the chin strap with care, and laid it on the end of the bed.

He touched her face, concerned and sad. "Look at you." He ran his hand over the ruthless clipper cut. He looked like he'd really love to kiss her. "We don't have to report to the ship for hours yet. What d'you want to do to pass the time?"

"I thought we should go over everything I need to know. Deck duties, gun drill, night watch, that kind of thing."

That raised a smile. "Oh, I love talking about all *that* when I'm on shore."

She got her way, though. Hours passed, talking, planning, rehearsing. She went over every detail with the tenacity of any military strategist determined to succeed. She grilled him. Question and answer. Question and answer. While he sat and took the tunic in, making it fit her better. When he was done, he severed the thread with his teeth – and tossed the garment back at her. But as time wore on, the mood became gentler. Calm came over them. Two kids in sailor suits, sitting on the floor, side by side. With their backs leaning against the bed. Just like it used to be with Geoff. In the end the sound of Patrick's matter of fact explanations soothed her, helped her relax, and she fell asleep on his shoulder. The room was safe and warm. He woke her up gently and they crawled into bed – and slept until the morning.

Chapter Twenty-seven
Cathy

"Cathy, it's time."

She woke up looking at the side of an unfamiliar bedside cabinet, unsure where she was exactly. Then she remembered. In the first hazy moments of the day the plan was like a dream – one that ought to fade and disappear. But then he stirred, where he lay, cupped around her back. He kissed the back of her neck, where her short hair was shaved to stubble – and her eyes went wide. *I'm in bed with Patrick Clarke, from HMS Tilbury.* His hand was on her waist. When she turned to face him, his blue eyes were both happy and sad. "Happy Birthday."

"Thank you." She let him trace the side of her face, and gaze at her as if she was some kind of wonder. He wasn't Geoff, but he was close enough. It almost felt odd that *he* wasn't having a birthday – she'd been so accustomed to having double ones.

Their clothes were discarded around the sides of the bed. It had been much too warm a night to keep them all on. And the look in Patrick's eyes was not exactly what you'd get from a brother. So she got up and started looking for something to pull on in a hurry. "Come on. Let's get ready."

He sat up in bed and looked at her, as she discarded her silk camisole and put on the serge top he'd lent her. His face looked tense. His brow was troubled. "Look. Cathy..."

"What?" she was struggling to remember how to tie her collar ribbons.

He touched her arm, appealing to her. "It's only been a bit of fun up til now. It's just a haircut. We got a bit tiddly and dressed up, that's all. You still can call it off, you know ... before you regret it."

"Come on. Have courage. I only need you to take me through the gate. After that, you can drop me like a stone if you want to."

"You know I won't be doing that. I said I'd help you. But they're going to get wise to it, love. And then what's going to happen to you?"

He didn't seem to be worried about what might happen to *him*. Brave man. She appreciated that. "It's alright. I'll tell them my father's an Admiral." She said it flippantly, as if it was a joke.

He laughed and said that was a good one. Then he got very serious, and his blue eyes were full of fear. "They'll slaughter you. When they find out. It's going to be effing slaughter."

"They'll be too busy dealing with the enemy to think about me – or they should be..." She wondered if she should tell him what the Admiralty had said. *This convoy will be deemed a success if even one ship makes it to Malta.* Better he didn't know, maybe. Cathy shook her head and pulled his hand. "Come on. Where's your sense of adventure? It might be fun having me on board."

He gave her a stern look. "Yeah. Fun."

"... and I'm really looking forward to seeing the ship." She meant it too. The destroyer, *Tilbury* – armed with guns and ready for war? She was *dying* to see it.

He smiled wryly. "You'll be sick of the sight of her before this is over."

"Never," she assured him.

He got washed and dressed. Took care to shave nicely – using Rawton's razor. Brushed his short blonde hair– found his sailor cap, and handed it to Cathy. She put it on and perched it just right, so it covered a bit of her forehead. "Yes, that's right," he said. "Don't wear it on the back of your head like a flat top."

They packed up their stuff and left everything tidy. Not wanting to have anything incriminating with them on board the ship, they stuffed her dress into Rawton's flannel bag and hid it in a dark corner of the wardrobe. They closed the door on the room they had shared and at the top of the stairs she pulled him back and kissed him on the cheek. "Thank you for doing this."

He smiled and gazed at her again – in a way that was verging on Guy-like. He touched her cheek, longingly.

"Oy – you two! *Not* in a public hallway." The landlady looked up from the bottom of the stairs. And judging by the look on her face she knew full well who'd come in last night, which didn't marry up with who was going out. She eyed them both with suspicion as they came down the stairs. They tramped out as if nothing was amiss, each saying sorry, and Cathy gave her some extra money to buy her silence.

◆◆◆

They approached the gate that led to the wharf, and Cathy recalled an old phrase from her days at Cambridge – about Crossing the Rubicon. The point of no return. The moment when everything changes...

Early morning – a fine fresh breeze – the Admiralty picked the right day for sailing. Look straight ahead, she told herself, don't cringe and don't look down. *Look at the ship – you said you wanted to see it.*

"Shoulders back, Smith," Patrick said under his breath. "Use your kit bag, if you want a bit of cover."

They approached the man guarding the gate. She handed over the letter. *She was living it. She was answering the Admiralty's call.* He looked at the paper. "Hmmm. They've sent you up from Suffolk?"

Cathy dared not answer, so she nodded and uttered one solitary syllable. "Suh."

He gave her back the papers. And she began to walk away. Trying to remember to walk like Patrick. The ship was up ahead, in the deeper water, grey and unforgiving. Painted in her dappled camouflage colours. Could it be she had got through, and the ruse had worked? Soon she would feel the deck beneath her feet...

"Hey – Rating!"

Cathy froze.

The man at the sentry post barked at her, "Look at me when I'm speaking to you."

Cathy turned, scared to catch his eye, but she did at least remember to salute.

"Your tunic looks filthy. Did you not think to smarten up before reporting for duty?"

She glanced down at the front of her sailor top, self-conscious about her slim body inside it. Patrick spoke for her. "He lost half his kit in a house of sin. That old tunic he's wearing is mine."

She almost gasped, thinking this was the worst possible thing to say. But it worked.

"Foolish behaviour. Don't dawdle. Get on board."

Guy

Part Three
Ship of hope

Chapter Twenty-eight
Cathy
Diary of C. Smith, rating on board HMS *Tilbury*.

August 3rd 1942.

The convoy moves towards the open sea. The sea scintillates and glitters. The sun burns and lights a path of pale sparkling light for us to follow, luring us out into the sea. And beyond, into a burnished place of danger.

The ship glides forward. Aboard her, a hundred and sixty-four men salute their commander, ranked on the deck for morning directions. Hidden among them, one imposter, with a firm salute and a clear conscience. Me.

The sea breeze is cool on our cheeks as every sailor stands to attention. The last glimpse of land slips out of view. A man sings a Farewell to Scotland.

She wrote the words in a small leather book with an anchor tooled on the cover. Patrick gave it to her. A diary. Something to do in the evenings. The fug of the men was ripe, she had to admit. Too many bodies in too small a space. They lounged on their bunks. Half-naked. She envied them. She couldn't take anything off. Didn't dare. So she lay on her stomach with sweat on her brow. In most of her kit. Being a sailor.

Pat's eyes tell me he regrets this to the pit of his soul. He looks at me with a mixture of sadness and admiration. *I love him, he is a bright blonde light on this ship of vulnerable souls. I love him – but as a brother.* He's on his bunk – across from me – so close we could easily link hands across the gap, but we don't dare to. He's reading a book from the ship's library – all the good ones were gone so he's reading about book-keeping. He wants to better himself when he leaves the Navy.

The night watch is topside working the ship, while we're at ease down here on our bunks. We are safer from the U-boats when moving at a fine clip. We don't talk of danger. We're cheerful and keep our spirits up. The men re-tell stories of how we sunk the Bismarck. Tales of victory make them feel invincible. We all need to feel like that.

Today I had my first go at refuelling at sea – a tanker came out to meet us, and we worked in seas so high that a wave washed right over me. I would have been swept clean off the deck if Patrick had not held tight to the back of my jersey. After that I listened better. I had to clip myself to the wire before using two hands to move the hoses. Afterwards, when my clothes dried out, they were stiff with saltwater.

The last time this mission was attempted – six out of ten of our ships went down, courtesy of our German friends and their Italian brothers. I saw the report on Rawton's desk. I'm aware of the danger. But there's nothing I can do but follow orders. We must move on and not risk any further delay. I'll sleep now. Work to do in the morning.

They had six whole days with no problems.

"This ain't no convoy," Patrick said. "It's a holiday in the Med." He lay on top of a steel ammo locker, with his shirt off and his bare chest gleaming, cigarette between two lazy fingers.

She wanted to kick him. He knew she couldn't take anything off. The orders came to change into summer rig – white tops, white pants – it helped a bit. Patrick went and got some for her from the quartermaster. She stayed fully dressed when some of the men were walking around the ship in their shorts, their upper bodies quite naked. When they were on watch this was bad enough, but when they were at leisure it was torture. She lurked in the shadiest parts of the ship. Crouching in the shadow of the gun turret, or lying with her face pressed to a patch of cold steel, in the lee of the ready-use lockers.

"Told you." He took a pull on his cigarette. He passed it to her. She liked that moment when their fingers could touch and no one would think anything of it.

"Thanks." She put it to her lips, drew in the smoke, and then blew it out gently. She gave the cigarette back to him. It hadn't helped. Even the smoke was warm.

On the morning of the seventh day, she stood in the mess queue with her metal tray in hand, thinking they'd soon see Gibraltar. Looking forward to going up on deck. The seaman beside her narrowed his eyes when he looked at her. Flicked a glance that assessed her for clues. She felt awkward under his scrutiny – dreading the moment of confrontation. But then he said nothing. Collected his food and sat down. She felt so grateful to him.

Another time – a tough old sailor caught Patrick's arm and said something about her under his breath. She didn't hear, but it made Patrick angry and a look passed between the two men that could easily have led to a fight. She'd seen a few shipboard rough-ups – a rude comment, a shove on the shoulder – followed by some fast punches and a man slammed, cheek first, against the metal wall of the ship. In the morning, there'd be a report read out at Captain's defaulters – and the two men would stand there with black eyes, split lips and bruised egos.

No. They wouldn't. Not if she could help it.

Her bright blonde sailor was too good for that. Too valuable. "Let it go, Clarke, I fight my own battles."

Patrick shrugged. "Only trying to help."

She looked at the old sailor who'd started the trouble. He stared at her as if she was half-crazed – and she stared right back, staring him down, until she saw laugh-lines appear on his craggy face. Then he reached out with a work-roughened hand and tousled her short red hair. "How old are you?"

"Sixteen." She raised her chin. "How old are *you*?"

"Forty-two," he said. And then they both laughed.

After that – she made a special friend of him. She played board games with him in the bunkroom at night. Told him how she once polished brass buttons – for an *Admiral*.

9th August – Sunday.

Fleet slipped through the straits under cover of darkness. The night watch has binoculars trained on the sky. I passed by the door of the radar room today – and heard the sound behind the curtain. Thought about Guy. Perhaps he would have been sweating in a little room like that.

But they're out there. The hunters. The killers. Probably hidden under the waves where the radar man cannot detect them. They know and they'll be waiting for us. Better hope the ASDIC system doesn't fail – we need all the warning we can get. The reassuring 'ping' keeps on coming. Uninterrupted. All quiet. All silent.

Patrick helped her every step of the way. He guarded her zealously when she had to take a shower – keeping his broad-shouldered body in the way so no one would see. Passing her the soap – trying not to look as the water ran down her soft white skin. "Hurry up," he would say. "Can't push our luck."

The heads was the hardest thing – the toilets on board – they were communal. "Go when it's quiet," he said in a low voice, "and take a newspaper with you."

"The indignity of it," she complained. The subterfuge. The ever-present danger of discovery.

He answered with a flick of his eyebrows. "And who's idea was this?"

But when she was up on deck – and the ship dipped into the rolling sea – she broadened her stride and laughed at the hardships she faced. A fine salt spray hit her face, and she breathed it – lived it. She loved the work, she loved the sea – and oh, God, she loved HMS *Tilbury*.

10th August – Monday.

All quiet. We got off scot-free again. I could get used to this.

We've been so bloody lucky. Pat winked at me before we went to sleep. We're going to be alright.

The next day when she went up top and reported for duty, Pat pulled her to the side of the ship where normally, the other hands worked. "There's something you might want to see."

"What?"

He pointed to a vessel in the far distance. "That there, is HMS *Eagle*."

My brother's ship. Oh, bliss to see it. Even matchbox size. Lying long and grey and low on the sparkling sea. Tiny aircraft and figures – easily visible to the naked eye. People walking around on board it. Men lying in the nets beside the flight deck. Sunning themselves. Just like the boys on *Tilbury*.

She caught her breath and ran to the side, hung over the rail and stared at it.

I must have reacted girlishly. Perhaps I leapt for joy – seeing Geoff's ship – or behaved in a way that was too unguarded.

Patrick said, "Gang plank, Smith." His teeth were clenched, his face worried. An officer from the bridge was coming. They'd been spotted.

The Officer saw the two ratings and did a double take. "What's all this?"

Both ratings saluted. The officer circled them, like a vulture, and his peaked cap cast a shadow over Patrick's face. But Patrick didn't flinch a muscle. He was good like that. The officer's gaze moved and he stared at Cathy. There was even an echo of the way men used to stare. Back in Portsmouth. Before she cut her hair.

They can't send me back. We're past Gibraltar. But I would be held somewhere. Disgraced. The laughing stock of the entire ship's company.

Frowning, the man asked. "What's your name?"

Patrick answered, though he was not the intended victim of the question.
"

We just sighted *Eagle*. Over there." He pointed over at the grey battleship gliding through the glittering sea.

That took the heat off them for a moment, as the officer looked over the rail, narrowed his eyes, and then lifted his binoculars. Lucky man. *Oh, to have a look through those.*

The bell rang for the change of watch. "Permission to go to our watch, sir?" said Patrick.

The man frowned, but then he nodded.

She worked for two hours or more alongside Patrick. The usual duty. Just a drill. Load and unload the pom-pom guns. Check the ammunition trays. The armourers worked like a well-oiled machine. She knew her place – the newcomer – the boy who fed the cartridges into the trays. "All in order, sir."

But there was no sign of any enemy.

The gunners took their place for the drill. Everything was ready. The breeze was gentle. The sea was flat.

She felt it as a premonition. Something wrong. The world too quiet, and Geoff so close, and yet, in so much danger. She turned her face to into the breeze, and sensed it.

The wolves are here, thought Cathy.

Under the sea, somewhere in the dark depths below the surface of the water, the order was barked in German.

Torpedoes released, shot through the tubes and seared their way towards the *Eagle*.

Guy

Guy was in a dingy room at HMS Long Sands. The size of a prison cell. The block walls were painted that lovely shade of puke-green that the Admiralty seemed to like.

They made him sit down, while they stood. *Power games,* Guy thought.

He swallowed and stared at the table in front of him. They shouted at him, for a time, about his relationship with Cathy. He said he had nothing to be ashamed of – and he didn't. Falling in love is not a crime. All the officers dated the Wrens. But things got ugly. At one point one of them slapped his face. Called him a coward for getting his girl to get him off active duty. Guy was cool, even under attack. "Did my commanding officer authorize that?"

"You deserved it. You're a defaulter."

"I told you. I didn't ask her to do this... I would have gone with the transport..."

One of them had such a look of disgust on his face... it really was quite hideous. Then, a knock on the door. Somebody handed something to one of the men. A bulging rectangular bag. "Try that."

They slammed it down in front of him. "Seen this before?"

The brown leather bag – with Henry Rawton's name on the side. Guy folded his arms. Resolute. "Well, it says who it belongs to. Right there."

Both men bristled with contempt. Determined to break him. The one nearest Guy inclined his head. Slanted his eyes towards the bag. "Open it."

This seemed an odd request. Guy unzipped it, because they ordered him too. Inside, rolled tight and stuffed in on top of the shaving things, was a flimsy cotton dress. Guy didn't touch it, but one of the policemen leaned forward, pulled it out and unfurled it like a flag. "Is that your girlfriend's dress?"

"I have no idea." Which was true. He hadn't seen the dress before. Every time he'd met her, she'd been wearing her Wrens' uniform.

The military policeman touched the dress, checking it for something. "No name on it. No laundry label."

The other one turned to Guy. "Are you sure you've never seen it?"

"Absolutely."

Next item. Her silk camisole and matching French knickers. Crumpled and worn. *Oh, God.* Unfortunately, those were more familiar to Guy. He folded his arms and tried to look away.

Too late. The policeman had caught the gist of his reaction. "Seen *those* before, haven't you, Palamara?"

He nodded. *Might as well admit it.*

The men smiled at each other, and one of them even chuckled. Guy felt a flash of irritation and thought he'd better defend her. "She didn't take them *off.*"

The policeman smiled. "She has now."

One of them went out into the corridor with the news. A familiar voice. A short conversation.

Guy groaned inwardly. Commander Rawton was waiting outside the door. Guy closed his eyes and wondered how to get through the next part of the interrogation. He listened carefully to get what he could from fragments of conversation. The lowered voices – the inferences – the silence. From what he could make out HMS *Eagle* had been contacted. And the results were... inconclusive.

Rawton came in. "I do have one piece of news for you. Cathy has surprised us all – it seems she spent the night with a sailor."

Guy flicked a glance at the repulsive man. He was enjoying this. How much more pain would this man inflict? Cathy often said she'd come to hate him. Guy realized he should have gone to Ralph – should have asked for help before this blew up in their faces. They were wasting time. It was days since Cathy disappeared. And all they did was *talk* about it.

"Did she?" Guy said, with an icy calm that did not match his inner turmoil. "And where is she now?"

"You tell *us*." The policeman said.

"I already have. *She's on the ship*. She's gone to be with her brother."

"She's not. Those things of hers were found in the Clyde. Her brother's ship left from Scapa."

Guy frowned, rapidly trying to process what Rawton had told him. "You must contact her parents. They'll be convinced she's with Geoff. They'll be worried."

Cathy

"They've got her in the guts, sir!"

Four torpedoes found their mark – not one. Four fatal spears in the side of the *Eagle*. One sliced in through her engine room – and the men inside were done for. On the *Tilbury*, all hands felt the impact too, like a roll of thunder. Within a minute she was listing. Anyone who could leave their duty ran to the side to look and cried out loud to see the stricken aircraft carrier, listing dangerously to one side.

Tilbury's men gave voice to the silent cinema that played out on the sea in front of them. "She's done for." "No – the *Eagle's* mighty – she'll be alright." Cries of despair. Shock. Fear. Vain hopes that the ship could right herself again. But no... she was not coming right.

The list got worse. The stricken ship lay tilted towards the waves. Her fate was clear. She was sinking.

Patrick told her not to look. But she couldn't look away. With staring, helpless eyes, she watched. She knew she would not write her diary tonight. There were no words.

She felt. She sensed. She imagined. Twin telepathy, call it what you like – she was with her brother. She was with him on HMS *Eagle*. She saw the unfamiliar angles created by the list – hatches out of reach, doors on the forty-five, men and equipment falling. The struggle as the water rushed in. Companionways seething with men – squirming like rats – climbing all over each other. She saw choices made. Fatal decisions. Traps below, and doors that clanged, heavy with seeping water. Steam that rose and killed.

Not my brother.

He would be on the bridge. If he was on the daytime watch. She hoped he was there. Deciding.

She shuddered. He was never any good at decisions. She sent him her best plan of attack. Willing him to hear. *Jump now. Yes. Into the oil. Jump before she turns turtle...Please, Geoff, jump.*

The smoke belched from the stricken ship, and she swung round in a circle. A fatal farewell dance. Muffled explosions from deep inside her. Cries of despair all around her. "Oh. She's arse up now." The red paint on the keel told the story. Her superstructure was under the waves. Upside down. Anyone left inside her was finished.

Look away. Look away. A sorry sight. There were men left clinging to her... tiny dark figures crawling on the keel – hoping for deliverance – slithering off as she went stern up. Up she went, up and up. And then... she slid... and she was gone.

For some reason, as she stood gazing at the place on the ocean where the ship had been, as the ship fell to the sea floor, she thought of the photograph. The Admiral, flanked by two children in sailor suits. Falling. Swirling. Tumbling down through the water. The glint of silver, the children's faces lost in the aquamarine depths. The darkness rising. The picture falling. The happiness of their golden childhood gone.

Diary of C. Smith. 12th Wednesday.

We are under continuous attack. Major Stuka raid. Incoming hostile aircraft high in the air above us. Our guns maintain a stream of steady upward flak. Hoping – even if we can't hit – at least to drive them away from us. My hands are weak from loading the ammunition trays.

My mind is numb. His ship is gone. I heard they lost 300 men. But picked up many others. Which is he? Dead and gone. Or gasping on some ship's deck, spitting oil? Why can't I feel it? I don't understand this strange absence of any feeling. I lay on my back at night – listening to the enemy fire – not caring. If he is dead, it's only right that I follow.

Patrick whispers "Smith. You awake?" But I can't breathe, let alone speak. He gets out of bed and checks me. Puts his hand on my chest as if I was the one who needed saving. "Smith?"

I turn my head to look at him. His blue eyes are grey in the half-light. Colourless. Like a world without Geoff.

He leans very close, keeps his voice low. "You want me to get into the bunk with yer?"

I shake my head. "Don't risk it. Don't risk yourself, Patrick."

13th Thursday – We lost tonnage during the night. Easier to say like that. Tonnage. When really, it was ships and men. It was death. Duty and bells force me out of bed. And when I go on deck – I see a flock of dive bombers. I'm too numb to care. They might as well be seagulls.

Chapter Twenty-nine

Anne

Anne heard the screech of brakes and the slam of a car door. She got up and looked through the taped windows to see Ralph Redcliffe running towards the front door. She made sure her jacket was buttoned up over her baby bump and went to meet him.

Grabbing her elbow he steered her inside. "I need to speak with you alone. None of this front office shit."

Anne flinched. He was normally so polite, but today he was not in the mood for pleasantries. "Of course. Come through."

She led him to a private sitting room, and he banged the door shut. "Where's Cathy?"

"In Southwold. Isn't she?" Anne's heart started to beat a bit faster. Making her feel slightly giddy.

"No. Don't lie to me. She telephoned you. There's a record of the call."

"Ralph. You're scaring me." Anne put a hand on her chest. "It was just a friendly call..." She groped for the arm of a chair and sat down. She gestured that he should sit too, but he preferred to pace up and down. Caged lion style.

"What did you talk about?"

Men and birth control. "I don't think I can discuss that, I'm afraid. It was a private conversation."

Ralph made a bitter facial grimace. "You can talk to the military police if you won't talk to me."

Anne let out a sharp breath and gave way. "Oh, for goodness sake. She told me about her new boyfriend."

"On HMS *Tilbury*." He seemed to think he was stating a fact.

Honestly, the man didn't know what he was talking about. "No. He's stationed at Long Sands. He's a scientist, I believe."

Ralph looked like he was trying to do a complicated math problem in his head. "She's writing to a sailor on the destroyer, *Tilbury*. I telephoned the Wren's Nest this morning and they searched her room for me. There were letters from him."

Anne shook her head. What a muddle poor Cathy was in. "You should have left her here with *me*, Ralph. Why didn't you leave her here with me?"

"You don't understand. I *had* to get her away from here. I had to get her away from the harbour."

Anne looked at him blankly. "She was good at harbour work. She loved it."

Through gritted teeth, he spoke. "The 'covert' operation to take a French port. We've been as discreet as we could, but the harbour is full of ships and troops. Don't you see? There is a serious threat of bombardment..."

In all the fuss, Anne put her hand protectively over her belly. Ralph noticed and stared at her – the light dawned – and he raised his eyes to heaven. "Oh. *God*. Petticoats in the Navy."

Anne glanced away. It was instant dismissal once a woman was found to be four months pregnant. She was more like five.

Then – at the worst possible moment – there was a knock at the door, and Mavis appeared. Ralph turned and shouted – "Not now!" – making the poor girl jump.

Anne thought the girl was going to burst into tears. She felt protective of her. "Is it urgent, Mavis?"

"Y-yes. The Master of Arms is on the front steps. And Mrs. Bancroft-Smythe."

Ralph went pale as Cathy's mother swept in – accompanied by the Master of Arms from the Admiralty buildings in Portsmouth. The feather on Harriet's hat pointed – like an accusing finger – at whomever she was facing. She turned to Ralph. "You *promised* me she would be kept safe."

And Ralph, face drawn and tight, said – "Ah – Harriet – you've heard."

"Why didn't you come and tell me?" Mrs Bancroft-Smythe's lower lip trembled. "Ralph. Are you aware that the *Eagle* is lost?"

Anne felt a wave of sorrow. First the carrier, *Fortunate*. Now *Eagle*. Cathy's brother was on board that ship. And how many men were on the carrier *Eagle* – was it a thousand?

Ralph passed a hand over his face, and nodded. "Harriet. If it's any comfort – I think she's on *Tilbury*."

Harriet looked at him, in horror. "*What*? What do you mean? My daughter is on a warship?"

And Ralph went pale, like he was about to faint. "Well...I thought you knew...about this possibility?"

He and the Master at Arms exchanged glances. *Apparently not.*

Harriet shook her head, and said she didn't. "I came to Portsmouth yesterday to say farewell to my husband. He's taking fifteen hundred troops across the channel. This morning they told me my son's ship was lost, and not half an hour later the Admiralty informs me that my *daughter* is missing."

Anne looked at this mother of two headstrong children and felt a wave of empathy for her. "I'll help you find her, Mrs Bancroft-Smythe. We must sort all this out. Welcome to HMS *Resilient*."

Cathy's mother looked at Anne gratefully. Then she turned to Ralph. "You'd better tell me where the ship *Tilbury* is going."

Guy

Guy had considered all his options over the last few days and come to only one conclusion. He must protect Malta. Because even if *Tilbury* got through – what hope was there for Cathy if the enemy chose this moment to take the battered island? He would send one message and pray to anyone who might be listening that it would be his first and last. He was not a spy – he was a scientist. He hated the subterfuge, the changing sides, the lies and the endless betrayals. The shifting scales of power that defined how he must live, and to whom he must swear his allegiance.

Just let me love Cathy.

All he had to do was jam the receivers for a few short minutes – he could write an incident report in the morning. Decision time. Choose a frequency. Choose a destination. He stared at the morse transmitter on his desk. It would be the work of only a few moments to rig that up so it was functional... his fingers rested on it. Thinking.

Do or die? Take a risk. Tap out a message in morse... and hope his betrayal would never be discovered?

No. Learn fast. Do it differently.

A piece of his own scientific research – a gift horse – something they'd accept and be pleased with. An attractive wrapping for the real message inside. Give them something of value, so the enemy would believe him. Then slip in the false intelligence, the information that might save Malta. The art of war – like the magician's show – is all about misdirection. So, he wrote down some key things from the work he'd been doing. Precious to him, but he gave them. It was like sharing part of his soul – but it was necessary. All that mattered, all that had ever mattered, was Cathy. He knew the Italians had become disenchanted with their alliance with Hitler. It wouldn't take much to persuade them. *Malta is stronger than you think... Malta is well defended.*

No – even that strategy might end in his execution.

What would Cathy do? Cathy understood the Navy, she knew how it ticked. What would she do? She'd be blunt. She'd say go to the top. Pull rank – but only when you have to – otherwise you lose the trust of the men. Okay, he'd go to the top. He'd tell them truth. And maybe they would help him. Because for all its flaws, the Navy always had a system for dealing with *everything*. A system you could trust.

He sent word to the War Office. Secret telephone number – Ralph warned him the time might come. He got through and said he had a contact in Ipswich.

Julius

"Admiral – we'll find her and bring her back."

The Admiral stood on the bridge of his ship. Staring out at the rippled waters of the Solent. He was within days of new sailing orders for Dieppe – on a mission that he did not fully support, but had to participate in. The mission had been aborted once already and the troops sent home – on account of the wretched weather. In front of him was an apologetic naval officer – cap in hand. Who'd just given him the news about his daughter.

Julius made a dismissive sound. "Don't be ridiculous. The Admiralty can hardly ask the convoy to turn around and come back to port because of one foolish girl, can they? Let's be realistic."

The officer nodded respectfully. "Very good. Sir. Nevertheless – the highest authorities have been informed."

Julius looked at him with a measure of impatience. "And what does that mean – you've sent a telegram to First Lord of the Admiralty, have you? Or contacted Mr Churchill, in Russia? I'm sure they've got better things to do than worry about my wayward daughter..."

Julius put a hand up to his eyes. He felt too old for this... The news of the *Eagle* was fresh, and there was no news yet of Geoffrey. And now *this*. He shook his head. He'd never imagined this war might take his lovely daughter.

There was a beautiful view out to sea from the bridge. The glittering sea – the big empty sky.

Except – maybe the sky wasn't empty. A speck far, far away in the distance. But gradually getting closer, and louder. Julius lifted his binoculars up to his eyes.

"Good God," he breathed. There were dive bombers heading for Portsmouth.

Even a man on the verge of retirement can move fast when he needs to. He sounded the alarm and it was all hands on deck. Everyone to their action stations.

The scream as the bombs fell. The silence and then the distant "crump" as they exploded. Messages flashed to and fro – things were going crazy on the ships at anchor. *Do we need to move out? Should we see if we can get the ships away and out into the deeper water?* Valuable anchorages could be lost, if a warship was sunk in harbour.

Stunned shock as they heard two warships intended for the Dieppe raid had been hit. Damaged and rendered useless, but not yet sunk.

Would they circle back and finish the ships off, people asked? No – they'd flown on – to drop their lethal cargo on civilian targets...

Chapter Thirty

Anne

Anne was stocktaking in the Wrennery linen cupboard when the siren sounded. Pillow slips, single sheets, quilts and bedspreads – all had to be counted and recorded neatly before anything new could be ordered. The girls rarely stole anything, even with all the shortages, but things did seem to get ripped or ruined from time to time. Apparently – before she arrived – they'd held a Roman toga party. That explained some of the damage – but how did they get *grass stains* on the bed linen?

But the wail of the siren was harsh and couldn't be ignored. Portsmouth had received plenty of punishment in '40 and '41 so it couldn't be taken lightly. A daytime raid too – not even the dark anonymity of a night bombing. And after what Ralph had said...

Anne set down her clipboard, went to the ship's bell that hung outside what used to be Ralph's office – she rang it vigorously two or three times to indicate action stations. Then she walked downstairs to supervise the girls hurrying towards the bomb shelter in the basement.

The noise outside was a warning in itself. Aircraft scream as they dive, and bombs scream too. The 'crump' sounds kept getting closer. The Wrennery shook, the light fittings jingled, the marble bust jittered on its stand.

I should have wrapped that in sacking and put it down in the basement.

Another searing screaming sound. Like a firework screaming past. Too close, thought Anne. That one was much too close for comfort. Girls came running in from the Nissen Huts to see what was wrong – when they should have been running to the shelter. Anne yelled at them with all the fury of a sergeant major.

They felt a powerful impact as the first bomb fell and exploded in their street – or maybe it was on the parade ground. It almost knocked her off their feet. And then she heard the second one screaming. No time to get to the basement now, so Anne ran through the kitchen, where she saw someone. "Have we got everyone out? *Linda* – what are you doing?"

"I left my satchel in the scullery, Mrs Tavistock – it has messages in it."

"Leave them," Anne ordered. "Get downstairs."

There was an impact – a sharp shudder that resonated inside the house – but it was smaller. No crump. Then everything went quiet. Anne looked up. "It's alright –I think it must have missed us."

It was Linda who heard the noise. The faint sound – falsely reassuring – a lot like an alarm clock before it rings. A harmless sound – of ticking.

And Linda remembered. *It's a ticker.* Toby said ticking was the last thing you'd hear if you didn't run.

She screamed a warning. "Anne. Get out. Now!"

Linda

Linda had tried to run. She'd tried to heed Toby's warning. But she'd panicked, not knowing if she had time. The ticking stopped. She fell to her knees and hoped to get under the table.

Time ran out. The blast reverberated, full and final.

Chapter Thirty-one
Cathy

Diary of a ship's boy. On board HMS Tilbury...

I am comforted by nothing. Only the cold grey steel of the guns. They say I'm nimble with loading the cartridges. I clip the belts on, one after another. I keep feeding the guns. They are always hungry. Black puffs of high explosive in the air, like smudges of black mascara on a perfect blue sky.

The sea stretches to the far horizon, grey and glittering. I see other ships lying low and dark in the water. Each morning we count which ships survived the night. Every day, there are less. We identify the survivors from their funnels – some are angled rakishly back. They are the merchant ships. The Navy ones have large gun turrets and camouflage paint. But Navy and merchantmen alike all have their guns angled up towards the sky.

Sardinia is now due North – this is the worst and most dangerous stretch. A man in a white square-neck tunic lowers his binoculars, points and shouts – "Hostile, hostile!"

The warning bell sounds and the men come running. They snatch a flak vest, a tin hat, but only if there's time...and I feed the ammunition into the clip. The gun carriage swings round smooth and steady. Our gun crew pummels the sky.

We are so close to enemy occupied territory. If I was the enemy – what wouldn't I have given to take Malta – and put an end to all this. Take Malta and you get control of the Mediterranean Sea and block the route to North Africa.

The men swarm up the steps to the highest guns and in seconds I hear them fire. The retort shakes the steel. Metal panels that seemed solid in port are flimsy now under fire – they are like bits of frail cardboard that will not offer me or my fellow ratings any real protection from enemy fire. Our eight-gun rig turns slowly – echoing the pathway in the sky of the warplanes sent to kill us. Alternate barrels fire. We pound the sky with shells, relentless, a factory of death in full swing. The plumes of explosion in the sky look like a thousand tiny parachutes fluttering to safety – when in reality they are nothing of the kind.

They give us a protective storm of fire – through which the Stukas and Savoias will not dare to fly. The bombs drop to the right and to the left of us. A tall plume of water rose beside me and with it a deafening blast. The column of water that went up was a salty grey and white – like breakers and seawater mixed with high explosive. The water splatters the deck – soaking us all – every deckhand, every man in the gun crew. As the water drenched me, I flinched but I did not scream.

Radio man

There was a lull in the fighting. The radio man on board ship passed the message he'd just received to his supervisor, as if he needed someone more experienced to interpret the true meaning of the innocuous batches of letters. "WRN missing. Believed to have boarded Tilbury. Confirm."

They both looked at each other. Perplexed. "What?"

One of them shrugged, rubbed his chin and laughed.

The older man scanned the message again, as if it might hold more clues if he read it a second time. No. Still inexplicable. Checked the call sign of the sender. It all checked out.

He handed it back. "Better take it up to the bridge then."

The radio man took it to the captain, who was drinking coffee on the bridge. He took the paper in his left hand, read it, gave a careless laugh, and handed it back to the messenger. "Some kind of joke? Of course I don't have a Wren on my ship."

The radio man looked serious. "It's from the military police, sir."

Which was sobering. A sip of coffee. A glance at the smoke on the horizon.

Another man looked up – a young officer – studying charts. With a guilty face. "Captain... the day *Eagle* was sunk...I thought I saw something. Or rather some*one*. Perhaps I should have voiced my concerns earlier..."

"Indeed you should." The captain said. Then he looked at the radio man who had brought the message. "Ask for more information. Have they got a name?"

It only took a about fifteen minutes before they had their answer.

The messenger returned. He drew his commander aside and told him in a whisper.

The captain went white. *Catherine Bancroft-Smythe*. He hadn't stood by the gate and let her on the ship, that had been another man's decision. But he knew who'd be held responsible. Ultimately every action taken on board a ship of war came back to the man in command. He shook his head. He stared at the messenger, blank and pale. His career was down the gash chute. "They'll keelhaul me."

He didn't even sound as if he was joking.

But no time for that. The cry came down from the men on watch. More dive bombers were coming towards them.

Linda

Linda's eyes were open. But there was no light. She was in darkness.

She tried to shift position, but she was in a confined space. *But where?* Under her bed, in her cabin upstairs? No, she remembered – she was in the galley – with Anne. When their world shook and she knew the house was hit. They were both in the kitchen. She'd screamed and Anne had run – Anne, who was having a baby.

It was dark. The world had gone dark, her mouth was choked with dust, and Linda couldn't see a thing. She blinked and wondered if she was blind. She reached up above her head – finger nails clawing at the debris above her. Yes – a flat surface above her – but angled. It had taken some of the weight.

But Anne? There wasn't a table in the scullery. Was *she* lying in the dark under a pile of rubble?

Chapter Thirty-two

Cathy

The day smoked with the smell of burning ships. They lost more of the merchant ships – one after another. They were only lightly armed and made easy targets. One of them exploded in a ball of flame – went up like a tinderbox because of the petrol she carried – cans and cans of it, lashed to her deck. Every cargo was like that – a mixed load of splintery wooden crates, food, supplies – side by side with the flammable stuff. Packed to the gunwales like a cheaply-made firework.

The Navy lost ships too. Cathy watched in dismay as another destroyer went plummeting through the darkening water – and then a cruiser was so badly damaged it would probably have to be scuttled so it wouldn't fall into the hands of the enemy.

We're being picked off, one by one. Like tin ducks in a fairground.

She did the only thing she could do. She fed the ammunition into the trays for the direction crew on the guns. A hail of spent cartridges shimmered down onto the deck. The eight-gun rig on its swivelling circular platform swung round to follow the flight path of the enemy aircraft. The noise was deafening as multiple barrels fired in constant pulsing movement.

"Keep loading, Smith." Patrick yelled at her. His face glistened with sweat from both tension and the hard work of keeping the guns firing.

In a lull in the fighting, Patrick stared blankly at the spaces left by the merchant ships they'd been sent to defend. Saddened, he watched what was left of the convoy go by. The damaged ones didn't look much better. He shook his head in despair, seeing the torpedo damage on the hull of the big fuel tanker – the oiler – Ohio. "She won't see Gib again, or sail into Valetta harbour. *Fuck it,* that's what we came for."

Cathy wiped the sweat from her brow and knew there was nothing she could say to comfort him. The odds were stacked high against them. How could they succeed when previous convoys had failed? She could only stand by his side, and work.

Tilbury was badly damaged too. The second gun turret was smoking. Crippled now like the other. The men inside – she didn't want to think about their fate – in that hot metal trap full of high explosives. Around them, huge plumes of water and smoke went up as the bombs fell and exploded in the sea beside them.

She waited in dread for the one blast that could come at any moment: the direct hit. The one that pierced the armoured deck and lit up the ship. The one that turned their floating home into a furnace. *When it comes, we will run through flames and leap into the sea. The ship will roll like the Eagle did, and we will know that we've only got minutes.*

The only thing she could do was feed the guns. Keep sending up that defensive hail of fire. Defend the ship.

A tap on her shoulder. "You're wanted on the bridge, Miss."

She turned in disbelief. Hearing that word – *Miss*. She was rumbled, and they'd sent a bloody midshipman to fetch her. She sighed. They'd give her a right dressing down, on the bridge. "Now?"

He nodded. "Too dangerous for you out here."

This is it. They know. She cursed and looked at the sky – it was filled with exploding shellfire. It wasn't going to get *less* dangerous if the ammunition trays were empty. Who would load them while she was gone?

She handed the belt of ammunition to the midshipman. "Alright. Load that then – while I report to the bridge."

He didn't of course. He looked at her like she was mad and let it fall back into the ready-use locker. He wasn't going to dirty his hands with that task – even if his ship sank from underneath him.

The captain of the gun crew – in tin hat and flash protection – looked angry seeing her walk away from her post. He called after her. "Smith? Where are you *going*?"

"Called to the bridge, Sir."

He shrugged and let her go. She looked up and saw the officers of the watch in a bunch on the bridge. Maybe five or six of them. All pointing at the sky and staring upwards.

Spread out, she thought. It's too dangerous

They were pointing at a swarm of incoming aircraft. She saw too, the moment when they realized they were in danger. The aircraft in formation scattered like a flock of sparrows over the ship, but not before they'd dropped their tiny black specks of destruction. *Anti-personnel bombs.* Falling, falling.

Not specks anymore. They were the size of metal dustbins – and full of explosives.

"Take cover!" she yelled.

The bombs came screaming down. The enemy aircraft had been flying too high for accuracy. But they'd dropped plenty enough for some to find their mark. They showered down over a wide area – some exploding as they hit the sea – but others raining down on the deck of the ship.

A blast – a close one, knocked her sideways. Cathy was thrown against the superstructure. As the bellow of sound dissipated, she touched the metal wall beside her. Wanting something firm, something solid, to tell her she was still alive and all was as it should be. But it was not...

Looking up – she saw the blast had decimated the bridge. There was twisted metal where the men had been standing. The officers had scattered. She wasn't sure who had escaped and who had been injured. But two of them lay dead or dying on the deck below the one where they'd been standing. She gasped in horror at the sight of the carnage. A man writhing in pain with a leg blown off. *Oh, God,* she murmured, and instinctively she gripped a steel wire near to where she stood to steady herself. A terrible mistake – it was hot from the fires that burned on deck – and she instantly recoiled with a red burn mark across her palm. Pain shot through her and she faltered, eyes smarting.

Jet black smoke streamed from the funnel stacks of the ship beside Tilbury. The other ship was making smoke to try and screen the merchantmen. A caustic cloud of thick black smoke came across the water that made her eyes sting so badly she could hardly see.

The engine room lads must be killing themselves. And they were in such mortal danger. For them – no warning if we get hit – and for them – no mercy either, as the seawater meets the heat... And steam forms. And men die. *We are in Dante's fiery hell,* she thought, ironically.

She closed her eyes in pain from the burn, wondering if she would live to write another page in her diary...

The smoke is so dense it feels like night – but above I see the crow's nest outlined against the sky – and brighter still – pellets of golden light crossing the sky in an upward path to bring down the hostile aircraft.

This was a day to remember, alright. This was a day to remember.

Only then did she recall that they wanted her on the bridge. Looking up, she saw that the metal steps leading up there from the deck where she stood, were now gone. She could, of course, find another way. But she could, of course, turn back and return to her post. Mission aborted.

She saw the harried face of a young officer running through the flames towards her. Fresh-faced like her brother, and lost now that command on the bridge was shattered. He yelled the bad news, "There are more coming. More dive bombers."

"What have we got?" – she yelled. "What firepower?"

He shook his head. "I don't know."

His world had fallen apart when his commanding officer fell. He looked at her. Wanting some help. She stared straight back at him. And did not try to hide her voice, her accent. She yelled in the way her father would have yelled. "Defend her – Defend your ship. All available guns must keep firing."

A strange moment. She was a teenage boy to him. He was her superior in every way except the one that mattered. He stared at her, shock-still that she had even spoken. "What?"

"All available guns *must* keep firing."

He looked at her like she was talking another language, but shaking he shouted some orders. The only other surviving officer came out of the superstructure onto what was left of the bridge. Nodded in approval when he heard that orders for the gunners had been given. "Good man."

Three enemy warplanes swept in from the east and the three of them looked wordlessly at them and knew they had almost nothing to offer in defence.

He shook his head. "Defences are shattered."

It was true. One of the big gun turrets was on fire – the other one jammed, and pointing the wrong way.

"We've got the other eight-gun, sir. Permission to get it operational?" She addressed herself to the man who had been in the superstructure. She didn't wait, but she told herself as she ran that he had said '*permission granted*.'

She leapt the railing rather than use the companionway. Vaulted like an athlete. She ran through the smoke until she encountered splintered metal in her way and then she had to climb and crawl. She cut her hand and tore her tunic, but she arrived at the eight-gun, climbed into the swivel platform and pushed the dead sailor in front of the gun sight out of the way. His body slumped over the railing.

She was used to putting the cartridge belts into the clip, she could do that in her sleep, but the other tasks were painfully slow. She turned the handle to get it into position, struggling because a gun like that needed a team of three men to operate effectively. Then she saw the old sailor who had guessed her secret and almost had a fight with Patrick. His leg was bleeding through the fabric of his uniform but he limped forward to help her.

"Come on," she breathed, winding the double handle that raised the gun barrels. She saw the trio of hostile planes entering the charmed circle of the gunsight.

Fire where he will be, not where he is now.

She eyed the first one with a necessary hatred. She pushed and held the trigger button. Jammed her thumb hard into the metal tube to keep the damn thing firing. She sent up a firestorm of flak. "Come on you little silver fucker, fly into that."

Her skin shone with sweat and her red hair glinted as she lit up the sky, brighter than sunlight.

A fiery swirl of smoke surrounded her, but she fired like a demon possessed. A piercing war-cry left her soul and reached the sky, as the first shells exploded above her.

The first plane wheeled away, changing course before her eyes. Smoking, it lost altitude and cartwheeled into the sea. The second was harder, her hands hurt with holding the handle to make the guns pulsate and keep firing, firing, firing. She sent up such a storm of flak that she knew some of it would find her mark. And sure enough the aircraft spluttered – and its path changed – it let out a trail of smoke – it fell and fell – and the danger fell away and they were safe ... and someone's son fell into the sea.

The last of the three planes came in for its death swoop upon her. She eyed it through the gunsight. "Yes. Come on. Fly straight at me, you misguided bastard."

It seemed to hear her, the silver Savoia, and like a moth to a candle it came closer and closer, til it was huge and the air shuddered with the sound. Glancing down, she saw the swarming men below the gun deck, the officers, the ratings, the galley cooks, and the others. *All my brothers.* They are *all* my brothers. She never faltered. She fired and fired. As the aircraft roared in, she knew this was the end. She might not succeed but she would try...

She sent up streams of explosive shells. Black puffs of smoke filled the sky, though her eyes were smarting so bad she could hardly see them. The spent shell cases tumbled out in front of the gun. A stream of jingling, glinting brass falling over the side of the gun carriage and shimmering onto the deck below. Eight barrels. All firing. Pounding the sky. A hundred and twenty rounds per minute.

Exhilaration came. Flooded her like hot brandy. What a way to die, she thought, what a way to die.

Patrick

Patrick heard her voice, shouting orders, high and clear. A girl's voice shouting an Admiral's orders. He knew who she was – he'd worked it out as he lay on his bunk one night, with his hands folded behind his head. That joke she'd made about being an Admiral's daughter. She'd pretended she was making a joke, but he'd lain there in the dark, thinking, and his eyes went round when he realized. Her initials, that she'd made him use when he wrote to her at HMS Long Sands. He knew. And she had come to *him*, and asked for his help, to make her stand, to fight her fight, like any sailor.

He stood on the deck now, looking up at her through the smoke of battle. She was a sight to see. Yelling through the flames – her pale white skin, her red hair glinting like her eyes, fearless in the demon heat. Her tunic – torn from her right shoulder, fabric flapped down, revealing one small white breast, like Britannia. She fired mercilessly into the sky. A lion cub – with a fighting spirit – a force of fire and fury. She was the fight, alright. The heat and the fight. Dressed in the colours of war. Bright orange flame, flickering black smoke, and beyond her, the undulating waves of the turquoise sea. The smoke swirled around her – like a cloak around a warrior on a shining gold coin, plucked from the depths of the ocean.

He gazed and caught his breath. Watching her firing rounds of ammunition into the sky. Power, guts, and resolve, hidden in soft-skinned womanhood. He'd never seen a man half so driven. Born leader, that girl. And who wouldn't follow someone like that? Someone who'd stand beside you, do the dirty work with you, cop the flak, take the heat, every step of the way. He'd follow her through the gates of hell if she asked him to.

But she needed his help, she couldn't do it alone. She was fighting to save the ship and he could see from the steel in her eyes that she'd die trying if she had to. Without hesitation he ran to help her. He filled the ammunition trays until the gun-layer copped it. Then, he took the dead man's place. Shoved the limp body away, and stood behind the winding levers. She turned to see what he was doing. Turned her shining eyes on him, and her lips made the shape of his name.

He yelled above the noise. "Keep firing, Cathy. I'll lay for you. Whatever you do, keep firing."

The sky above them darkened. The air screamed with sound. Staccato shots tore along the metal deck, every bullet closer. Every single one.

Anne

Anne was sitting inside the cab of a lorry, parked in the road outside the Wrennery. They'd wrapped her in a blanket because she was shivering, even though it was August. But even in that state she was trying to do her job. She was holding a stub of a pencil, making a list of who was there and who wasn't – from memory. It was a strange thought that all the meticulously kept records she'd worked on these past few months were now buried under a heap of bricks, or blowing down the street, or fueling the clouds of white and grey smoke coming from the rubble. The firemen trained water on the wrecked building, hoping to prevent a serious fire from spreading.

A cry went up. They thought they'd found a girl when the decorative hem of her dress was seen – sticking out from under the debris. But they realized their mistake as Delia's party dress was dragged from the rubble.

Anne sat in the vehicle, tapping the end of the pencil they'd found for her. The boat crew girls were at the harbour. They'd be alright. Ironic that Ralph had been so scared for Cathy that he'd moved her, when in the event it was the Wrennery that was hit. She believed that most of the girls in the signaling class had got into the shelter safely – but the entrance to that would have to be dug out to release them. The word from the men digging was that they could hear singing coming from down there, so she could assume that for now – they were alive and keeping their spirits up until they could be rescued. Mavis could not be accounted for – that was more of a worry – she would've been in or around the kitchen. Delia was in the second Nissen hut working on her signaling. Binky? Was she with Delia? No, she was out at Lee – working with the ground crew...thank goodness. But what about Linda?

With a pang, Anne realized that even though Linda was the last person she spoke to – the girl was missing.

While the men worked to see if they could recover any more of the Wrens – living or dead. Anne took a break, now that the list was finished. She sat shaking in the car with a thermos flask, she couldn't drink, she couldn't talk. She just sat with the cup in her hands, staring into space, with a blanket around her. Penelope leaned in and told them they were digging in what had been the kitchen now. She said they were looking for Linda.

"Penelope," Anne whispered. Stricken. The light was fading now, the sun was low.

"What is it, dear?"

"I haven't felt the child move."

Penelope's face clouded with concern. "For how long?"

"Since the explosion."

"You must stop what you're doing here, and go and seek medical attention."

Anne shook her head. Not wanting to face it. "Later."

Mavis was found about an hour after that. She'd been killed by the blast – probably instantaneously. Anne took the news as stoically as she could – but it seemed so unfair. Mavis was the nicest, kindest girl you could have met. She was eighteen years old. She'd never had a boyfriend – save that brief encounter with the Canadian soldier who asked her for a dance. Poor lad – destined for the beaches of France, no doubt. She was glad those two had met and been happy for a time. Even if it was just for a few moments. She wished Mavis had got a bit more of life than that, though. Anne had hoped to get Mavis a chance to try for something beyond the domestic duties she'd been given. The day they did the armoury training – she'd shown herself to be capable. And now, no more. No more chances. No more dances. Nothing.

Anne shook her head in sadness. "She mended my veil... for my wedding." She'd been so kind about that. So encouraging. She was a wonderful cook, a charming helpful girl. It seemed so sad that she should die while others were alive and kicking.

Kicking. The baby wasn't kicking.

Penelope leaned into the cab again. "Anne. The ambulance is waiting."

"Who for?"

"You."

Chapter Thirty-three

Officer, HMS Tilbury

The Acting Commanding Officer spoke low to one of the hands in the steel doorway of the gun deck. "Where is 'Smith' now?"

"The surgeon's got him, sir. He's cutting the clothing off him."

A look passed between the two men. "Him? Don't give me that. Everybody knew, didn't they?"

But the men, when questioned one by one, all told the same story. Smith was a sailor, same as them. "He was good at his work, sir. He had a good pair of sea legs. Played Uckers. Swore like the proverbial. He cleaned a gun as good as anyone." Every one spoke the same way. "He knew the Admiralty instructions back to front, sir. Quoted them like the bible. Obviously served on a ship before..."

The officer rubbed a forehead stained with soot. The Admiralty instructions were no help at all at a time like this. Nothing in the big lead book covered *this* eventuality. He stared at the sailor standing before him now. "You couldn't have believed, though. I mean ...you saw her."

That white translucent skin. That small form, laid on a stretcher. One slender arm hanging down, hand lifeless.

But nobody had wanted to admit, or get themselves into trouble. No one told the bridge. It was a fo'c'stle secret.

Under pressure, one rating finally gave his explanation. "We sort of knew, sir. But she became one of us, part of the crew. And we thought what she did was courageous."

The officer nodded. "Hmm. Stupid – but courageous."

Cathy's letter

In the grounds of the Wrennery, men, women and children worked to release the survivors from under the rubble. They scrabbled through the dirt to find them, digging with their bare hands if they had to. The letter that Cathy had slipped into Linda's messenger bag the day she left lay undiscovered. The bag itself – ripped and dirty – lay discarded where it had been pulled from under the wreckage. The metal clasp had broken, spilling the contents. The edges of the hand-written letter fluttered in the wind.

Dear Linda,

I'm sorry to burden you with this – my last message – but I know I can trust you. People will be wondering why I did such a damn fool thing, and they deserve some answers. I know I can rely on you to deliver this, even if it's painful, even if it's difficult, and even if you don't want to.

Truth is, I *had* to do it. I did it for the people I love, and I felt I had no choice. I loved Geoff and wanted to keep him safe always. I loved Guy and wanted him to continue his wonderful work for the war effort. Maybe I thought he'd be better off without me – troublesome spirit that I am – and that's why I resisted him so long. But when I realized I was truly in love with him, I knew that if it were not for the war I would devote my whole life to him – and in a sense that is what I am doing now. I'm giving my life for his. I hope he'll forgive me. I hope he'll flourish in a time of peace when this war is over.

To fight alongside my brother is my birth right as my father's daughter. I loved my father and I wanted to prove myself to him. I was not 'just a girl'. I was as good as my brother. I loved my mother too and wanted to show her what true heroism looks like. This convoy is vitally important and I am fully aware of the danger. The odds are so unfavourable that no young sailor should ever have to face them.

Ralph – you said I had to keep an eye on Rawton for you. I did, and it is time for him to be relieved of his command. Yes, it is audacious of me to say that. But although much has been achieved by the people at HMS Long Sands, a lot has not been achieved too. There is a pettiness and a spitefulness about him that is not helping to win the war. If you value me as a person, and not just a pretty face, you will take this as an important message from one strategist to another – and you will heed my advice.

Tell Anne I am both glad and sorry. Glad she had the courage to say yes when Dicky Tavistock asked her to marry him. Sorry she had to face more heartache. I only hope her little baby will bring her lots of happiness and be a comfort to her. She said don't talk about Dicky in the past tense, so for her sake I won't. Instead, I will address my last message to him, as if he could still hear me. Dicky, fly home if you can. Fly home over the white cliffs of Dover and into our lives again... But of course, I'm a realist, I know that many of our pilots, our sailors, and our soldiers will never come back, and *we must not send them* unless we are prepared to face the guilt that goes with that decision, the sadness of their loss, and the finality of their sacrifice.

Love to you all,

Cathy.

The ink on the paper seemed to fade from black to brown as the heat beneath it took hold. The rubble smoked and threatened to flicker into flame. The heartfelt words would be lost. The rough work-boots of a workman trudged past – a man carrying a bucket of spoil from the area where they were digging. His feet disturbed the wreckage, dislodging the bag and its contents.

The fragile message blew away in a breath of wind. Undelivered.

Captain, HMS Tilbury

Two men stood in the doorway of the sick bay. The shrouded shape lay on the bed, motionless and small.

"How is ...the patient?" said the officer in command. Acting Captain, since the others were dead.

"Lost a lot of blood," the ship's surgeon told him, "...and unresponsive."

"But still alive?"

"Barely."

Looking past the surgeon and through to the patient, the officer experienced a wave of compassion. "Do you have what you need?"

"Yes," the surgeon said heavily, still blocking the doorway. He looked tired and drawn. "I appealed for donors, blood type O, and a hundred and twenty-eight men came forward." He gestured the hallway, empty now – "They were all lined up along here with their sleeves rolled up."

The officer smiled. "Smith is well-liked. A folk hero in their minds. You must do everything possible to save her."

❖❖❖

The men were in their mess hall, grabbing a meal now the fighting had died down. The hollows in their metal trays had food in them – lumps of potato, salty stew and thick gravy – and they hunched over these with spoons and forks in their hands, downing mouthfuls as if they hadn't eaten for a week. The First Officer came in and stood at the head of the long table. "Stay easy," he ordered.

He was greeted with questioning faces and several asked – "Any news, sir?"

"Officer Bolton has died," he said. Knowing perfectly well they didn't care about Officer Bolton. But they murmured the right sentiments and some crossed themselves. "God rest his soul. But what about Smith, sir?"

When he told them that Smith might not live, they were silent for several minutes. Some men pushed their mess trays away, no longer hungry. Others glanced at each other. Some shook their heads and refused to believe it. "Where there's life there's hope, sir, surely?"

But the officer said he was pessimistic. She was in a death-like slumber, her system shocked from loss of blood and from the impact of the injury.

One sailor looked up from his dinner. "Can we go and say goodbye?"

But that was forbidden. The bridge thought it best not to turn this into a circus. Fraternization was not permitted. No one was allowed near her. No one could hold her hand or speak soft words, or send any message to her.

That's harsh, they said. It made the men depressed. Listless.

One rating started it, saying soft like an epitaph. "God rest Smith's soul, I say. Rule Britannia."

They all nodded. Someone whistled a strain from the chorus of the old song. A thin sound, but defiant. Rule Britannia, for that is what she had been to them. Their warrior girl. Their Britannia. If only Smith would arise – arise like the seafarers of the golden days from out of the deep blue sea – the azure main – they called it. All the men at the scarred old mess table wished so much that she would wake, they started singing it for her. And others soon joined in. "Come on boys. Sing it for her. Give her some hope. Sing it loud enough to wake her from the dead. Tell her we're with her."

Defying the ban on all communication – and on unauthorized singing – they banged on metal walls, stamped on the floor, thumped on their mess table with fists, tin cups, trays and spoons, and sang *Rule Britannia*.

They sang to wake their Britannia from a deep, deep sleep. *Wake up, Britannia.*

Chapter Thirty-four

Cathy

The sound reverberated through the metal ship. All the way to the sick bay.

And it worked...

Cathy heard them. Her eyes fluttered open. Her throat was dry from the smoke she'd inhaled. She almost didn't recognize the sound of her own voice when she tried to speak. She nearly gave the ship's surgeon a heart attack when she gripped his hand as he walked by, and said, in a broken whisper – "Why are they singing?"

He had gone to fetch a metal dish and some cotton wool. He began to clean small burns on her lily-white skin. She had not been wearing any flash protection. "They're singing for you, Smith. Because you scored three hits."

She almost closed her eyes in despair. "I didn't get the last one. He got us."

"You did get him – he flew over us but he flamed out too. Crashed into the sea some way astern."

The singing died away. The ship went quiet. She lay looking up at the bulkhead.

He continued sponging antiseptic into her wounds. He looked at her with a mixture of sadness and irritation. "Is it so very wrong of us to want to keep our womenfolk away from all this? This hell, this horror."

She was silent.

"Did you really want to end up like that?" He pointed to the adjacent bed. A man, or rather a body, lay there with a blood-stained sheet over it. Charred fingers visible where the sheet didn't quite cover him.

"Who was that?" she asked.

"First officer Bolton."

"I didn't know him. I wasn't on the bridge."

"You shouldn't have been on the bloody *ship*," said the surgeon. He worked on her, dabbing her wounds with that awful stinging liquid. Face grim. "There's no easy way to say this. But it's possible you're going to lose this leg."

"Oh." A small, hopeless sound. "Are you trying to scare me?"

He looked at her, and seeing the look, she blanched.

Perhaps in response to the pain in her eyes, the surgeon looked down at the leg again, hoping for inspiration. "I'll do my best, but ..."

She was silent, for several long minutes, while the doctor worked on her. Then, making a conscious effort to get the words out, she said – "It doesn't matter. It's not as bad as losing Geoff."

"Who's Geoff?"

"My twin. He was on the *Eagle*."

"Poor bastard."

She closed her eyes, numb with loss, but no tears came. There was something else, too, that she needed to know. "Patrick Clarke? He was with me on the guns. Is he alright?"

The surgeon shook his head.

"What happened?"

"Shrapnel through his neck."

•••

She was too weak to go on deck while the Tilbury's men prepared to bury their shipmates. Even if she hadn't been too weak to stand, she would have been forbidden. But she heard the men moving about the ship and she knew what they were doing. They would shroud the dead in canvas, prepare the boards to lay them on, and find the flags to drape across them. She did not dwell on the idea that she might have been one of them. Lifeless on a board.

She didn't think sailors thought like that. Patrick hadn't.

She could see the moment, in her mind's eye, right before the last Savoia. The shard of metal through his neck, and it was done. His lifeblood spilt on the deck of the ship. His body falling heavily. A red stain spreading on the deck. An open hand that would not hold a rope again, or grip a ship's rail, or trace the shape of a pretty face with infinite gentleness. A life too easily erased. Drenched by a wave or washed away with a bucket of seawater. She closed her eyes and saw him lying there, clothing wet, his sea-blue eyes unfocussed.

From where she lay, she heard the guns fire their salute, when they honoured him and the others who had fallen. She lay and spoke the words her father would say, when he lost good men like that. He'd pick up an old hymnal and read from it, finding words of farewell. "A thousand ages in thy sight, are like an evening gone; Short as the watch that ends the night, before the rising sun."

His watch was short. His day was done. And as she finished saying those words, she heard the men on deck lift the boards and let the dead slide into the sea. Too many brothers. Too many sons.

"Patrick – you were right. It was slaughter."

Anne

"The doctor will be with you in a minute, Mrs Tavistock."

She was alone in an ante-room at the doctor's surgery. She placed her hand on the still small curve. The child inside her didn't stir. The room was furnished sparsely. A desk, a chair, and an examination bed – narrow and hard – where she was sitting. On the wall, a shelf containing some cardboard boxes of supplies. Clean and clinical. Beside her a screen – with a metal frame and a pale green curtain – a classic medic-room colour. The sounds coming from the street included children's laughter. She sat feeling numb. Wondering, wondering. Was tragedy threatening to envelop her again? Had she taken it too much for granted, that her child would live to laugh and run around.

"Please," she said, out loud. "Tell me you're alright. Tell me you're still with me."

Nothing. All was quiet.

She couldn't even cry. She felt too numb. She didn't even want the thought to enter her mind, but it did, of course. *Maybe I'm not going to have a baby, after all.*

She'd have to be practical. People would expect that of her. If the child was gone, she'd still have her work. She could carry on. She'd have to find a new home for her Wrens, organize meals and beds, and there would be so much to do. She could lose herself in the work, in the requisition lists... work had always been her refuge before...before Dicky... before the baby...before the Wrennery was bombed.

But a sob caught in her throat. Could life really be so harsh?

The doctor breezed in and he was cheerful. "Now let's have a little listen." He made her lie back on the examination table, and pulled up her clothing

Chapter Thirty-six

Cathy

Still on board the ship, Cathy lay in the sick bay, and the Navy's bureaucratic machine turned. An officer came to see her in the surgeon's room just after they docked. Although he could see she'd been seriously injured – or perhaps because of that – he was horribly curt with her.

"We've sent word to your father."

"Yes?"

She knew what was coming.

"He finds this whole incident lamentable and embarrassing in the extreme."

Cathy just lay there. *I shot down three enemy planes. I hoped he'd be proud of me.*

"For the sake of his and your brother's career, this incident must not be publicized in any way."

"My father is at the very end of his career and my brother went down with the *Eagle*."

"For the sake of your brother's memory then – which is even more sacred."

More sacred than his life? Cathy wondered. He gave her a single sheet of paper with some legal mutterings on it. She was too weak to read it, even. "What am I promising?"

"That you will never speak publicly about this regrettable incident. It is to be treated like any other official secret."

"Why?"

"Do you want the Royal Navy to be a laughing stock?"

"No. I love the Royal Navy."

Every lock, stock and smoking barrel. Every sailor. Every man, woman and child who ever was a sailor.

"Then you must sign. Catherine, you were *never* at sea."

Numb from the fight, the injury and the loss, she stared at the document he had given her. She was too tired to argue. Too weak from loss of blood, loss of hope and loss of purpose. Guy would hate her forever, and she doubted the Wrens would have her back. Rawton and Redcliffe would probably *both* want her guts for garters.

"I'll sign it," she said slowly. "If you promise to give Patrick Clarke the highest honour you can give."

The man nodded. He amended the form by hand – and she signed it. She gave the officer his precious bit of paper and he went away a happier man. Cathy lay back – pale with exhaustion. She had done what was expected of her. She had done her duty.

◆◆◆

Most of the naval escort peeled away before the last survivors sailed into Malta. The tanker – Ohio – limped into port with two ships on either side like a pair of crutches. The tanker was so badly damaged it was a miracle she was still afloat. Low and broken in the water, she was nothing like the fine ship that had set out on this mission. She was only fit to be scuttled. But she still carried the fuel that Malta so desperately needed to survive a little bit longer. The *Tilbury* followed her. All the way into the battle-scarred harbour where people lined the wharves to welcome them.

From her bed in the sick bay, Cathy heard the cheers as they came into the Grand Harbour at Valetta. The two ratings who came to carry her off the ship were under orders not to speak to her. But one of them gave her a wink. As her stretcher was carried down the gangway and onto the shore, people reached out to touch her hand. A hero's welcome. Her small sacrifice was nothing in the scheme of things – it was part of a much greater whole. The harbour erupted with cheers and people threw flowers. Faces beamed with smiles. Pretty girls waved. *Patrick would have loved this.*

Malta was battered and broken, but Valetta was still a city of gold. The Opera House was a pile of rubble. Many houses completely destroyed. The buildings that remained were battle-scarred, chipped and marked – every one of them. Their smooth colonnades had chunks missing, their tall facades were laced with holes. Steps, once smooth, looked as if they had been nibbled by rats in the night – and some buildings stood open and crumbling, the desiccated masonry falling into the street. But the sun still rose and the blue water sparkled in the harbour. As if war was an evil myth that had never been invented.

Cathy was taken off on a stretcher, and sent to a hospital that was itself, a battle casualty. The nurses – some of them British, some Maltese – wore white headdresses like nuns. With remarkable inner strength, these women worked in the semi-bombed out building, tending the sick as patiently as if they had every resource, instead of almost nothing. Their hospital had large holes in the roof that showed the blue sky. They should have been in despair, but they were calm and unruffled. They kept their cool in the Mediterranean heat. They took infinite care with Cathy. With dedication they tended the wound on her leg – trying new therapies, keeping it meticulously clean. They managed to save her leg. It would never be the same, but at least she would not have to lose it.

Once she was well enough to receive a visit one of the local Wrens came in and presented her with a summer uniform – a white dress with an A-line skirt and white shoes. Despite all the shortages they found this for her. Cathy looked at it and wasn't sure if she should accept. "I'm not really a Wren anymore. Not after what I've done."

"Yes, you are. You did what so many of us wanted to do. You spoke for us all."

She couldn't travel home in a hospital gown, so she accepted the uniform with grateful thanks. But she looked at the white shoes doubtfully. She'd only be able to wear one, because of her plastered leg.

She put on the new white uniform and tried out a pair of crutches. She was wobbly and weak. The brutal shorn haircut softened as her hair grew in a bit. The nurses styled it for her and she started to look like Cathy-girl again.

The Navy arranged for her to be flown home – now that Malta was more secure. New aircraft for defense. The oil they needed so much. And food on the table.

For about a month. That's all. Only a month. It was done at a cost of thirteen ships, thirty-four aircraft and five hundred and fifty men. "And that was just our side," Cathy thought. *There is a price for Victory.*

◆◆◆

Admiral's house, Middlesex, England…

Cathy went to her parents' house to recover from 'what she'd been through'. Life on the leafy fringe of London was not the same without Geoff, and Julius was away, so the two women were left together, working on various 'war effort' projects – often in companionable silence.

Cathy's mother hid most of her pain. On the surface she was stoical about her loss, as a Naval commander's wife was required to be. It was always assumed that Geoff would live and die in the Navy. But at nineteen, he had been taken far too soon, everyone said. She nursed her daughter, helped her convalesce, and made no further reproaches about what Cathy had done – not after that agonized bout of weeping when Cathy was first brought home. She kept Cathy with her almost constantly though, as if, by keeping her close, she could prevent her being hurt or taken away again.

That Monday, they had spent the morning knitting socks for the army in the conservatory, where the light was good and the view of the garden was pretty. But Cathy was listless. Pale. Her concentration shot to pieces. She would pick up a sock, do a few stitches, then falter and put it aside and lay her head back on the divan. She slept for a time... and woke only when she heard door-bell chime.

Their last remaining servant came in, bobbed and whispered something into Mrs Bancroft-Smythe's ear. This seemed to Cathy to be a highly irregular way to relay a message in a forthright Naval household. But she guessed they had a visitor. Mrs Bancroft-Smythe placed stitch keeps on the ends of her knitting needles, set aside her work, and then got up to see who it was.

Cathy glanced out into the garden and then reached for the khaki sock she was knitting. She held it up and felt a kind of lacklustre despair when she saw she had dropped several stitches, which meant the sock would have to be darned before it could be worn.

Several long minutes later, Mrs. Bancroft Smythe returned with the news. "Guy Palamara is in the study. He wants to know if you will see him?"

Cathy looked up, and when she answered, her voice was calm. "Yes. I will. Someone will have to help me up." She was wearing a long pale garment, not really a frock even, more of a housecoat, and hoped her mother didn't insist she had to change.

But her mother helped her wounded daughter out of the chair without a protest. She reached for the crutches, which were standing beside a potted palm. "I'm surprised he has the gall to come here. A good thing your father wasn't home. If you don't want to face him in your current state of health, dear, I will send him away."

"No. I owe him an explanation." Cathy took the wooden crutches and put one under each arm.

"You owe *him* an explanation?" Mrs Bancroft Smythe was icy, and Cathy understood her mother's pain. Her son gone and her daughter injured. What more could the war take? What was left? And yet, there was always more. Cathy's father was now on active duty, engaging the enemy supply ships enroute for North Africa. And, if Julius had his way, sending the enemy's best ships to the bottom of the sea. If they didn't get to him first.

Cathy limped across the mosaic hallway – where she had run so lightly that day in her new Wrens uniform. The door of the study stood ajar, and Cathy could see him, standing, holding his peaked cap, staring out of the window into the street. He was tall and melancholy. Dark hair shining. A renaissance painting come to life – a lone figure with a handsome visage and a long patrician nose.

She sent her mother an eyeball telegram. *Mother, let me speak with him alone.*

They exchanged a glance, but her mother retreated.

He was startled and swung round as she stood in the doorway. She felt the full force of his reaction to seeing her, written in pain in his dark eyes. He tried to form the word, her name, on his lips. "Cathy."

She stood, listing slightly to one side, crutches under both arms. "Let's not shake hands." She gave him a weak smile, which he did not return.

"You went instead of me." He glanced away. His pride was injured. A painful place to sustain an injury.

She took another step into the room. "Well, someone had to."

"It should have been me." His tone was flat, emotionless, but the room was charged with all that his level voice would not convey. His dark eyes were full of sadness, mixed with an unspoken rage and even a measure of soulful humiliation.

"Could you have done it? Could you have shot those Italian boys out of the sky?" She stood, looking directly at him, easing her hand on one of the crutches. In her mind she was half here and half there, reliving the moment that triggered it all. "You were needed where you were. Your work was imperative to the war effort. Well, I thought so, anyway."

He looked away from her, as if he didn't know what to say. He fingered one of the brass buttons on the front of his uniform. He shook his head. "Henry Rawton didn't. Much of the work has now been handed over to the Americans."

"Then you must collaborate. War is a team effort."

He looked stony when she said that. As if there was still a huge gulf between them. "War is not a sport."

"No. You are right." War had been a deadly game, taking family, friends, health, and dignity. And now, Guy. She felt she was losing him. But how could she convince him? When every action she'd taken to protect him had hurt him, and he could not seem to say the things he wanted to say. She shifted uneasily on the crutches – longing to ask him to lift her into his arms and help her back to a comfortable place. "Why did you come here?"

"To hear it from you."

"Well, then hear me," she said. "I saw your name on the list and I knew I had to remove it. I knew what you were doing was far more important than anything you could have done on the bridge of a ship. But as I came to type up the new list, I asked myself – how do I choose who to send in your place? Which radar technician, which cook, or maintenance man, do I send? It seemed an impossible choice. Every single one of them had work to do. And all of them were important to someone. Irreplaceable. Loved. Needed. How could I make that choice? In the end, I felt that unless it was something I was willing to do myself, I couldn't justify putting anyone's name on the list. So, I typed it – a version of my own name. C. Smith. And after I'd done that, every single thing I had to do became inevitable. No matter how much pain it caused."

"It did cause a lot of pain. But it was the most singularly brave thing anyone could have done, Cathy. You should have been decorated for what you did."

"Patrick Clarke will be decorated. I have asked for that. For his family – his parents, his sisters." Her heart felt shadowy and soft. Thinking of Patrick. Who lay down his life for his friends.

Guy broke with emotion and flung his cap down on the desk. "Cathy – I don't care if you slept with him." Although, quite clearly, he did. Startled by the words and by the gesture, she saw how this wounded him, and what it cost him to say it didn't matter.

She couldn't respond. She gazed back at him. Thinking of how detached she used to be. Half a year ago. How she would give *anything* to go back to that – to the way it was before this happened.

When he spoke again, it was in a much gentler tone. "Let me come and support you through Geoff's memorial service," he said. "He was my friend too – the closest thing I ever had to a brother. Let me stand with you in the church and hold your hand. And then, later, when you feel stronger, let me be part of your life again – friend, confidante, lover – whatever you want. Husband, even."

She came towards him, slowly, crutches awkward. And she touched his arm. "Patrick Clarke was everything a British sailor should be. He was loyal and kind and he really knew the sea. He was guided by three things – patriotism, duty and friendship. And yes, I spent the night with him, but not in that way. Sometimes, I've even thought I *should* have given myself to him that night – if I'd known how short a time he had left – and that he'd give his life for the war and for me. But I didn't, and it wouldn't have been right if I had, because I was in love with *you*."

"You were?" he asked. "You *were* in love with me?"

"I was, I am, I always will be."

He reached for her. "That's what I came to hear." And he leant forward, closed his eyes, and met her in a soulful kiss. A kiss – a promise – a hope for the future. He caught hold of her, and the crutches fell to the floor.

Mrs Bancroft-Smythe

Harriet Bancroft-Smythe had stolen back into the hallway to listen. She was stooped with her ear close to the door when all had gone quiet, and she was caught out when it opened abruptly.

Her daughter emerged, followed by that determined young man – about whom she had very mixed feelings.

But Cathy had fire in her eyes and roses in her cheeks, for the first time in all the weeks she'd been home, and before Harriet could say a word, her daughter said – "Lieutenant Palamara will be staying to dinner."

Harriet looked from one to the other, and the truth was plain to see. Cathy's strength would return if she had someone to love and to live for. She nodded. "Alright."

The campaign was won, and so was her daughter. Against her better judgment. She wondered what to cook and if they had some wine in the cellar. She caught Guy's eye as he came through the entrance hall. He was always hard to read. What was he now – contrite, emotional, adoring? His cheeks held a high colour, like her daughter's did, and he glanced away with suitable embarrassment. But when his gaze fell on Cathy, she saw his eyes darken with sultry ambition. *Good God*, she thought, she'd be lucky if he wasn't staying for breakfast.

"Oh!" She dropped Guy's hand and tried to run towards him. "Geoff!"

Cathy could not run. Her brother closed the gap much more quickly than she did, and again the unwanted crutch was abandoned as he whirled her round and lifted her into his arms. "What happened to you?"

"I'm not allowed to talk about it," she said, holding him tight. But she whispered, "Tell me. Do *you* think a woman's place is on a pedestal?"

The message passed between them. "You were *there*. I knew you were there. I felt it. My God, Cathy, you could have been *killed*."

Cathy loved him so much, even though he was a buffoon. "Five hundred people were killed. We thought you were one of them." *Geoff, you silly idiot, how could you put us all through this? We thought you were dead.* "Why didn't you get a message through? You must have known we'd be worried."

People gathered around them to marvel, to point and poke, to check for sure that this was actually Geoff they were seeing. "You're alive!"

An accurate diagnosis, Cathy thought. One had to be impressed with their powers of observation.

"I believe I am," Geoff said. "I got torpedoed. Bit rough, yes. I was in the bloody water, Cath – covered in oil – thought I'd bought it. But they took me on board the Dorset, and then the bloody Dorset got shelled *too*. Hauled ashore by the Vichy French, then managed to give them the slip. It's been a fiasco, alright. I sent a telegram, but when I got home it was obvious it had never arrived. The caterer nearly died of fright when I told him who I was."

The Admiral came up and clapped his son on the back. And his mother said, laughing through tears that she wasn't sure what the appropriate etiquette was, with all the guests who had come to mourn his passing. "Geoffrey, darling – we've planned a *wake* for you, for a hundred and twenty people..."

"Ah, well, sorry. Slight change of plan. Is there any alcohol involved? I'm sure we could all do with a drink."

Guy came through the crowd and hugged his friend. Teased him about wearing the garb of an ordinary sailor, until Cathy nudged him sharply in the ribs. Geoff didn't care. "Best they could do at short notice. They ran out of scrambled egg. Hey, Guy – how come my sister's in such bad shape – I thought you were looking after her?"

Then Guy turned to Cathy, and they shared a look. Guy said, "are you going to tell him? Or have you changed your mind about me, now he's back?"

She looked at him, almost witheringly. "As if I'd do that to you. After everything we've been through?"

"What's all this?" asked Geoff. Raising an eyebrow.

Cathy knew it was time to tell him. "We were going to wait for a decent interval, a period of mourning, and then announce it. Later."

Geoff started to smile.

Guy said, "We could *shorten* the period of mourning, under the circumstances."

"Yes, yes. That would be fine by me – I don't require a *long* period of mourning." Geoff looked closely at Cathy, who was now holding Guy's hand. "You were saying?"

"Guy and I..."

Geoff nodded, encouragingly, trying not to laugh. "Yes? You and Guy?"

"Love each other," she said, looking up at the sky, a way to hide her embarrassment, even though she meant it from the bottom of her heart. "And want to be together, always."

"Ah. I thought there might be an Anglo-Italian entente developing. Eh, Cathy? An entente *cordiale*." Geoff smiled at her, and then at Guy. "The ice finally melted did it, while I was away? Well done. Can we go and get that drink? I've been through rather a lot. Can't wait to tell you about it, actually..."

He was heading off, talking about getting a lift to his parents' home and getting his seaboots off. Cathy grabbed him by the arm. "Look, I hate to stand between a man and his booze. But don't you need to let *Alison* know that you're back?"

"Oh, God, yes. Alison. She'll be worried. I'll send a telegram. Thanks, Cathy – you're an angel."

Chapter Thirty-eight

Cathy

The door of the Admiral's house was shiny and black – a handsome panelled door at the top of a short flight of steps. The gleaming brass door handle shone. Cathy had polished it herself so that it would shine respectfully for the guests at the reception after the funeral. But instead of the sober gathering they'd expected, it was rapidly turning into a party, and if Geoff had his way, it would soon be a rowdy, boozy knees-up. All four Bancroft-Smythes were elated. Geoff himself went round with a wine bottle topping up people's glasses and re-telling the tale of his survival. All with that slapdash charm that usually infuriated his mother. But today he could do no wrong in anyone's eyes. And all because he had performed the extraordinary feat of staying alive.

Cathy was jubilant. She even hugged Ralph and said she was sorry for causing him so much trouble. To her surprise, he said he wanted her to re-join the Wrens.

"But after everything, Ralph, surely the Wrens won't want me?"

He leaned in close, holding his wine glass close to his smart navy jacket. "I want you, Cathy. I'm forming a new group, very hush hush, operating from the tunnels at Fort Southwick. Better if people think you left the Wrens in disgrace. Then you won't have to tell them what you're really doing."

Oh, she'd *love* to be back at work, since her sock-knitting skills were so limited, and she missed the Wrens dreadfully. "Could I, Ralph? Would you let me?"

He nodded. Smiling down at her. Then her face clouded with concern. "Ralph, there can never be anything between us. I belong to Guy now. I hope you understand."

He smiled again, perhaps a little sadly. "I do understand. I understand completely. I don't know when I will ever meet Miss Right – or Miss-Right-for-Me, but I hope it's soon. I feel as if I've been waiting for her for rather a long time." He glanced around the room. As if the woman of his dreams might be hiding behind a pillar somewhere. "What do you say, Cathy? Come and plan the invasion with me, at Fort Southwick?"

She nodded and they clinked glasses. "Try stopping me."

He looked at her sternly. "You can't be a loose cannon any more. You have to learn from your experiences."

"Of course." She pretended to be contrite and meek – she knew she'd worried everyone sick. Just like Geoff, in fact. *Twinny*. But then she laughed and the old Cathy was back. Fire-cracker Cathy who was capable of anything.

He smiled at her, mellow and charming again. "I must say – you achieved *one* thing I wanted – you kept my best radar scientist out of Davey Jones's locker."

She looked across at Guy, who was standing next to her brother, looking happy and relaxed. Only now it was Guy who stood out – who shone for her. *And that's how it should be.*

Ralph said, "He was a good choice, Cathy. For you, and for the Navy. A genius with radar – and once he fessed up about that Ipswich fellow – he was putty in our hands and completely trustworthy."

They spoke a few moments longer. Ralph was still interested in recruiting people with special talents. For the last push to win the war. Anyone else she could recommend? He was looking for tact and discretion – delivering orders leading up to the final invasion.

Yes. She knew one person like that. She put forward Linda.

Anne

31st December, 1942

The waters broke at 4am. And she managed alone, through the early contractions. Until nearly seven in the morning. There was fear, pain and loneliness, as ever, to get through. When the pain became intense, she telephoned the only person she could think of who might be able to drive her to the hospital, and that was Linda.

To Anne's undying relief she heard her friend say, "I'm on my way".

"Woodville Nursing Home please," she said to Linda, as if she was getting into a taxi.

Linda smiled. "Right you are, madam. Woodville Nursing Home."

"Oh gosh, sorry Linda – it's the pain, I can't think..." Anne groaned.

Within minutes they were pulling in through the gates of the maternity building. "Will you be able to get near the front door, do you think?" The labour pains were pressing in, and Anne wasn't sure how far she could walk in her condition.

"Yes. Quietly confident."

In the Royal Navy's new bomb disposal van, Linda never had any trouble finding a place to park – people and traffic seemed to melt away wherever she went.

Before long, Linda was gone, she had to get the van back to the dockyard before it was needed. Anne was alone in a sterile room that reminded her of that doctor with the stethoscope, just after the explosion. She was lucky. Incredibly lucky to have got this far, she told herself. But the pain made it difficult to think that way, instead she felt like a trapped animal. A lonely, scared woman with no husband to pace up and down outside. The nursing home probably thinks I'm an unmarried mother. Anne lay there with tears on the pillow.

Baby. Pain. Can't do this.

The nurse came close to the bed and tried to help. "Don't push, Mrs Tavistock, it's too soon to push."

"But I need to. Why are you telling me I mustn't push?" She was almost in tears.

Pain told her why. "You're not ready. Not yet. Wait." The nurses busied themselves getting ready. Putting a hot water bottle in a cot at the foot of the bed. To make it warm for the baby.

Enduring another fierce contraction. And all because she'd said those words, in the hallway. *Why did I say that? He was a stranger, all this pain, for a stranger.* I'd marry you like a shot, those were her words, and like a shot, fired by a gun – the pain cracked through her. Splintered her body from within, until she moaned for it to be over.

The nurses were brisk and efficient. One of them stood beside her, in a nun-like headdress, and patted her hand. "Not long now. You can push soon."

Anne, sweating and desperate, thought about everything that had led to this. *The day he sent the dress. I said I was so happy I could scream. Why did I say that?*

She was screaming now, with every contraction. Oh, God, they were so strong. And deep. They were agony. Agony inside her.

Oh, why did I let him do this to me? Why did I ever? No wonder love is so sweet, no one in their right minds would ever do this if it wasn't. Oh, Dicky, you selfish bastard.

He should have been there – her young husband. He should have been there, pacing up and down, soothing his nerves with a glass of cognac, waiting for the lusty howl of his first-born child.

"You're going to have a baby now, Mrs Tavistock. I can see the baby's head."

No. She thought she would die; the pain was so bad. A nurse mopped her forehead with a damp cloth, another nurse leaned in past her knees.

"No," she begged. "Make it stop. Make it go away. I can't…"

"One more push. All your strength now, come on. *Push.*"

And she could hear him. His warm resonant voice: *Come on, Anne. One last try. Be the mother of my child.*

She pushed like she had never pushed before.

And then there was a different scream.

On the last day of December, Anne held her newborn baby. Eight and a half months after she last saw her husband. Three years and eighteen days on from that other December day when her fiancé Jim was killed.

Last New Year she had watched happy couples kiss under the mistletoe and felt unsure of her ability to love anyone again. But then – at Tavistock speed – it had hit her. A new love came quick and burned slow, leaving this perfect child with her.

She hoped that cradled in her arms was a person she could love forever.

Anne

January, 1943

Outside a modest semi-detached house in Woodford, was a shiny Bentley, pre-war, but chauffeur driven. Getting out of it – and armed with that most defensive of weapons – a bunch of flowers – was a man.

Richard Augustus Percival Tavistock, the 8th Lord Glenlark.

He walked with difficulty. Walking stick in one hand, bunch of flowers in the other. Up the paved garden path to knock on the door and speak for a moment, with Anne's mother. He asked – would it be possible to meet his grandchild?

Anne's heart sank. Dicky's father. The last meeting with this man had gone so badly. *And you bring me a woman from a shoe shop.*

Anne's mother couldn't send him away. The flowers, the car, the determined look in the old sea captain's eye. She invited him in, and now, he stood, rheumy and out of breath, taking in the atmosphere of Mrs Foxton's parlour. A perfectly ordinary home, with a shabby brown sofa and two easy chairs by the hearth. A mantelpiece with ration books in a row and some family photographs on it. Her mother took the flowers. The old man didn't look as if he could cope with holding them much longer.

The cot, holding the sleeping child, was right there, near where he stood. The room was too small for anything to be hidden. Inside the cot, a hand-knitted blanket had been tucked over the sleeping bump. A tiny pink face, two chubby little hands, with tiny, perfectly formed fingers. The old man gave the child a nervous look, and then glanced away again. As if it was all a bit painful.

He looked doubtfully at one of the low easy chairs, as if the descent would be perilous for him. He noticed, with a start, the wedding photograph on the mantelpiece, and bent to inspect it closer.

"Ah, there's Richard. Yes, what a pity."

A pity he's gone? Or that he married me? She wondered.

He saw, with a widening of his rheumy eyes, that Anne – in the wedding photo – was wearing his wife's gown. "Hmmm," he said, in what sounded a lot like amazement. "Well, I never."

He turned, leaning heavily on his stick, wheezing a little with the effort and with the emotion. "Thank you, Anne, for what you have done for my shattered family. You have helped us, immeasurably."

She wasn't sure what he meant by 'us'. He was the only one left, to her knowledge. He was the last one standing. The end of a great Naval tradition. The end of a family.

She stared at him. In his overcoat and muffler, one brown speckled hand on his walking stick. Her mother – a small thin woman – stood beside her, holding the flowers like a bridesmaid. She was the reason for this moment – she liked to do things properly, and she'd placed a small announcement of the birth in the newspaper, and sent a little card to the castle.

"You see, without this little fellow, it would have all come to an end, with Dicky gone, and me not long for this world, either." He touched the tiny hand of the newborn baby. "A legitimate heir, for the castle."

Yes. Dicky had done that for him. Whether by accident. Or design.

Anne swallowed her pride. "Perhaps you'll have a new lease of life, now you've got a little grandson to run around after."

His face broke into something close to a smile. He nodded. "That's the thing, my dear, you've given me *hope* for the future."

She said, "No. It wasn't me. It was Dicky who had hope. I had almost none left, when he met me. But he gave it back to me. He had enough hope for everybody."

"He did," said the old man, sinking into a seat, offered with a nervous head tilt, by Anne's mother. "He had impossible, unstoppable hope, that boy." He stretched out his painful legs, he had aching bones, and needed some time to settle.

"I think your son loved you very much, Captain," Anne said, careful to acknowledge his naval status. "He seemed to know what we all needed, didn't he?"

He made a gruff sound of acknowledgement, but he did not meet her eye.

Anne's mother, glancing nervously at Tavistock Senior, said, "Do I make tea?"

Anne nodded. She lifted the child out of the cot, and put the baby in his grandfather's arms, now that the old sea-dog was safely seated. He cooed at the child in his arms, very much like a normal grandparent.

In that moment, she saw Dicky for what he really was – an impossible, reckless dreamer. A boy, raised by his nanny, instead of his glamourous mother. A child of five, who had gazed up at a beautiful painting of a girl in a wedding dress and wondered if that was the answer. A second son, not used to responsibility, who took his brother's yoke and wore it valiantly. A man who went on hoping until he was out of time, out of luck, but who kept on trying. Always hoping for a better outcome. Always seeking another chance. A stroke of luck. A victory. That day, when he left her and went to sea, perhaps he'd known – maybe he'd understood – that he could hand the baton of hope to her, and she would take it to the finish line for him.

In the same tones that Dicky used – but even more archaic – her father-in-law spoke. "He wrote to me, from his ship, don't you know?"

"Oh, did he? What did he write about?"

"You. Anne. He wrote about you. He said he wished he'd had more time, because you would have made a lovely mother."

The old man looked down at the child, and bowed his head and cried.

Chapter Thirty-nine

Linda

Linda and Toby had both worked over Christmas and New Year so they decided to spend a few days together.... Talking about new year's resolutions... Toby didn't really go in for special promises. His word was his bond. She admitted that there was something she wanted him to promise her and it was very important. "I want you to give up bomb disposal."

He shook his head. "Impossible. Why d'you even ask me that? I've told yer-"

"I know, you have to keep defusing, until the day you die. But what if you could defuse a hundred bombs safely, at the same time, on the same day?"

"There's no way. I've tried not sleeping. Doing a second shift. Doesn't work."

"If you trained the experts. With your drawings. Bombs could be defused your way. Everywhere."

She turned to him as they walked along a row of little shops. The butcher, the baker, the candlestick-maker, she thought, remembering the nursery rhyme. Only it wasn't a candlestick-makers shop at the end of the row. It was a jeweler's.

"I couldn't teach," he said. It was true, he could barely speak.

"You'd only have to stand there and draw your drawings on the blackboard and then explain what you've drawn."

"No. They'd throw things at me when me back was turned."

She hesitated. It was never any good lying to Toby. "Yes, they might. I can't promise that they wouldn't. But you'd be in a classroom filled with people with a vested interest in paying attention. That might help. You always said the penalty for inattention in bomb disposal is harsh."

He was silent. Thinking. But after a long pause he said. "I'm useful where I am."

"Toby. Are you telling me that you'd rather face an unexploded bomb than have someone throw a ball of paper at you in a classroom? Are you actually saying that?"

"Are you calling me a coward?"

"To turn down this chance for that reason would be cowardly. Yes. And I'll call you anything if it would get you off the beach and into one of those training centres. Please, Toby. Ralph thinks he can swing it."

She saw him mouthing the words 'swing it' in confusion. He didn't like imprecise words. She corrected herself. "*Arrange* it, I mean."

Toby studied his hands. Fingernails scrubbed clean. All trace of explosives washed away. It was a good offer, but he shook his head. "I don't think so, Linda."

The memory of the day they lost Morrison was painful, and she was beginning to lose her cool. "Toby, if you love me, you'll go and teach bomb disposal for the Admiralty."

His face clouded. "If I love yer?" He looked confused. "Can't see a correlation."

"You can't?" She searched frantically for a way to explain. Why did he always need a bloody correlation? "Yes. There *is* a correlation. It's cause and effect. If you go and teach in a training centre, great things will happen. All over the country. Bombs will be rendered safe. Lives will be saved. Everyone will be happy. And if you don't go and teach in a training centre, I will never visit an oat field with you again. Simple as that."

But Toby remained blank and impassive. But after a long thoughtful pause. "And if I said yes?"

"Ralph says he wants you in the training school at HMS Volcano, effective immediately. Then I won't have to worry about what's going to happen if you insist on putting your arm inside another bomb. Well not as *much*. I think they practice with live ones, unfortunately..."

He smiled at her, put his arm around her, and they stood gazing into the window of a small shop. Until Linda realized where they were standing. Outside a jewelers' shop.

He had brought her here. Deliberately. Step by step. He pointed at the display behind the bars. A modest collection it was, mostly made of 'utility gold' due to wartime shortages of metal. "See these here rings that people go giving each other?"

She smiled. She knew he thought that was a silly idea. His people didn't wear rings or make oaths they might not be able to keep. "Yes?"

"I'm buying you one."

That was a bombshell alright. She looked at him. "You what?"

"If one of them rings makes you mine – we'll have to get one." He spoke as if he was talking about buying a plunger or a new sprocket set. "That one, there. Deposit's down."

Her whole perception of the high-street went haywire for a moment, and then settled down. She turned to him. *Sly dog*, not to tell her what he was planning. "Bit confident, aren't you?"

His face showed no emotion. "There was a tell."

She laughed and turned to kiss him. Her heart had already chosen. It was a done deal, just like the ring.

Chapter Forty

September, 1945

After Victory over Japan Day.

A man stood in front of the site of the bombed-out Wrennery. He knew his age was more difficult to assess now, he was so changed, so thin, so damaged by the war. But he was lucky. He had sight in both his eyes, and all his limbs, which was more than many returning servicemen. He was battle-scarred, inside and out, and to the depths of his soul he was weary, but he was alive.

Like the man, the shape of the house was still recognisable, it was not entirely reduced to rubble. But weeds grew, the garden was untended, the building was a burnt-out shell instead of a place of grace and beauty.

"Pity," he said to himself. "Pity Hitler didn't get the bloody castle."

He had an appointment he must keep, so he turned and limped towards the bus stop. The Red Cross had offered to help with the process of repatriating him. A bridge between the places of horror where he had spent the war, and the stranger he was meant to return to. He'd come straight from the ship that had brought him home. But the rooms where he and Anne had lived were rented by another family now. And the Wrennery was in a sorry state. Uninhabited and abandoned.

At the offices of the Red Cross the woman brought him some tea, and said she was glad to learn he'd already been issued with a de-mob suit and that he had a place to stay for the night. "I expect your uniform was in tatters after being a prisoner that long."

His uniform? His *uniform*? His *life* was in tatters. His body and his soul. He said nothing, stared blankly beyond her, as he often did. Hoping the flashbacks would not come. The prison hut. The butt of a hostile gun. The maggots.

She had a manila folder open on her desk with some notes scrawled on it. She went and picked it up.

"Good news, sir. We've found your family."

"My family?"

In the camp the only family he'd known was his observer, Cyril. As at sea, he'd been loyal and they'd looked after each other. A brother through the bad times. The only other person who had experienced that decisive moment, when they set the Swordfish down on the deck of a Japanese carrier.

Images came into his mind. Climbing out of the cockpit and down onto the enemy ship. Raising his hands above his head. A few words exchanged. A nod that meant 'we surrender.'

Cyril said later they should have ditched in the sea. Taken their chances in the dinghy. Better the deep blue sea than the prison camp. Sunburn and dehydration and madness induced by drinking seawater. Better *anything* than a Japanese prisoner of war camp. *It's your call, Dicky.*

He'd lived a long time with that decision. It would haunt him always, he feared.

"Your wife and child," the woman said. "It was very straightforward. They were at one of the addresses you gave us."

The man with the scars stared at the desk and said, "She has a child now?"

The woman nodded. "She does."

No. He dared not hope. They must have told her he was dead – years ago. Why would she have waited? He believed he knew her. She was practical. She would not have waited. But he had to ask, because the word stirred hope. "How old is the child?"

The woman said she'd have to look it up. She had some sad news, she said. She had to tell him that his father had died. He took that news stoically. He had not expected to see his father again.

"Your wife was with him at the end," the Red Cross woman told him. Dicky struggled to imagine her, holding the sea captain's hand. Speaking softly to him. Closing his eyes, maybe, when he was at peace.

Like he had done. In the prison camp. For Cyril.

He was glad he had the Red Cross people to act as his intermediary. This was difficult, and he was fearful of contacting his wife. Too scared to see the aversion in her eyes. He was no longer the handsome young man who had swept her off her feet in the foyer of the Wrennery.

"How old is her child?" he asked again. Needing to know but almost scared to hear the answer. He felt sure it was *her* child, not his. But then he heard that the child was *nearly three*. Born in the same year that he'd married her.

The surge of emotion that should have come with that news was dulled by his prisoner-of-war experiences. He felt weak and shaky, but the woman behind the desk was kind. She urged him not to rush. She said these reconnections had to be done correctly. They would telephone Anne first and lay the groundwork.

"So she doesn't die of fright when she sees me?" he said.

"She'll be happy to know you're alive," she assured him. "But we'll set the scene. Pave the way. Tell her a little of what you've suffered."

And find out if she's got someone else.

He nodded. Heard the words. Sipped the warm sweet tea, slowly, remembering times he'd seen men die for want of food and water. And some who'd died when they finally got some. Too much, too soon for the broken bodies of half-starved men. He signed the forms. Took the rail pass gratefully. Put it in the pocket of the unfamiliar suit. The clothing hung off him, he was nothing but bones. Poor, poor girl. She deserved better.

◆◆◆

The journey to his home town took about four hours. He got off the bus and saw people from the town whose faces he knew. He saw a woman who had once been his nanny on the other side of the town square, carrying her basket for market. Dimly he remembered her name. Nanny McAlister. He almost turned away – not wanting her to see – but she didn't recognise him – a gaunt, thin man in a poorly-made demob suit. Scarred and changed. That was a shock. The woman who had brought him up didn't even recognise him.

No matter. He would face the townsfolk soon enough. He needed to see Anne first.

And the child.

He walked up the hill, slowly making progress. The aspect of the castle was still the same, but then it would be. It was reaching a new level of dilapidation, but there were tiny signs that somebody cared. He passed the place where the tree was cut down – and saw that a slender new tree had been planted in the gap, it had a lot of growing to do, but eventually it might come to something. He passed under the gatehouse, where he saw her car – with a woman's scarf tied to the mirror. But it was once *his* car – the one he had called an old pram. He almost smiled. She must have learned how to drive it

He approached the kitchen door – the one he had run in and out of when he was a boy. One of his father's old dogs lay outside, sleeping in the sun. The hound opened an eye, but didn't growl. Must have recognised him, which made him happy. He stroked the animal's head, receiving an appreciative look from the dog's brown eyes.

So much of this place was familiar. He tried to reconcile the idea that his wife, a stranger of only a few days acquaintance, had made her home in a place he knew so well. She had lived *here* and started raising their child. Among his things, his books, his childhood toys, his rocking horse, his cast-off clothes and old school photos. She must know him better now, much better than he knew her.

He put his hand on the door, and found it was open. He went inside. She was there, in a floral dress, with a sleepy child resting heavy on her shoulder. She had not changed very much; her features had only softened with motherhood. For a second, as their eyes met, there was a moment of shock, but then she really *saw* him. Her eyes lit up and she smiled – yes, that was the moment he wanted to remember.

"There you are," she said, "We've been waiting for you." The child turned and looked at him too, with eyes that reminded him of his brother. The child was shy – took one look and then pressed his face into his mother's neck.

"He needs time," she said. "He doesn't rush into things, this one."

Which seemed ironic. The history of their life together had been all about rushing. He looked at her – his wife. Her eyes shining because he had come home to her. Shattered though he was. "H-How are you?"

Well, it was a start.

"Oh Dicky, I've been trying to look after things for you. I've planted trees and laid out new paths. I found someone to patch up the roof. And I'm in negotiations with the National Trust – so that we can continue to live here, but open up to the public on Sundays."

"Anne. I knew you could do it, from the minute you first said you'd take me on."

She smiled, and nodded. "It was a challenge. But people helped me. Your father helped me."

"I hoped he would. And I'm glad you brought some light back into his life. But what about *you*, Anne? Why did you wait for me? All this time?"

"Because I knew you were still alive. And that you would come back to me if you could. And here you are." Her bright eyes shone with tears of happiness. She reached out and laid a hand on his face. Accepting him. Loving him.

He nodded. Feeling tears of relief coming. She was welcoming him home. He need not be ashamed of what the war had done to him, or the part he'd played in it. "Her fortress is a faithful heart," he murmured. A quote from an old song, full of patriotic fervour. "And they tell me you live here, alone?"

"Well, not very alone. I have Nanny McAllister, and your father's old gardener, and Sandy, of course, and there are two girls from Poland in the turret."

"Sandy?"

Oh, yes – sorry. I should have done proper introductions. Your son. Isn't he lovely? I took the liberty of naming him after your brother. Alexander James Tavistock. People kept telling me that he should be Richard after you, but what with your father being Richard as well – I didn't want them calling him Richard the third in the school playground."

"Perfect." Everything was perfect. *In a moment we will kiss.* The child's hair was soft and fine. Golden brown – like hers. He wanted to reach out and touch. *Soon.*

The war's over, there's no need to rush. There would be time now – time for everything. Time for getting to know one another – the way couples do – after they're married. Time to grow stronger each day supported by their love for each other. For good times and laughter and maybe even a flip in a Swordfish. He'd promised her that, and he liked to keep his promises.

Then she looked at him. "One thing has worried me. All this time, I've wondered. Did you do it for me, or was it all for the castle?"

He shook his head. "Anne, my love – what do you think kept me alive – all the years I was a prisoner – thinking about this old place, with its dry rot and death duties? Or dreaming of the hours we had together?"

She looked at him, as if testing him for truth, and gradually a smile came, lighting up her face with love and hope for the future. "Then kiss me and make me believe it."

And they both knew. All covered. All questions answered. Peace was theirs to keep and to treasure. Their trees and their children would grow tall, and no scarlet banner would ever unfurl from the ramparts of their home – their castle.

The end

Author's Note

Thank you for reading this book.

Many elements of the story follow history closely. Wrens worked in boat crews in many harbours, in radar stations along the east coast, and rode Triumph motorbikes with urgent despatches for Naval commodores. In Britain, the Wrens were marshalled under the indomitable leadership of Vera Laughton Mathews, who was – in real life – known as Skipper. A 'stone frigate' was bombed in Hampshire in 1940, killing ten wrens, and a Wrennery was bombed in 1943, killing eight more.

Operation Pedestal – the most famous convoy to Malta – sailed in August 1942 with the loss of many ships and 500 men, a sacrifice that helped the Allies retain access to the Mediterranean. The Italians were fed a false report that there were bombers defending the island, in the hopes that they would not attempt to invade when Malta was close to surrender. The Dieppe Raid in which many thousands of Canadian soldiers fought so bravely, and for so little gain, took place on the 19th August, 1942, and two ships waiting to take troops across the Channel were bombed at anchor not far from Portsmouth. Those elements of truth are all woven into this narrative.

For Anne's story, I was inspired by Isabel MacNeill, who was an art and drama teacher who ran HMCS *Conestoga*. She was the first woman to command a stone frigate – but she was based in Canada, not Britain. In England, many female officers were in charge of WRNs Quarters and responsible for training young women, and their contribution to Naval history is only just being recognised. For this story, I invented a fictional stone frigate named HMS *Resilient,* loosely based on HMS *Daedulus* in Hampshire.

In real life, pilots like Dicky often trained at Brough, before being transferred down south to work on their deck-landings at Gosport. The air station at Lee-on-Solent was a primary shore airfield of the Fleet Air Arm during WW2 and vital for the formation and final training of newly commissioned squadrons. I was intrigued to find that another training station – HMS *Raven* – also known as RAF Southampton was located only a few miles from where I was born.

The Fairey Swordfish was a biplane torpedo bomber, designed by the Fairey Aviation Company in the 1930s. This 'obsolete' plane, capable of only modest speeds, was operated with stellar success by the Fleet Air Arm of the Royal Navy, and made a significant contribution to the war.

Most people think of the army when they think of bomb disposal, but the Navy had bomb disposal teams of its own – and divers who disarmed mines at sea. The stone frigate HMS *Volcano* was a real place – Holmrook Hall – where bomb disposal officers were trained for Navy work with support from the Wrens. For the purposes of my story, I used a fictional house that I named HMS *Nautilus* as the barracks for Linda's bomb disposal boys.

The destroyer HMS *Tilbury* in this story is also fictional – because the fate of each of the ships on the historic convoy is well known and I wanted to retain both suspense and artistic freedom. But it is based on descriptions and specifications of the destroyers that escorted the convoy. Part of the naval escort left from the Clyde with the merchant ships, as described here, while the other ships left from the great naval base at Scapa Flow a day earlier.

HMS *Fortunate* (Dicky's aircraft carrier) is fictional – but modelled on HMS *Hermes,* one of the world's first air-craft carriers, which sank in the Indian Ocean in April, 1942. The sinking of HMS *Eagle* is a true story – she was torpedoed by a German U-boat and sank in a few short minutes. The description of her sinking in this book is inspired by eyewitness accounts.

The most controversial part of the story was Cathy's decision to board a warship, which is a fictional element– but maritime history contains at least twenty known cases of women who managed to hide their identity to serve at sea, including Anne Chamberlyne, a 23-year-old woman who 'dressed in man's apparel' in 1690 to fight the French alongside her brother. It was only in 1943 that the commemorative plaque celebrating this woman of "undaunted valour" was destroyed by a bomb. We will never know the real number of women who disguised themselves to serve at sea or in the armed forces, and many of the stories have passed into legend and song, rather than being verified and recorded.

Officially, women were barred from serving at sea by a law passed by the Admiralty in 1808, and it was not until October 1990 that the first female navy personnel were allowed to go to sea. They joined HMS *Brilliant,* t Devonport, Plymouth. The motto "Never at Sea" appeared on early recruitment posters for the Wrens – and as you can imagine many Wrens wanted to change that policy – during World War Two they travelled a long way towards this goal.

The role of these avant-garde female sailors was celebrated in an exhibition 'Pioneers to Professionals' held in Portsmouth in 2017, which was also hosted by the Fleet Air Arm Museum near Yeovilton. For this book, though, a key source of inspiration was Maud Butler, who boarded a troopship in 1915 hoping to fight in the army with her brother. The men on board had almost universal admiration for her courage, and the captain said if there had been any way he could have kept her on and allowed her to serve, he would have.

The 'combined ops' station in this book is fictional – but it represents some of the amazing work that went on at various Chain Home stations along the English coastline and at HMS *Flowerdown*. The British system of direction-finding stations could establish the position of any ship or aircraft over the North Sea, and in 1942 scientists like Guy were racing to deliver radar controlled anti-aircraft tracking devices for guns that would help the RN to defend its fleet.

The Cinderella story of Anne and Dicky was loosely inspired by two stories that I was told as a child, the first was a tale about a young man who inherited a castle – and proposed to several nurses in a matter of weeks before finding the right one. The second was about my grandmother's cousin Anthea – an artist who married a Fleet Air Arm man just after the war. He was a shy young man who later became Lord Craigmyle, and first sat in the House of Lords wearing his naval uniform. As far as I know, Anthea wasn't a Wren – and she certainly didn't command a stone frigate. But she did rise to the challenge of being the wife of a peer.

I'm very grateful to a family friend – Colin – who was a helicopter pilot in the FAA, for explaining how the Navy ticked in the post-war period. Any mistakes here are mine, not his.

Thank you so much for reading my book. If you enjoyed this one and would like me to write more, you can contact me through my website. I'd love to hear what stories from history interest you most, and the people and places you'd like to read about in the future.

THANK YOU

About The Author

Stella Hutchinson

Stella Hutchinson was born in the New Forest in Hampshire. She grew up in a zany book-loving family in Cambridgeshire and Suffolk. She loved writing stories from a young age and spent many happy hours scripting adventures with her two younger brothers. At the age of eighteen she went to work for a shipping company in London, but later won a scholarship to study maritime history at the University of Auckland. While in New Zealand she met her husband, who is from Italy, and together they are raising twin boys. When she's not working on a new book, she likes learning languages and making costumes for community theatre. She also writes contemporary fiction.

Printed in the USA
CPSIA information can be obtained
at www.ICGtesting.com
CBHW050824260224
4659CB00009BB/439